KEEPING TIME

A NOVEL

KEEPING TIME

THOMAS LEGENDRE

ACRE

CINCINNATI 2020

Acre Books is made possible by the support of the Robert and Adele Schiff Foundation and the Department of English at the University of Cincinnati.

ISBN-10 (pbk) 1-946724-28-9   ISBN-13 (pbk) 978-1-946724-28-1
ISBN-10 (ebook) 1-946724-29-7   ISBN-13 (ebook) 978-1-946724-29-8

Designed by Barbara Neely Bourgoyne
Cover art: Cairnbaan rock art, panel 2, Kilmartin Glen, 3D model. Photogrammetry by Dr. Aaron Watson, February 2017. https://sketchfab.com/3d-models/cairnbaan-rock-art-panel-2-kilmartin-glen-a8471fafee294b49a09197ea2335f661.

Distributed by the Chicago Distribution Center

This is a work of fiction. Names, characters, businesses, places, events, and incidents are either products of the author's imagination or used in a fictitious manner. Any resemblance to actual persons, living or dead, or actual events is purely coincidental.

The press is based at the University of Cincinnati, Department of English and Comparative Literature, McMicken Hall, Room 248, PO Box 210069, Cincinnati, OH, 45221–0069.

Acre Books books may be purchased at a discount for educational use. For information please email business@acre-books.com.

for Nicole and Callum

Time present and time past
Are both perhaps present in time future,
And time future contained in time past.
If all time is eternally present
All time is unredeemable.
What might have been is an abstraction
Remaining a perpetual possibility
Only in a world of speculation.
What might have been and what has been
Point to one end, which is always present.

—T. S. ELIOT, *Burnt Norton*

And yet the present is only a construction. It can be argued that any act 'in the present' is always already past. It has to be past so that we can perceive it. Even our thoughts are past. Otherwise we could not know we were having them.

—IAN HODDER, *The Domestication of Europe*

KEEPING TIME

CHAPTER ONE

1988

If I make a circle it doesn't matter where I start, so let's begin with Aaron appearing from the future. How does a time traveller arrive? By buzzing the entryphone. It halts me during Bach's Passacaglia in C minor for organ—or rather, a piano transcription that seems too thin, too sterile—and I rise from the bench humming the final variation, trying to give it some life. I lose it completely, though, at the sound of Aaron's voice bristling with static. This can't be good news. He's supposed to be in Mid Argyll. As his footsteps come up the main stair, I think maybe the next phase of his Great Dig was postponed and he lost his keys in a Neolithic ditch. But then the sight of him sends me backing into the sitting room. He recites my favourite colour, my lucky number, my comfort foods, my shoe and dress sizes—as if I need convincing, when in fact the problem isn't that I doubt who he is, but that I immediately believe it. Yes, it's obvious. My future is his past. Though it's April of 1988 for me, it's November of 2006 for him—or almost November. Halloween night. That's when our son will stay home with me, apparently, while he takes our daughter trick-or-treating, despite my protests, so he can introduce her to his American childhood ritual, his annual allowance of junk food and fright. I can't imagine myself protesting such a harmless thing, which is partly why it seems like a different woman in that time. An alternate self. The mother of two children. I'm already suspicious of her. Where does she begin? Where do I end? But I'm getting ahead of myself. I'm here. I'm now. I'm making it up as I go along. If I make a circle it doesn't matter where I start.

"But you need to know it's really me," he says. "And I can prove it. The first time we met was at that pub off Buccleuch. You were upset about playing the Rach 3, and I told you . . ." He stops himself, clenching his eyes shut. "No, no. Wait. Anyone could know that."

He turns away and grips the mantel, in the throes of some internal debate, then turns back and starts reeling off details about something that happened to me before that—a private trauma I've never shared with anyone. Proof. Evidence. He needs to convince himself that I'm convinced. He needs to believe that I believe.

"Aaron?" I wave him down. "This isn't necessary."

"But you locked the door behind him," he says, "and you sat there hugging your knees until dawn when you could walk home safely, and you couldn't even bring yourself to tell Clare or Isobel afterward, instead making up some story about, what was it, he vomited and passed out. It was your first and last one-night stand. Am I right?"

His face is both familiar and strange. There's a wider spread to his features, the continental drift of age, but otherwise he seems recast with sharper angles and ridges, with deeper definition. The endearing little curve to his lower lip is more pronounced, his hair reduced to a close-cropped style that actually suits him better. It's the haircut he should have had from the beginning. I hesitate to mention it because I'm afraid he's going to say it was my suggestion. The other Violet. The older one. A deep unease comes over me, unreasonably, at the thought of her.

"Violet, please. Am I right about this?"

I manage to nod.

"Have you shared that experience with anyone?"

I shake my head.

"Anyone at all?"

2

I close my eyes to absorb not the fact but the feeling of it. A new time signature.

"I know it must be strange to have me describe it this way, like watching your own dream on television. But you'll tell me in a few years. At a performance one night you'll see someone who resembles him, and you'll confess the whole thing afterward right here in this room. Except it's not really a confession because you didn't do anything wrong. I should mention that now, ahead of time, to preempt some of the guilt. Because the guy tried to rape you, for Christ's sake, so don't be ashamed of that, and I *still* want to track him down and break his kneecaps, which you'll attribute to my crude notion of Appalachian justice. If memory serves."

And his accent has changed. Those hints of southern comfort, those drawling vowels—all tempered to British speech. The sound of him, the sense. Yes, it's the man he will be in eighteen years. One of my legs is trembling like a bow string, and I have to collar it with both hands to make it stop.

He comes forward. "Are you all right?"

I step back and knock into a lamp. He lunges and catches it before it falls, then looks at it oddly as he sets it back.

"Tessa broke this. She was crawling under the table and—" He glances at an empty corner of the room. "The table we're going to buy after we have the flat repainted. In 1996, I think."

"Good thing you caught it, then."

He snaps his attention back to me, flummoxed by the comment until it takes hold, and he laughs. Then his eyes widen with mischief. "Hey, should I smash it and see what happens?"

"Please don't. It's hard enough living in an unfurnished rental— and excuse me, but how are we going to buy this flat if we can barely afford the rent?"

He hesitates, sensing a tripwire. "Did I say we bought it?"

"You said we repainted it. Eight years from now."

"Oh. Well. Don't worry about that. It's not the sort of detail that matters."

3

I fold my arms. "As opposed to what, my shoe size? Which you got wrong, by the way."

"Your shoe . . ." He sways slightly and catches himself. "Ah, right. Before the children you're a five, not a five-and-a-half."

"Pardon?"

"Because your feet swelled with the pregnancies."

"You mean permanently?"

He shrugs.

"Leave off, Aaron. Time travel is more plausible than *that*."

He seems to drop a notch. It's all crucial to him. Endings and beginnings, cause and effect. With renewed desperation he starts patting himself down, as if searching for a futuristic calling card. But what can he offer? He isn't wearing any silver lamé. No spacey designs or insignias. Just a jumper with a hole in the shoulder, a collared shirt, jeans. The trainers are a type I've never seen before, but that doesn't mean much. He could be from any time, any place. He doesn't even have a wallet. The only artefact he can produce is an electronic domino, which apparently is a mobile phone.

"Will you stop that, please?"

"I'm trying to provide hard evidence."

"Hard evidence of what? That mobiles are shoddy in 2006?"

He holds it up. "The supporting technology doesn't exist yet. If you brought a radio back to the eighteenth century and switched it on, it wouldn't—"

"But it *doesn't* switch on."

"Or maybe the circuits were fried in the . . ." He gestures broadly. "I don't know, the time warp or whatever you want to call it, because it sure as hell did something to my nerves. In fact, I thought that was the problem at first. It felt like a concussion. A seizure, maybe. Except the weather was different. The daylight. I knew it was spring. I could taste it in the air. And then on the street I saw . . ." He trails off, his eyes magnetized by something across the room.

I swivel but don't find anything worthy of fascination. The stereo and records, the old armchair, the telephone on a faux Ancient Roman pedestal that he bought a few months ago at a charity shop. I turn back to him. "You saw what?" I ask.

He walks over and puts his hand on the phone as if he doesn't quite believe it exists. "That would be the real test," he says.

"Pardon?"

"No room for doubt after that."

"What are you talking about?"

He picks up the receiver, then immediately slams it down again and steps back with his hands over his mouth.

"Hey," I say, coming over and touching his cheek cautiously, expecting some kind of metaphysical crackle, but it's simply Aaron with extra weather in his skin, etchings around his eyes. "It's all right. I'm here."

He folds at my touch, settling against me. A firmness to his chest, a harder texture to his arms. Does he exercise now? I try to imagine him at the gym, substituting fitness for youth—a youth still intact in the other Aaron, working on an excavation three hours away. I run my hands all over him, him but not-him, finding the differences, the octaves between one and the other, as if playing the Passacaglia in a lower register to bring out the resonance, except something is missing from the transcription, because even though the notes are right as my fingers press to his shoulders, they don't sound true. Do I still think this way in the future? Am I always this strange? When I pull back to ask him, though, I find the full presence I've always anticipated without realising it, his face in mine.

"Ultra-Violet," he says. "It's you."

There's no reason to stop what happens next. He's here and there, now and then. We're making it up as we go along. By the time I work his shirt off I've discovered a scar on his shoulder, old to him and new to me, and a mild subsidence in his body. But it doesn't matter. Oh, it really doesn't matter. He hits notes of pleasure in me that I didn't even know were there, new pitches on my scale. Of course he has an unfair advantage. An extra eighteen years of practice, I think, as he carries me across the threshold of our bedroom like it's our wedding night again, a replay of our honeymoon with all this messy, raunchy tenderness. Better than our honeymoon, actually. And gripping his hand against the mattress, I feel his wedding band—our ring of eternity, as Isobel phrased it, in honour of our legal manoeuvre to keep him in the country. But it has lasted. It has endured. If only I could share the news with her and Clare, not to mention Mum, still unsettled by my lack of propriety and pageantry, my unserious life. See, Mum? He's my husband, after all.

Afterward there's a sizzling purity to everything, all nerve endings and open strings. Sunlight flickering on the wall, the howling raw motions of sky. A breeze sighing through the fireplace. Traffic rumbling like a waterfall in the distance. Everything acute and true. His leg still draped over mine. An octave occurs when one pitch has exactly double the frequency of another. But this is a different harmonic. A different sequence of semitones. A perfect fifth. Yes. The interval above the root of all major and minor chords, and now excuse me while I smile.

He slides out of bed and starts gathering his clothes. "This isn't a coincidence."

I turn toward him. "What?"

"The date."

"You mean, Good April Fool's Friday?"

He gives me a perplexed look.

"That's the joke you made when you called last night. Or maybe I should say eighteen years ago? Because it's Good Friday and April Fool's Day, together at once—which proved, you said, that the Resurrection was really just a prank that got out of hand. Why else would they celebrate the occasion when the saviour was whipped and beaten and nailed to a cross? If that's a good Friday, I'd hate to see a bad one."

He halts for an instant after stepping into his jeans, blinking the thought away. "I'm talking about spring 1988. Kilmartin Glen. The excavation at Inbhir. Right now I'm discovering that it's not only a chambered cairn, but also a . . ." He breaks off. "I'll tell you—I mean, *he'll* tell you all about it when he comes home tonight."

"Lovely. Something to look forward to. But why is that not a coincidence?"

"I go back there in 2006."

"And?"

He shakes his head. A forbidden topic. I'm about to press him when he reaches for something on his bureau—the mug he won at a state fair when he was a boy. Another casualty of the years between us, no doubt. Is he going to blame our daughter for this one as well? As he runs his fingers over the raised lettering, I can't help recalling that moment at the telephone. Who was he going to call? Then he sets the mug down and, still naked from the waist up, strides out of the room. I lean over and watch him through the doorway of his study, examining all the drawings and photos tacked to the wall—the collage he hopes will provoke some kind of insight—along with the Ordnance Survey map that he marks with the locations of all known rock carvings in Kilmartin Glen, like a general plotting troop movements. I am under solemn oath under penalty of death not to tell his coworkers for fear he will be mocked mercilessly. Because he is convinced the rock carvings occur not at random locations but at natural thresholds of the landscape, with the motifs taking on greater complexity at key approaches. Furthermore, he says, they have a systematic relationship to the cairns and standing stones along the floor of the valley. They lead you to those sites. They guide you in. They bring you down.

That must be it. The source of his accidental time travel. A mystical portal of some kind, marked by signs and stones—the very sort of wishy-washy New Age hokum he loathes, which would explain why he's so tight-lipped about the whole thing. He'd sooner whip up a hypothesis of geological features and material culture than allow any kind of metaphysical mystery. But today's superstition is tomorrow's science. He probably just stumbled into it like Alice falling down the rabbit hole. After all, there's a hidden aspect to that place, or rather something absent. Undisclosed. Withdrawn. I kept looking for what I was missing even the first time I visited, long before Aaron, on a family holiday. It was Dad's idea of a diversion before catching the ferry at Oban—some pagan viscera to offset the tepid encounter with St Columba he knew Mum would impose on us once we reached Iona. At least that's my understanding of it now. At a layby he read out a placard explaining how the cairns were arranged in a straight line over a distance of two miles along the floor of the glen. A linear cemetery. A valley of death. A natural amphitheatre fringed with terraces, as if designed by the gods themselves, whoever they happened to be back then, for ritual processions and ceremonies.

And what remained? A few standing stones. Some rock piles resembling igloos where prehistoric corpses were supposedly stored like tins in a larder but that now held nothing at all. Nevertheless, we made a go of it. We tramped among livestock and heaps of manure to lay our hands on the slanted monoliths. We squeezed inside one of the cairns with Mum holding her jacket over her shoulders and Dad declaring his wonder at what it must have been like, really, if you gave it a bit of thought. And of course the rock carvings, worn down and barely visible at midday, with their cups and rings and stray lines radiating outward. A few looked like dartboards, Peter said. Because he played darts. I spotted a treble clef, then realised it was just a part of the texture, of the cracks and fissures in the rock itself. The whole thing was a Rorschach test. A trick of desire. I felt it most at the summit of Dunadd, when I stepped in the carved footprint used in the first coronation rituals of Scotland. Dad dubbed me Violet MacAlpin, conqueror of the Picts, founder of the Kingdom of Alba. Peter dubbed me a royal pain in the arse.

Aaron is the only one I know intent on assembling a larger picture, even as he distrusts larger pictures. It's who he is: his helpless speculation, his urge to know. His pleasure in paradox. He doesn't expect to solve the rock carvings but rather to become satisfied in the effort. Yet he will never be satisfied, even in that. Does he know it yet? Does he know himself?

I hear a tapping of keys, a familiar staccato from his desk across the hall. What on earth could he be typing? I call his name. I wait. I lean off the bed again but see only the scraped file cabinet, the chair plundered from a skip, the lamp with its paper shade burnt by a bulb that gives more heat than light. When we buy this flat I bloody well hope we can afford to furnish it properly.

"A friggin' *typewriter*," Aaron says, jerking his thumb over his shoulder as he comes back through the doorway, his voice flaring with Blue Ridge summer, the gut-level syllables of his younger self—all still inside him, of course. A ground bass of basic pleasures and straightforward thinking.

I work up a tolerant expression. "Yes, a typewriter."

"And the circle jerks."

"What?"

"Those pages I tacked up. As if I had some great insight into the universe." He draws a long breath. "All those years I was putting the cart before the horse. That's one thing Tessa . . ."

I watch him carefully as he trails off, a flicker of caution in his eyes.

"Anyway," he says, "that typewriter still drops the f's. Oh, and look at *this*." He goes over to his closet and flips through the hangers.

"Um, Aaron?"

He pulls out a striped shirt—not one of my favourites—and holds it at arm's length. "I really used to wear this, didn't I?"

"You don't have the greatest fashion sense, if that's what you mean."

He gives me a burlesque frown before setting it back.

"I gather you were typing a note to yourself?"

"Hell no. I just wanted to bang the keys again for old times' sake."

"But don't you have some advice to offer? Words of wisdom?" I prop my head on my hand. "Stock tips, perhaps? There must be something you'd like to say to him."

"I doubt he'd listen."

"Then tell me instead."

He straightens up with wry gravitas—about to make a joke, it seems, at the expense of his younger self—when a heavier notion takes hold instead. He falters for a moment before he finally says it. "Don't worry about him while he's on this dig. He's not doing anything wrong."

"Wrong?"

"I mean, he's not misbehaving. That's all." He reaches for his shirt on the floor, trying to be nonchalant. But then our eyes catch. "All right," he says. "There's a colleague—a woman working with him at the site. Pottery expert. They'll flirt and have some laughs together, but that'll be the beginning and end of it. Nothing is going to happen. No big deal. Ok?"

"Ok," I reply, drawing it out with a light twist. "If you say so. After all, I guess it pales in comparison, doesn't it?"

He stops with his arm in a sleeve. "In comparison to what?"

"This. I've just cheated on him, haven't I?" I ruffle my hair and let the sheet slip down a bit. "And with good reason. Some things improve with age."

He eases back and adjusts his shirt like a stunt driver checking his seatbelt. I seem to be a dangerous temptation now. A hazard in time.

"You still haven't told me how it happened," I say. "All I know is that it was Halloween night."

"Sort of," he says, fastening his buttons.

"Oh, dear. Suddenly you're evasive. A while ago you were babbling away about a windstorm and guising—sorry, trick-or-treating—with our daughter. Tessa. I must have chosen that name. After my gran. And our son, what do we call him?"

He inhales. "Can we change the subject?"

"Why?"

"I've already told you too much."

"What difference does it make if you tell me our son's name? You've already warned me about your pottery expert and her clay jugs, or whatever it is that you find so attractive. But really, Aaron. You can't start that kind of thing and just *stop*."

"I told you about Siobhan because it's worth the risk. Now will you drop it, please?"

"Worth what risk?"

He holds up a hand. "Can you just trust me on this? I have to be careful. I don't know how it all works. What kind of damage I might do. What damage I've already done."

I roll onto my back. "Well, unless you murdered someone or robbed a bank on your way here, I don't think you have much to worry about. The only difference is what you've told me. We'll have a daughter and a son. Our daughter will break a lamp. We'll have the flat repainted, presumably after we manage to buy it. Oh, goodness, think of the disruption, the great rip in the fabric of the space-time."

Wrong thing to say. He crouches down and ties his shoelaces. What happened to his gleeful nihilism? His urge for existential mischief? All those late-night rhapsodies about geological time scales and the insignificance of the human race? He's taking the wrong track. He's confusing the score with the music, the treble with the bass, the right hand with the left. As if one thing causes the other. Oh, Aaron. That's not how it goes. Let's sequence the motif. Let's try a different key. Let's improvise.

"Are you going to tell her?" I ask.

"You mean—"

"Me. Her. The future Violet."

"I guess I won't need to. She'll already know because . . ." He pauses to untangle the pronouns, the past and present selves. " . . . well, you're her. Or you're going to be her."

11

"Don't be so sure."

He gives me an indulgent smile. "You planning on a severe case of amnesia between now and then?"

"I'm just saying we could be different people. In fact, I'm quite certain of it."

"And why is that?"

"Dad took us guising every Halloween when I was a girl, and it's exactly the kind of thing I'd want for our children. I don't know who that older woman is, but she's not me. Don't you get it? This isn't just a different time, Aaron. It's a different place as well."

He opens his mouth to reply, but seems to lose track of the thought, his expression lifting free of its moorings as a pulse of sunlight comes into the room, bringing a higher voltage, a renewed circuitry to every surface and texture.

"A separate reality," he says. "A parallel universe. Which would mean that whatever happens here . . ." He shifts his gaze back to me.

I flick my eyebrows at him and stretch out with a feline extravagance.

He comes over for what he probably tells himself is just a kiss, but then his face is buried in my hair and I'm working his shirt off again. He grips me with an almost helpless greed. I have to reach back and brace myself against the headboard, working into the pleasure until we're breathing together, his hands cupping my face as if he's afraid of losing it, his body sliding down afterward, his forehead pressed to the space between my breasts. I feel him trembling. Then something seizes him, and he shoves away. A fracture between us like shattered glass.

He dresses brusquely, giving his lapels a hard tug. "I need tools," he says.

I run the words over, thinking I must have I misheard.

"A hammer," he adds. "Or at least a screwdriver. Otherwise I can't go back."

"Well, you know where they are," I manage to say. "Or were. I guess we might move them to a different cupboard by 2006."

I wait for more—an explanation, a response of some kind—but he finishes dressing in silence, his mouth clamped shut. And a terrible stillness comes into me. Something is wrong. Not now. Then. In the future.

"What is it?" I ask, my voice falling to a whisper. "What's happening to us?"

He leaves the bedroom without replying. I hear the creaking hinges of the cupboard. The rattle of the toolbox. The lid's metallic thud. There's a rustling, a scraping inside the closet itself. What could he possibly be doing? And then the sounds of him repacking everything slowly, with that special care of his.

No. I won't let it end this way. I'll bring him back. The other Violet and I can share him. What's mine is hers, what's hers is mine. Yes, that's the key. It's how everything falls into place. The sharps, the flats, the accidentals. The intervals and chords. The perfect fifth. As he walks down the hallway his footsteps become the rhythm, my heartbeat the time. The door shuts behind him with a click like a metronome. I can play it now. And it goes like this.

13

CHAPTER TWO

2006

Another day, another fight. What was it now? I asked point-blank while she was putting Jamie to bed—too early, in my opinion—because she had decided he was ill, giving his perpetual sniffles the status of a cold. It wasn't right. I wanted him to come with us. A wee ghostie to accompany Tessa. Violet was making excuses, but when I tried to bring it up, her response was so naturally hostile that it seemed to be the reason we were arguing in the first place. Well, that's right nice, I said. Thanks for the vicious circle, Vi. I stalked off to Tessa's room and consoled myself by helping with her costume while a gale blew with gothic force and our Georgian windows bucked and trembled in their frames. Hallow-een night. Heavy weather inside and out. It felt like middle-aged defeat, or maybe a failure to reach escape velocity somewhere back in the early stages of adulthood, when it might have made a differ-ence. All this bickering and bitterness. All this grey feeling. And all that darkness beyond the windowpanes, as if the hour gained by setting back the clocks had already been lost.

I straightened Tessa's hood, tied the braided rope around her waist, and stepped back. Her plump cheeks lifted into a smile. Despite the pseudo-ancient trimmings, she looked like a flower girl at a wedding, or maybe an attendant to the May Queen.

"You're ready to rock," I said.

"Daddy, it's too tight."

14

I reached down and loosened it. "Better?"

She nodded and stretched out her arms, as if striking a mystic visionary pose.

I asked the question we had rehearsed. "Where's the midsummer sunset?"

"Over there!" she shouted, pointing toward her bed.

"Really?"

"No, there!" she said, pointing to the window.

"Are you sure?"

"No, over there!" She pointed up at the ceiling.

I broke into laughter. Great touch. I hadn't taught her to go vertical. Three-dimensional thinking, all on her own. My daughter was a genius.

"What are you trying to accomplish with that?" Violet was standing in the doorway with her arms crossed. She had changed into a baggy sweater and frumpy sweats and those tight slippers that made her look like a ballerina from the ankles down. Her ponytail was frayed at the end like an overused toothbrush. Tessa had inherited all her physical qualities—the crude-oil lustre to her hair, the pale skin, the North Sea eyes—but I hoped her attitude would resemble mine. I was cultivating playful responses in her, an irreverence and hard wit. She would need them to balance those troublesome good looks. I was thinking ahead.

"I'm trying to 'accomplish' the difficult task of having fun," I said as my pleasure drained away.

"It's not exactly a fair trade, is it?"

I tried to follow what she meant, deliberately glancing over at Tessa as she swayed and hummed a bogus ancient chant we had made up.

"I stay here," Violet added, "while you have all the fun."

"Then let's go. All of us."

"I told you, Jamie's ill."

"The usual sniffles. Come on, it won't kill him. It's a special occasion. You're the one who suggested it last week."

Her gaze veered off. "I didn't suggest it."

"And now you're backpedalling."

She touched her forehead and then shook her fingers as if they irritated her. "It's not what I thought it would be, all right?"

"Halloween night." I spread my hands. "What the hell did you expect?"

Her shoulders rose, but then her eyes flicked over to Tessa. I felt a watchful silence behind me. When tooth enamel forms at a young age it absorbs traces of local geology through the groundwater and takes on a permanent chemical signature. And Tessa's fifth birthday was only a couple of months away. She shouldn't be drinking this, I thought. It should be a cocktail of sunshine and apple juice and undiluted love.

"Come on," I said. "Stonehenge awaits!"

She grabbed her empty pillowcase and squeezed past Violet like a convict through a hole in the prison fence. When I came to the doorway I stood nose to nose with her—a woman who had once interrupted a rushing flurry of Bach to screw me on the sofa. Now she turned without uncrossing her arms to let me by.

I followed Tessa down the long hallway, past the cornice work and brass fittings, the dining room with its surfaces polished to an obsidian shine. The building seemed to breathe in the iron lungs of the weather. The fan over the stove gave a metallic rattle. The bathroom vent surged like a turbine. I grabbed my jacket and opened the door to the stairwell. Plain walls and fluorescent lights, the steps eroded by two centuries of ascent and decline. Although the stonework needed renewal I hadn't brought up the issue with our neighbours, and just then, as something fell from the eaves of my mind, I understood why.

I stood numb in the clarity of it—in the clarity of realising what I had been thinking—while Tessa plunged ahead and swung herself around each landing, whipping the pillowcase into bloom. The night ahead offered a late bedtime and roughly a kilogram of refined sugar. Yes, this was paradise. But when I followed her down and opened the main door, the world confronted us in a thunderous rush. The gardens lashing and churning madly, shedding leaves in a ticker-tape parade that would leave the bones of every tree exposed by morning. Shadows were veering and clawing each other in the white light, the streetlamps glowing like moons on their poles. And watching Tessa with her hair scrabbling loose and her face tensed against the mad force of it all, my revelation seemed like a dirty trick. A false bottom. I wasn't leaving. I wouldn't move out. I loved my children more than I hated my situation. End of story.

Or maybe the beginning. How often did I understand something in my life while it was actually happening? How many moments of clarity turned out to be mirages instead? Tessa was tugging on my jacket, so I made a show of shielding myself with my forearm as we marched against the massed winds of the north. At one point she turned backward to test her weight against the gale, her hood flipping up and her pillowcase puffing out like a drag racer's parachute. Every act was a discovery with her. Everything new.

Our goal was a certain street that, according to rumour, had collectively embraced the tradition of costumes and candy that the Scots called guising and I called trick-or-treating on a night everyone agreed was Halloween.

"It's too far," she said at last, struggling with her hood.

I urged her onward through the precincts of Edinburgh's New Town. Here the streets ran parallel and perpendicular, with curves and crescents and circuses to accommodate variations in topography and civic purpose. Gardens filled the spare sockets and elbow joints. Thoroughfares suited the turning radius of a horse and carriage. The sandstone blocks, though pale brown when freshly cut from Craigleith Quarry nearly two centuries earlier, had been caramelized by the elements into a dark and sere beauty that stood low enough to admit plenty of daylight while also preventing the sort of overcrowding that showed particularly bad taste. No medieval squalor here. These angles were sure of themselves. These lines were true. Together they expressed the geometry of an ordered mind. The balance and proportion, the configurations of the Enlightenment. I took comfort in a place with solid aesthetics, with traffic markings grafted onto cobblestones and satellite dishes concealed behind chimney stacks that now smoked with curated firewood instead of coal. It was a place that could survive any retrofit. I wanted my children to stay here. And I would find a way to stay here with them.

We rounded the next corner to find a world of aliens and monsters and superheroes accompanied by adults in civilian clothing. Tessa went pattering up the first set of steps and then halted at the top, too timid to ring the bell. The townhouse displayed its address in Roman numerals and a fanlight glowing above the door like a diadem. The heavy ceramic planters had been evacuated, but the wooden stake tied to the railing was still in place, its sign convulsing in the wind. To Let By Owner. A basement flat. I had seen it earlier that day and now found myself staring at the phone number listed at the bottom.

"Daddy, ring the bell!"

I was about to reach for it when the door opened to a woman in a flower-print dress with a frilled collar. She swung her smile toward us like a searchlight.

"Well now, what have we here? Are you a ghost?"

Tessa jiggled, averting her gaze.

The woman made a show of examining Tessa's priestly veneer. "One of those little creatures from *Star Wars*? I forget what they're called."

Tessa shook her head.

"Oh, I give up."

Tessa remained silent. I gave her a playful nudge. "Can you say what you are?"

"A Druid."

"Well! My goodness. You don't see many of those around these days, do you?"

"Wait for it," I said.

"Sorry?"

"It's coming back in vogue. Polytheism. Pagan chic."

She seemed to flicker at the unexpected notion, the jolt of brain activity among the pleasantries we were supposed to exchange. She wore mild shades of makeup and flesh-coloured stockings and thick-heeled shoes, placing her somewhere near me in the middle-aged plains where the years manifested themselves with drastic variations. I was about to neutralize my comment with some small talk when she set her hands on her hips with comic impatience and raised her eyebrows at Tessa, waiting for the obligatory joke.

"How did the ancient Romans cut their hair?" Tessa said.

The woman pretended to mull it over. "I don't know."

"With a pair of caesars."

She laughed appropriately and reached for a bowl of what appeared to be milk-chocolate thistles, holding one up like an auctioneer before dropping it into Tessa's pillowcase.

Tessa wheeled and started to leave before I caught her.

"What do you say?"

"Thank you."

"You're welcome, dear."

"And just out of curiosity," I said, "is the flat still available?"

She blinked at me. I blinked back at her. We both seemed surprised I had asked the question. Then she looked at the sign as if confirming its existence before replying that indeed it was still free.

"What's the rent, if you don't mind me asking?"

She told me. Very reasonable. I tried to think of a pleasantly hazy reply, but nothing came. Her smile was losing pressure, so I simply said good night and followed Tessa down the steps. We joined some robots with trademarked colour schemes and space aliens from a film that had spawned a series of video games or vice versa. Tessa said hi to a skeleton from her class and a fairy she knew from her swim lessons while I smiled along with other parents in self-conscious fellowship, acknowledging our participation in this true and honourable custom that had endured through the ages. I recalled all the Halloween nights my parents had driven me and my brothers into town like a pack of Huns to ravage the neighbourhoods, the streets transformed into dioramas of fright—the MacFadyens' lawn studded with the tombstones of characters who had died under punny circumstances, Old Man Nuttall's walkway flanked by pirates dressed as local politicians and a headless mayor guarding a community chest full of chocolate kickbacks and payolas. Nuttall himself had winked at us and encouraged repeat visits. Come on back if'n y'all want more. The rules were suspended. Earth was permissive to its core. I felt a retroactive gratitude at the thought of it all. My parents had stayed together without a cold war, without a separate peace. They had worked out their conflicts in front of us like a pair of keystone cops. Nothing major, nothing traumatic. I wanted to call across the Atlantic and describe this night, or a version of it, to thank them even though only one of them was alive to hear it.

I tapped Tessa and pointed to a jack-o'-lantern in one of the windows, comparing its gashed features to those I had carved in competition with my brothers at her age, but she bolted ahead. As we worked our way down the block she developed a realpolitik in her transactions. She smiled because she knew it was cute, and she declared her Druid-ness immediately because she realised it was the fastest way to relieve these foolish adults of their sweets. Her consciousness was taking shape. I wanted to kiss that pure forehead of hers. Those years of brutal service to her biological needs were finally yielding results.

The wind was increasing. Cartons and wrappers ripped past us, a pizza box cartwheeling into lift-off. A roadworks sign fell over with a clang. Car alarms were howling out of phase with each other as people began to return home, sensing that everything was coming unmoored. Tessa's eyes took on a frightened look. I leaned down and suggested she had enough booty. She agreed.

With a mighty heave I lifted her up onto my shoulders and felt her rough costume scratching my neck, knowing every day she would get heavier and I weaker until the two trends met with an impact more powerful than any birthday. The pillowcase swung like a pendulum as I walked, but when we reached our address, instead of climbing the stairs, I gripped the wrought-iron fence and gazed down into the gap that resembled an empty moat between the sidewalk and the building where it dropped down to basement level, the front stoop spanning it like a drawbridge.

"What are you doing, Daddy?"

"Help me count all the doors down there," I said.

"I want to go inside!"

I pointed at each door in turn, trying to make a game of it, until I reached the one in question. Our coal cellar. Our grotto. A small underground room that had once held a winter's worth of fuel but now stood empty. Or almost empty. Many years earlier our downstairs neighbour had suggested it might contain some Victorian-era tools and other relics of value, but I had counted from the wrong direction and pried open someone else's door without realizing it. I had blamed Mrs McNaught's unsound mind, which in its final phases had led her to burn empty pots on the stove and serve meals to a husband who no longer existed before she herself followed him to the grave. But last weekend I had discovered my mistake while looking through the title deeds. And I saw it with different eyes now. If the relics existed, they might yield some cash I could put into a bank account I had established in my name only for work-related expenses. Hermetically sealed from the married morass. Though it didn't matter, after all. I wasn't leaving. No, I told myself. Those thoughts aren't really happening. I wasn't thinking what I thought. I held Tessa fast as another gust threatened to unseat her, the trees around us heaving and hissing and twisting in spasms that showed how much every new direction could hurt.

* * *

The next morning I walked through the city centre with clouds
still reeling in the backwash of the storm. It was the first of
November. The dark side of the moon. A world of blood blisters
and cold sores, the anaemic pulse of streetlights against the coming dawn. Janus Archaeology was located at the edge of Holyrood
Park in what had once been sidings for a railway delivering most
of Edinburgh's coal and therefore most of its reputation as Auld
Reekie. Now, though, the train line was a bicycle path. The extinct
volcano beyond it had collapsed in sections like a circus tent, leaving angular slabs protruding among the folds of eroded earth that
held lochs and bogs and mini glens. A couple of volcanic vents had
become a Lion's Head and Haunch. Lava columns had turned into
Samson's Ribs. A vein of magma running under the tropical forests
and lagoons had solidified into Salisbury Crags, exposed now with
its ruddy flanks, its talus slopes dropping to the greenery below—
all excavated by glaciers scrubbing away the softer layers around it
like dead skin. This was what I saw from my office. The workings
of Earth. No vestige of a beginning, no prospect of an end. I had
a habit of finding myself in these things, seeking guidance in the
world. And this morning my eyes were drawn to the highest point,
Arthur's Seat—a formation that had provoked my brother Marcus
to make an observation that still echoed through the office occasionally. That Arthur must have had a big ass.

I had exchanged the swelter of North Carolina for a landscape with the same latitude as Moscow and nothing but the Gulf
Stream staving off Russian Winter. Over the years my blood had
thickened, my skin had hardened like a shell, but I still felt the
mad slide of the season within me. The sun losing altitude until
it flatlined at the solstice. Midwinter, as the British mistakenly
called it. There was nothing *mid* about it. It was the bottom of the
barrel, the back of the cave, the outer limit of Earth's orbit, where
the northern hemisphere was tilted farthest from the source of
all life. And lately I was beginning to understand something else,
something more subtle about those elderly timeshares in the trop-

ics. It wasn't simply the climate. It was the emotional comfort of living in a place where nothing seemed to change, the days running together so seamlessly that you could almost forget time was passing. Here, though, with these constant variations of weather and light, the sky was a clock.

I removed my outerwear like chainmail. I pressed the buttons for power and light. I dealt with the usual traffic of colleagues and consultations. Victoria explained her spreadsheets of ancient pollen. Alan A, as we called him, touted his dendro data and rugby scores. Eventually I rolled up my sleeves to perform a meticulous itemization of core samples and artefacts recovered from an excavation I had conducted the previous summer in the Highlands. Six weeks of digging had uncovered timbers, trackways, quernstones, hearth features, and a varied tool assemblage from an Iron Age crannog whose discovery had suspended the construction of a luxury hotel on the shores of a picturesque loch. The developer, an American conglomerate unacquainted with my adopted country's devotion to rules and regulations, had hired us with the mistaken impression that Janus Archaeology was some sort of tartan fixer. A senior executive with a set of golf clubs had been air-dropped in for negotiations with the local authority, but his pleasure at finding a fellow patriot on his team had dissolved almost as quickly as the ice in his whisky as I described larger projects than his halted by less than what we had already found. I capped it off with a description of what I had gone through to get a British driving license. He was gone within a week. Contractually obligated to pay for all excavations, Last Resorts had interrogated every inch of earth we had dug after the boundaries of the site had been established. When I told my father about it afterward he reacted with his usual empathy and understanding for the builders, wondering how many jobs, how much income, how much prosperity I had denied everyone who would have been involved in the hotel project. I wondered back at him how much we would know about the origins of architecture, not to mention the human race itself, if modern engineers were allowed to destroy ancient artefacts for the latest flavour of the month in commercial design. And after a transatlantic silence I tried to make amends by pointing out it was only the second time in my career that I was preventing the construction of a hotel, and furthermore, none of it was my doing. I hadn't built the crannog any more than I had built the passage grave under Fergus McCain's pasture in Kilmartin. I only discovered them. I brought them to light. The builders of this time had been thwarted by the builders of a previous one. And my father, unable to process such a notion, had responded with a derisive cough.

My working hypothesis about the crannog was that it had been used for grain, textile, and perhaps also leather processing. Along with some hammerstones and flint tools, there was a jumble of horizontal timbers with no clear pattern of distribution and, beyond it, two structures with alternating layers of sandy gravel and wood-rich organic deposits that indicated repeated renovations to the floor surfaces—but as the layers tended to merge and mix with each other I was having trouble defining the extents. And I was reaching the point where I didn't want to define anything anymore. Each keystroke seemed to take me further from what I had found. Which was what, exactly? Blisters and abrasions. Raw hands gripping a handle pasted with grit. The cold sense of knuckles and fingernails etched in grime, the whorls and ridges and crinkles of skin stained clear as lifelines. An expansive slow awareness at once dumb and acute as I stared down at a tool on the ground, as if thinking about picking it up was the same as picking it up. Everything unstrung and released. Thoughts going out and coming back, in some deep respiration of the mind.

I reached for the phone and dialed the number I had noticed with Tessa the previous night. It happened thoughtlessly, like scratching my neck. The receiver was in my hand, the line ringing. Was I really doing this? The woman who answered recognized my voice immediately. Obeying an instinct for respectability,

I thanked her for indulging my daughter's trick-or-treating and then told her I needed a quiet place to work on a long-term independent research project while my wife renovated and redecorated our home. And as I spoke the words, they became true. Mrs Natalie Sharples, as my prospective landlady identified herself, seemed relieved at such upright necessity and offered to show me the residence that evening. We chirped and sang through the arrangements. We thanked each other kindly. I put down the phone with trembling fingers, a glandular heat released by what I had done. But then it wasn't such a big thing. No commitment had been made. Nothing had been signed. I was just window shopping. Testing the waters. How many times, after all, had I tasted a new ale at the pub knowing I was going to end up with my tried-and-true favourite anyway?

At lunchtime I went to the gym. I worked machines without purpose and lifted weights without function and watched flickering screens while headphones blasted sweet nothings in my ears. I hated doing it, but loved how it made me feel afterward. I pushed, I shoved, I breathed. Thought became muscle, muscle became thought. At the end I submitted myself to the sauna for an extra purge and returned to work in a haze of endorphins, adding indentations and folds to the crannog report to create the appearance of a conclusion where none truly existed. I closed my eyes occasionally as I typed. That evening I donated my pocket change to the Royal British Legion and took a poppy for my lapel before stopping by to see Mrs Sharples for a guided tour. When it was over I requested time to finalise a few details on my end before making a formal commitment. Could she wait another day or so? Indeed, she could.

At home I confronted the end of days—a hellish wail resonating in the stairwell like the entrance to a third-world prison. When I reached the landing I took an extra breath before thumbing my key into the lock. And then, easing the door inward, I discovered a pack of dinosaurs occupying Violet's shoes, a panda modeling one of my t-shirts, and a robot who had appropriated my old wrist-watch as a belt. A mixed fossil record of other activities lay farther down the hall, but I had become numb to it. This was life.

"Nice of you to turn up."

I swivelled toward the living room to find Violet clenching a candy wrapper in her fist and the children heaving and shuddering in reaction to some epic reprimand. She nodded at the sofa, its cushions reconfigured into a fortress.

"There's more in there," she said.

I came through the doorway. "More what?"

"Halloween sweets."

"No way," I said. "I stashed them on the highest shelf of the larder. How did they reach it?"

Violet slanted a look at me. "If you had come home on time, you'd know the answer to that. And maybe," she added, "you could have prevented it from happening in the first place."

She pressed the wrapper to my chest as she passed. I reached up for it and peeled the gummy plastic away from the lapel of my coat only to find the poppy stuck to it. Something about the label seemed familiar. Ah, yes. Mrs Sharples's treat. A coincidence that sent my gaze straight to Tessa, who shrank back as if sensing the betrayal. Jamie came forward with an outstretched hand—his stride still bowlegged despite his recent release from nappies, his lips rimmed with forbidden sucrose—and made a declaration too snarled in snot for me to understand. Unlike Tessa, he had inherited my sandy brown hair, near blond in summer, near dark in winter, and what my father called the Keeler ears. Poor kid.

"Treat," he said again.

I shook my head. "Nice try."

Tessa flared out. "He wouldn't give it back to me!"

The dual wailing resumed, and I made the mistake of trying to shout it down, which only made it worse. I took a breath and glanced at the mess in my hand. The apple of discord. No doubt they had been enjoying a secret banquet within their fort until the dispute caught Violet's attention. Now it was all insult and injury. Paradise lost. Tessa usually bossed Jamie around without resistance, but now she was learning what it was like to hit another person's bedrock. Our children. Despite their differences in colouring they resembled each other in the very foundations of their faces— those faces all pruned and simian now in the aftermath of their tantrums, full of primeval want. Their endless, heedless, brutal, relentless demands. I loved them, but I hated raising them. The feeling ran through me with blades attached, drawing blood.

I crouched down with the poppy as a peace offering. Tessa came over and, after inspecting it with chocolate-stained fingers, allowed me to pin it to her shirt. When I turned to Jamie I recognised a certain awareness blooming in his eyes. I had about three seconds. I fumbled in my pocket and pulled out an I Dig Archeology badge, thankful beyond measure for the paraphernalia that came with my job, and adopted a pseudo-royal accent as I dubbed him Digger of the Month. The weather lifted. Clouds dispersed, bringing sunshine back to young faces.

Struggling to my feet I caught sight of Violet in the doorway, halted on barbs and fishhooks, it appeared, as she watched us, a glint of tenderness in her eyes.

"What?" I asked. "What is it?"

She seemed to harden up like a sniper taking position on a rooftop. "Tea's ready," she said. And then she turned and walked away.

Sure, I thought. See you later. As the kids went traipsing after her I took the opportunity to convert the fortress back into a sofa, confiscating the rest of the sweets while also kicking aside the crayons and workbooks, the building blocks and train cars, the stuffed animals and doll clothing. It used to be simple. It used to be clear. We had started one kind of life together and ended up with another. She had wanted children—two of them, with a tidy spread of ages planned to the very month.

Her hands had gone numb during the pregnancies, pressurized by hormones, the tendons loosened and stretched. She had slept

27

with her arms raised on pillows. After the births she had massaged and strengthened them between feedings until they were restored, but she hadn't gone back to performing in public, preferring to give lectures instead. A quasi-academic, she called herself. Part-time teaching. One class here, another there. Some kind of commitment had drained out of her. Some kind of drive or desire. Now she was exploring something special about Bach's tuning that she claimed was revealed in his calligraphy. Her hands were fine, she said. But one time I had caught her looking down at them with mournful eyes. Why didn't you tell me? she had asked. And she had sat there waiting for her hands to reply.

D on't sleep. I said the words to myself, reverse psychology, as Violet snored and shuffled beside me. She wore protective flannels and a pungent confection of skin creams that promised to counteract not the appearance of aging but its effects. I had restrained myself from pointing out the difference. As if it would have increased our odds of having sex. There was nothing happening on that front. It was a drought that went beyond the seasons of age or familiarity or even that perplexing clash between motherhood and womanhood that required elaborate romantic procedures to resolve. How exactly had it happened? At what point had it become normal for her to wash ashore at the end of the day like a shipwreck victim? The loss was too gradual to identify. Now I eased in closer and touched her hip. Her living heat. Her workings of blood and bone. We didn't tell each other everything. We never had. But the square footage between us had become a moorland.

The mistake was somewhere beneath us but manifesting itself now, it seemed, playing itself out. Our marriage too hasty. Too sudden, too soon. At the time it had seemed like a prank on the British government, pretending to be settled and responsible adults for the sake of my visa. But the vows, simple as they were, and the wedding ring, just a metal band around the finger—they had done something, meant something, after all. Constriction. Constraint.

The feeling had dissipated gradually, but its source remained like a fault in the bedrock.

I turned onto my back and felt a troubling stillness, as if the windstorm of the previous night had been reversed to dead air. Inhale, exhale. Earth was still turning, after all. The core was still boiling with iron and nickel, the mantle still cracking and venting and shearing under all that tectonic mass, the crust still ripping along fault lines, still thrusting up mountains, still grinding plates. And the rains and the winds and the oceans were still wearing it all down. Earth was swelling and contracting. It had a pulse. It had breath. It had a metabolism measured in deep time. And with my eyes adjusted to the eons like a film at high speed, it gave my life proportion and scale. A sleepless night in which I wasn't really thinking what I thought I was thinking. I couldn't leave. But I would do it tomorrow. I would do it next week. I would never do it. I would get up and pack right now. I veered through the emotional and practical issues, the ramifications among family and friends and social sects. My father's blunt disappointment, the implied failure of my life overseas in Marcus's and Robbie's eyes. And Violet's parents. They'd think it was my fault, wouldn't they? I grappled with questions great and small, parsing out the logistics, until I realised the coal cellar would probably open with an old mortise key Violet had found under the carpet in the storage cupboard a few weeks earlier. Yes, of course. Obviously. I would unlock that door like the entrance to Aladdin's Cave. Open sesame. The riches would be mine. A minor victory. In the middle of the night, all victories are minor.

I heard a round of pops and cracks outside. Then another. I hauled myself up and went to the window in time to see a red glare tracing itself out at low altitude and dissipating with a squeal. A prelude to Guy Fawkes Night. Some teenagers in our neighbourhood who couldn't hold their fireworks until the official occasion. The whistling rockets, the Royalist payloads. Yes, that Catholic terrorist still had a lot to answer for. Instead of bringing down a government he had become an excuse for mischief. His death was his life. Failure made him immortal.

I returned to bed and settled myself with massive rearrangements of the pillows and covers. The topography was perfect. Now sleep. I played the command over and over while staring at the ceiling for minutes or hours until I must have slept, because I was awake with a sense of missing time. The clock confirmed it with measurements in red. I switched off the alarm just before it sounded and, remembering the mortise key, quietly dug it out from the hall cupboard, went over to the coat rack, and slipped it into my pocket. When I turned Jamie was standing at my knee.

"Brekkie?" he said.

He was at a stage where most of his statements were phrased as questions, as if he wasn't sure that the experience of one day would apply to the next. I picked him up, bottom-heavy with his overnight nappy and still a bit snotty. Maybe Violet was right about the cold after all. I kissed him on the temple, tasting his silken hair, his sweet skin.

"How did you get out of your cot?" I asked.

At that moment Tessa emerged from his room, all skewed and brilliant, as if she had spent the night connected to an electric socket.

"He climbed out," she said.

"By himself?"

She blinked at me with megalithic guilt.

"Or," I added, "did pterodactyls help him escape?"

She smiled. Jamie smiled because everyone else was smiling. And it was all downhill from there. After coercing them out of their jammies and into proper clothes, I oversaw the daily prison riot known as breakfast. Milk was spilled. Toast was flung. Tessa reacted to some unseen offense by hiding Jamie's favourite brontosaurus in the fridge despite previous warnings not to do such a thing because he truly believed it would freeze to death. As a result I deducted precious minutes from her video time, thereby provoking a tantrum that required more discipline, which in turn aggravated her tantrum and therefore my response to it until I gave her a timeout in her bedroom, holding the door shut to prevent her from escaping while I listened to Jamie drag a chair across the kitchen for what was undoubtedly a nefarious purpose. The trove of Halloween candy. I shouted out his name as Violet emerged from the bedroom, still gnarled with sleep.

I gave her a grim look. "Rise and shine."

There was the sound of Jamie's plate clattering to the kitchen floor. The keyhole erupted as Tessa put her mouth to it and gave a mighty scream of injustice.

"It's like rehearsals for the Ring cycle out here," Violet said.

"It's not as bad as it sounds."

"That's what Mark Twain said."

"What?"

"About Wagner." She came over and took hold of the doorknob to relieve me of guard duty, her hand briefly over mine. She seemed to be full of shadows and fault lines, as if she had been the one with insomnia.

I opened my mouth. "Are you . . .?"

She swung her gaze toward me.

Pregnant, I almost said, but stopped myself. An unexpected and unwanted pregnancy would have explained a lot, but I wasn't going to grab at straws anymore. My questions were always treated like the opening moves of an interrogation. It was up to her now.

"Don't forget I'm at uni today," she said, leaning back to resist one of Tessa's sudden tugs. "You're doing the weans. Pasta Bolognese in the fridge."

"Check," I said.

"Make sure Tessa's fleece comes home with her."

"Anything else?"

Tessa gave another pull.

31

"That's all," she said.

"How about mad sex on the floor? I could work it into the schedule."

She squeezed out a smile. "But what about your wife?"

"We could make it a threesome."

"With you in the middle, you mean."

"If that's what turns you on."

"Oh no," she said. "This isn't about me."

"Then what is it about?"

"You really want to do this now?"

"No time like the present."

She lowered her head and started laughing with her hair fanned around her face. Then she drew herself up and gave me a look of twisted affection that in days past would have led to a lighter moment, a reminder of love in this mad mess of things. Now, though, it seemed to go sour at the very moment it ripened, her words coming out flat. "You're going to be late for work."

The stones, the timbers, the tools. They all appeared on my computer screen with blemishes and flaws rendered in perfect detail. I was nailing them down into cold hard truth, one letter at a time, when I heard a knock on the doorframe behind me and adjusted my eyes to Graeme's reflection.

"The future is certain," he said in a fake Russian accent.

I swiveled toward him, picking up the cue. "*Da*, comrade. It is the past that is unpredictable."

He exhaled grandly. "Ah, Soviet irony. Is there anything better?"

"I can think of a few things."

He flicked his wild eyebrows. His grey hair was groomed with an elegant sweep from the brow, his eyes full of primitive drive. He had emerged from the council flats of Leith by climbing a ladder, as he phrased it, made of scholarships and posh guilt. Now he wore clothing in deliberate juxtapositions—designer shirts with old jeans, torn jerseys with pleated trousers—to mock the upper-class forces that had opposed him, like a warrior wearing the ornaments of a dead foe around his neck.

He glanced around my office as if he hadn't been there in months. "Guess what they say instead of *anti-clockwise*?"

"Who, the Soviets?"

"The Russians."

I gave it some thought. "Counter-revolutionary. All clocks moving in such a manner will be sent to the Gulag."

"Good one, comrade. But *nyet*. Against the fingers of the clock. That's the literal translation."

I nodded slowly, trying to express appreciation. He had come for a specific purpose that would be revealed at his pace rather than mine.

He pointed at me. "Aye, you're feeling it."

"Feeling what?"

"Darkness visible. It's written all over your face."

I stretched back. "It's just sleep deprivation."

"Shagging the missus into the wee hours, were you?"

I wasn't capable of mentioning my trouble with Violet, at least not yet, so I told him about the fireworks instead.

"Lovely coincidence, that. The Gunpowder Plot. Samhain. Like he couldn't have picked a different day to blow up Parliament. Now he goes into the bonfire every year like it was invented just for him."

I was rubbing my eyes. "Who?"

"Guy Fawkes, you daft bastard. Have some coffee."

I held up my hands in surrender. He disappeared down the hallway, returned with a mug for each of us, and leaned against my desk while we drank. Tough love. He had hired me straight out of Edinburgh University because of a conversation in a pub. He either wouldn't or couldn't identify what I had said to make myself worthy of Janus Archaeology, but over the past two decades I had come up with explanations that I later rejected in favour of others like a series of myths that seemed to be true until they seemed false and then ridiculous in retrospect. He was a generation beyond me, steeped in astronomy, literature, anthropology, geology, languages, folklore, and the microclimate of Scottish politics. And he had recently married his third wife. He had started over not once but twice. He took pride in reinventing himself for survival.

He glanced over his shoulder at the Crags, which were gleaming in a low exposure of sun. "Christ, look at that. Why didn't I take this office for myself?"

"Because you want to be near the main entrance to see who comes and goes. Keep an eye on the serfs."

"Aye, right."

We drank in easy silence. It was either this or the crannog report. Maybe he had a similar piece of nonsense on his desk.

"Samhain," he said. "The final harvest. When the lighter half of the year gives way to the darker half. A time to size up the grain supplies. Decide which animals to slaughter for winter provision and cast the bones into the flames afterward. Bone-fire. Bonfire."

"You've said this before."

"Leaves fall. Grasses wilt. The border separating us from the netherworld becomes thin. Thin indeed. The dead reach across the threshold unless we placate them with rituals and costumes. Halloween, aye. No coincidence, that."

He took a slow sip of coffee. A man who worked his way toward an announcement, enjoying every step.

"You'll be happy to know that Fergus McCain is alive and well."

I didn't move, but somewhere inside me I felt a sail filling out, a hull swivelling in the current. "Fergus the Destroyer," I said. "Still grinding up artefacts under cover of darkness?"

"Nobody's perfect."

"The guy threatened to kill me."

Graeme shrugged. "Apparently he's letting bygones be bygones."

The bygones came from a proposed expansion of his B&B into a massive hotel and spa complex in 1988. The bygones also came from the ruined medieval chapel and graveyard adjacent to his land, which was not only part of the tourist appeal but also why an archaeological survey had been required before planning permission could be granted. Additional bygones had been found via the keyhole excavations I conducted, revealing a vallum enclosing an early Christian settlement, while the bygone stones I uncovered below it had turned out to be the orthostats of a Neolithic chambered cairn with both inhumed and cremated burials, flint arrowheads, hazelnut shells, and a carinated bowl assemblage that served as evidence of maritime contact with France early during the fourth millennium BC. Those bygones would have stopped the show even if I hadn't unearthed the bygones of a Mesolithic shell midden at the bottom of it all. The development of Fergus's B&B had been arrested permanently, which at first I had assumed would be a minor issue as it seemed to be a sideline compared to his quarry located only a few miles away. If anyone had a right to feel let down, I thought, it was his darling and generous wife, Catriona, who actually managed the accommodation and did all the cooking. She took it in stride like a Buddhist monk. Fergus took it like Attila the Hun.

"Did you know he's having some trouble with that quarry of his?" Graeme asked, examining his fingernails with an affected air.

"You don't say."

"It seems that some trees were uprooted by the gale the other night. And guess what was underneath?"

I lowered my mug.

Graeme's expression finally cracked, releasing a smile. "Rock carvings."

"Which side of the quarry? How far up the slope?"

"Look at you. Like it's Christmas morning."

I reached out as if to grab him by the lapels. "Graeme, please."

"About halfway up the northeastern side, apparently. Where he aims to expand. In fact, he already started and, ahem, might have blasted straight through it without notice, but the local authority received a call from a mountain biker who happened to see the carvings on the exposed rockface." Graeme flicked his eyebrows. "Mind you, I'm sure it had nothing to do with the quarry cutting toward the trail, which local cyclists have been protesting."

I began pacing the office. The carvings were located not in Kilmartin but a side valley called Kilmichael. And I could see it— the clumped spruces, the earthfast rock, the curved hills in the distance like a pod of whales.

"So now," Graeme said, "the future is certain for Mr Fergus Mc-Cain. He needs an impact study before he can carry on with the work."

I looked at him. "When?"

He drank off his coffee, savouring the delay, and set down the empty mug for me to wash. "Monday. And see if you can do this one without a death threat, aye?"

CHAPTER THREE

1986

The circle of fifths shows the relationships between the pitches of the chromatic scale. And it looks like a clock. The twelve tones correspond to hours. The major and minor keys answer the shadows on a sundial. Starting from A minor at noon, for example, each sharp takes you clockwise while each flat moves you anti-clockwise until the two hands meet as an enharmonic pair at six o'clock. Then they carry on past each other all the way round to noon again. Or midnight. And so this is how we meet: a spilled pint glass, beer sluicing across the bar. The bloke in front of me lifting his hands from the surface and taking a step back and then swivelling to apologise when he steps on my foot, his forearms raised like a doctor waiting for surgical gloves.

I look at his hands. He sees me looking at them and tries to make something of it.

"Guess what I do for a living?" he asks.

The fingers are nicked and callused, with rough knuckles. And they're large. What I could do to a keyboard with those. "Stone mason," I say. "Gravedigger."

He smiles. "Neither. Both."

His eyes are shaped in a way that offsets the wide block of his forehead. An endearing little curve to his lower lip. His hair is pale brown, almost blondish. American voice, with southern ballast. I reckon he gets his way with women just a little too often. And he has some friends or companions, it seems, resonating beside him. A popular guy.

"What are you studying?" he asks.

We're surrounded by dark teak and old smoke and lamps with stained-glass shades. It's the Rig & Run in early December, the dead end of term, and I've been trying to play Rachmaninoff all day and haven't washed my hair or changed out of the trousers I was wearing when a car bashed through a puddle next to me and even now a television in the corner is blaring with Chernobyl and contaminated sheep, a toxic spring everlasting, all bad news within and without. Clare is somewhere behind me, trying to find a table before Isobel arrives, and I just want to forget it all and have a few drinks with my friends.

I make a point of looking over his shoulder to catch the barman's eye.

"English," he says to me.

I snap him a look. "You think I'm English?"

"I mean English literature. What you're studying."

I shake my head.

"Hot or cold?"

I take a deliberate breath. Stop it before it starts. Otherwise what? Back to his room somewhere—or worse, mine—for another nasty surprise. After what happened with that other bloke, I've adopted a Presbyterian attitude. Men belong on the other side of the aisle. Make them work. Make them wait. It's the only way to vet them. It's the only way to let them know I'm real.

"By any chance are you sensing a resistance from me?"

"Oh, yeah."

"Then why don't you move on?" I say, brushing up against him out of sheer necessity as I lean in to order the drinks, giving him my shoulder to make it clear what's what. And then, easing back, I notice Isobel at the doorway shaking the rain off her jacket. The plain beauty of her oval face, her bright eyes. She attracts upstanding blokes seeking marriage just over the rise. But this one? He'd go for Clare's hot blond confidence and leopard curves. She's the lightning rod for these types. As Isobel catches sight of me I bulge my face out and roll my eyes toward him. Look at this, will you.

"I'm not moving on," he says, apparently unruffled, "because I was here first. And besides, I'm trying to find out if you're as smart as you look."

That comment catches me, almost. I turn back to him with an eyebrow raised, just a wee bit amused. "Good one. I bet it works with a lot of girls."

"You think it's a line?"

"Yeah. And a clever one for someone like you."

He seems to straighten, his expression struck clean. "Someone like me?"

"A Yank on the make."

He watches me for a long moment. "Oh," he says. "I guess you're not so smart after all. Sorry for wasting your time."

He turns to his companions and joins in their run of laughter. The drinks appear in front of me. I hand over the money and wait for change. I glance at his back. His attitude in a major key. An upbeat Tom Sawyer–type who doesn't deserve what I just gave him. I'm not that kind of person. I'm better than that. Now act it.

"I didn't really mean that," I say.

He doesn't hear me. Or he can't be doing with me at this point, and who can blame him.

I tap him on the shoulder. "I'm just having a rough day. All right?"

He swivels at the waist and gives me a different look, blank as paper. "Sure. No problem." He turns back.

I tap him on the shoulder again.

I'm about to admit I've been punishing him for someone else's crime, but the whole mass of it seems too much. "I'm studying music," I say instead. "And you know what? I'm bloody awful at it. When I play the Rach 3 it sounds like the Lone Ranger theme. I can't hit anything right. And obviously it's one of the hardest things in the universe to play and obviously Rachmaninoff wrote it for his own *huge* hands, but what really kills me is how it exposes all the flaws I didn't even know I had all the way back to Mozart concertos I nailed years ago—or thought I nailed, because when I play them now I hear mistakes big enough to drive a lorry through. How could I think I was any good? These *things*," I say, holding up my hands the same way he did, "are all wrong."

I blow out a breath. I didn't know this was in me. I didn't know it was how I felt. He seems to be sizing me up, measuring the full length of what I've said, and it feels pleasant to be looked at for once, unpleasant to be truly seen. Ok, that's us finished. I pick up the drinks.

"They're not foreign objects," he says.

I give him a careful look. "Sorry?"

"Your hands. Don't blame them. It's probably the music that's fucking you up. What's it called again?"

"Rachmaninoff's Piano Concerto Number Three," I say. What I don't say is that it's notoriously daunting and convoluted. After the failure of his first symphony Rachmaninoff sank into a depression and then emerged from it several years later with his second piano concerto. The tolling of those notes in the opening movement like a state funeral before that lyrical theme in E-flat major crops up. A rebirth. A transformation. But he had nowhere to go after that and so he whipped up a storm with Concerto No. 3. A daredevil who loved the tonal system for all the hurdles it gave him, all the opportunities to show off. That whole development with the left and right hands playing overlapping figures like a canon and those ferocious climaxes over and over leading to the cadenza—two versions of it, the longer and thicker chordal one that he preferred, inaccurately labeled the ossia, and the lighter one in toccata style. I can't play either. Instead I've been soothing myself with the E-flat major melody in the second movement, an echo of that lyrical theme in Concerto No. 2, pretending it will give me a stronger sense of the whole piece, pretending it will lead somewhere, pretending it will revive some small measure of talent that I foolishly thought I possessed.

"Rachman . . ." he trails off. "What did you call it before?"

"The Rach 3."

"The rack. Like a medieval dungeon." He fixes a clinical look on me and then nods. "My guess is you're some kind of hypertalented piano goddess who's finally come up against something difficult."

I'm about to protest when that comment hits me square in the chest. What I didn't want to tell myself. What I didn't want to hear.

"It always came to you much faster," he goes on, "than it came to everyone else. You absorbed it like you already knew it. Like you were remembering instead of learning. And it seemed as if you were . . ." he gestures at the ceiling " . . . beyond yourself. But now this Rach 3 is manual labor. It's just work. It makes you feel dark and dead inside. That thing—that magic—it doesn't happen even in the sections you *can* play. And like you said, it's ruining all the stuff you did before. You're doubting what you've already done. But what you're feeling now, the darkness and death . . . maybe that's part of it. Maybe you need to go through it because that's what *he* went through. At the darkest point, you'll find it. You'll light up again. The same way he did. The Rack Man."

"Rachmaninoff," I manage to say, still standing with the drinks in my hands and my body angled away from him, lost and found at once.

Isobel slips into view behind him and flashes me a look like do you require roadside assistance, madam? She knows how I've been lately. She knows I'm living in no man's land, though she doesn't know why. And I can't say it because my throat knots up. How stupid I was to let him take me back to his room, all carefree and sexed up that night with who knows what, hormones and whisky, I guess, and then suddenly facedown on the bed with an arm twisted behind me and his cock almost in my arse before I twisted and kicked and caught him in the balls. But now? An instinct running like a river in the other direction. I seem to want this one. I seem to want him a lot. As he's tipping back his pint I give Isobel a wee shake of the head, or rather quite a sharp one, my eyes going off like magnesium flares. Back off, actually. Second thoughts. He's mine.

I'm looking straight at him when he lowers his glass. His face crinkles with a self-conscious look. "Was that over the top?"

I'm not sure how to reply, what with Isobel in the background, her jaw dropped like what do we have here? Leave some for the rest of us, Vi. I flick my eyes at her. Move along, please. There's nothing to see here after all.

"Ignore it," he says.

I hesitate, for an instant thinking he's cottoned on to Isobel.

"Forget what I said," he says. "It wasn't really me."

I smile despite myself. "Then who was it?"

"Not who. What. Maeshowe."

"Sorry?"

"The passage grave in Orkney. The big one. The famous one." He watches my expression. "Oh, come on, you're Scottish. You should know this. Late Neolithic. A couple centuries shy of five thousand years old. From a distance it's just a mound, all turfed over. The entrance passage is long and narrow, about yay high." He holds a hand at shoulder height. "You have to stoop or crawl through the dark. All that flagstone surrounding you. You can feel the weight. But then you reach the central chamber, which opens up to, what—" He raises his eyes above me. "—twelve, thirteen feet high? Which isn't so large, but it feels like a stadium after that claustrophobic passage. There are a few side chambers where bones were kept, but of course they're all empty now. Looted by the Vikings and everyone else who stumbled on it. Nothing to see. Except when I visited yesterday."

I turn slightly, putting Isobel out of sight. She'll find Clare at one of those long benches back there, the plain hard wood polished by who knows how many bums on a thousand nights like this. I'd set one of the pints down on the bar, but it's walled off with other bodies, a mass of elbows and broad backs. What the hell.

"You went there now?" I ask. "I mean, in December?"

He hesitates, as if I might laugh at what he's about to say. "Because the passageway is aligned toward the sunset for about three weeks before and after the winter solstice. But not on the solstice itself."

I raise my eyebrows politely. "And that's important."

"It's vital."

"But the solstice—that's the shortest day of the year. I would think that's the one that counts."

"Which is why they marked it on *either side*. Maeshowe doesn't have a hearth in the central chamber like other passage graves because I think it was always meant to be dark. A place for the dead. But then, in the heart of winter, when the days are almost at their shortest . . ." He sails a hand out. "The sunset comes shining down the passage, illuminating the inner chamber. A golden glare reaching all the way to the back wall. That dead zone inside—it's suddenly bright and alive. The sun keeps shifting, though, beyond the passage until the chamber goes dark again during the actual solstice. The shortest day of the year. But then the sun returns, lighting it up again. And that's when you feel it."

"Feel what?"

"Rebirth. Renewal. The whole sky—the whole world happening in that moment. Maeshowe gives you the full sense of it, inside and out."

Someone jostles me from behind, the beers sloshing and dribbling over my hands but I don't bother glancing back. Do I want this? Can I handle it? Whatever is ahead with him? A key change, surprising when it happens and then inevitable afterward—these things always coming into existence just beyond the edges of the heart.

"My name is Violet," I say. "Violet Wringham. I'm listed in the campus directory. Ring me up, and I'll meet you at a café or something. I know that's geeky and old-fashioned, but I'm not normal."

"Violet," he says, more to himself than to me, with a mild drawl, an easy slide through the first vowel. And then I see a secret humour edging through his smile.

"What?" I ask.

He widens his eyes in a show of innocence.

"You're thinking something."

"I'm always thinking something."

I tilt my head, playful but utterly honest. "If you're going to act like that, it's over before it starts."

"Promise you won't pour those drinks on me?"

"Don't be ridiculous. I wouldn't waste perfectly good cask ale on you."

He laughs. "That's why I was thinking it."

"Thinking what?"

"Ultra-Violet. Because if I'm not careful, you'll burn me."

In other circumstances this would be an insult, but here and now it seems like a sign of respect. Maybe it's the tone in his voice. Or maybe it's my need to be taken seriously. And to be liked. By him. Ok, yes. The notion settles down all snug inside me.

"Aaron Keeler," he says. "You can make fun of it all you want, as long as I get to hear your voice when you do it."

He smiles at me. I smile back despite myself, a heat coming into my face as I make my way toward Clare and Isobel with their sound advice and common sense.

CHAPTER FOUR

2006

My parents expected me to go to Chapel Hill. They expected me to become enlightened at a convenient distance. They expected me to take wing not suddenly but in stages, like my two older brothers, returning home on a regular basis with altered clothes and hairstyles to signify my independence as I tried to argue them out of their political delusions. Instead we had transatlantic conversations about the finer points of radiocarbon dating and bone collagen analysis. I described the geological cycle with its continuous transformations of igneous and sedimentary and metamorphic rock. And I broke the news that, like me, Scotland is alien to the rest of Britain—a piece of shrapnel lodged in the northwestern corner of Europe's skull, fortunately without impairing upper brain function. London is fine, thanks.

"Now you're losing me with that local colour."

"Because London is the cultural capital," Dad said, speaking up suddenly on the extension in the living room. "Like New York."

"Well thanks, Gene. I'm talking about the shrapnel. That's *ex nihilo* to me unless you say what it comes from."

From a pair of continents colliding in the Iapetus Ocean just south of the equator about five hundred million years ago, I told them, buckling and crumbling and folding together to force new segments above water for the first time. At one end of the wreck, England emerges. At the other, Scotland is born. Now without getting too political, doesn't that make sense? This impact gives Scotland the West Highland and Grampian Mountains and, after another hundred million years of volcanic activity, a position at the hub of the supercontinent known as Pangaea. Contrary to popular belief, Pangaea isn't some tectonic Garden of Eden but a fairly recent condition, where the billiard balls happen to collide in the middle of the table. And here's Scotland at the very heart of it all, with mountains indistinguishable from the Scandinavians to the north and the Appalachians to the south. But then a plate boundary becomes active and rips it all apart, creating the Atlantic Ocean in the process. The larger mass moves off to become the Americas, while the smaller portion drifts northward and, after an outbreak of volcanoes on its western isles, is reshaped by glaciers gouging out glens and corries and granite ranges and bare crags like the ones I could see from my office.

My office came in later versions of the story, of course, but in retrospect I couldn't distinguish exactly when it appeared any more than I could remember when gas became petrol, when pants turned into trousers, or when I started eating takeaway instead of takeout. I had retained a few hard nubs of vocabulary—parking lot, sidewalk—and the long vowels of tomato and vase, but after two decades of erosion my voice sounded foreign everywhere I went. I belonged to neither country, and I belonged to both.

A few days after my conversation with Graeme I drove toward peaks that had more in common with the Blue Ridges than with anything in England. The ocean that divided me from my homeland also plunged its arthritic fingers deep into Scotland's windward flanks, forcing the roads into twists and coils like varicose veins that made my drive a three-hour journey instead of a straight shot from one coast to the other. In early morning darkness I took the motorway across the Central Belt to Glasgow, following the unseen imprint of the Antonine Wall, then headed north before turning west and then south and then west and then north again, following the lobes of coastline farther and farther out. The world took shape with balding hills and bare-knuckled pastures and empty croftlands, tufts of dark forest, the glades breathing out mist. By the time I reached Loch Fyne the sun had risen high enough to put everything in a cold sweat. There was an enameled shine to the grasses and ferns at the roadside, the fields churned to a muddy gleam. I took my bearings from the loch beside me, running with the others in parallel slashes that held either fresh or salt water depending on how severely the glaciers had carved them out. Over the hills only ten kilometres away Loch Awe had released several hundred Niagaras as it melted, digging out a gorge that slowly silted up and became a flat-bottomed valley and estuary, the tides washing in and out with changing sea levels to erode the steep bluffs into terraces. This was the anatomy of Kilmartin Glen. Or the bones of it. Like most of Britain, it had been deforested by the time the Romans invaded.

At Lochgilphead I wheeled through a couple of mini roundabouts and passed through the low frontages of stone. A few shops had been replaced by others, like spark plugs in their sockets. The board for the inn had been repainted, but not the one for the pub. I caught sight of my favourite sandwich vendor, still serving his daily bread, and the outdoor supplier where I had bought extra waterproofs eighteen years earlier, now flanked by Chinese and Indian takeaways. Since when? How long had I been away? At least one season of change. The world was opening up.

Low tide had exposed spews of kelp at the esplanade. I eased down the window for the harsh brine scent. The humped landforms in the distance gave that sense of things too near and too far, too light and too dark all at once. I was here again. There was something strange in my heart. Another roundabout took me out of town along a level stretch fringed with bracken and scrub and mixed woodlands and, despite the sunlight, a sense of colours draining from everything everywhere. It held the dirty wash of foliage I had come to expect—the tea and tobacco stains, the tarnished brasses and russets. Tessa and Jamie had never been to North Carolina during the autumn peak. They hadn't seen the fierce hot flush, the colours all touched with fire. I imagined the three of us driving along the Blue Ridge Parkway and stopping to play in fallen leaves together, pretending it didn't matter that Violet wasn't there. I experimented with the feeling. I dropped it like a rock into a well, listening for the splash. Or the thunk. I lowered the window fully and took a cold breath. Last Friday I had phoned Mrs Natalie Sharples to tell her I was leaving town unexpectedly, a half-truth that allowed me to put off the decision.

A decision whose consequences couldn't be reversed. Even if I moved out for only a month or two and then returned with my marriage renewed, Tessa and Jamie would feel the gap. It would linger in their emotional registers. If Daddy went away in the past, he might go away again in the future. I didn't want them to feel that. But as I followed a broad passage through the hills I couldn't think of another way to provoke Violet into recognising her behaviour. How much of it involved me? How much came simply from her? I had tried talking. I had tried silence. Now I needed to do something more drastic. But how would it feel, living apart, living alone? I steeled myself to that possibility as I passed slopes that had been clearcut, or *harvested* as the phrase went, to leave a vast exposure of stumps and ragged aftergrowth, a timberline of Sitkas packed together in the distance, their branches knitted tight.

The hills parted beyond the next bend. The land opened up and spread out flat. The entrance to Kilmartin Glen. A petrol station gleamed just a bit farther along—the site where Fergus had unearthed a prehistoric stone and deliberately fed it into his crusher before anyone could notice. This according to a reliable eyewitness. Report him? Aye, go ahead. The deed was done, the evidence gone. Her word against his. Good luck, lassie. His true grievance had been not against me but the world I represented, everything that stood in his way. At least that's what she had told me afterward. I felt a tick upward in my blood pressure. I eased it down. And as the crag of Dunadd came into view I swung onto a track marked for the Inbhir Bed and Breakfast, my reflex intact. Despite my fervour for the new rock carvings I stopped here, as always, to pay my respects.

There was no sign of life at the McCain household. The byre was open, but the cottage seemed to be shut, with draperies drawn and patio cleared in sober preparation for the winter ahead. The tractor was dead, unhitched from its trailer. The B&B sign hung heavily from its chains. In the wake of his scuttled plans Fergus had commissioned a local artist to paint an iconic silhouette that to my eyes resembled the sarsens of Stonehenge more than Inbhir's distinctive forecourt, but I could hardly blame him for trying to whip up some prehistoric mystique and gain momentum to take him through the winter—without success, as it turned out. The hotel, like the farm, was helplessly seasonal.

I switched off the engine and looked back toward the road running along the base of the terraced hillsides, the petrol station with its placards and pumps. The spot had been screened by trees at the time of the excavation. And the very first scrape of Fergus's backhoe had exposed the stone, she said, breaking off a chunk but also revealing not simply one spiral carvings but two—one on the broad side, the other on the edge—with a tail linking them. A motif that resembled the ones at Newgrange. And if it was true, if her brief glimpse of the stone could be trusted, then a link between Inbhir and a passage tomb across the Irish Sea, with some of the most elaborate rock art in the world, was gone forever. No. Don't think of it. Don't think of what has been lost.

I climbed out to the long view, the release of open space. Yes, remember this. The person you were. The sound of the River Add running below on the Moine Mhòr, the great moss, with pools all soft and spongy where it hadn't been reclaimed, the hummocks and hollows giving off a scent of fresh decay. The mixed clumps of sphagnum moss and sedge grasses and heather. The bog myrtle whose paddle-shaped leaves she crushed between her fingers and rubbed on your neck to ward off midges with its resinous scent.

Summer then. Winter now. With breath pluming I gazed out at patches of grassland where a few dozen sheep stood marked with fluorescent pink bursts as if they had lost a paintball fight. A couple of burns trickling nearby—one hugging the single-lane road like a gutter and another coming out of the foothills—had been redirected during peat harvesting in the nineteenth century to suit the new workings of the land, but the River Add still followed its natural course, emerging from the side valley of Kilmichael, where the new carvings had been found, before flowing past this spot and, farther on, the knoll of Dunadd, which had been an island as recently as a thousand years ago. Tribesmen had reportedly sailed up to its slopes to participate in coronation rituals involving a carved footprint that, Graeme never failed to point out, was now covered with an unmarked fibreglass replica that even preservationists admitted couldn't be removed without damaging the original relic. As if you could keep anything from changing in this kind of landscape. It went from woodland to freshwater peat bog to saltmarsh, with lochs running deep inland—a natural crossroads for travel across the Irish Sea. There were copper deposits nearby. Local pottery and fossil material had been traced to other parts of Britain and northern Europe. A dynamic place, all flux and flow, though it wasn't easy to notice as I stood inhaling not the scent of low tide, hidden just behind the line of hills nearby, but the funk of manure and the nameless sheddings of harvest.

I pulled on my gloves and zipped up my coat. There was a warmth to the daylight but a chill to every shadow as I walked. The chapel held its plain windows against the day. The graveyard bared its broken teeth at the sky. And there, less than a football pitch away, was the Inbhir chambered cairn wanting none of it. The divisions of life and death, earth and sky. Was that part of the appeal? A consciousness five millennia before ours. How we were back then—not quite ourselves.

The cairn was a mound of rubble stretching back over a hundred feet, slightly oblong, with a flattened façade of orthostats originally joined by sections of drystone walling but now standing apart as they fanned out from the entrance, diminishing in height. Two sets of portal stones formed a central passage that was divided by septal slabs into burial chambers, the largest one at the rear. And the forecourt, paved with quartz, still held a stubbled glow among the various gravels mixed in over the millennia—a fierce and vivid presence in the light. There had been a roof, of course, probably corbelled and trapezoid in shape, but I had refused to reconstruct it because the amount of conjecture involved would have made the results dishonest, if not fanciful. Furthermore I had argued against covering it with a concrete dome, which was a common practice back then, because it would have been self-defeating to distinguish the artificial elements from the original ones when dressing it up for public display was the very thing that introduced the need for those artificial elements. I had stated my case to Graeme, knowing how he felt about Dunadd's fake footprint, and he had convinced the right preservationists in the right places. The result was a restoration of only the basic elements, with the orthostats set back in their sockets and the septal slabs upright to let the sections resemble vertebrae, the very bones shifted and processed within it, the fractals of design. Extra grooming would have given it a false sense of accessibility. It didn't belong to a world that calibrated science with religion or distinguished thought from feeling, that regarded the wheeling of the seasons without blood. It didn't belong to civilization and its discontents. Keep it that way. The quiet provocation of ancient humanity. Yes, that was your line. You were a purist, determined to make your mark with bold simplicity.

And nobody noticed it now. I removed a glove and patted each of the orthostats as I passed. The cold density. Epidiorite shot through with veins of quartz. The two tallest ones flanking the portal had simple cup marks like acne scars. I stopped between them and gazed down the sectioned passage. Remember the work. How many hours you spent on this. How much time. Facing inward toward death, facing outward toward that distinctive notch in the hills to the northeast, which wasn't a coincidence. You had known that immediately. It was an alignment. Obviously. And along with the quartz hammerstones and mixed lithic assemblages recovered in the early stages of the excavation, it had suggested some kind of ritual. Unfortunately it suggested the same thing to a group of Druids, who had mounted a protest against the removal of the bone fragments and cremated remains of what they claimed were their ancient guardians. Wearing a variety of robes and antlers, they spent an afternoon beating drums and chanting just beyond the yellow tape, condemning the excavation crew with curses and then delivering an official letter, signed by the loyal Arthurian warbands and their orders, covens, and groves, as well as the Council of British Druid Orders, calling for the reburial of prehistoric human remains.

You made the mistake of arguing with them, pointing out, in your brash American voice, that most British people are a mixture of early hunter-gatherers, Bronze Age immigrants, Roman invaders who themselves included various Mediterranean races, followed by waves of Saxons, Jutes, Danes, and a rather large assault force of French Vikings otherwise known as Normans—most of whom pumped their DNA into the gene pool long after the owners of these particular bones had been laid to rest, which meant that ancient remains effectively belonged to everyone. And you were actually surprised that it didn't go over well. They still claimed the excavation was tantamount to digging up a cemetery. You responded with a shrug, informing them that modern cemeteries were routinely emptied of dead bodies in advance of development, usually by professional cemetery-clearance companies, and that furthermore anyone buried in a such a place should expect to be dug up after about a century since most burial plots in Britain were rented rather than owned.

You used the truth like a cudgel. That's what Violet had said a few days later back in Edinburgh when you told her the story, expecting compliments rather than the sort of unpleasant appraisal that comes in the early stages of a marriage. But of course, you told her, she hadn't been at the site. She hadn't seen those self-important bastards. And you hadn't been *here*, she replied. You hadn't heard her play the Passacaglia in C minor, really heard it in Tolbooth Church, otherwise you might understand how something can take hold of you despite all reason. Except, you replied, Inbhir wasn't music. It was architecture. Stone cold. Rock solid. Hard and heavy fact.

The following week you lost all patience with the Druids when they informed you that Inbhir had been built to honour the midsummer sunrise, which according to their calculations would take place in that notch between the hills. You took great pleasure in pointing out that the sun would rise about five degrees to the south of it, which was a large margin of error even by Neolithic standards and didn't even qualify as an orientation, let alone an alignment. Well of course, the chief or grand shaman replied, five thousand years ago the sun would have set much farther north. Well no, you said, it would have set only about half a degree farther, which still put it well outside the launch window for his enlightened spirit, both then and now, and at any rate if he wanted to commune with his bespoke god he'd have to wait until next summer, when the excavation would be finished and the site open to the public. He raised his staff at you. You brandished your trowel. His loyal followers intervened on his behalf, your work crew on yours. The police were notified. You enjoyed the institutional power on your side. Your expert status, your authority. And you relished the days as the solstice approached and it became clear that the fabled alignment wasn't going to take place. You watched their daily assembly shrink, drying up like a puddle in the sun. The natural order was restored, it seemed to you. After all, this wasn't another Stonehenge. It wasn't even another Maeshowe or Callanish. Without a solar blessing it was an unspectacular configuration of stones whose allure relied on a taste for what was missing as much as for what was there.

And what was here now? Nothing. Admit it. Visitors consisted of some niche tourists, academic specialists, and New Age crackpots. Nobody cared. Your great excavation, the launchpad of your career, had turned out to be of only passing interest to others. It had proved simply that you were competent, that you deserved the job you already had. All those months of discovery, that inflation of your ego. What did it add up to? What did it get you in the end?

Walking out farther, I cleared the shadow of the hill behind me and stood in a sheaf of sunlight. I blinked into it. I breathed. And when I turned back I discovered a full moon setting in nearly the opposite direction, matted clean and white against a blue sky. As I stepped forward I kicked a beer can scattered with a few others and noticed some firework casings at the edge of the slope. The refuse of Guy Fawkes Night. Hard to resist a natural platform like this one. At least someone was enjoying the site. In Edinburgh there had been the usual pyrotechnics, some of it official, some of it not, but here it was all DIY. As always. The chapel, the graveyard. The cairn and carvings. And beneath it all thousands of shells left by Mesolithic hunter-gatherers. Cockle and carpet, mussel and oyster. Periwinkle, razor, limpet. This had been a special place from the beginning, or what was called the beginning because it was the earliest deposit that had been found, the sequence determined from the top layer downward, the first thing last, the last thing first, on an ancient shoreline unseen now in time and tide.

Fergus McCain came at me before I shut the door of my car. He was wearing what looked like the same work fatigues and heavy boots, the same knit cap over that same bald head. As he approached, though, I realised that his face had deepened over the years, taking on the creases and encrustations of a doormat at a crofter's cottage. He extended a rough hand in both greeting and threat. "I like you, lad, but I hate seeing you."

Ah, yes. Lad. It was all coming back. This was his attempt at diplomacy. As I shouldered my bag I resisted an urge to reply with the phrase reversed because it would have been too sharp for a joke. "Graeme sends his regards."

"Aye, the flea loves the dog."

"Dog? Does that mean you're going to sniff my groin?"

He coughed out a laugh and nodded at our adversarial edges reestablished. And then, as he launched into a tirade about his disrupted schedule, I noticed that although his elephantine stature had shrunk and his stride had become a wobble, he still jabbed the air with knobbed fingers and barked out each word as if he were ten minutes into an argument. I pitied the family members by his deathbed. He would not go gentle into that good night.

"No offense," I said, interrupting him, "but instead of gabbing like a schoolgirl you can just point me toward the rock carvings before something happens to them."

He looked at me for a moment, thrown clear of what he had been saying. The vast impact crater of the quarry loomed behind him. The framework of grinders and mullers and conveyors, the ribbing of heavy pipes. A dump truck was parked at one of the funnels. Yeah, I thought. Ask me if I'm suggesting something. Go ahead and ask.

His chest rose like he was about to make another comment, but then gravel started rattling behind him and he gestured at the prefab shack that served as an office. We walked toward it through a gale of diesel fumes. I expected him to turn on me once we were inside, but instead he squeezed between a couple of desks and reached for the coffeepot. I stood in the stale heat with my arms folded. The shelves were packed with binders and folders and loose paperwork, the rack on the wall beside me thick with reflective jackets and hardhats. There was a ratty armchair in the corner that I guessed was Fergus's throne and fluorescent tubes overhead bleaching everything in sight. And sitting at another desk was a young woman whose smile loosened a deadbolt inside me.

"That'll be Lorna," he said without looking at either of us. "My granddaughter."

I was caught for an airless instant before I said hello, but she didn't seem put off by it, or even to notice, as she called out a greeting and then lowered her eyes back to her computer screen.

"She'll be showing you that precious stone when she's done the invoices."

"I don't want to interrupt anything," I managed to say. "Just tell me where to go."

"Interrupt anything, oh, aye." He left a caustic silence. "Too right I'll tell you where to go."

"Granddad," Lorna said, giving him a surprisingly sharp look, "you think our visitor'll be wanting some of that coffee?"

"Thanks," I said, turning back to her, "but I'm fine."

She had a forthright expression. No makeup. Early to mid-twenties. Her hair was tied back to reveal her face, almost cat-like, with a firm balance to her gaze.

"A civil phrase from a civil man," Fergus said.

I didn't reply, letting my silence do the work. Lorna inhaled and pushed herself back from the desk. "Right. Shall we make a start then, Mr Keeler?"

Fergus shifted the mug from his lips. "After the invoices—"

"That's me done," she said, reaching for her coat. "And anyway I could use the air just now."

She brushed past me in a backdraft of floral hints that wasn't exactly perfume but lotions and scrubs absorbed into her body, the scent of her own life, and I stepped outside like a dog following a butterfly.

"Sorry about that," she said, zipping up her coat—a weather-proof shell with a fresh plastic poppy pinned to the lapel. And as we walked I tried to pick out what it was—the wide set of her eyes, the shape of her mouth, the complexion and colouring of her long brown hair in a twist, or all those things together—that made her not exactly a dead ringer for Siobhan but the kind of near miss that leaves a crazed rush in the heart, telling you what was already there.

"You here just the day?" she asked.

"And tonight. I'm staying at the Torran, then back to Edinburgh first thing."

"Sounds nice."

"Especially if they have Black Gael on tap. A couple of those before bed and I'm a happy man."

"I meant going to Edinburgh."

I raised an eyebrow. "Doesn't he give you time off for good behaviour?"

"Other way round. I'm keeping him on the straight and narrow." She broke into a wry smile. "But I don't need telling you that."

I gave her an appreciative glance and noticed she was slowing her pace. "I could have used your help eighteen years ago."

"He's got a big heart, that man. Believe it or no. The trouble is his head." She halted and pressed her fingers to her temples. "And speaking of heads . . ."

"You all right?"

She stood hipshot, breath smoking in cold sunlight while she massaged her eyeballs, impatient with her own pain. "Aye," she said, taking her fingers away and blinking experimentally. "A few too many last night, is all."

"I hope you didn't scare your granddad's sheep with those fireworks."

She jolted.

"I stopped at Inbhir this morning and saw the litter," I said.

"Och, no fair."

"If you take me to the carvings I promise not to report you."

She nodded in mock gratitude and led me past a few outbuildings and the claw marks of some recent digging, a slurry of some kind. We made our way through some rough grass and started heading up a slope, the tangled gorse and brambles forcing us to climb single file. In obedience to an inner law of decency I tried not to watch her ass in front of me. She was what, nearly half my age? And Fergus's granddaughter, no less. Siobhan would get a kick out of that.

Where was she now? The Middle East? Canada? A couple of years after the whole thing happened she had married a petroleum engineer named Smith heading off to a foreign posting, and in an age before the kaleidoscope trackings of the internet, that was that. She took his name and became invisible. But now a thought came over me like blown glass. I hadn't looked for her at all—not a single search during those idle phases at work when I had unearthed others all the way down to the classmate who had stolen cookies from my lunchbox and the first girl I had kissed at the Spring Fling. That's how deep I had buried Siobhan. Deep enough to forget I had buried her at all.

There had been eight people on site then, but none with pottery expertise when we started uncovering sherds from carinated bowls, those assemblages with incised markings. A week later she was digging beside me. Her hair a muddy ochre full of curls all bunched back and frizzed in damp weather. Something in her voice pitching forward when she spoke, something uncontained, something unstopped. The sound of her breath when she reached orgasm sharp as a spade plunged into dry dirt. The grain under her nails, the taste of her nipples, drought and flood, all and nothing at once. Blame Inbhir. Blame the goddamned pots. All those weeks we pretended we weren't going to have sex until the Beltane up on Calton Hill. The May Queen and her fire-breathing sprites. The night when Violet didn't show up. Yes, blame Violet. If she had been there it wouldn't have happened. Those days when her attitude seemed to be tinged with doubt or regret, the untimely commitment of marriage. The way she looked past you in those most intimate moments, as if she was going her way while you were going yours. It was only when the dig was finished and the two of you gradually came together again that you recognised it— that sense of being apart, after the fact. Over the years it seemed to dissolve like the memory of Siobhan herself. But maybe it was crucial. Maybe it was where you went wrong.

"So it's no' my fault," Lorna said.

58

I caught up to her words—a confession of her antics with some friends at Inbhir the previous night, when they had fled the scene as granddad Fergus switched on the floodlight because the last thing she needed was that kind of hell, Guy Fawkes or no, and even though they'd come back later out of sheer guilt to pick up their litter they couldn't see a damned thing because the moon was setting behind a wee sharp peak by then and they didn't dare risk torches of any kind.

The churnings of the quarry were fading behind us. Farther up the glen I could see a field occupied by some cows and a couple of standing stones that I had visited years earlier, the stones maybe twenty metres apart, cup marks on their broad sides. The River Add a grey ribbon stretching along the floor of the valley. We were almost there. The elevation, the gradient of the slope. Yes, this was right. As the gorse dwindled and we had enough room to walk side by side I realised her pert young ass had been blocking my view of the fallen trees ahead. I lengthened my stride. She was huffing now, trying to keep up, but her hangover seemed to be getting the better of her. Go on ahead, she said, as if I weren't already.

When I got there I lowered my bag to the ground and took it in slowly, a general sense of the site. There were the stubs and slash of harvested trees along a plot of private land jutting into the public forest, which accounted for the bicycle path that connected two otherwise inaccessible sections, winding through the devastation as if avoiding aerial bombardment. I found the mature Sitka that had blown over, lifting the root plates of long-gone neighbors, the dark and wormy veins smelling of primeval ooze. And the carvings, an elaborate panel of them on a rounded outcrop of schist. Some were still caked with mud. I crouched down and touched the surface cracked and scoured from glaciers, a fine line of quartz visible through dry shavings of dirt. I felt the indentation of a cup, the groove of the first concentric ring. I went back to my bag and pulled out a pad to kneel on while I worked out the grit.

"To be honest I'm hoping we can work around it somehow,"

Lorna said as she arrived, puffing somewhere behind me. "Grand-dad's hell-bent on digging this way as it's the only bit no' on Forestry Land."

Cup and ring. Plain and simple. A central crater surrounded by up to nine concentric circles that resembled solar systems, atoms, dartboards, raindrops with ripples fanning outward, and countless other natural phenomena. The most interesting ones included tails or gutters connecting with others to form compound motifs or leading into natural cracks and fissures—into the rock itself. Or perhaps emerging from it. Who could tell what direction? I had read an article by someone who compiled 104 wildly divergent explanations or meanings that ranged from sperm entering eggs to sacred cowpats to messages from outer space. Over the years I had tried to understand the carvings by placing them in the context of other archaeological features in the region, establishing a sequence for Kilmartin as a whole—the chambered tombs in significant but scattered locations, followed by cursus monuments at either end of the glen to give it a formal shape, infilled with henges and stone circles later on. And then came the rock carvings. Up on the slopes. They seemed to synthesize or tie everything together, making the landscape into a coherent whole. At first I had thought the circular designs were an insight into the nature of the universe before physics had come up with the equations to spell it out—a grand theory refuted by Tessa when she was barely a toddler, putting pen to paper for the very first time. I had kept her drawing like a master's blueprint to replace all the foolish diagrams and photos on the wall of my study. Yes, there it was. The instinct we all shared. The circle wasn't the fundamental shape of the universe. It was the fundamental shape of the human mind. It was how we understood everything.

"Mr Keeler? I said if you need anything just give a shout, yeah?"

The words didn't come to me until sometime later as I glanced up and saw that she was gone. I sat back on my heels. Then I looked down at my work—the outcrop divided by cleavage planes and larger joints into irregular panels, framing the carvings. The complexion of cracks and veins and glacial scourings obvious now in the shifting light. Or my shifting mind. The carvings seemed to mimic the natural features of the rock as if responding to them, interacting with them, treating them not as geological quirks but designs left by someone else in the past.

How many times that summer? Four or five. Half a dozen at most. Siobhan seemed to have a limit in mind. This doesn't mean anything, she'd said. This is recreation. Just hormones. She was still seeing her boyfriend every fortnight when he came off a rig in the North Sea, a vague but serious partner, and she knew about Violet, oh the love of your life, isn't she, till death do you part. The way she twisted your collar in her fist like she was going to scold you when she pulled you in for a kiss. That evening climbing the hill above Crinan you asked wryly if she was out of breath, and she grabbed your hand and pressed it against her chest for the slick sheen of sweat and her heart thudding a raw sense into you more than yourself, so much more, her eyes aimed out at the islands of Jura and Scarba and the bottleneck between them, the Gulf of Corryvreckan, the mad waters pulsing with the tides, all frothing and treacherous blue as the Cailleach ushered in winter by washing her great plaid, or in other words as the pinnacle on the seafloor forced the currents into a maelstrom. The third largest whirlpool in the world. And over by Craignish Peninsula a tidal rip called the Dorus Mor, the great open door, leading guess where. The boat she hired to see it up close, to be in it, she said, hanging onto the rail while the fisherman laughed, piloting along the edge. How much she paid him she refused to say, a gift of some kind. The spinning caldrons. The standing waves. The whirlpools spiralling down.

I leaned down and blew at the carving. There was something different about this one. I sat back on my haunches again, trying to see. I traced it with my finger. No. That couldn't be right. It had to be a mistake. I must have skipped a worn edge of it somewhere, or maybe caught an accidental groove in the rock. My fingertips were numb, my nails black with grime. My lower back ached as I rose to my feet. I was sweating in my thermals, my breath visible in the bright air.

I pulled a bottle from my bag and poured water over the rock and then stood with my back to the sun. A simple thing. The optics of moisture and low-angled daylight revealing even the faintest designs—second only to laser-scanning, in my experience. And as the excess trickled away it began to gleam. The cup was a lens to the sky, the rings a luminous coil unwinding and blending with a natural crack and then emerging from it again to form another carving. Another spiral. Two of them. Linked.

I brought a fist to my forehead and stared. And then I turned and gazed down at the River Add running along the floor of the glen. I hadn't checked the sightlines and orientation on arrival the way I usually did, too consumed with other things, too preoccupied. I swivelled to take my bearings. These carvings faced southwest. Inbhir pointed northeast. Whatever the two sites meant, they meant it together, like the hands of a clock. They were working in space and time.

The following day I came home to an empty flat. I dropped my bags and shouted hello to nobody. Violet was lecturing. The children were enjoying accredited care. I made my way through the eternal debris of playtime and raided the fridge for leftovers. The table still held the droppings of breakfast, so I stood at the window and watched daylight climb the walls of the neighboring building, exposing the complexions of the stone, the glint of minerals in the civilized grain. Normally I would have made an effort to tidy up the mess around me, dutifully sweeping back the ocean with a broom, but instead I glanced at the calendar. I glanced at the clock. What day was it? What time? Our schedule required both coordinates, like plane geometry. Violet would pick up the children on her way home, which meant that I had about forty-five minutes to inventory my possessions. The complicated act of deciding what was mine. Or what I wanted to take with me. My eyes had come open that morning in the middle of dream that was also a thought: are you living your life or not? And it seemed like the decision had been made long ago and was finally falling into place. Nothing was stopping me. But nothing was helping me either. I was elated. I was terrified. I reeked of nervous sweat, and I needed a shower to set myself right.

In the bedroom I emptied my pockets and was about to kick off my shoes when the sight of my keys on the bureau triggered a memory. The coal cellar. The fabled antiques. I went out to the coat rack and found the mortise key zippered into my inner pocket, where I had stashed it a few days earlier, heavy and thick and buck-toothed. But then my mobile rang. I went back to the bedroom and saw Graeme's name on the display.

"What news, my son?"

"Round and round she goes," I said. "Where she stops, nobody knows."

"I've told you not to talk that way during business hours."

"A pair of spirals." I stepped into the stairwell and descended as quickly as I could with the mortise key clenched in my fist.

"Say again?"

I opened the main door before I replied, directing my voice outward to avoid the acoustics that would have given away my location. I hadn't stopped at the office before coming home, and it was still early enough in the day for him to hold it against me.

"Two spirals. Linked."

"Bloody hell."

"You got that right. If Fergus so much as drives his backhoe within a hundred metres of it I'll have him up in court for the rest of his pinched and nasty life. I recorded every detail. I took photos till the sun went down. I'm going to recommend hand-cleaning and excavation to determine the extent of the carvings, plus follow-up work depending on the results. Wait till you see these pics."

There was a troubled pause at the other end. "With that kind of recommendation, what makes you think Fergus is going to give us the work?"

I stood in the sharp bite of air. The entire street was in cold shadow. The residential silence of our block at midafternoon with a sense of the city teeming faintly beyond it. There was a mild stretch of light along the rooftops, igniting the gutters and copings, the flanks of slate. I went down to the sidewalk and confronted the wrought-iron gate with its rusted latch.

"That's the other thing," I said. "I did a bit of unofficial research while I was there. His granddaughter likes to drink, and she likes to talk. Turns out that granddaddy Fergus has pissed off every contract archaeology firm north of Hadrian's Wall. That's why he came to us. Nobody else will deal with him. He'll howl when he sees the tender, but he'll go along with it."

"Or he'll chuck his nationalist credentials and ring up somebody in England."

"England? No way. Lorna says he dinnae trust the buggers."

Graeme paused. "Is there something I should know about you and this McCain girl? For your sake I hope she doesn't resemble her forebears."

I twisted the knob and threw my hip against the gate until it popped and swung open, shedding flakes of rust. "A friendly drink after a hard day's work. That's all it was."

"If you say so. I don't suppose you waxed poetic about the double spiral?"

I started making my way down the rough steps. "Hell no. I didn't even mention it. The less she knows, the less Fergus knows. And the less he knows, the better. At least until he signs the contract."

I reached the bottom. The flagstones had a sheen of moss, grass sprouting from the cracks. A few scraps of litter in the drainage trench. I walked past the other coal cellars and halted at ours, inspecting its corrosions and crustings, its dust and soot. A siren passed nearby. I preempted the awkward question Graeme would feel obligated to ask.

"Listen, I'm arriving home as we speak. I'll give you the full report tomorrow morning. It'll be a new era for archaeology."

"And for your ego. Feet on the ground, aye?"

"As always," I said, signing off.

I put the phone in my pocket. I put my key in the lock. The latch clicked and the door swung out smoothly, a complete surprise. A dank smell wafted over me. Churned and festering earth, deep rot. I peered into the black entrails and, as my eyes adjusted, picked out some plastic sheeting against the wall, the dismembered leg of a table or perhaps a chair. A shovel blade without the handle. Dregs of coal. And nothing else. My disappointment was unreasonable. I reminded myself that one of the items Mrs McNaught's sons had discovered in the postmortem clear-out was a jar labeled PIECES OF STRING TOO SMALL TO USE. Maybe these were the fabled antiques after all. I stepped inside for a better look, nearly recoiling from the filthy stink of it. But then I saw something. A faint shimmer. A thread of light. I moved closer and felt a difference in the air just before it took hold, stretching like a rubber band for an instant until I sheared into nothing. I lost sight. I lost breath. I lost thought.

With a strange click of the senses I came together again, eyes tearing, hands numb, skin all hot and confusing to touch. Trembling. Intact. Alive. I seemed to be outside the coal cellar with bright air on my face. The door was shut and locked, the key gone. I hauled myself up and leaned against the wall until the world became familiar again. But not quite the same. No. The sun was higher and hotter, the weeds at my feet ungrown, the flagstones unmossed. I blinked. I breathed. It was an effort to keep myself in existence, as if I didn't quite match the space I occupied. Eventually a balance returned, an equilibrium between one thing and another. I straightened up, gave my head a final shake, and climbed the stairs.

It was all there. The cars in earlier vintages. The street adorned with younger symbols and signs. The garden budding with a sycamore that had been cut down years ago, and just ahead of me, shuffling along with her tote bag and her cane, the reliable figure of Mrs McNaught.

CHAPTER FIVE

2006

Think of it this way: a woman can be in the same place at different times, with a daughter in Aaron's study, a son in that room with toys and sheet music piled together on the shelves. There shouldn't be a gap between us. I'm her and she's me. But it's not that simple. Our pitches aren't the same. A perfect fifth will never correspond with an octave, so unless I shrink some of my intervals to match hers our two scales will keep going round and round without ever meeting each other until the circle of fifths becomes a spiral instead. And is that her fault or mine? Neither. Both. But of course I'm the one who has to resolve our differences, the dissonance between our voices as the metronome ticks away.

I raise my teacup and watch Euan poke at the keys. He nods his head. I nod mine. The world outside is growing pale, the rooftops in silhouette against an afterglow of sky. The boiler is humming distantly in the kitchen while Aaron pursues his latest discovery in Mid Argyll, a fact I push away with the full weight of my mind. I'm here. I'm now. I've washed off my makeup and outsourced the children to Mum for the afternoon. Normally I would charge more for these lessons than I would pay for childcare, but today everything is quid pro quo, one thing for another—or, in this case, an hour for an hour, time for time.

I shut off the metronome. "Well done."

Euan smiles at the score in front of him, all acne and freckles, a slight flush coming to his face as if the accomplishment has a specific heat. His hair is cut short and straight above the collar, but his jumper is baggy, his lips innocent and sensuous. He's fifteen. Too old for a beginner—or the sort of beginner his mother would like him to be. Rebecca claims the lessons are a productive substitute for video games, while also suggesting his hand-eye coordination just might lend itself to Chopin's Nocturnes in a few weeks. I don't have the heart to tell her the prodigy window has passed, and furthermore, he simply doesn't have the head for it. He picks off the notes like mutant aliens in a kill-or-be-killed scenario, as if marksmanship were the issue. Video games. Something to look forward to, Rebecca says, with a wry glance at Jamie. I let it slide. She generously includes him and Tessa in her morning school run when I'm scheduled for early lectures this semester. Yes, quid pro quo. This lesson should be a chore. Why, then, is Euan such a pleasure?

"That's great, the way he does it."

I look at him carefully. "The way who does it?"

"Beethoven. It's really simple, like. Five notes on this hand, but it sounds—"

"Five pitches."

"Five pitches. Right. But played at different speeds, different rhythms. He makes you think you're hearing a new note when it's really just the old one again. And the other hand comes in and out like camouflage."

"Camouflage?"

"I mean, to cover it. Because it's the same note! The left hand shifts to make it sound different to the right, and then fills in those missing bits, those gaps, to make it seem more different still. They interlock and . . ." His gaze meets mine with a sudden awareness, as if his thoughts have been caught naked in broad daylight.

"Yes," I say. "Exactly." Such sweet passion for these details. Is that why I like him? Or is it because he has fun with whatever he plays, untroubled by the inability of his hands to keep pace with his mind? No Salieri complex here. He'll be a midlevel executive swinging his briefcase in the easy rhythm of his days, bubbling with quirky notions. Yes, he'll be content. Euan's adulthood is folded within him like a flat pack with instructions and screwdriver included.

"Now let's try the new one. The Minuet in G."

He slides me a look as if dreading what he is about to unleash. I nod to let him know I can take it. I rise from the bench and refill my teacup. I stand behind him as he plays. It doesn't last long. He cranes his neck in apology.

"That's as far as I got."

This doesn't surprise me. Without setting down my cup I reach past him and play the next motif for the right hand. "Try that."

He knocks it out slowly, unevenly.

"Again," I say.

He plays it again.

"Now from the beginning of the bar. Take your time."

He plods through it with heavy fingers, his right hand moving farther out to play the new motif, which is simply a sequence of the old one, and then returning for the G repeated at the end.

"I'm Bach," he says.

I halt with the cup raised to my lips. "What?"

"I'm back. I mean, my fingers are back where they started." He gazes up at me. "That's really cool."

"Cool as a brook," I say.

His face crinkles at the obscurity of it, at what must seem like a middle-aged attempt to sound young and happening.

"Because *bach*," I add, "means *brook* in German. And do you know what your friend Beethoven said about him? 'Not Brook, but Sea should be his name, because of his infinite, inexhaustible richness of tone combinations and harmonies.'"

"He knew Bach?"

"He knew Bach's music."

Euan nods in appreciation. Then I glance at the clock on the mantel and see we've gone over. He jolts as if it's his fault. With a quelling gesture I sit down next to him and run through a bit of simplified Vivaldi for him to take away, pointing out the tricky bits, the fingering. I assign the next major scale on the circle of fifths. Can he practice all that? He nods and gathers up his papers and slides off the bench in a great tangle of limbs, then makes his way over to the coat rack, working his arms into the wrong sleeves before he realises the whole thing is inside-out and finally gets it sorted. I smile as I open the door for him, feeling the stairwell's cold breath in my face. And then, after he has left, a stillness in the empty flat. Silence. Or the closest thing to it. The thrumming presence of the city. The radiator ticking with heat. A faint charge to every object and every space in between. The pulse of being and time.

And the fishy ribbons I forgot to defrost. Bloody hell. In the kitchen I pick through the freezer with stinging fingers to find them wrapped in a single brick. The whole thing folded and fused together. Ten minutes, maybe fifteen before I can peel off the foil and pop it in the microwave for a quick thaw. Along with? Carrot sticks. A wee bit of ketchup, which I'll have to ration. Barely enough milk. I should have been shopping this morning instead of meeting Isobel for coffee and then tracing through the scribbles of JS Bach. My selfish pursuit. All these household tasks undone. Tessa's torn dress draped over the chair. The blast radius of Jamie's breakfast I neglected to clean up. And the laundry on display right there, in the washer's glass portal. I stoop and yank out the damp fabric, the whorled and tangled guts of it all—the shirts and trousers clotted together, the teeny pants and socks. The stains from various meals and mishaps still faintly present despite my spot treatment. And I told Mum I would fetch the children when today? What time am I picking them up? I stand upright, thoughts coming loose. No. I have time to spare. For what? For all these things that need doing. Or only seem to need doing. Their urgency fading as I make my way out of the kitchen with the tumble dryer rumbling behind me, an odd tingling sense in the hallway, in the length of space leading away, into something else. It's not a decision. I find myself in the sitting room again without taking a single step, it seems. I'm off the clock.

I lift the lid of the piano bench, a slim treasure chest holding my copy of *The Well-Tempered Clavier*, among other things. The sturdy script, the fine dry scent. The facsimile of the title page with those linked spirals scrawled across the top. Bach's tuning method, hidden in plain sight. How long I swithered before accepting it. His alternative to equal temperament, which came into widespread use during his lifetime even though it sterilized the tones, he said. It made them untrue. Instead he believed each fifth should have its own particular character. And he spelled it out in that calligraphy, in what appear to be doodles, an entire tuning system with this cycle of keyboard works serving as a test drive in every key—the crux being whether his Prelude in E-flat minor would fall into alignment with his Fugue in D-sharp minor, paired together at six o'clock on the circle of fifths. The only way to know is to try it on my own piano, not quite the clavier he had in mind but an instrument I've tempered according to his instructions nevertheless, like a mad scientist conducting experiments on herself, or maybe just seeking recovery, because it brings us together, her and me, reconciling my flats with her sharps and isn't that a strange thought.

I open the collection to the Prelude. I flex my fingers. Don't think about it. All that's been lost. Because she didn't tell me. Or I didn't tell myself. Not a single warning about what the pregnancies would do to my hands. The loss of dexterity felt more than heard, too subtle to measure, but permanent. Everyone believes I recovered after Tessa was born and then again after Jamie, waxing and waning with each child, because it's the only way to ensure Aaron believes it. Otherwise what? He would tell her somehow. And what if she decided to prevent it from happening? No pregnancies, no children. A sickening thought. No. It needs to happen this way because it already happened that way. My decisions predetermined, twisted in knots. Yet I'd thought I was ready for motherhood, hadn't I? The nausea, the aching breasts, the sea levels rising within me, the dark exhaustion of the first trimester followed by late-stage swelling like a pressure cooker with my skin stretched hard and tight and stiff. The nutrients leached from my blood and bone where in the past mothers never regained themselves, losing a tooth for every child. And then? A delivery that turned me inside out, leaking and trickling in the aftermath. A newborn sucking everything I could give her. The hormone havoc, the traumatic love. My loose skin at the midriff like a deflated raft. Yes, I was ready for all that, all of it, but my god not the loss of my hands.

I shut my eyes. I let my breath settle. I put my fingers on the keys and hear it straightaway—a sour tinge to that wide major third on the G-flat of the first chord so fitting and perfect in this temperament, the chords repeating against a florid line. The flat keys and dotted rhythms of a tombeau. A funeral melody. One of his biographers described it as a lament for his first wife, Maria, who died around the time he composed it—a fanciful speculation, it always seemed to me, until now. This feeling of remoteness, like exploring the moon, all brilliant and barren, and I'm not quite myself passing the motifs from hand to hand. This is how it happens. This is how it goes. It's not about that mechanical plonking, that rote precision staid and stiff, tapping it out like the dots and dashes of Morse Code. All those teachers saying how it should be done. You play Bach your way and I'll play him his way—with rubato, with conjunct suggestions, with variations and romantic flair, because it's there, it's there. It's in the score with the proper temperament. It's in the spaces between the notes. Those nuances impossible to duplicate in performance, impossible to play twice, and is this a flaw or my only talent? Remember how it felt to discover his chords and cadences and syncopations and strettos, his subjects and restatements and episodes with their ordered ecstasy, his throbbing sense inside me after all those countless hours working through it after school when Mum and Dad were out and I finally got it right with his consciousness glinting in mine and I shouted oh you clever man, you adorable *genius*, holding the fermata with the whole room humming like a beehive only to find Mum in the doorway when she was supposed to be at a meeting or a fundraiser or something and all the air left me, otherwise I would have screamed.

"Who are you talking to?" she asked, leaning in the doorway with her arms folded.

My shock was so pure that the prospect of lying didn't even occur to me. "Bach," I said.

"And does that make it easier to play his music?"

"The other way round, really."

"I see," she said, with an effort coming into her eyes. "I suppose playing music is like a conversation with the composer, isn't it."

I blinked into her then, into everything she was. The ruffled apron. The dress full of plain pride. Her bland hair pinned subtly into place. Those bony elbows she preferred to hide. And her spare expression, with her chin lifted slightly as if she had caught a foul scent in the very nature of things, as if the whole world were a pint of milk that had gone off. How odd to feel it then, my true rebellion, an urge to be everything she wasn't.

"Mostly it's like following an instruction manual," I said. "And then suddenly it's not."

She nodded in a way that I recognised from public occasions when she was confronted with opinions that clashed directly with her own.

"But it only happens," I added, "with Bach."

"Ah," she said. And then she straightened up and released her arms and informed me tea would be ready soon. Because it was all safe now. I wasn't courting ghosts or arguing with the voices in my head, but simply being her silly little girl with a hobby. Which would fade, wouldn't it? I'd find a serious profession, a real and

73

proper job. Not a homemaker like her. Goodness no. I'd do more. In fact, I'd bloody well better do more. Why? Because she would have excelled in my place, and in just about any other place apart from her own. Born to the same family only a century or two earlier, she would have been the woman-behind-the-man introducing parliamentary legislation or running his various estates, whereas in my generation she would have come to early adulthood in a Thatcherite craze, swinging her business degree like a mace while she paid other people to raise her children. But poor Mum had ended up in the worst of both worlds, where her gentry were no longer landed and all her career paths ended in the foothills. And if there wasn't a route to the summit, then she wasn't going to climb at all. That was her problem, wasn't it? She never had the nerve to go off-piste.

Instead my school uniform held the force of her ambition. My hemlines were surgical. My collars were blades. While Peter found his wardrobe restocked and his rugby colours restored without question, I negotiated every neckline and shade of makeup not for what it implied about my morality but for what it might do to my prospects. My exam results elevated her. My hockey goals qualified me for the Olympics in her mind. I would realise her potential in public displays worthy of our townhouse with its flagstones buffed to glassy perfection, the vases and doilies centred, the complexions of antiques revealed. While Peter was away at uni I came home every afternoon and snacked alone in the kitchen with pans gleaming around me like cymbals, the crystal tinkling in faint celestial pleasure whenever a lorry rumbled by. We lived with her ancestors presiding over each mantel—white marble in the sitting room, black marble in the dining room, according to custom—and her arsenal of silver in the Edinburgh press. But the piano was mine. It was where I found the only thing that mattered, the very stuff of life, while she ran her social club and charity events and landscaping parties in the communal garden down the street, because they were all worthy causes that demonstrated her modesty. She

74

navigated life with a damp finger raised to every passing breeze. And the trade winds, she believed, were in my favour. How lucky I was, how lucky. I could do anything in the world, as if her world was the same as mine.

The Prelude's chilling bleakness resolving into warm chords now at the end. The low rich register. The comfort. The release. Surprising but natural. E-flat minor into E-flat major. A farewell to his wife Maria in the resonance, the sound dying away. My fingers not quite rendering the speed or deeper delicacy of those notes. But it's serviceable, isn't it? Yes, it's adequate. Good enough for a lounge act. Just stay away from the performance hall. I take a slow breath as I turn to the Fugue in D-sharp minor. Leave off. This is about Bach's tuning. His temperament. And it breaks over me slowly—the difference in tonality even though that's impossible. The M shape of the subject. M for Maria. The curve of quavers rising and falling into an open cadence, sober and expansive, the subject coming back over and over again, layered upon itself, and then once in canon in the first development, revealing a shadow, an identical twin.

I was the sort of girl who would bring Aaron home to meet Mum and Dad for the first time without briefing them. My personal philosophy seemed to thrive on their confusion and discomfort. And besides, I told myself, it was just dinner. Arriving in the hall, though, Aaron craned his neck up at the grand staircase, taking everything in with anthropological wonder—the brass umbrella holder, the gilt-framed mirror, the carpets and wall hangings, the dining room in full regalia with the massed brilliance of the chandelier. It was like Masterpiece Theatre, he said, though I didn't have time to ask what that was before my parents appeared and introductions commenced.

To my surprise one thing led safely to another throughout the meal with the full range of pleasantries and neutral topics, the exchanges of harmless opinions that demonstrated how much everyone wanted to like each other. And the necessary history:

Aaron's first visit to Scotland when his father's engineering firm was consulting on a project in Glasgow. His unexpected visceral interest in the landscape. His discovery that a British university would allow him to plunge straight into archaeology without the general education requirements of American schools. That was uni sorted. And of course we told them about the trip we had just taken together after finishing our exams, not to Paris, as he suggested, thinking I would be happy to do all the talking, or the parlay-voo, as he called it, but to Orkney, which I proposed in honour of how we met. We actually had a disagreement over it, each arguing in favour of the other's preference. In the end I prevailed. I wanted to know who he was, who he might be. And who I might become with him. But of course I didn't know that at the time.

The narrow streets of Kirkwall packed tight against the wind. The extra depths of stone to our hotel with a single tiny window like a prison cell we kept open every night while we shagged. The treeless distances. The sea lochs fingering inland. Wind and rain and sun. Hills ringing the far horizons. That Norse inflection I heard in the voices but didn't mention for fear of being drawn and quartered as an Edinburgh toff. The smooth green mound of Maeshowe, surrounded by a trench or rather a henge, as Aaron called it. A ditch reinforced with a bank on the outside. Probably filled with water when it was built. Like a moat. See that break for the entry? A causeway. And a modulating bridge, I added. A passage from one place to another. Or did I keep that to myself?

Following a mandatory tour guide, we went stooping down the long passage to the central chamber. The side cells. The absent bones. The corbelled roof constructed of overlapping stones, the layers moving upward and inward to a capstone like a vortex into both earth and sky. Yes, I felt it then. The modulation. The key change. The harmonic sense. By that point the guide was shining her torch on the runic graffiti from Vikings who broke in more than a millennium ago, along with the chisel marks left by the original Neolithic builders several millennia before that, which strangely had no clear purpose or function. Or nothing, I thought, that could be seen. Because it was the sound of the picking that mattered. They were making music in here. Didn't anyone realise that?

Dad had been to Orkney ages ago with nothing more than a thermos and a rucksack, as he phrased it, and he loved comparing his impressions with ours. Those stone circles marking the sky in the land. It was a phrase he still remembered from the guide book. The Ring of Brodgar. The Stones of Stenness. And the village of Skara Brae built into a midden, the roofs long gone, so you actually peer down into the dwellings, at the beds and dressers made of stone. Tourist placards proclaiming it as the Pompeii of the North—though, Aaron pointed out, that wasn't really accurate because it wasn't frozen in time, buried by a volcano one day. It was abandoned deliberately. And we're actually closer in time to Pompeii than Pompeii was to Skara Brae. It was already ancient when Caesar was born.

"But what about that other place?" Dad asked, his eyes going distant, squinting at a notion half-remembered, half-forgot. "The island. Not Pompeii, but . . ."

"Egypt," Aaron said. "The Egypt of the North. Otherwise known as Rousay." He gave me the slightest glance, trying to resist banging on, but he was so obviously delighted by my father's interest and I was delighted that he was delighted, all of us together, I thought. We were sitting with the plates and cutlery cleared, the tablecloth wrinkled, a dollop of brown sauce screened from Mum's view by the flower arrangement. The perimeter of Aaron's place setting marked by crumbs and various sheddings that I was planning to tidy discreetly as soon as she went into the kitchen to make coffee. The candles were flickering. Brahms was at low volume. The auld alliance of my father's wine cellar doing its usual work to make the conversation freewheeling and open. Except I was leaving someone out, wasn't I?

"A circular island with a high concentration of prehistoric sites. It's not simply the sites themselves, though. It's the relationship

77

between those sites. Their distribution along the slopes. A larger cosmological pattern. The ones on the lowest terraces held entire individuals, bodies intact. The middle terraces, about halfway up, were filled with disarticulated remains and skulls placed in side cells off their central chambers. And on the upper terraces the remains were all fragmentary, burnt in bone dumps, the skulls placed in the innermost stalls."

Mum's slow frown during his description. And my slow satisfaction at the sight of it, confirming the gap I needed between us in the Fugue's second development with the subject inverted, turned upside down in contrary motion and blending naturally, the tones holding their colours, the flats and sharps aligned but somehow not quite the same. The subject becoming a negative version of itself.

"And get this," Aaron went on, "they all included animal bones in the mix, as usual, but they were set at different elevations— cattle and deer and other 'earthly' land dwellers on the lower slopes, eagles and other birds on the higher ones, closer to the sky. The animal bones remained in the same place while the human ones were circulated not simply within the monuments but between them, shifted to higher elevations as they disintegrated. I guess you could call it a stairway to heaven."

"Sorry?" Mum raised a finger like a student trying to catch the teacher's attention. "You said *disarticulated*?"

"Pulled apart," Aaron said, "by animals."

"Animals."

"Yeah, you see they—" He paused as he sensed some kind of transgression, a tremor in the lower cobwebs of her beliefs. "But you probably don't want to hear about that."

"Oh, but we do," Dad said, leaning forward to refill Aaron's wine glass. As he eased back into his chair I recognised the saucy colour and elegance that served him well in social settings, conveying a mildly roguish demeanor while staying safely within the bounds of decorum. And at home, on a night such as this—well, he liked to let his curiosity off the lead, didn't he? He would have welcomed Genghis Khan and his mounted horsemen into the dining room just to ask what ruling over those Mongol hordes was *like*, really.

"During the Neolithic," Aaron said, "they practiced something called excarnation. In other words they left the corpses exposed until all the flesh and tissue were gone."

"Gone?" Mum asked.

"Defleshed. Scavenged by wildlife until they were stripped down to the bones."

Mum caught herself and smiled, trying to bring a lightness into it. Her Anglican discomfort. How did Isobel describe her? Spiritually brittle. Her metaphysical feathers easily ruffled. Yes, it could have been worse, Mum. I could have read philosophy instead.

"It's not as strange as it sounds, if you think about it. The dead were released into the world around them. Reabsorbed. The animals and land took them back in, physically. Existence was all-inclusive, both living and dead, the same thing in different forms. Like water and ice. And steam, I guess. At least that's my theory. Which explains why they dismembered the skeleton and sorted out all the bones—the femurs, the skull, the scapula, et cetera—and added them in with all the others."

"The others inside the passage graves, you mean?" Dad turned his chair at a slight angle from the table to cross his legs before taking up his wine glass again.

"Human and animal alike. And that's why they were mixed up, moved around. Why they were circulated. Because they were active participants in daily life. People carried them like what, talismans maybe? Tools?"

"Oh really." Mum laughed nervously.

"A different relationship to the natural world," Dad said, swirling his wine. "And I suppose a different notion of ancestry as well."

"Relationships that branch out horizontally in the present," Aaron added, "instead of vertically into the past."

Mum peered at him.

"Think of it this way," he said, trying to draw her in. "You have two parents, four grandparents, eight great-grandparents, and so on. It doubles with each generation, right? That's exponential growth, taking up a larger percentage of the population with each step backward. After twenty-two generations, taking us back about five hundred years, you have four million direct ancestors. That's the entire population of Britain at that point. And if we go back to the beginning of the Neolithic, roughly four thousand BC, you're talking about two hundred thirty generations, which comes to more than the population of the entire world. So the whole concept of a specific ancestry loses meaning really fast. And I think they understood that."

"And all of this came with the Neolithic?" Dad asked.

"Or continued from the Mesolithic."

Dad paused, raking it over in his mind.

"I'll give you a crude primer," Aaron said. "There are three major periods—"

"Aaron," I said.

Dad batted a gentle finger at me. "Don't interrupt the lesson, Violet."

"The Paleolithic, or Old Stone Age, began about two point six million years ago with the invention of primitive stone tools and ended here in Britain about ten thousand years ago, at the end of the last ice age. Then you have the Mesolithic, the Middle Stone Age, which was characterised by what we call microliths—smaller and more sophisticated stone blades. That lasted for another four thousand years or so. But over that whole time our subsistence practices stayed basically the same. Hunting and gathering."

He put his hand on my knee and eased it up my inner thigh as he was talking, and it seemed like it would always be that way— doing what we wanted, whenever we wanted, cheating decorum and propriety. It seemed like the natural fabric of life. We believed we were busy with our schedules and minor limitations. We couldn't have understood how our lives would change until the act of planning or manufacturing time together would require so much effort that our time together would be spent resting from the effort of creating it. There was whim in every breath. There was serendipity in sex, all twisted with pleasure and the third development of the Fugue with the subject returning incomplete, layered in canon, and then juxtaposed in contrary motion before coming back in one coherent restatement, letting you know what it is, what it was, how it will be. Bach knew what he was doing. Why didn't I?

"Until—" Aaron snapped his fingers. "The Neolithic Revolution. Within a hundred years the diet shifted abruptly from marine to terrestrial sources. We started farming and herding. We started making pottery. We started building permanent monuments."

"And this happened when?"

"Four thousand BC, more or less."

"And why was this? Why this sudden change?"

"That's a huge question that archaeologists are trying to answer. Personally I think it was caused by a shift in something called the THC—the thermohaline circulation of the ocean. The global conveyor belt. Marine resources became much less reliable, so people focused more on game animals for their protein. That's my theory. Or I guess I should say someone else's theory that I agree with. But anyway, the important thing is that agriculture became entrenched. The landscape settled into field systems with the dead treated in a really different way. By the time you reach the Bronze Age you have separate and distinct places for them. Individual burials with bodies intact. Crouched down, usually. In a foetal position."

Foetal, fatal. Tomayto, tomahto. I remember that wordplay at the mischievous giddy edges of my mind. Missing the obvious. Foolish girl.

"Or else," Aaron went on, "they were cremated and buried in pots."

"Did they not scatter the ashes?" Dad's eyebrows raised.

"Maybe they did that with some of them, but that wouldn't have left any trace in the archeological record. And at any rate that's where you start seeing concern with lineage and descent. People rooted specifically to a place. If you scatter the ashes then you lose that sense of permanence."

"Hence the pottery. To keep it contained, so to speak."

Aaron nodded. "Yeah, it's kind of funny to think they used it not only for cooking and food storage, but also as an urn. Grandma's ashes were buried in the Neolithic equivalent of a saucepan."

Mum's eyes seemed to shrink. She made a motion with her hand under the table, thinking only Dad could see it.

"But in those early days," Dad said, ignoring her.

"In those early days, the dead weren't finished. They weren't sealed off permanently in some box. That's why you see those chambered tombs. Linear structures with compartments. The bodies processed from one end to the other. It wasn't really a grave in the way that we think of it now. It was a place where people were unfleshed and freed. It was a site of transformation."

I should have kicked him under the table right about then, but I loved his reckless playful edge, his headlong comments as he trusted the situation simply because he loved me and these were my parents and I wanted to pull him down to the floor and make love to him there and then. Here and now. Aaron. Euan. Yes. Of course. I should have known that from the start.

"And why is that, do you think?" my father asked. "Why did they have such a notion, whereas we don't?"

"But we do." Aaron leaned forward, as if involving my father in a conspiracy. "Science tells us that nothing really disappears. Energy is neither created nor destroyed. It simply changes form."

My father shot out a finger. "Hang on, I know that one. Thermodynamics. Entropy and all the rest of it."

"Then you follow me. It's no coincidence, I think, that so many of those monuments are oriented toward the sunrise and sunset at pivotal points in the year, and no coincidence that they start building them at the same time they started farming. The link between the seasons and land. Sowing and harvesting. Death and fertility. Regeneration. It was all around them. It was inside them. They could feel it happening, the whole cycle over and over again." He fell back in his seat and let out a big breath. "Sorry. I've really been holding forth."

Dad tipped his wine glass and winked at him. "Only because I keep asking."

"Yes," Mum said, finally spotting an opening. "He's aiding and abetting. You should have seen him with Violet's science projects in secondary school."

There must have been a tremble in her expression—no, in her voice—that stopped me. A pain I didn't expect. Just then the Brahms died off, and I understood that something in this speculation was too sharp, too deep, an injury of some kind that I didn't expect. A cut instead of a scratch.

"And one of those projects," I said, trying to help her along, "was actually about thermodynamics. Remember?"

Dad's face went wide. "The steam engine. Oh, that was fun." But in the ensuing pause his thoughts slipped back into their grooves. "Isn't it funny that we've confirmed their myth, as it were?"

"Confirmed it?"

"I mean, verified it. With science."

Aaron straightened up again. "Now I can see why you think of it that way, but really—"

"Aaron, could you help me with something in the kitchen?"

"Nonsense, Violet," Dad said, spreading his shoulders with radiant and jolly warmth. "He's a guest!" Then he looked back at Aaron and waved him on.

I could have asked my mother to help me instead. It would have been quite plausible for us to make the coffee together while Dad and Aaron carried on like a couple of undergraduates sharing a spliff. Yes, how obvious it seems in the final development of the Fugue, with the subject inverted up high, augmented down below, the middle layer in stretto and then shifted and reordered until they're brought together at last. I could have simply taken her out of harm's way. But I didn't think of it at the time. Because I wanted it to happen. I sensed it then. I know it now.

"All I'm saying is, when we refer to their beliefs as myths, we should keep in mind that the reality of one age is the myth of another. The ancient Egyptians believed in over two thousand gods, the Greeks and Romans several hundred. All retired from active duty. Irrelevant. Like what, disposable razors. But the same goes for science. I mean, do we really think that after forty thousand years we finally got it right? Does it really end here? Were we just fumbling in the dark until Einstein hit the lightswitch? Maybe we should ask ourselves if people five millennia from now will really believe in atoms and molecules. How about quantum mechanics? String theory? Will they seriously think that reality consists of tiny strands of vibrating energy? Imagine what they'll make of an atom smasher or a super collider if they happen to discover one. An enormous circular structure with mysterious components. How is that different from Stonehenge?"

"And five thousand years from now," Dad said, scything an arm over the decanter and serving bowls, "there will be an entirely different technology, won't there? A different understanding. Protons and neutrons will be obsolete."

"A naïve way of seeing the world. A historical curiosity like stars in the firmament. The music of the spheres, maybe. Assuming they have records of what we thought at all. And the kicker is that they'll think they've got it all figured out. They'll think everyone before them was wrong. They'll think their version of reality is the final and correct one. They'll think, this is how the universe really is. This is the right science. At every age we think we finally got it right, and at every age we're wrong."

Which means nothing is right. Nothing at all. It was what Mum must have sensed, sitting there with her pained grin, her broken chords, her keys all loose and strings buzzing inside. String theory. It wasn't her religion that had been undermined. No. It was herself, plain and simple—too plain and simple for me to see at the time. She had assumed her life was the right one, the correct one, simply because it existed. As if every choice had led inevitably to the woman she should be. But what was so inevitable about it, after all? What if she had chosen differently? Would she be happier? More fulfilled? What about those alternate selves? My little Bach orgies threatened everything she could have been in those other lives she imagined for herself, those fantasies of unrealised talent, all safely channeled into the woman she had become, and was that her or is it me?

The fermata. The room trembling in sound. The layered resonance of E-flat/D-sharp minor, identical and not, with a subtle difference in shading, impossibly aligned and separate, together and apart at once. I glance at the dark windowpanes holding my reflection. The woman I've become. What happened to that young Violet? Where did she go? Why did she believe it would be fine on this end of the affair? Foolish girl. As if you could be both the mistress and the wife. But it's not what you thought it would be, is it? What I thought it would be. What have I done to myself?

In the growing silence it all returns now, as always—the traffic rumble, the whine of a bus, the tumble dryer throbbing in the kitchen. The thawing fish. My god. I head down the long hall and find it on the counter and peel off the damn foil, the little things that kill me, death by a thousand cuts, these invisible domestic scars that Mum bore with pride. How did she do it? Her daily life must have been a deception. Like mine.

Coat, keys, mobile. And of course I'm running late. Outside I push an empty pram through the madness of winter wind, and no excuse for this, rushing about all distracted like one of the suited and skirted, the high powered, the six figured, a woman who earns the right. What am I, really? A mother lagging behind in every way, her depleted hands in gloves. The tendons no longer taut like they were—a micron of loss registered not only in the ear but the deepest sensings of the heart. Is there a calligraphy for that? Bach didn't find a temperament for the sharps and the flats of a woman's life, her ambitions and her children at once. I need to become a better mother to them. The mother they deserve. As I reach the house it comes ripping through me again, that urge to reset my life, and I have to stop and take a breath, gripping the fence with its fleurs-de-lis aimed toward heaven. How appropriate. How it all comes back. The cemetery in France where I stood pregnant, my hands set in stone, recognising it too late. Yes, reading a score is one thing and playing it is another, even when you've written it yourself.

The front path, the steps, the door. Home for so many years. I ring the chimes to announce my arrival before stepping inside. A smell of beef stew and cabbage in the hall, a settled impression in the flagstones but commotion in the back room where Mum tries to keep them contained like seals in an aquarium tank. As I peel off my gloves Tessa comes rushing toward me, waving something she made. I crouch down to examine the artwork. The odd shapes and clashing colours, the paper still soft with glue.

"It's a design for you."

"Beautiful." I touch her velvety head. "Thank you, Tessa."

"Don't tell Daddy, though."

I give her a curious look, trying to keep it light. "Why not?"

"Because he loves it so much."

I try to follow the logic. "But I love it as well, sweetie. And Daddy hasn't even seen it yet."

She seems to hover with something she can't articulate, a loose notion playing through her eyes before she turns and dashes back down the hall. I follow her to find Mum setting a table upright and Jamie coming to grief of some kind—something I could have prevented, no doubt, if I had arrived only two minutes earlier. A few ounces of distress I could have spared him. If this happens every day it adds up to what? He trembles and shudders against me with the moist warmth of a puppy.

"We had a bit of a stumble," Mum says in her soothing Gran voice, "but no harm done. Just a wee fright, wasn't it?"

With my chin resting on Jamie's head I wonder how she can do this again—the live-wire impulses of toddlers, the unfiltered wants. Was she this gentle with me, or is this her special provision for grandchildren? I recall the struggles of adolescence but never the soft grain of those early years, when she nourished me in too many ways to distinguish. How much of it has been lost? I look into her now, into everything she is. Her parched lines, her sagging edges. Her dropped shoulders and watery gaze. The grey reduction of herself. So much of her life fed into mine. I've been unfair to her inside and out.

"Did you get everything done?" she asks with an edge I recognise, implying there must be an important reason for my lateness. A legitimate excuse.

"All finished," I say, letting it wash past. No fight this time. No counterpunch. Instead my tone is tolerance. It's gratitude. It's some of the love she missed.

"Cup of tea?"

I flick my eyes down at the children. "If they'll let me."

She sets off down the hall, heels clacking, like a secretary with an important file to deliver. That tight urgent walk of hers. A minute or so later I hear the kettle shrilling out. As I set Jamie to rights with a racetrack, I notice a stray mark by the windowsill. Does she know? I glance at the nude walls, the phantom squares where a few nondescript paintings used to hang—all removed for the sake of this durable play chamber. As if Tessa and Jamie might spray it with gunfire. Mum's sewing machine once stood against the far wall, flanked by an ironing board and a trouser press. And sometime after that it became a war room for her different causes and drives, with charts tacked to a proper bulletin board, a fussy desk, a file cabinet of respectable wood. All that energy. All that time.

She comes back with cups jittering in their saucers. "The way you like it," she says, handing one over to me. "No milk, no sugar."

And no tray. Too risky, apparently. Her indistinct worries of what might happen with the children about. So I balance the saucer on my knee and finally set it under my chair as she eases into an anxious disquisition on Peter's renovations in Perthshire. The builders are mucking it up terribly, putting Heloise in a state, you can imagine. Actually, I can't imagine. Heloise has been raising two children with hardly a flicker of distress, her household duties subjected to brisk triage as she occasionally taps out a thoughtful abstraction for the op-ed pages of *Le Monde*. Peter's success as a property agent has brought them affluence and ease, as far as I can tell, all fin-de-siècle sunny relations. But Mum goes on a bit, as she does. And I listen, finding some comfort in her ungrounded worries. The care and concern underlying it all. And the warmth of the house. And the rustle of the children, the pleasant battering of their toys, Jamie's giggles as Tessa obliges him with a race. Everyone is getting along. Yes, this is nice. This is life, isn't it? My mother, my children. Why have I resisted these pauses, these Earl Grey afternoons? I used to accept every third invitation out of charity to her, regarding it as a kind of tax—a stamp duty on child care. Twenty minutes. You can spare it, can't you, Vi?

"There's something off, I fear." Mum cradles the cup with both hands in her lap, skirt folded in, knees pressed properly together.

"Off?"

"I hope they're all right, I mean. It just seems, the way she behaves sometimes . . . I know I shouldn't say such a thing. It's not my place. But where Peter's concerned I can't help it."

I click through the last couple of occasions when I've seen them—once here, once there—all seemingly content. I raise the cup to my lips. "What's wrong with Heloise's behaviour?"

Her eyes dart off too sharply, too deliberately avoiding mine. And that's when it occurs to me. What she's really saying. I'm the one she's worried about. The things a mother senses in her children but doesn't recognise. What she senses in me, what I sense in myself—the woman I might have been. A presence like static electricity, needing only a touch to release. Is it possible? Could she come to life again, or is it too late?

CHAPTER SIX

2006

Here and now. There and then. How did it work? I returned through the coal cellar and found myself trembling on the flagstones like an epileptic, my head full of blown fuses, eyes flaring in their sockets. Eventually I got to my feet and steadied myself. Fading sky. Naked trees. The stones slick and cold. I shivered as the November chill took hold of me. Yes, this was my proper time. Or place. The door was ajar behind me, the key still in the lock. Which was impossible. Since I had just taken it from the hall cupboard in 1988, I thought, it shouldn't be here anymore. In fact, it shouldn't have been here at all because by removing it I had preempted anyone from discovering it and travelling back in the first place—a self-defeating scenario. But here they were. Two keys. The same key. I rubbed my eyes and tried to imagine how it all fit together, but found myself caught in an endless loop, like Escher's stairs, in which both directions were true yet cancelled each other out. Unless Violet was right and they were separate worlds. Maybe one thing didn't lead to another at all.

Or maybe the locks had simply been changed. I took the younger version from my pocket and examined it with a jeweler's eye. Then I shut the door and removed the older key and locked it with the other one instead. It worked perfectly. A duplicate, then. Easily done by a locksmith. Or not. I didn't know. I leaned against the frigid wall and blew out a breath, and suddenly I could taste her, smell her, my ultra-Violet all toned and taut, clear and casual, with her luscious snug ecstasy, until I started trembling and crying. The easy rush of her. Her unblocked affection, a warm rich sense of who she had been in body and mind. I had forgotten. I had really forgotten.

And now I couldn't forget. Despite my shaky condition I wanted to turn around and throw myself back into it just to see if I could repeat the trick, even if it meant meeting myself, doubled, on the other side—assuming I reappeared at the same moment, which would mean I could keep doing it over and over again, multiplying into an army of Aarons. I pressed my fingers to my eyeballs. The last thing I wanted was more of me. And anyway it didn't seem right. There had to be some principle behind it. Had the passage been here the whole time? But then other people would have used it, not least the ones who dug out the cellar in the first place. No, it had to be new, like a sinkhole appearing in what you thought was solid ground. It was a miracle and disaster. And for the time being, nobody else knew about it. It was mine, all mine.

By the time I climbed the steps and yanked the gate shut and brushed off my hands the streetlamps were glowing at the onset of darkness. I looked around to see if I had caught anyone's notice but saw only a dogwalker emerging from the bare ribs of the garden and a passerby talking on her mobile. Which is when I remembered mine. I pulled it out and pressed buttons. I slapped it against my palm. Nothing. Dead.

In the stairwell I paused outside what used to be Mrs McNaught's flat, the site of her unheralded resurrection. That wry smirk of hers, the inquisitive tilt of her head. Her hair covered with a kerchief in weather fair or foul. Her vision foggy and nearly glaucomic in those final years, though she had compensated with a strong internal compass. I had followed her all the way to the corner shop with a bizarre fondness for what I saw and remembered at the same time—her habit of wagging her cane with a vaudeville flair, as if it were a prop instead of a necessity, which had fooled my younger self but not my older one as I suddenly understood her need to be eccentric instead of helpless, amusing instead of pitiful. Oh, Mrs McNaught, I got you all wrong, like so many other things in my life.

I continued climbing the stairwell. The newer colours, the older steps. I heard strains of the family circus awaiting me and leaned my forehead against the door before opening it to meet Jamie's cavalry charge, his jumper stained with something red, either blood or lunch, he refused to say, instead demanding a form of tickling I had invented known as Mortal Combat. Soon Tessa joined us, giggling and squealing, until I went down and called a truce. Sitting back on my heels, my shirt untucked, I tried to breathe while she rubbed a bump on her head, a mild injury some-where below her glossy black hair all ruffed and mussed. She was getting ready to lunge at me again when Jamie pointed.

"Tickle Mummy!" he said.

I swivelled to find Violet standing outside the kitchen with a guarded expression, as if expecting something unpleasant. I braced myself for a great reckoning, as if our tryst would suddenly manifest itself in her memory, but she simply wiped her hands with the tea towel she was holding and draped it over her shoulder and gave us all a wry smile. She didn't remember. She didn't know. I smiled back at her with relief, and then guilt that I was relieved. She was still wearing her university garb, the straight cuts and plain colours setting off the floral pattern on the towel and what I realized was a spice packet in her hand—a contrast that nor-mally would have occasioned a joke. Spice up your lecture. Those exam questions are half-baked. Now, though, it all remained on the loading dock. Unwanted merchandise. I was confronted with the tired drift of her, the crinkled work and wear of her features, the slight pinch to her eyes. Would I even notice her on the street? A short hard woman who needed to be taken seriously. It wasn't a fair thought or a fair feeling, but I thought it and felt it and so with a long blink I reversed everything and put myself on the receiving end, my emotional litmus test, and wondered how she would measure me against my younger self.

"You look knackered," she said.

I shrugged. "All that digging."

"That must have been rough. But good, yeah?"

"Oh, really good. We uncovered a double spiral."

"We?"

"Daddy!" Jamie writhed on the floor. "Tickle!"

"And you got back just now," she said with a different intonation to her voice, her thoughts fastening onto something.

I glanced at the clock. Though I couldn't be sure without my mobile, it seemed like the same amount of time had passed on this side. "I went for a walk. After that long drive."

"Daddy, come on!"

"Without a coat?" she asked.

I looked down at myself as if taking note of the fact, buying time until Tessa saved me with a tackle. Jamie joined in. We rollicked and rolled. I was an octopus with tickle-tentacles and they were jiggling jellyfish wanting my touch and fleeing it at the same time. We stumbled over boots and rucksacks on the floor, race cars on their final lap with dinosaurs waiting to eat the winner at the finish line. The dark carpet concealed stains—juice, milk, piss, puke—and the chipped moldings displayed the impacts of toy trolleys and buggies. With every blink I phased back to the clean lines, the uncluttered space of our young adulthood, the flat undamaged, the children unborn. Now you see them, now you don't. But here I was striving with them, pulsing and palpable. As they mounted a final assault I rolled onto my stomach and folded my hands over my head until Violet announced cheese toasties and they lifted off like locusts. The air settled around me as they went clattering into the kitchen. I released my hands and pushed myself up. I was parched. I was spent. The two mortise keys felt like medieval daggers in my pocket, so I went over to the coat rack and stashed them in the inner pouch of my jacket. I ran a hand over my face. I was still wearing ultra-Violet's secretions, her scent. The bathroom beckoned.

"I tried calling you."

I jolted and turned to find her in the hall again.

"Ah. That's the other thing." I reached into my pocket, so eager for the evidence that I almost dropped it. "My mobile died."

She kept her eyes on mine. "But you got it just two months ago."

"Yeah, no kidding. Damn thing." I slapped it against my palm. "But I bought the insurance, so—"

"A double spiral."

"What?"

"The rock carving. You said it's a double spiral."

This seemed to be a prompt of some kind, so I reached deep down into my reserves for some canned enthusiasm. Outstanding, I said. Phenomenal. It would change our understanding of . . . of what exactly? I was trying to stay where I was instead of where I had been, with the woman in front of me instead of the woman behind, both the same, but it was all double vision and second sight and I was faltering between them when I heard a crash in the kitchen followed by a child's wail, deus ex machina, except this was all natural and ordinary, the stuff of everyday life as Violet went rushing to the scene.

With the shower running I inspected myself in front of the mirror. Sticky groin, raw foreskin. The odour and pasty residue of sex. Red marks on my shoulders where she had gripped me that last time. I could make up something about carrying a heavy bag, the strap rubbing as I hauled all those tools up to the site. Yes, that would work. I rubbed at my greying temples, my thinning crown. I probed the culverts under my eyes. What the hell did she see in me? I had crossed a threshold of wear and tear that showed in every component of my face. I watched it all disappear in the rising steam. Good riddance, I thought, stepping into the shower to scrub away evidence that I had spent the afternoon with my wife.

* * *

I couldn't shake the need for an explanation. Time travel. It wasn't coherent. It didn't make sense. Seeking answers online, I found an echo chamber of outlandish notions, all theoretical, all sci-fi, all the time. The Grandfather Paradox, for example, stated that if someone went into the past and murdered his grandfather, then he would prevent his own birth and therefore couldn't travel back in time to commit the murder in the first place—assuming, of course, that it was a causal loop, which the double keys in my pocket seemed to disprove. The Many-Worlds theory, on other hand, asserted that entering the past would be a quantum event causing another timeline to branch off into one of many possible histories and futures, all of which were equally valid. And if this was true, then I wondered if it was possible to feel those potential realities, those other lives, as déjà-vu moments or goose-walking-over-your-grave sensations. Or just plain regrets. I wondered a lot of things, like why it was called the Grandfather Paradox instead of the Father Paradox or, more directly, the Mother Paradox. Kill your mum during her first trimester. Better yet, force her to have an abortion. No need to murder anybody except yourself. Keep it simple. Limit the crime to suicide.

I reached this conclusion while sitting on the closed lid of the toilet with my laptop as Tessa and Jamie thrashed in the bathtub next to me. I wiped my forehead occasionally as I clicked and typed. My shirt clammy in the damp warmth. I was getting nowhere, solving nothing. I should have buried or hidden something in 1988, I thought—yes, an artefact—and checked if it was still there, or still here, when I returned. And I shouldn't have mentioned Siobhan to her, no matter if it was a separate world or not. A slip of the tongue. A slip of my guilt. Stupid. Here and there, now and then. Keep your mouth shut.

"Play a video," Tessa said, rearing up from the froth with her hair slicked back.

"Not here."

"Why?"

"Thirty minutes of television," I said, like a prison warden reciting the rules, "after you've changed into jammies and brushed your teeth."

"But you were watching!"

"I wasn't watching. I was searching."

"For what?" She assumed a righteous posture that would have been a perfect imitation of Violet if she had put her hands on her hips. I hesitated at the sight of it, amused and troubled at once. In the silence Jamie abandoned his tugboat to give me the plain force of his gaze.

"Information," I said at last. "For work." And then I reached into the bath and pulled the plug to let the dirty water slurp away.

In the kitchen Violet and I ate roasted chicken and some green beans that the children had rejected, raising our voices to each other whenever the clothes washer went into its spin cycle. Halogen lights glared overhead. Pots and pans sat uncovered on the stove, exhaling aromas that fogged the windows. Appliances stood with their jaws dropped and flaps open, wanting loading and unloading, all our time to be saved, our conveniences to be done. At one point the phone rang and then fell silent after the answering machine kicked in. A telemarketer. Or maybe a call that would have changed our lives. I could have dialed my parents' number in 1988. I could have heard my mother's voice again. And I could have said, what—don't have a stroke in thirteen years? Ask your doctor to prescribe a blood thinner as a preventive measure? I would have been a crank caller, a crank son. I closed my eyes and turned away from the entire shoreline of it all. It was too tempting, too treacherous—a continent offering a fountain of youth and a city of gold, but also malaria and hostile natives and venomous wildlife. If I set foot on it I wouldn't come back.

Long before she died I had visited a crematorium out of professional interest to see exactly what happened to a body on a pyre. I had peered through the spyhole with utterly heartless fascination as the flesh flamed and bubbled and burned away to leave a bright hot skeleton that in ancient times would have become calcined as it cooled, leaving the bones cracked and warped, their bluish-white hue easily distinguished from the ash. In the crematorium, though, the operator broke it apart with an iron poker and sent the glowing pieces down into a cremulator, which resembled a tumble-dryer but pulverized them instead. I thought of that years later, trying to match my mother's absence, that sickening sense of the world without her, with the object my father held in his shaking hands. She had been processed and packaged at a factory, removed from the kind of grief we all needed. And I felt cheated. We should have been the ones to burn her. We should have lit the fire and beat our chests and screamed ourselves hoarse.

"You all right?"

I had my elbows on the table, thumbs pressed to my eyelids. I felt rickety and congested, like maybe I had caught Jamie's cold, but I leaned back and forced a smile. "Just tired."

She glanced down at the wine bottle in her hand. "Maybe I shouldn't have opened this."

I picked up my glass and held it out to her. She came forward and tilted her head as she poured, hair hanging to one side, her eyes at a low wattage, mild and neutral, full of ordinary thought. Her suspicious edge had disappeared. We were back to logistics and mission briefings for the coming weekend, the deployment of one child at a birthday party, another at a swimming lesson, and a play-date that conflicted with either the first or the second—I couldn't remember which. Before the children were born we used to pursue our own interests and come together at natural intervals. Now we were shackled together like a pair of convicts on a chain gang, each one jerking the other. The interdependence was exhausting. Years ago it had been different. The connection between us hadn't been a tether but a lifeline.

"Do you remember?" I asked.

Her eyes flickered and settled on me. And then I saw her—ultra-Violet, with that little quirk at the corner of her mouth, amused by my non sequiturs, my stream-of-consciousness crossing the threshold between what I thought and what I said.

"More specific, please?"

"Mid Argyll." I took a full sip of wine, watching her for a reaction. "Kilmartin Glen. The first time I went there."

She seated herself and began filling her own glass. "You mean back in . . . God, when was it, twenty years ago?"

"Eighteen. Eighteen and a half," I said, recalling the exact date I had found in Tariq's corner shop. The black-and-white proof. After Mrs McNaught's departure I had made my way down the aisle with a hand bridged across my brow, peeking at Tariq himself through parted fingers—his taut face, his dark mustache unflecked with grey—before taking cover behind a rack of newspapers in their silent chorus. This is the year, this is the day. Why eighteen and a half? Then again, why not? There was no reason for round numbers. Afterward I had stumbled back outside to the junction where the street crossed the main thoroughfare. The bygone traffic, the expired concerns. The past in motion. It was too simple to comprehend. In either direction the street was bracketed by gardens that held unfamiliar shapes, like vases with different flowers, while the road running uphill offered some kind of release, maybe because of the space or light or simply the climb. I was drawn toward it without knowing why. I glanced at the outdated styles around me as I walked. And when I reached one of the higher junctions I looked back. The trees of the parklands seemed lower, the frontage along the firth thinner, the huddled slopes of Fife wearing higher hemlines through a soft bright sea mist in the distance. Or was that just me? I couldn't trust my own perceptions, the condition of my own mind. Turning uphill, though, I found the world unchanged—the bronze figure of George IV in his oxidized green robes skylighted and flanked by the twin towers of New College, which were actually half a kilometre behind him and, farther still, the steeple of the Tolbooth Church with its crocketed spires and spikes, designed during the nineteenth century in the style of the fourteenth, all aligned and matted together as a single thing, layered in space and time.

"What of it?" she asked, taking up her knife and fork.

"I was wondering how it was for you."

"For me?" She paused over her meal. "But I didn't go."

"Exactly. I was away every week, and you were here alone."

She chewed with her gaze averted, casting her thoughts back. "Well," she said finally, as if thinking aloud, "you came home at the weekends, of course, plus bank holidays. And we visited your family in July. What did we call it? 'A Fortnight in Dixie.' But otherwise, really, I was banging away on my own stuff so I hardly noticed. I mean, I missed you terribly. Especially at night. But we talked on the phone, and it was all right because I knew how much it meant to you." She lifted her wineglass. "Your first dig as project director."

"While you were banging away," I said, "on what, exactly?"

She gave a slight torque to her head, as if she were going to look sideways but then caught herself. An effort came into her eyes, seeking the grooves of whatever was running through my head.

"I'm just curious," I added.

"About what I did twenty years ago?"

"Eighteen and a half."

The washing machine began spinning again with enough force to make the place throb like the engine room of a ship. I took another bite of food but lost its flavour for the bitter aftertaste of what I was thinking. What I was understanding. The way she gave herself to me—the older me—while my younger self was at Kilmartin. The lack of fulfilment it implied. Her dissatisfaction with him. With me. With the way I was back then. It was so obvious now. Of course I had no right to be jealous, especially given my misbehaviour with Siobhan, but in retrospect that only made it worse. All these years we had been fooling ourselves. Or maybe she was just fooling me.

"I was finishing up my Master's," she said. "I was practising for the ABRSM and giving some lessons on the side. And I was running in the park almost every day. Oh, wasn't *that* the life."

Oh, wasn't it. Two versions of the same man. After trying us on like outfits at a designer boutique she must have decided that she preferred me, the older vintage, which meant she had to wait for the younger one to ripen. But maybe I wasn't turning out to be what she expected. Maybe she was discovering I wasn't worth waiting for after all.

I shovelled green beans into my mouth. I drank wine as if it were water. I salted the chicken until it bristled white, and still it wasn't enough. I was trying to think through my behaviour with the younger Violet. Had I given her a false impression? No. I had been nothing but myself, and if she thought otherwise then it was her own delusion.

"What brought that on?" she asked.

I made a vague gesture with my knife. "The trip. My old stomping grounds. It brings everything back."

"Including me."

I coughed and pressed a napkin to my lips.

"You all right?" Her eyebrows went up slightly, a token show of concern.

I waved her off and sat back with my wineglass. "You were saying?"

"Just that you asked what I was doing back then as if it occurred to you for the first time."

"I couldn't quite remember everything. That's all."

"Mmm," she said as she chewed. "To be honest, I'm surprised I remember what I did twenty years ago."

"Eighteen and a half."

"Right. And how is Inbhir these days?"

"Inbhir."

"You stopped there, yeah? To pay your respects."

I nodded. "As always."

"And how does it look?"

"Neglected." I picked up my fork again. "The Druids haven't been taking care of it."

"A pity. But at least it's safe."

I looked at her. She was scraping at a chicken bone with delicate flicks of her knife. "Safe from what?"

"The Stonehenge Syndrome. Isn't that what you call it? All that crude attention. You want it to remain obscure. Hidden. Secret."

Although she didn't lift her eyes from her plate there was a subtle tilt to her head, listening for a misplaced note in my reply.

"Popularity," I said, "is a double-edged sword. Look at what it's done to Bach."

"And what it almost did to Inbhir. Those Druids using it as a backdrop for their primitive fantasies."

"Like those philistines treating the Brandenburg Concertos as a soundtrack for Sunday brunch."

"Not really respecting all that subtle and sophisticated material culture."

"The polyphonic texture, complex and exuberant," I said. "Subject and countersubject. Point, counterpoint."

"The grammar of the rock." She plucked a green bean from her plate and crunched it between her teeth. "Everyone misunderstands it. The same way they misunderstand Bach."

"I guess we're a couple of elitists."

"Damn straight," she said, imitating my southern twang. She lifted her wine. "Hey. Cheers to us."

As I touched my glass to hers it seemed like something was coming loose inside her and she might kick off her shoes or shake out her hair, and I felt a glint of excitement at the prospect of whatever it was simply because it existed, simply because it was there. But then a white shape appeared in the hallway. Tessa. The ghost of our future.

"I'm thirsty," she said, blinking at us in the bright kitchen.

I aimed a stern look at her. "There's water by your bed."

"But I want milk."

Violet went to the fridge and filled a cup for her. "Here, sweetie."

Tessa took it in both hands like the Holy Grail and drank it down, gulping audibly. A dribble ran from the corner of her mouth. I watched her pulsing throat, her bare feet, her living lean body all knobbed and arched with the promise of growth.

As Violet took her back to bed I wiped some wine off the table-cloth, or what we called a tablecloth but was actually a sheath of plastic suitable for most construction sites. I had glimpsed the true wood of the table maybe once or twice over the past couple of years. The drawers in this room were still fastened with child locks. The outlets were covered with protective plugs. Children made everything dangerous and dull at once. Siobhan couldn't have children. She had announced it, like so many other things, while staring up at the ceiling in the aftermath of sex. Endome-triosis, she said. The odds were low. Nil, really. And then, turning toward me in the half-dark, she pressed her face to mine. So that's one worry out the door, aye? You won't be getting me pregnant.

"Can barely keep her eyes open, that one," Violet said, coming back into the kitchen. "She'll be out soon enough."

I took a breath, wanting something else in my thoughts. "So how did it go today? At uni."

"The lecture?"

"Higher education. Share your knowledge with a good ol' boy who doesn't know his shit from his sherbet."

She wrinkled her nose.

"Ok," I said. "Bad metaphor at mealtime. But come on, let's hear it."

She lifted her chin for a moment, as if consulting the ceiling. "Passacaglia. Ground bass."

"Do I know this one?"

She smiled. "You used to."

"You mean I forgot? Shame on me."

"It's a strict form," she said, "based on a process of variation. You have either a bassline or a harmonic pattern built on that bassline, which is repeated cyclically, over and over. On top of that you have upper voices changing from one cycle to another, or one variation to another. Simple, yeah?"

I put my knife and fork together on my plate to show I was finished, just as Violet herself had instructed me all those years ago. Table manners of an older society. Etiquette lessons. I picked up my wineglass and nodded.

"Or at least it seems simple. Take Bach's Passacaglia in C minor for organ. The theme is a bassline eight measures long, which returns a total of twenty times. Twenty, Aaron. You've no idea what an achievement. He starts with the bassline exposed, of course, to let you hear the theme—the structural assumption underlying the entire piece—"

"Wait a minute," I said. Something was coming back to me. "Have you played this one?"

"The organ at Tolbooth Church. Before they moved it. You should have heard those pipes. The acoustics in the vaulted ceilings."

The steeple of the same church I had seen hours ago, years ago, in the layered perspective of the street. A coincidence. No. Yes. A coincidence, of course.

"Of course," she continued, "Bach isn't content simply to run a series of variations over the bassline. He groups them into a kind of macro structure, the first ten serving as themes and variations with a steady buildup of rhythmic complexity, adding more and more voices, the music getting larger and louder. Then with the eleventh variation he shifts the theme into higher registers, taking it up from the bass by an octave or two to create the illusion of departure, but it's still the same theme, just a little higher and quieter. At variation sixteen we get the recapitulation, where he returns the theme to the bass and that earlier mood of heaviness and power resumes—a sense of arrival despite the fact that we never really departed. And those upper voices. They draw our attention away from the main structural element—the repeated ground bass theme. He elides through sections, understates cadences. He grips you by the heart with all that rhythm and exuberance and structure and power."

The washing machine was churning again. Her smile had taken on an exquisite charge. In her monthly cycle there seemed to be a phase when Bach worked on her like an aphrodisiac and the most uplifting passages became G-spots that were everywhere and nowhere, maddeningly present but untouchable unless she gave herself to me, like that time I came home to find a cantata at high volume and tears streaming down her face, and she simply pulled me toward the sofa and removed her clothes. In a postcoital haze I had promised to buy every Bach recording ever made, and she had given me a warm rushing smile and said she already owned all the ones worth buying, but maybe I could take up German and wear a wig instead. She was still ultra-Violet then.

"And I discussed 'Dido's Lament,'" she said.

"That sounds familiar."

"Because it's a famous aria."

"A famous aria." I tried to hold back a smile. "Now there's an oxymoron—like what, jumbo shrimp?"

"It happens to be," she said, "one of my favourite pieces of non-Bach Baroque."

Her expression seemed to be hardening, but I said it anyway. "And what's your favourite non Russian borscht?"

She set down her glass, which made a sharp clink as it caught the edge of her plate. "We seem to be hitting some turbulence here. Should we buckle our seatbelts? Is this about to get rough?"

"Sorry. I'm just . . ." I waved a hand vaguely at the wine, at my fatigue with the hidden indentations of her moods, the wynds and closes that always seemed to take me where I didn't want to go. But I was provoking her now. It was my fault. I bowed my head in contrition. A long moment passed. The washer finally wound down and clicked a couple of times before falling silent.

"It's a *famous aria*," she said, "but most listeners don't realize it's also a passacaglia. That's because Purcell keeps the theme in the bassline, which is the structural level of the composition, and uses it to control the melodical development of the piece. All the changes and embellishments occur in the upper voices, one of which is literally a voice. The singer. And the ground bass—it's a chromatic descending line for a funereal mood—repeats eleven times, acting as a control factor under Dido's voice. Really amazing. The singer's lines don't always correspond to the beginnings and endings of the ground bass theme, masking the repetitions so you don't always hear them. But you feel them."

"Which opera is this again?"

"*Dido and Aeneas.*"

I blinked slowly, registering the names. A story extracted from Virgil's *Aeneid*. "Mom would have known the verses by heart."

Violet nodded once, with a crease between her brows to acknowledge both the truth and sadness of the fact. Whenever I thought of my mother now I tried to take some comfort in her sudden death. How much worse it would have been for everyone, herself included, if she had survived the stroke. A prize-winning translator, speechless and twitching in her wheelchair. My father feeding her like a baby. No. Kill her, Zeus, strike her with lightning. Bang, she's dead.

"Do you remember the plot?" Violet asked.

"Vaguely."

"Even so, Purcell gives the story an extra tragic twist. I mean, the main elements are the same. Aeneas stopping in Carthage after the Trojan War to resupply his ships and falling madly in love with Dido, the local queen. And the feeling is mutual, of course. But an evil sorceress has it out for Dido and wants to destroy her, so she disguises one of her elves as Mercury, messenger of the gods, and makes him deliver a fake command: Aeneas must sail onward and found the great city of Rome. Aeneas falls for it. He thinks the gods have decided his future. He thinks it's his destiny. He agonizes over leaving Dido behind, but in the end chooses his career over love and bids her farewell. And Dido is so devastated that she commits suicide. The aria is what she sings while doing it."

"*While* doing it? So it must be, what . . . poison? Something slow and fittingly operatic."

"Depends on the production. I saw one where she seals herself in a cave and gradually suffocates."

I blew out a breath.

"Exactly."

"Do you have a recording of it? I mean, here at home?"

She put down her cutlery, lifted her head, and softly began to sing.

> When I am laid, am laid in earth, may my wrongs create
> No trouble, no trouble in, in thy breast.
> Remember me, remember me, but oh
> Forget my fate.
> Remember me, but oh
> Forget my fate.

Her voice wasn't great, but it was hers, and she didn't attempt some kind of silly pulsating vibrato that made the words unintelligible. When she finished singing the kitchen became truly silent for the first time. Her eyes held a faint mist. She looked down at the napkin bunched in her hands. Something sliced through every cell in my body.

"Did you miss me?"

She looked up.

"After I left," I said, "and you were stuck with my clumsy and clueless precursor. A naïve guy in his early twenties. A boy, really. That's how I must have seemed to you. Which explains a lot. That was the summer you admitted you had a thing for older men. Yeah," I said. "That explains a lot."

She pushed her chair back and went to the sink. "Well then maybe you can fill me in," she said, rinsing her hands, "because I don't know what you're talking about."

"You know exactly what I'm talking about."

She gave me an odd glance as she made her way back to the table and, once she sat down again, nodded at the empty glass in my hand. "How much have you had?"

"I don't know. Check the bottle to see what's left. And anyway what difference—"

"I mean before dinner. When you went for a 'walk' without a coat and came back rather disheveled and incoherent, actually."

I held up a hand. "Hang on. You think . . . you think I went to the Cross Keys?"

"Your mobile doesn't get reception there. I was about to try their landline when you showed up."

"You're not serious."

"I don't mind if you have a pint or two. Especially after finding that double spiral. But I was counting on you to watch the children while I made their tea. And you didn't call to say you would be late. I was worried."

Worried? No. She was jealous—jealous of my free time. Now it was making sense. We had to barter and negotiate for every spare moment, and apparently I had taken more than my share. Payment was due.

"If you tell me you went for a walk," she said, "then I'll believe you. Ok? But don't babble like some nutter and expect me to go along with it. Don't put me through . . ." Her voice quavered and trailed off.

I spread my hands in a what-the-fuck gesture, but she lowered her eyes to the table, her mouth set. My thoughts went crashing forward into the whole ridiculous truth. Sure, blurt it out. Violet, my love, I found a time portal or wormhole or cosmic helter-skelter in the coal cellar and screwed you eighteen years ago. Don't you remember? I rubbed my face and then looked at her again.

106

"All right," I said. "I'm sorry. I'm really sorry. But I didn't go to the Cross Keys. You can ring them and check if you want. I went for a walk this afternoon to clear my head because I haven't been feeling right today. Maybe I caught Jamie's cold. I don't know. Winter always hits me hard."

She straightened and searched my face with a kind of technical appraisal—the look of someone dismantling a bomb. I wanted to dissolve it, whatever it was that had fitted itself to her emotions like a second skin with every nuance intact, the appearance but not the sense of who she was, or who she had been, her deepest feelings coated with enamel. I wanted to crack through it. And I was reaching across the table for her face and soft slope of her neck and all the hollows of her clavicle when I heard a noise and saw Jamie standing in the doorway and my hand settled on the neck of the wine bottle instead.

Jamie came forward with his blanket wrapped around his neck like a scarf, his thumb in his mouth, fleeing a nightmare or the threat of one, the exact nature of the beast unclear. Yes, he knew how to climb out of his cot after all, just as Tessa had said last week. A new era was dawning. Violet rose from the table and gathered him up in her arms. While she carried him back to his den I sat back in the reverberation of the thwarted moment. Not that I could have delivered the goods. With dreary recognition it occurred to me that after sleeping only a few hours the previous night and passing through what felt like a cellular meat grinder into a parallel universe, then having rigorous sex with a woman half my age and coming back through the portal again into some heavy emotional fallout while also consuming half a bottle of wine, I couldn't get an erection if Aphrodite straddled me in her boudoir. Maybe my younger self would be able to handle it. Or maybe I was overestimating him in retrospect. The older I get, the better I was. I stared down at the chicken bones on my plate. I swirled the last of the wine in my glass. I was a mess, inside and out. I gulped it down. Cheers to us.

Violet returned with a look that seemed more herself, or the self I remembered.

"You're Bach," I said, unable to resist the joke.

She stopped with her hand on the back of her chair, her expression crossing into something and then back again, both cold and hot. "Don't do that."

I raised my eyebrows at her.

She sat down and finished the last few bites of her meal and then, as if she had made a decision, took on a bright look and said, "Tell me more about this double spiral."

I told her more about the double spiral—the look and feel of it, the location, the angle, the sightlines and significance. I played up Fergus and played down Lorna, emphasizing the grand archaeological intrigue in which this particular carving needed to remain a secret until the tender had been accepted and the contract signed.

"But Fergus wouldn't dare destroy this one, would he?"

"No way. That's not the issue, though. If he knew the value of the find and how desperately other firms would want to work on it, he'd probably shop around and try to pit us all against each other. We'd bid ourselves into the basement, and even if we won the contract, I imagine we'd barely cover operating costs."

She rose from her chair and started gathering dishes. "Do you think it's the same thing?"

I rolled my head toward her. "Same thing as what?"

"As the first double spiral."

A bitter smile spread across my face. I pushed myself up and followed her to the sink. "Oh, how I'd love to know."

She started rolling up her sleeves. "Too bad you can't compare them."

"Too bad is right." I halted at the blunt force of it. April 1988. Fergus broke ground on that petrol station when? September? October? When Siobhan was in town to meet with the curator of the local museum and she happened to see his backhoe not too far from Inbhir. Several months after the excavation was finished.

Which meant if I could go back through the coal cellar, and if the time interval remained the same . . .

I was clutching a smeared glass. Violet was feeding plates into the open dishwasher. She didn't notice. And why would she? It was a whole different existence, separate from the one she knew. My hand started to tremble. Yes, it was that simple. I had the key to another world where the rock carving was intact. Where my mother was alive. Where my wife was ultra-Violet. Here and now, there and then. I couldn't tell if I thought it or said it, but it seemed to hang in the air anyway. Another chance. Another life.

CHAPTER SEVEN

1988

Coming home I sense it in the sunlight flickering through a reel of clouds and gardens dripping with rain, everything glossed into bright presence, damp and alive. The instinct of birds scattering before an earthquake. I'm fumbling with my keys and a bag of groceries on the front stoop when I feel him next to me. It worked. Whatever I did, it worked. I should commend myself. Well done, Vi. But I don't glance up. My heart going like a kettledrum. Keep your eyes on the score with the music working through you without stopping to think, without thinking to stop. No, I can't look at him yet because I'll lose everything—the bread, the butter, the eggs, myself. He clears his throat. A hot blind pleasure as I flick dumbly through my keys, no longer knowing what fits what.

"Need a hand?"

I steady myself before I reply. "I'll need more than your hand."

Then I lift my eyes. He's leaning against the wall with his arms crossed and chin lowered, trying not to smile. And he's dressed properly this time, showered and shaved, with a quilted jacket and crisp shirt and pleated trousers. A rucksack at his feet. Like he's just stepped off a commuter train. Or about to step onto one. After giving over the groceries I drop the keys and pick them up all jingling until I finally get them sorted and we're climbing the stairwell in a swelling, rasping silence. He seems to falter on the first landing, but then I glance back to find him watching my arse.

Another flight, another turn, jagging upward with the keys like razors in my hand.

We manage to shut the door behind us. His rucksack drops. My groceries hit the floor. A few buttons pop off my blouse, my elbow catching him on the cheekbone before I go down to all fours with the wall inches away, the seam of paper revealed, the doorframe chipped to expose a hint of plain wood through several layers of paint, and I know that's me, that's what I am with his body hunkered against mine. The trembling hard ride of him inside me, not my favourite position but otherwise the carpet would scorch me in all the wrong places, and how would I explain it to the younger Aaron when he returns this weekend? My palms planted squarely on the floor, waiting for him to finish. A final pulse of pleasure. Yes, a big quick shot for the sake of something more fulfilling later. He must know that about himself by now. Our breaths settling. Then it's the awkward separation, the shift and swivel, the about-face when I always expect to find a bloke laughing. I cup my hands over his shoulders. The bulked arms, the trim stomach. Not that my younger Aaron is flabby, but this one—this is the one I want. This is really him. As I rise to my feet I realise I'm still wearing socks. How does he avoid laughing at that?

"Well," I say, running a hand through my hair, "thanks for your help."

"Don't mention it. My good deed for the day." He touches his fingertips to his cheek.

I wince. "Sorry about that."

"And sorry about *that*," he says, gesturing at the floor.

I turn to find the paper bag slumped and stained at the bottom. The eggs, no doubt. I lift it by the corners and carry it into the kitchen and place it gently in the sink. Cold tile, airy echoes. A place where it never feels right to be naked. I tear a sheet from the kitchen roll and swab the dribble off my inner thigh. The stuff of life, as Isobel calls it. When I come back out to the hallway he's buttoning his shirt.

"I don't remember seeing that," he says, nodding at the stain on the carpet. "I mean, I never noticed a mark or discolouration or anything. Later on."

I peer down at it. "It'll come out with tonic water and bicarbonate of soda."

"Actually, don't."

"Sorry?"

"Do me a favour and leave it there. As a test."

"A test?" I'm about to ask what he means when I catch his clinical edge. I wrinkle my nose at him. "Don't tell me we have this same carpet eighteen years from now."

"Oh no. But at some point over the next few months he might notice. And if he does, then I'll know for sure whether or not these worlds are the same."

I watch him.

"Because," he adds, "it would affect my memory. Or not."

As I pick through my clothing on the floor it occurs to me, with an unpleasant backbeat, that he'll be tracking everything—every crack and crinkle and crumb—for the tiniest break in continuity. I'm having an affair with Sherlock Holmes. Maybe between the two of us, the older Vi and me, we can adjust his attitude just a bit here?

"What day is it?" he asks.

"Wednesday."

"I mean the date."

"The sixth."

"Of?"

"Aaron," I say, giving him a look.

"Violet," he says, giving it right back.

I breathe out. "April. And if you ask me what year, I'll scream."

"Interesting," he says, nodding to himself. "And good. Easy to track." His eyes snap back to me. "Because the same number of days have passed on either side."

"Lovely," I say, stepping into my pants. "Easy maths."

He reaches for his trousers and shakes them out. "What was in the bag, by the way?"

"Eggs."

"I'd offer to buy more, but I left my wallet back in 2006."

"Again?"

"On purpose. Because what's the point? The credit cards are useless, the driving license hasn't been issued yet, and the bank notes are counterfeit, technically speaking."

"So you left behind all that evidence," I say, "that you were so desperate to show me last time."

He folds his arms. "But you don't need it. It doesn't matter. Maybe I'm Aaron, aged to perfection. Maybe I'm not. Who cares? I still fit the bill, right?"

I hesitate at the subtle shift, the hardness coming into his eyes. "Easy does it. I just thought you'd bring back a newspaper or something."

"No such luck. You'll have to take me on faith."

"It isn't faith," I say. "I just know it's you. The same way you know it's me."

His attitude seems to smooth as we finish dressing. My blouse with two missing buttons. I find one in the corner, another near the egg stain, which apparently has become some kind of laboratory experiment. We've got our work cut out for us, don't we, Vi?

"And anyway you should have seen my mobile."

I look up to find him inspecting his spare jacket on the rack.

"Turns out the SIM card and the microchips were fried, which is why it didn't work," he says, giving me a glance of vindication. "So I just brought the basics this time. Clothing, toiletries. No technology."

"Your mobile was . . ." I pause at the troubling weight of that detail before catching the larger sense of what he's saying, the obvious sight of his rucksack, and despite myself I clasp my hands like a schoolgirl. "You're staying?"

"For a couple of days. That's all I can spare right now."

I walk over and wrap my arms around his neck. "Oh, how shall we pass the time?"

"By making a great discovery."

"Sorry?"

"At Kilmartin."

My arms go slack.

"To save an artefact before it's destroyed," he says.

I step back from him. "So that's why you came."

His expression takes on a familiar shape despite those mature ridges and depths. And of course his tactic of barging forward like this, brandishing his agenda without any notion of how it might come across—the same mistake after all those years.

"No," he says. "I mean, it's not the only reason."

"I'm glad I'm somewhere on the list."

"Hey." He takes my face in his hands. "I'm here for you, first and foremost. This other thing at Kilmartin is just the icing on the cake."

"Some icing," I say.

He gives me a slow and lingering kiss. "Mmm. Some cake."

An hour later we're on the road with my bag full of fleece and lingerie, wool socks and silk stockings, cash and contraceptives. I've notified my seminar tutor of a sudden illness, which is not entirely untrue, and I've cancelled my lessons for the next two days. I'm a fool. Can we sing it? This is what I sensed—yes, this is what I sensed when I first met him in the pub. I tried to deny it with structure, with old-fashioned dates that caused Clare and Isobel no end of amusement before the inevitable arrival in my bedroom. And I remember trying to make light of it—the serious move that came soon afterward—while running with Clare around Arthur's Seat last September. Our ritual of endorphins and plain talk. The ring road with its headwind both east and west, as always, those blistering shears coming round the slopes. The bracken thrashing, the cliffs scrubbed raw. The tall brown grasses and goldenrod along the far side with the Pentlands humped in the distance. The mingled autumn scents all robust and clear. A shout from a passing vehicle in praise of our tight leggings, Clare's blond ponytail like a flare.

"So when 'God Save the Queen' came on," I tell her, "he asked why they were playing 'My Country 'Tis of Thee.'"

Clare falls into laughter, breaking her stride. "You've got your hands full with this one, Vi. Are you sure?"

"Of course not. That's the problem. I need some assurance."

"Or *ins*urance."

"That would be nice."

"Love insurance."

"Who sells that?"

"My sister could sort you out. Mind you, it's not cheap. And I hear the excess is high. But it covers cheating, dumping, all types of crash-and-burn."

"I'm worried about something less obvious."

"The long-term stuff, you mean? The slow and dreary drop. Subsidence. By the time you realise your mistake," she says, with an aerobic pause, "you're a middle-aged frump with children. Sorry, dear. No insurance for that."

"Quite a risk, then," I say, "if we get married next week."

She slows and stares at me as if I've sapped all the strength from her legs.

"It's just to keep him here. In Britain. Otherwise he gets deported."

"But his visa . . ."

"His student visa. It's about to expire."

"But what about . . . I don't know, a normal visa? He's got a job, right?"

"Two jobs. Part time. Not enough."

A rhythmic silence as we run and breathe. "It's just a legal thing," I add. "No biggie."

"How long have you been together?"

"Nine months."

"Sod the insurance, Vi. You need a stunt double."

The wind hits us with a tidal wash as we crest the hill. The Crags slanting and crumbling down into skirts of greenery, the city out there bristling with steeples and spires and the Castle high on its rock like a petrified wedding cake. We're silent during the long descent. The impact of each stride, the steady punishment to our knees. Calton Hill wheeling into view with Nelson's tower and the Parthenon columns set against open sky, incomplete. And when we reach level ground by Holyrood Palace I hear Aaron's voice ridiculing the monarchy—the royal waste of resources, the imported German bloodline. On the outcrop above us the single corner of St Anthony's Chapel like a broken bookend, its windows unglassed. How much of it do I notice because of him? His interest in every ruin, in every ripple of rock. Impossible to keep his thoughts out of mine. We're already married, I think, in our own way.

Alongside the pond we run past knots of walkers and pram-pushers, children tossing bread into convulsions of waterfowl, babies squealing, toddlers testing limits. Clare gives it all the smile of someone pleased not to be them—that is, the mothers. The product of a persistent marriage, as she phrases it, and blood-sport holidays at the family table in Sussex, she has declared her intention to be sterilized, after which she plans to have a long succession of lovers and die at the age of ninety surrounded by her lovely cats. It isn't until we're winding our way up the Queen's Drive that she speaks again.

"He asked you, didn't he?"

I try to frame a suitable reply.

"And you couldn't say no," she adds. "You couldn't say, let's find another way. You're afraid he'll think you don't love him enough, or some tripe like that."

"Not really. It's more like I don't want to miss my chance."

"Your chance for what?"

"For what happens next."

Clare slings me a look. "Sharing a toilet and scraping eggs off his breakfast plate. That's what happens next."

"I mean, beyond that."

"You mean children. At which point goodbye, Vi. Your life ends where theirs begins."

"That's not my agenda."

"It's rarely the agenda. But it's what happens." She pauses as if deciding not to say something, but then says it anyway. "Just don't take his surname, all right?"

"Not this again."

"You know how much grows out of that choice," she says, letting out the phrases in beats, timed to her breath. "Don't give yourself up, Vi. Don't surrender. Because that's what it means. Deep down. You're saying, 'I'm not as important as you are, darling. Your identity is the one that really counts.' It's not a conscious thing. But it's there. And then we expect, what? Equality? What does a woman think, Vi—what does she think when she surrenders her own *name* to a man because he puts a ring on her finger?"

"She thinks she loves him, I reckon. She thinks the name doesn't really matter."

Clare snorts out a laugh. "Ask a man to take your surname and see if it matters. It's fundamental. Your soul is at stake."

"That's what I meant earlier. About missing my chance. It's not just the relationship. It's more than love. He actually sharpens my technique. I play better with him."

She goes silent for a few strides. "On the piano?"

"Uh-huh."

"Because of . . . what, the sex?"

"Not really. I mean, I don't know. The sex is good, which helps, but he gives me something else. An attitude. A temperament." And my eyes widen as the drive levels off and Arthur's Seat comes into view ahead of us, the lower slopes terraced with ancient farms, just as Aaron pointed out, but they seem like organ manuals now, one above the other, the landscape full of music, a fugue in the layers of earth with the grain of every rock sounding out like a piano string after the hammer has struck. "That's it," I say. "My temperament. My tuning."

"No offense, Vi, but that sounds fucked up. Like he's messing with your head."

"Not just my head. My hands as well. And he's not really doing it. But it's happening because of him."

"Now you've lost me. What are you saying?"

What was I saying back then? That I'd always sensed another harmonic in the very nature of things. That I'd always known I would risk some essential part of myself to find it, in the spaces between the notes. And now I think maybe it's her, the older Violet. And him. This Aaron I crave inside the younger. Ever since we met in the pub I've wanted him less for the way he is than for the way he will be. And this compound pleasure I feel in making it happen on either side—yes, I know I'm doing it but I don't know how, each surprise inevitable, every chord consonant, every note true. A perfect fifth. As he drives we hardly speak, due not only to the uncanny ease between us but also the radio he insists on keeping tuned to the news. The American presidential primaries. Thatcher and the Middle East.

"So the Russians are pulling out of Afghanistan. That'll solve everything. Yes, indeed," he says. "The *Soviet Union.*"

I reach for the dial and switch it off. "Sorry to spoil your fun, but you can't carry on this way. Treating everything like an inside joke. It's not fair."

He gives a sober nod. "Point taken. But it's not just amusement. The news, I mean. I want to see if it matches my own history."

"How would you know? I mean, all that nitty-gritty stuff?"

"I checked online."

"You checked . . . ?"

"For the details. In case it wasn't obvious. If it turns out Paul Newman is president and the Beatles are on a reunion tour, then

I'll know we're pretty far off. But there doesn't seem to be any difference at all. It's identical but separate, as far as I can tell, because she doesn't seem to have any memory of this. As if it never happened for her. The older Violet, I mean."

I absorb the notion cleanly and quickly—how it needs to go in the future—without showing a flicker of notice. "Yeah, I get all that. But you said you checked something on a line. Like you were fishing or something."

He drives in silence, eyes working through some thought. "Oh, that. Well. Nothing, really. It's just the name of a newspaper. The *Edinburgh Line*."

"Wow," I say.

He glances at me.

"I'm actually insulted that you expect me to believe that."

"Hey, come on. I'm just saying . . ." But he doesn't finish.

I wait for an extra moment or two, affronted and reassured at the same time. "What you're saying is you're still a transparent liar eighteen years from now. It's really quite amazing."

"Can we change the topic?"

"Only if you give me a glimpse into your crystal ball. Don't worry, I'm not after football scores or anything like that, but some basics would be nice. I presume we avoid nuclear armageddon, for example?"

"You presume correctly."

"Ecological disaster?"

He takes on a weary look. "Nothing dramatic, if that's what you're worried about. But we're farther down the slide. The rainforests are smaller. Ditto the polar icecaps. More pollution. More people. Fewer animals and plants and insects. We're still fiddling while Rome burns."

"Politics?"

"I guess you could say there are more . . . colours on the chess board. It's not just black and white anymore."

"Go on."

"That's it, really."

"That's abstract, really. What about the Soviet Union?"

"Meet the new boss, same as the old boss."

"You sound like Nostradamus with a head injury."

"What else can I say? If I share details, I could make things worse."

"Details like, what? A new political regime? A little war, perhaps? Or maybe, on a more personal note, your time travel method? You could share that, at least."

He eases back, releasing a smile. "Now look who's transparent."

"Am not!"

He lifts a hand from the wheel in a placating gesture. "Don't get me wrong. I hate holding back like this, Vi. I really do. But I'm trying to be cautious here. As cautious as possible. The less you know, the better."

"That's patronising."

"That's the truth. I'm scared to death of harming you or anyone else." He says it casually enough, but then it seems to trigger a response and he takes his eyes off the road to look at me with all his age. "And since I'm a transparent liar, you can call me out on that if you want."

As he turns back I study his profile against the blurred greenery, the crackling sun. His cropped hair and shifted features. It seems like a wave has gone through him. This isn't the kind of crystal ball I wanted.

I touch his arm. "All right, then. Let's stick with the more immediate future. How about if you tell me what we're looking for at Kilmartin."

Bracing against the wheel, he straightens up and resets himself. "A standing stone—or a stone that used to be standing—carved with a rare and remarkable design."

"And?"

"The Lost Treasure of the Incas."

"I mean, what happens when we find this precious stone? What then?"

"We'll cross that bridge when we come to it."

I look forward to find nary a bridge in sight but instead the road fringed with budding trees, all nubbled and laced with growth, a patchland of farms and fields and tawny humps rising up, some mountains farther out spangled with snow. This loch I remember, just before Crianlarich, where we used to stop for lunch sometimes, the whole family, on the way to Oban.

"And why are we taking this route? Isn't it longer?"

"But safer. I don't want to run into myself."

I purse my lips, resisting a smile.

"If we approach from the south," he says with the tone of a headmaster, "we'll pass Inbhir at quitting time, and who knows what could happen. Ok?"

"Trust me," I say. "Someone would have to get pretty close to recognise you. It's not just the older face. Sorry, mature face. It's your haircut, your clothes. And besides, no one is looking for an older Aaron. People only see what they expect to see most of the time."

"He'd recognise *you*, though."

"I'm a lot easier to explain. A surprise visit. Love among the ruins. And anyway you should be more worried about getting pulled over without a license. That's the real danger. Why don't you let me drive?"

"Hell no. I'm enjoying this."

"What, breaking the law?"

"Driving here. Driving now. With you. It reminds me how it all used to feel. The newness of everything. The reversed rules. Left is right, right is wrong. Public is private. The first floor is the ground floor, the second is the first."

"Oh, that. Well, you haven't been blethering on about it recently, so I reckon you're adapting."

"Going native."

"Mmm. Which is quite a long process, apparently."

He catches my tone and glances over. "Meaning what?"

I hesitate in the steady rush of the car, tyres humming on tarmac. How much fun should I have with this? "Oh, nothing. Nothing at all. You seem to be coming along decently enough."

He ripples out a smile. "Well, that's right nice, Vi. Y'all do me a favour and let me know when I've passed the test, huh?"

At the next junction we turn and follow a track through clumped forest and throbbingly bright pastures, lambs scampering in newborn fear. Odours of manure and soggy growth and decay. Loch Awe appearing through breaks in the trees with waters all roiled and murky, resisting the blue sky overhead. In the distance the shell of a ruined castle. I try to remember which clan killed and connived the others into submission but draw a blank, the road narrowing to a single lane along the shoreline with swings and swerves and undulations bringing a nausea I try to relieve by lowering the window and hoping for a quick end to what he so helpfully reminds me is the longest freshwater loch in Scotland. In response I close my eyes and begin humming a tune. By the time we emerge from the folded hills I'm embroidering the melody for dear life.

"All right," he says, with an academic sigh. "I give up. Why do you keep humming that?"

"Humming what?"

"God Save the Queen." He does a double-take at my expression. "What?"

"You passed the test."

To my relief the road lengthens and rises easily through the town of Kilmartin—an array of cottages, a whitewashed hotel, a call box in red relief—before heading down a slope with growth massed thick on my side. Aaron glances out his window at the fields. The flat stretch of the glen. The burn running alongside parallel because it was straightened, he says, at about the same time the peat was cut for better farming. Which also exposed many of the sites. Without him I wouldn't notice any of it. I'd hardly see it at all. That trip with my family years ago to stare at those rocky humps, those standing stones, those nearly invisible carvings. It's all there. It's real. But it holds as much interest as a fence or a fallen log. There's too much missing. He has to fill it in for me.

"Wow, I remember this," he says, angling his head to glance at something overhead.

"What?"

"The trees. Withered at the crowns. The effects of Chernobyl. Don't worry," he adds quickly. "They'll recover. And these Forestry tracts in different places. Different stages of growth, I mean. What a haircut."

Lochgilphead is still some distance ahead when he pulls onto a lay-by or maybe the beginnings of a gravel car park. He switches off the engine, his eyes fixed on an anonymous stand of saplings, some overgrown grass.

"Is this really the—" I manage to say before his door pops open and he disappears as if sucked out of an aircraft.

By the time I climb out he's stamping through the weeds and prodding the turf. I ask a few questions, but he doesn't respond. Well, that hasn't changed, has it? He'd miss Armageddon in this condition. I lean against the warm bonnet of the car and fold my arms. A chilly breeze. A scent of spring fields. The grumble of a lorry approaching. And looking out at the sunlight on the hills, I recognise it for the first time—the landscape of the glen, shaped like a vast trench. Or an amphitheatre. With acoustics to match? Like a giant Maeshowe. I clap my hands. I sing out a note. But it's not enough. One voice, one pair of hands. It would have been bigger and deeper, sharper and higher. They would have had flutes or pipes of some kind. And drums. My fantasy, perhaps. Music everywhere and always.

I glance over at Aaron still grubbing away. If only Clare could see me now, sidelined like this, subverting my interests to his. I take a slow breath. Five lessons I've cancelled, plus a practice session and a meeting with my seminar tutor, who despite his gruff demeanor indulges every half-baked idea that comes into my head. But he'd crack my knuckles with a ruler, Hugh would, if he knew I wasn't in bed with a fever, as I still owe him a response to that puzzle canon from Bach. A riddle originally assigned to the master's own students in the eighteenth century. With only one voice notated, I'm supposed to discover the rule that applies to the rest, which in this case consists of two melodies with separate canonic imitations above a bassline Bach used in another work. The only clue is his inscription on the facsimile, *Christus Coronabit Crucigeros*, Christ will Crown the Crossbearers—a symbolum with contrasting moods, hinting that the sad upper layer, which begins with a mournful chromatic descent, shall be happy in the end. It took me a while to crack it. I knew the solution involved contrary motion, as suggested by that script, but I was lost until my eyes settled on those three capital Cs. In plain sight. The original lines and their inversions pivoting on C. Yes. There's something to Bach's approach—an underlying method, an essential coherence—just beyond my reach. Something that will allow me to bring it to its fullest expression. Otherwise what? How many auditions lie ahead? How many chances have I got? It might not happen straightaway—in fact, it might be better to make an astonishing debut after honing my dexterity and expression for a bit. In the meantime an academic career can serve as a solid foundation. A backup. I almost let it slip to Hugh the other day—my secret egotistical ambition—while he was showing me the facsimile for Bach's Sonatas and Partitas for solo violin, my mind slowing, coming round to find something gripping about it. This wasn't meant as a puzzle canon, he said, but notice the pen strokes of the letter P in *partita* gradually pulling apart with each repetition as the cycle progresses until they resemble the initials JS? And see that mistake on the title page? *Sei Solo.* Translated as Six Solos when that second word should be plural, *Soli*—this from a man who had been writing Italian words in composition and daily practice for most of his life. And bear in mind he completed this work, along with others in *The Well-Tempered Clavier*, shortly after his first wife died. Some say it means nothing. But perhaps it suggests something deeper. The expressive clue to the entire cycle. The emotional key.

You only. Only you.

I blink slowly and ease myself away from the car. Forget the academic puzzles. Stay here. Stay now. I've run off with him, so let's make the most of it. I go round to the boot and pull out the gardening tools borrowed from my parents' shed. Or nicked, I suppose. I didn't leave a note. I bring them over as he is straightening up and brushing his hands on his trousers. He breaks into a smile as I prop the shovel next to him, but instead of reaching for it he takes me by the shoulders and gives me a kiss. I rise into a fullness. A heat, a light. Am I that easy? A flower opening, a plant growing helplessly toward the sun. And then my mind kicks in.

"Ah," I say. "You want me to dig."

"No, I want you to talk to me while I clear this away."

"Talk to you? About what?"

He starts rolling up his sleeves. "What you're playing these days. At Tolbooth Church."

"You remember that?"

"You reminded me, a few nights ago over dinner."

You mean *she* reminded you. But I don't say it. I'm still finding my way into this music, learning how to play it. As he drives the shovel into the turf I try to imagine Violet telling him about me, but it feels dissonant. The wrong key. So I tell him about the Passacaglia in C minor—not the piano transcription but the original work for organ with the pulsing effort, the footwork, the hard time. How much bloody dogged effort goes into learning the technical twists and turns so it becomes automatic and I can articulate the upper voices properly. And the distraction of the bench. The stained glass. The chill of all that stone, the sweet sickly aftertaste of incense in the air. But what I don't mention is that just yesterday it started falling into place, and it involves him, or how he came to me, the notes fitting together, the chords sounding full and true in the organ pipes. And this is how it happens. The consonance of a thought. You only. Only you. Why should I share him with some middle-aged copy of myself? Sorry, Vi. I've decided to keep him after all. He's mine.

"Here it is," he says. "Oh, yeah." He crouches and starts working with the gardening gloves, brushing and scraping, defining the edges. A fallen stone maybe six or seven feet long—or tall, I suppose, if it were standing properly. As he dashes back to the car I stare at the caked surface, the deep black grime, the crenellations of—what is it, granite? Schist? I can't tell one rock from another. An upper edge broken. If I saw it in different circumstances I wouldn't look twice.

He returns with a plastic jug and pours water along a bit at the far end.

"Yes," he says. "Yes, yes, yes!"

I move in close enough to make out a curved design. A circle. "Is that a . . ."

"A horned spiral. It starts here," he says, patting the top, "with a line that runs around the corner over to this side, making another spiral. Or vice versa. No beginning, no end. Absolutely fucking fantastic."

It isn't until he cleans it off that I notice the dirty line, worn but clear, winding inward and outward, the same again on the other side. The sky, beyond sunset now, taking on a pale hue as he works. When he's finished he sits back on his heels and gazes along the length of it, managing an expression both clinical and dreamy at once.

"Funny how the spirals are facing away from each other," I say, trying to offer some kind of intelligent observation. "Or catty-corner, I should say. At a ninety-degree angle."

"Just like the other design."

"What other design?"

He rises and, standing behind me, puts his cheek to mine, aligning our sights. His rich seasoned skin, his sweat, the rough grain of his face. "Over yonder," he says, pointing to a break in the hills, "is Kilmichael Glen, where a remarkable set of carvings is waiting to be revealed."

"Revealed by what?"

"A windstorm." He kisses my neck.

I tilt my head back. A windstorm, then. Violet, take note.

We have dinner in the back room of a pub with hearty food and robust ale that strikes me as unremarkable but seems to bring him untold pleasure, suggesting the venue's closure by the turn of the twenty-first century. Afterward he locates a self-catering cottage apparently out of harm's way, but sends me in to deal with the owners while he hangs back like a celebrity avoiding the paparazzi. Is this how it's going to be? We'll have to work on that, I think, lying in bed while he showers. But when he emerges we have sex with delicious care, as I anticipated, to compensate for the quickie on the floor earlier, and the secrecy seems minor, such a small price to pay. Then he rummages through his rucksack and pulls out a flask of whisky. We bundle up and head outside to a pair of loungers facing the hills to the south. The stars a cold glint, a bright lobe of moon above the treeline.

"Gigantic," I say, gazing at it.

"An optical illusion. It just looks bigger when it's closer to the horizon."

I give him a wry look as I reach for his hand, but then sit forward when I touch it. "Why are you shaking?"

He glances down at himself as if he has become an object of scientific interest. "Cold, I suppose."

"But your hand actually feels warm to me."

He sets down his glass and tucks both fists into his armpits. "Speaking of hands," he says, "I could use a bit of help tomorrow. Digging, I mean. Carrying the dirt. Are you up for that?"

127

"I'll need gloves."

"We can buy another pair in town."

"You mean I can buy them while you hide in the car."

He makes a show of letting the comment pass. "I want to dig it out completely and take photos."

"More? You used up a whole roll of film this afternoon."

"Which needs to be *developed*. Ain't that something."

This time I'm the one who decides not to react.

"And I want to find the socket for it," he adds.

"Why?"

"To know exactly where it was standing, what direction it was facing. Because if you remove the trees, which the Forestry Commission will do soon enough, it has a clear sightline to Inbhir. Those two sites are connected, I think."

"You mean, they're different parts of the same thing?"

He picks up his whisky glass. "Sort of. These sites were built by different groups of people at different times, hundreds and even thousands of years apart. There wasn't any grand plan. But of course they still interact in a certain way. They line up, they work with each other, they correspond."

There's a silence. The dark shapes of the hills, trees in shredded outlines. The fierce glow of the moon.

"And maybe they were honouring that," I say, raising my glass to it.

He nods slowly. "It's possible. Everyone nowadays get excited about solar alignments at places like Stonehenge—"

"And Maeshowe."

"And Maeshowe. Don't worry, I was going to say that. But prehistoric people actually seemed more concerned with the moon. Which makes sense, if you think about it. In a world without artificial light it's much more obvious. It changes more rapidly than the sun, with shorter cycles. And the association with night, with darkness and death."

"And life, actually."

He pauses, trying to work it out. "How do you figure?"

"The menstrual cycle. Women would have known it was linked to the phases of the moon. I mean, how could they *not*? Without contraceptives and the rest of it, you get all tidal. On a clear night you could look up and know when you're going to ovulate."

There's a troubled silence before he replies. "You're on the pill, right?"

"What?" I sit forward, nearly splitting myself in half. "Are you drunk already? Do you really not remember?"

"In my timeline, yes. But here . . ."

I clutch my head.

"Come on, Vi. Please."

"I'm on the pill. Here, there, and everywhere. And for future reference, Aaron, don't ask a girl that question *after* you've shagged her."

"Sorry. I'm still sorting out this whole scenario." He pauses deliberately. "All right, so you were saying that women's fertility cycles could have been a factor in tracking the moon's movement. I never thought of it before, but you're probably right about that."

I settle back into my chair. "Well then maybe you could share that startling archaeological insight with other members of the boys' club."

"Hey, come on. There are more women in the field now."

"You mean like what's her name? Siobhan? The woman with the nice pots."

It seems to hit him harder than I intended. Another moment passes before he replies. "She doesn't go blabbing about her menstrual cycles, if that's what you mean."

"Well maybe she should do. Maybe we *all* should do. Too many women out there seem to be pretending they're not women just to get ahead."

He waves it off and picks up the flask.

"Ladies first," I sing, holding out my glass.

He leans over to fill it and then tops up his own. "Cheers to us," he says, clinking his glass to mine.

We gaze at the moon again, at whatever it means, whatever it meant. And looking down the glen it occurs to me.

"If we were there now," I say. "At Inbhir. And we were facing in the direction of that stone we dug up today . . ."

He straightens. Then he gets to his feet. "There might be an orientation. Possibly. But probably not an alignment, which is much more precise. And in any case we'd also be facing a constellation or two. A notch in the hills. Perhaps the midwinter sunrise. That's always the problem with this sort of thing. There are so many possibilities that it's hard to tell if it's by chance or design. Drive a couple of sticks in the ground and they'll line up with *something*."

"But this isn't just *something*. It's the full moon."

He shakes his head. "Except it's not quite full."

"Mmm. I guess it was four or five days ago when—" I smile at him. "Hey, when you first came!"

He tilts his glass at me. "See what I mean?"

"You're saying it's a coincidence."

"I'm saying don't get carried away. It's like a horoscope—a self-fulfilling prophecy. If you give meaning to a coincidence, then you tend to behave in a way that creates more coincidences to verify the meaning you created in the first place."

I perch my chin on my fist and decide to argue by agreeing with him. "Ok," I say. "So the moon happened to be full when you first arrived. And now the not-quite-full moon just happens to be rising in some kind of alignment—sorry, orientation," I say, as I notice his finger rising to correct me, "with the stone we just uncovered."

"Tonight, yes. Tomorrow, no."

"Pardon?"

"Because it shifts along the horizon, rising in a different place every night. Like the sun, right? It swings from a southern track to a northern one and then back again during its monthly cycle." He

130

sips his whisky. "But what the sun does in a year, the moon does in a month, so the change is much faster. And sometimes greater. I mean, during a lunar maximum there's a wider range between the southern and northern extremes. In about two weeks it swings from there to *there*," he says, sweeping his arm from front to back.

"Sorry, this happens during a what?"

"Lunar maximum. There's a lot of convoluted geometry that I could never really follow, but it has to do with the tilt of the moon's orbit relative to Earth's orbit, which causes the moon's range to expand and contract. When that range is at its widest extreme, it's called a lunar maximum, and at its narrowest it's called a lunar minimum."

"How come I've never noticed any of this?"

"Because you can't really mark it from one month to the next. The whole cycle takes . . ."

At first it seems like a joke, the way he freezes, the glass slipping from his hand and thunking softly on the grass. And then I know what he's going to say. Of course. I stand up and put my arms around him. I tell him everything will be fine. He rests his forehead on my shoulder, as if taking consolation in my flesh and blood. His whole body trembling. I hold him close. The perfect fifth, consonant and true. Yes, he's mine.

"I know," I whisper. "You don't have to say it."

18.61 years.

CHAPTER EIGHT

1988/2006

Eighteen years, seven months, six days. Using Violet's diary as a reference, I discovered that it matched my dates exactly. But without internet access, or internet existence, I could only beseech the heavens for evidence that lunar maximums had occurred, or were occurring, in 1988 and 2006. As usual, Violet needed no confirmation. She said my experience alone was the proof. Her composure gradually offset my shock until the whole phenomenon seemed natural and comforting—an explanation of sorts, suggesting a correlation of things both seen and unseen. But what things? And why? We talked through various possibilities while we dug for the socket the next morning under a sullen sky. And when the rain finally arrived a memory came with it: Siobhan lifting her face to those very same clouds and turning to me with a slanted smile, saying don't you love the cold truth of this weather, don't you love a good honest storm? Yes, it was happening then and now as we took shelter in the car, Violet and I, making it sour with our heat, our breath. I looked over at her damp hair. Her soggy spirits. She hadn't uttered a single word of complaint.

"Let's call it a day," I said.

We drove back to the cottage and, after a hot shower, had the kind of daytime sex that had once been our entitlement but now happened only on those rare occasions when we managed to get time off work and deposit the children at the Wringham town-house for a few hours without revealing our true agenda.

We lay there until the rain died away to leave a sound of wind hollowing out the hills somewhere, leaves ticking faintly by the open window.

"Where did that come from?" she asked.

"The rain?"

"No, the manoeuvre."

I turned my head and looked at her.

"Where you lift my leg and hold me from the side like that."

"You didn't like it?"

She cranked her head back and laughed, lines flaring into her smooth face, the hollows of her young throat, and for just an instant I saw her, the older Violet in the younger, the one I had come to know.

"Fishing for compliments?" she said. "In case my reaction wasn't enough?"

"You never know."

"Oh, leave off, Aaron."

I ran a hand along her thigh, the firm swerve of her hip. Her stomach taut and tight as ripe fruit. The navel still concave. After the pregnancies, I had found some pleasure in the stretches and ripples like saltwater taffy, knowing it was where our children had taken shape. But it was an acquired taste, not an erotic thrill. In the desperate tundras of the last ice age I might have lusted for a woman all bloated and baggy and pendulous like one of those Venus figurines we had seen years ago in the visitors' centre for those cave paintings in France. The swelled features carved out of mammoth bone thirty-five thousand years ago, sealed inside a glass case. A glorification of fertility, I had said. Or a fear of it, Violet had replied. Neither. Both. She had been heavily pregnant with Tessa at the time—a coincidence so obvious we hadn't even mentioned it—and since my mother had recently died everyone seemed to think the birth of one would counterbalance the death of the other. But it hadn't felt that way to me. And then Violet had fainted or suffered a spell of some kind during the cave tour. In retrospect it seemed portentous. The beginning of the end.

"I've learned a few things over the years," I said, "if that's what you mean."

"Mmm, that's what I mean. Now out with it. Where did you learn that trick?"

There was a rural silence, a sense of everything at ease. One of the simple and beautiful moments that would leave no trace in the world. She must have known the answer. Maybe she was the one fishing for compliments. What the hell, I thought. It's only the truth. "You taught me."

She did a slow blink, then turned and gazed at the ceiling as if I had delivered news too profound for either a smile or a frown. Her face drawn clear of all emotion, a pale gleam to her eyes.

"Do you miss me?" she asked.

Something overturned and spilled inside me. I couldn't speak. I was trying to keep every solid object from washing away. Then she turned and cupped my face to console me as if I had suffered at the hands of a different woman, as if it didn't involve her at all.

In Edinburgh the next morning I kept the engine idling down the street from her parents' house while she returned the tools to their garden shed. Then we dropped off the rental car, and I walked a safe distance behind her in case we happened to encounter anyone we knew—a precaution she mocked by halting now and then to give me a spy-movie stare. I waved her on with a parental frown, missing the older Violet's attitude for once. Her gravity and deeper understanding would have been helpful right about now. As we made our way onward my head was rattling with old associations, old needs, a strange lonely feeling, the sky all charcoal and slate, the buildings in mineral gloom despite the spring growth everywhere. I seemed to be trembling and buzzing, my vision sketchy at the edges. I needed a rest. And I needed answers.

Inside the flat I went straight to the bedroom for the dish of spare change on my dresser. I didn't bother to hide what I was doing, only why I was doing it.

"Is it possible to steal from yourself?" she asked. "I mean, technically speaking—"

"Tell him you needed coins this week," I said, weeding out the pennies and pocketing the rest. "For the launderette. Or a vending machine. Or a wishing well. Whatever. Just make up an excuse. He'll believe anything. He'll be so giddy over the developments at Inbhir that you could replace the furniture and he wouldn't notice."

She folded her arms. "Let me guess, they don't have coins in the twenty-first century. They're collector's items, worth a fortune."

I went up to her and gave her a slow kiss. Her arms unfolded and came up around me. I stepped back and looked at the clock.

"Don't worry," she said. "He won't be home until midafternoon. Remember?"

Yes, I remembered. Fridays I had always knocked off at noon and drove home straight from the site to beat the weekend rush hour through Glasgow. But that wasn't the thing on my mind. I was subtracting numbers from the clock. North Carolina was five hours behind. I looked at her again, trying to phrase some sort of goodbye.

"I'm free Monday afternoon," she said. "If you can make it then."

"I don't know if I can come back, Vi. Or if I should. You understand?"

She smiled. "I'll stash a key under that loose stone by the railing. You know the one I mean? If I'm not here when you arrive just make yourself at home and ravish me when I come through the door. Surprise me, yeah?"

My throat tightened. She was making it easy for me. For both of us. I hefted my rucksack and walked down the hall with everything pushing and pulling inside me, all force and friction in my heart. In the stairwell each step was a little death. And when I reached the street outside I glanced up at the sere face of our building. Blank windows. No Violet. Maybe she really believed I would come back. I zipped my jacket against a chill whistling from the north. The vast lungs of the sky. The coal cellar awaited me, but instead I walked a long block over to the newsagent where I had followed Mrs McNaught. The crossroads. The junction of streets great and small. You didn't see some things disappearing until after they were gone, but now that it was both before and after at the same time, I found a call box where it no longer would be. I stepped inside and tugged the door shut. Then I took a deep breath and, after feeding coins into the slot, dialed the first telephone number I had ever known.

It seemed like the nature of things. Cause and effect. On rainy days my mother had translated ancient Greek and Latin texts in the corner of our living room while cartoons and game shows blared away, infusing her Ovid with a demotic boldness that would be praised, I later discovered, as the hallmark of her style. And whenever the poetry thwarted her, or whenever she needed to clear her head, she played with us. Cicero was left speechless while she joined our board games or directed the construction of railway lines through legs of furniture. Odysseus remained caught between a rock and hard place during our missions to the moon. Rome was left unfounded while she negotiated truces between the not two but three brothers striving at her feet, punishing our misdeeds by forcing us to memorize verses from a fateful war in which everyone's armour clanged upon him. In fair weather she must have been much more productive, because we usually came inside at some point in the afternoon to find our breakfast dishes exactly where we had left them and, more tellingly, discarded pages of her wild longhand on the floor. She would remove her horn-rimmed glasses, attached to a chain that she wore around her neck, and let them fall as she rubbed her forehead. Lunch, she would say, pronouncing it as if it were some kind of anachronism, like a corn cob or a satellite, that we had introduced into her ancient thoughts. And she would blink over at us as if she were the last person on Earth who would know how to deal with that. Y'all take a look in the icebox.

The kitchen bamboozled her. Appliances revolted at her touch. Her sessions at the stove produced unrecognizable results. My father compensated with an engineer's logic, stocking the freezer with peel-and-serve meals and, at the other end of the continuum, hunks of meat that he grilled by proxy, assigning each of us a particular item to monitor over the coals until we learned by trial and error exactly how it needed to be done. Libertarian parenting, as my brother Marcus phrased it. When the barbecue rusted through and collapsed he handed us shovels and oversaw the digging of a firepit, setting discarded patio bricks as cornerstones to support a large grate. For firewood we rode in the bed of his pickup to clearcuts in the National Forest, where we descended like hyenas on leavings of broken hardwoods, the shattered oak and hickory branches that imparted the best flavour. Meanwhile Mom approached housework, on those rare occasions when she approached it at all, as a Sisyphean task whose results were ephemeral at best. The revenge of Thanatos, she would say. His sadistic joy! Motivated by hygiene rather than propriety, she would attempt a biannual dusting, lifting the rag now and then to examine the fabric as if it held runes instead of grime. Afterward she could be found with her feet up and a gin and tonic pressed to her forehead. The siege of Troy was easier to manage.

Her commissions paid for a few indulgences, such as a trip to the Outer Banks and a new exhaust system for her car, but otherwise my father was the Atlas holding up the financial heavens— not Earth, as Mom pointed out—on his shoulders. He had established himself by designing a viaduct known for its innovations in structural engineering, particularly the use of cable-stayed bridges and segmental concrete construction for spanning the larger gaps. Built from the top down to protect the landscape of the Blue Ridge Parkway, the viaduct flowed against the mountainsides and incorporated every type of alignment geometry that had ever been used in highway construction, including reverse curvature. It was honored with eleven design awards. His work on that project and others that followed was admired for its natural blend of form and function. A prickly and unsubtle man who routinely offended people within listening radius of his voice, he treated my mother's domestic shortcomings like the Venus de Milo's missing arms. Occasionally I overheard her reading out lines to him in their bedroom, his voice murmuring in reply. Nobody seemed to notice her besides him. There was an obscurity in their love.

He deserved credit, she said in later interviews, for a few key suggestions in her rendition of Lucretius's *De Rerum Natura* or, as she translated it, *The Nature of Things*, which gained notice by slipping into a subtle and irregular rhyme to suit passages that struck her as invocations to the profound existence of objects rather than philosophical diatribes against the Stoics. This interpretation provoked an eminent scholar in the field to reassess the very nature of things in *The Nature of Things* and thus the nature of Abigail Keeler's previously obscure translations, which in turn triggered a reissue of her Ovid, which consequently gained the attention of an immoderately popular talk show host, who invited Mom to appear on her special Book Club episode. Shortly afterward Violet and I opened a padded international envelope and settled down to watch a videotape of my mother describing Orpheus and Eurydice in such unselfconscious and exquisitely romantic terms that the studio audience swooned and then, minutes later, roared with laughter as she dismissed Zeus as a serial rapist. They subsequently applauded in agreement as she praised Diana's treatment of Actaeon.

Abigail Keeler's *Metamorphoses* appeared on the bestseller lists with her Virgil and a couple of Homers trailing in its wake, all of which were admittedly bought more than read. The Keeler bank account swelled nevertheless. My parents' ramshackle home at the edge of the Appalachian woods was exchanged for a full-blown deluxe model along the road toward Winston-Salem for the sake of its lower elevation and milder winters. And thus began an epic phase of retirement. Just as astronauts enjoy zero gravity in an orbiting capsule, detached from their usual exertions yet unsettled by the knowledge that every passing moment in such a state causes their muscles to atrophy and thereby makes their return to Earth more difficult, so my parents attained a prosperity that both pleased and troubled them. The Senior Citizen Syndrome, my brother Marcus said, in which everything was assessed in terms of its comfort and convenience. No doubt it was caused by an enzyme or some other biological process, like the release of hormones during adolescence, but instead of triggering acne and self-absorption it resulted in a yearning for ease. The absence of friction. As a result my father took early retirement and devoted his time to spectator sports and the rigors of what he called aqua-jogging in their swimming pool, strapping himself into an assemblage of flotation cushions that he had fashioned to keep himself upright. He was on the verge of filing a patent only to discover that similar products had been on the market for over a decade, giving rise to jokes about reinventing the wheel. Meanwhile my mother immersed herself in a fully furnished study and the daily pleasures of a spa that caused her productivity to plummet, while her gin and tonics, according to Marcus, advanced steadily toward the Rubicon of noon. Such was the nature of things until one morning, in midsentence at the breakfast table, she fell forward into her scrambled eggs.

Cause and effect. As I listened to the phone ringing across the Atlantic, I knew she was at work on the very lines that would launch her career. I had read her Lucretius with particular admiration because it was a philosophical work, a fusion of poetry and polemic, rather than a narrative populated by the usual cast of characters with unexplained motives and pathological deities squabbling over who would control the puppet show down on Earth. I remembered it as an astute attempt to understand the world through its physical qualities. No gods, no spirits, no afterlife. Lucretius believed that everything, both living and dead, consisted of small blocks of matter known as atoms. There was no qualitative difference between us and the ground beneath our feet or the stars over our heads. It was all the same, a chance combination of particles that would dissipate and recombine into other things. Our existence, he said, is material and ephemeral. We should release all fear, which springs from the ego's anticipation of something it will never experience, and instead embrace the beauty and pleasure of the world.

"Speak of the devil," my mother said.

Even though I was braced for the sound of her voice it still brought a trembling into me. A release of emotion. I leaned against the glass and closed my eyes. "Well, then," I managed to say, "I guess that makes you the devil's mother."

"Now don't go cracking your whip on me. What I meant is I just wrote this line—I swear the ink isn't even dry on it—with you in my head. You ever heard of Lucretius?"

I hesitated, then said I hadn't, which was a lie from my perspective but the truth from hers. These conversations we would never have again.

"He was a contemporary of Julius Caesar's. Anyhow, get a load of this. 'If we stub a toe against a stone, we touch the outer shell alone—the surface hue, though what we feel, is the inner hardness that its depths conceal.' Ah, needs work. The rhyme isn't my choice, by the way. When you unpick that man's verse it just seems to be there. In certain places, at least. My editor's going to say get in or get out with the rhyme scheme. All or nothing. But I think there's a golden mean in there."

When I was three or four years old she lifted me above a split-rail fence to see horses running in a field. I remembered the shaggy grasses, the packed earth. Her body braced behind mine as I gripped the wood. And a plank bridge over a tea-colored stream with her crouching next to me in the shadows, the cool breath of running water, a spread of oaks and pine overhead, as we dropped leaves and watched them race over the rocks. How much she seemed to love it all. The nature of things. *Unus folium, duo folia,* teaching me to count the leaves in Latin. *Unus saxum, duo saxa.* Those are the rocks. My hand raised high in hers as we walked somewhere after that. Back to a church. A wedding. Yes, I had been unruly or too loud, and she had taken me outside. It was my very first memory, earlier than anything else. The horses, the field. The stream, the leaves, the rock. I could find it only in retrospect, in the mist of emerging consciousness where there was no single moment in which I realised I existed. It wasn't the first thing I felt. But it seemed like the first thing I knew I was feeling. And she was there, showing me the world with her intelligent heart.

I inhaled and held myself still for a moment, trying to stop the wrong sound from coming out. "I have no doubt," I said, "that you'll find it."

"Now you sound strange. Like you're inside a tin can or something."

"A call box."

"A what?"

"A phone booth. I'm on that dig in Mid Argyll."

"Oh that's right. Britannia Barbarica. North of the Wall. How're y'all doing up there?"

"Fantastic. Lots of stuff happening. I'll give you the details later, but right now I need to ask you something."

"Your voice is different too. You coming down with a cold?"

"A touch of hay fever." I brought a fist to my forehead. Keep it steady. Keep it normal. "Listen, I'm wondering if you remember something you read to me once about the moon and an eighteen-year cycle. Or maybe nineteen years. I'm not sure."

"Oh, you mean that thing about Hyperborea. A secret code

word for Britain, you said. Diodorus wrote that, though he was just recycling a story from Hecataeus. Yeah, he's around here somewhere." Her voice wandered from the receiver. "The original is still packed away, but I probably have a half-assed English on the shelf."

As she searched for it a voice came over the line asking for more money. I dropped more coins into the slot. There were clicks and beeps of satisfaction. Then I heard more rustling on Mom's end. A book hitting her desk. I remembered she was in Robbie's old bedroom now—sunny and quiet, with a view of the backyard—which she had seized days after his departure for university, undeterred by the irony of having her own study only when the house was finally empty and she no longer needed it.

"I guess," she said, settling down again, "y'all are uncovering some great new old thing. Do I get credit for this contribution? My name in lights?"

I laughed softly, with a swell in my throat. I remembered the first couple of years living overseas when I thought her accent was mysteriously changing—each 'thing' shifting to 'thang' and 'you all' to 'y'all'—until I realised the difference wasn't in her voice but in my ears. And now it was all here again, different and the same. The blend of delicacy and grit. The homespun tone to her educated comments. As a girl she had been forced to take a course called Table Manners and White Gloves without, she insisted, ever once glimpsing a white glove. My grandmother had passed judgment on the whole ordeal after a few glasses of wine one Thanksgiving, claiming that high culture must've been too high because Abigail went to her coming-out ball and never come back.

"Now good ol' Diodorus says a few things about the Hyperboreans, but I think this is what you're gunning for. More or less. The island in the north, inhabited by Hyperboreans . . . the island fertile and productive . . . two harvests every year. Uh-huh. Dream on, Diodorus. Now here it is. There exists a legend in which Leto was born on this island and—"

"Who's Leto?"

"One of Zeus's victims. No maiden was safe from that electric sperm of his."

"Electric?"

"Hurling lightning bolts. Control your metaphors, Aaron, or they will control you. Anyhow, she gave birth to Apollo and Artemis, which is why it says here that Apollo is honoured above all other gods and the Hyperboreans praise him daily in song, blah blah blah."

"Don't skip anything."

"Only the chaff, Aaron. Only the chaff. You think after thirty-five years I don't know my shit from my sherbet?"

"Mom."

"Now it says—"

The voice came over the line again, asking for more money.

"What's happening over there?"

"Economics," I said after chucking coins into the slot. "Now carry on."

"Carry what?"

"Keep going."

"You're picking up those Britishisms by the bushel, aren't you?"

"Mom, please."

"A sacred precinct of Apollo and a notable temple which is adorned with many votive offerings and spherical in shape. That sounds like Stonehenge."

"It's hard for me to tell what's text and what's colour commentary."

"And there's a city sacred to Apollo where the inhabitants play the cithara."

"The what?"

"That instrument you see on all the vases. Looks like a lyre. And now here's what you're asking for." She cleared her throat. "They say that the moon, as viewed from this island, appears to be but a little distance from Earth and to have upon it prominences, like those of Earth, which are visible to the eye. The account is also given that the god visits the island every nineteen years—see, it's nineteen—which is the period in which the return of the stars to the same place in the heavens is accomplished. Egad, who did this?" There was a pause, a flipping of pages. "I thought so. Thornton Solow runs those prepositional phrases clickety-clacking like train cars and he calls it fidelity. My fault, I suppose. The original is buried in a cardboard box along with Jimmy Hoffa somewhere, but I still haven't unpacked since moving it all into this room. I know, what's the point of having it all one place if I'm too damn lazy to unpack. You still there?"

I was holding the mouthpiece down, but I was sniffling, and my eyes were brimming. "Still here," I managed to say.

"So anyhow it's nineteen years," she said. "And if we can survive Mr Solow's train wreck of a translation, it says the nineteen-year period is called by the Greeks the 'year of Meton.' He plays the cithara and dances through the night of the vernal equinox until the rising of the Pleiades, expressing his delight, et cetera."

I blotted my eyes. The recorded voice asked for the rest of my money. I fed it all into the slot.

"Apollo," I finally said, trying to aim my thoughts clear of the ripped feeling inside me. "The god of the sun."

"And poetry."

I breathed out evenly. "The sun and the moon, brought together. And who was this Meton?"

"Greek thinker, polymath. The whole nine yards."

"But what's the link between Meton and nineteen years?"

"Can't say as I know. You'll have to hunt that one yourself. Y'all have libraries over there?"

"And running water, too. It's downright civilized." I smiled and felt a crazy welter, all mixed and mashed, joyful pain, painful joy. Stop it from happening. Steer it in a different direction. Swerve. *Clinamen.*

"Cinnamon?" my mother said.

I must have said it aloud. "A Latin word. You mentioned it a while back."

"I did?"

"Yes," I said, because it was true, or would be true in a year or so.

"Well ain't that something. It's from Lucretius, as a matter of fact. *Clinamen*. An unexpected movement of matter. A swerve."

"Mom . . ." I hesitated with everything I felt piled up over the years, so much to say, and so dangerous to say it.

"*Tempus fugit*," she said. "We're about to be cut off."

I had always heard that I would cease judging my parents when I had children of my own, but instead I found myself judging them more rigorously and precisely. And then I found myself forgiving them with the same rigor, the same precision. The stroke had occurred only a few months before Tessa was born, preventing contact between a new life and an old one. She would have been an indulgent and protective grandmother. She would have read the less disturbing myths as bedtime stories. She would have been a loony and loving Grandma Abby.

"We're going to have children someday," I said. "A girl and a boy."

"Family planning, huh? Sounds good. Just leave room in there for the swerve. Children don't follow anybody's plan."

Something clicked in the earpiece. The recorded voice announced the end was nigh.

"I have to go now," I said. "Thank you, Mom. Thank you for everything."

"Well, all right. Say hello to that lovely woman of yours."

"Take care of yourself."

She laughed indulgently. "I always do."

"Go to the doctor."

"Planning on it. I'm due for a physical."

"I mean, you should—"

But the line went dead, and I must have slid down to the floor, because when I took my hands from my face the receiver was swinging in front of me like a pendulum.

I descended the steps and then, with the door open and darkness of the underworld confronting me, remembered the film inside my rucksack. I set it down and pulled out two small canisters, each one containing photos of the carved stone, each one needing to be developed the old-fashioned way. I peered into the space. It had fried my mobile. And it seemed to leave me with some kind of aftershock, the shakes running through me in unpredictable cycles, though I couldn't be sure if it came from the actual travel or the emotional impact of the destination. Violet's touch. My mother's voice. Not to mention everything else. Maybe it was more than human biology could handle, the way oceans and mountains punished you for diving too deep and climbing too high.

I pulled out a plastic bag, which I had packed in case we found any samples, and sealed one of the canisters inside. And then, just inside the threshold, I felt along the upper wall of the cellar and wedged it into a cleft in the stonework. Sheltered from the elements. How long would it last? This, it seemed to me, would be the true test of time and place. If the film was still there when I came out the other side, then I would know it was all the same universe after all. And it would also serve as a backup in case the other roll in my pocket got ruined by the portal.

Or I could forget the whole thing and stay here. The notion took me with a calm intensity and power. There was no law that said I had to return to 2006. I could wait on the front stoop for my younger self and explain the situation. We could work out an arrangement. Share the identity, perhaps? No. I nearly slapped myself on the cheek. No, no, no. Come on. I had to reestablish a better life with the older Violet in 2006, where I belonged. If I had learned anything from my mother's death, it was to salvage the moments I had, whatever and whenever they were. You can't trade your wife for a younger model like a car. I needed to go through. I needed to go back and make it right.

I shouldered my rucksack and pulled the door shut behind me and, bracing myself, stepped forward into *tempus*.

Fugit. I found myself thrown clear of the cellar, trembling on the paving stones. I rose to my feet and stumbled over to the wall and held myself there, breathing the cold, the dusk, the dead scent of November and the gloom so much deeper than the grey lowering force of the April I had just left. Yes, all those myths and fables, accurate to the core. Spring, life. Winter, death. Head throbbing, I pulled at the door to find it locked, just as I had left it. I reached into my pocket for the key and opened it and stepped inside, staying close to the threshold as I felt along the upper wall for the film, but it wasn't there. And with an enormous gale of relief I understood just how much I wanted the realms to be separate, the Violets independent of each other, the nature of things unlinked. Different causes, different effects.

I locked the cellar and climbed the stairs into hard blades of wind. The bare trees, the rough faces of the tenements, the sticks and stones breaking my bones. I entered our building and climbed more stairs and unlocked the door to our flat, weary and wary, but found an unexpected silence as I set down my rucksack. No clamour, no chaos. I lifted my wrist but remembered I wasn't wearing a watch, so I leaned into the living room to see the clock but stopped short when I realised something was wrong. It was completely dark. No light through the windows. Because the interior shutters were closed.

"Did you miss me?" Violet asked.

I made out her shape in the easy chair by the piano. "It's as dark as a cave in here."

"That seems to be the idea."

"What?"

She didn't reply. I took a few careful steps over to the nearest table and switched on a lamp. She was utterly still, hands clasping the armrests. Her hair pitchstone black, as always, but now renewed every month at the salon, her face full of pale discontent instead of the natural tint of her being, her actual self. I wondered if my experience with ultra-Violet had spoiled me, if I could ever be fair to this woman again.

"What are you doing in here?" I asked. "Meditating?"

"I guess you could say that."

A silence passed. I had taken a big risk with this trip, informing Graeme that I was ill and Violet that I was going to Mid Argyll, because each party required a different lie. All it would take was a single phone call, and the jig would be up.

"Where are the kids?" I asked.

"At my mother's."

"On Friday?"

"It's Wednesday," she said. "I suppose it's become rather difficult for you to keep track."

I could feel my nerves thrumming. "What are you driving at?"

"Strange, isn't it? How some things happen all at once? Tessa's latest thing is to arrange the whisky bottles on the floor like bowling pins. I have to keep putting them back on the sideboard. And there I am wondering what happened to the twenty-one-year Islay single malt, which I swore last week was nearly full, when the phone rings. . . ."

She paused as if allowing me to note, with growing dread, the flask of whisky in my rucksack. And what else? Graeme, I thought. He must have called to check on some detail, even though I had sent him a terse email saying I had strep throat and couldn't speak.

"It was your friend Natalie."

I grappled at the name. "Natalie?"

"Natalie Sharples. She wants to know if you're still interested in the flat. Apparently she's been holding it for you."

My whole body seemed to bend like balsa wood. I had given her my mobile number, which was no longer working, and so she must have just looked up my land line.

"It's sensible, isn't it? If you're going to see another woman, why fork out all that money for a hotel?"

I held up a hand. "I can explain."

"Natalie already did."

"She doesn't know anything."

"You mean she doesn't realise what she knows. She asked how my redecorating project is coming along. She must have thought I was her."

"Her?"

"The other woman, you shite."

"It was a lie—"

"Oh really?"

"A lie I made up," I said, raising my voice, "to explain why I needed the flat without ruffling her feathers. She seems quite proper. Your mother would like her. A kindred spirit."

She gazed at the window, or at the wood panels covering it like an old-fashioned coffin. The brass fittings polished. A funeral. I thought about telling the truth, about acquitting myself of one crime by confessing to another. Her name was Siobhan. Her name is Violet. Take your pick. But in any case Natalie Sharples is the wrong woman, the wrong place, the wrong time.

"There's nobody. Only you. I was considering the flat as a . . . well, I guess for a trial separation. But then I decided against it."

"Oh," she said in a flat voice. "Is that what you decided."

My eyes went to the sofa, where I noticed a pillow and a neat pile of bed linens. "It's a misunderstanding, Violet. Let's try to make it right."

But everything was fixed and impassable in her face. The thought and the act of moving out had become the same. I was already gone.

The next morning I was a member of the walking wounded, with barely enough sense to drop off the film at a photo shop before soldiering onward through the streets—the cold and clear lines of the New Town originally mapped out in the pattern of the Union Flag to make amends for being such a pushover during the Jacobite rising. That was Graeme's take on it, at least. Licking those English boots, aye? But I understood the impulse now. The need for an apology writ large, in the very land itself. An urge to make a resolution in the layout of your life. I had phoned Mrs Natalie Sharples to tell her I would be moving into the flat immediately. And as I approached city centre I felt its neoclassical stone everywhere, its domes and pillars and turrets weighing over glassy retail. The mixed blessings of commerce and culture. I tried to keep myself grounded in practical issues. I told myself the move would be a matter of simply filling up a few pieces of luggage when the children weren't around. I told myself I'd be popping back and forth quite a bit, as Violet had phrased it to them. I told myself that I would get to the bottom of what was happening with all this—the moon, the carvings, their connections in time—with a calm attention to detail. The first piece of evidence was the film, and if it turned out to be ruined then I could go back for the other roll and develop the photos in 1988 before travelling back through the portal with them. Or I could go back and get the photos, anyway. Or I could just go back.

I halted at the site of George IV standing at the hub of the roundabout with his cloak gathered about him and his gaze averted from the layered view I had noticed so strangely during my first visit to 1988. The same statue conveyed a different impression now. Like someone refusing to see the obvious. Streaked with pigeon shit, stiff and green with decay. Ultra-Violet said she would hide a key for me near the front stoop. She wanted me there. She wanted me then.

The sky held a faint promise of daylight at Princes Street, where the Royal Scottish Academy confronted me with its ancient Greek physique. This was the threshold. This was the fault line. The Castle perched on black basalt crags. The Scott Monument a grimy syringe all barbed and buttressed, its pinnacles rising above the train station named after his novels. At its base there had been a miniature field of crosses bearing poppies—a mock-up of a veterans cemetery for Remembrance Day—but now it was gone, replaced by a Ferris wheel and a merry-go-round and other amusements along with a German market selling trinkets and high-octane snacks. Could I take Tessa and Jamie this year? Would their pleasures be affected by my pains? The force-fed cheer of Christmas. Without the constraint of Thanksgiving the mood pivoted sharply every year from mourning to celebration, from the deaths of our heroes to the birth of our saviour. That date he inherited from Saturnalia, Mom said. If you want to celebrate that holiday the traditional way y'all better put Roman candles on Jesus's birthday cake.

At the crosswalk I watched the jeweled spokes of the Ferris wheel glowing against the dark complexion of sandstone. Beyond it was the clock tower of the Balmoral with its balusters and false balconies and, stepped farther back, the heights of Calton Hill displaying the Nelson Monument like an Italian campanile gone grey and the freestanding columns of the National Monument mimicking the Parthenon, started in 1826 but never finished, which had become its final condition, a work forever in progress and therefore complete. Everything working together. All vertical, all skyward, all onward and up. But what if our love didn't work that way? What if it simply stopped?

I would tell her everything. No matter how deeply insane it sounded. So what? Even her disbelief would be an acknowledgement of some kind. A relief. Sure, take me to a psychologist, Vi. Let's talk. Let's discover what's underneath it all, your demons versus mine.

I tried to boost myself with that notion as I glanced at the gardens below me, the former bottom of the Nor' Loch, which had been drained three centuries earlier for the city's expansion after it had been created three centuries before that for the city's defense. The bucolic pleasures of boating and picnicking by the shore had given way to ailments caused by effluent trickling down the flanks of Castlehill—the Royal Mile literally a High Street that served not only as a marketplace but also a watershed with its labyrinth of lanes and wynds forming elaborate gutters into the cesspool below. The waste reached such a heavy concentration that methane wafted up and caused hallucinations, which the citizenry attributed to either God or the Devil depending on whether or not the visions assumed a pleasing shape.

I breathed deeply as I walked. A few years before Mom died she had sent me an article by a climatologist claiming that every breath we take contains at least one molecule exhaled from Julius Caesar's lungs as he died on the floor of the Roman Senate. But afterward I had discovered the analysis was actually far too conservative. Ten years, in fact, was enough for the complete distribution of a single breath throughout Earth's atmosphere. The very first creature to emerge from a primordial ocean was recycling its own breath within a decade, passing it on through countless organisms before it reached even the dinosaurs. How many lungs had it touched by the time we stood upright? By the time we used flint and fire? By the time it nourished Julius Caesar and Sun Tzu and Montezuma, Lady Godiva and Nefertiti and Abigail Keeler? I inhaled multitudes. We all do. Now breathe.

I climbed the long incline of the Mound, built upon the rubble from the Nor' Loch drainage and the construction of the New Town. A midden. Everything reused. Everything secondhand. This world of mistakes and wrong turns still visible among the corrections, the overlays and fixes, until this was what surrounded me, these things that survived. Don't think of all that has been lost.

Violet wanted me out. She wanted me gone. It was something fundamental she wouldn't reveal or maybe couldn't even find. I knew it, or thought I knew it, as I reached the heavy ranks of the Old Town with its spikes and spires, its thick brows, its stiff upper lips. The vast ravine of the gardens gaped below me. The sunken railway let out a pneumatic cry of departure or arrival—I couldn't tell which. When I was younger and flabbier I would pause near the top to catch my breath, turning a necessity into a virtue by taking in the city below. But now I had a cardiovascular system. Now I had some muscle. For the first time I understood that my hours at the gym had been fueled by discontent and thwarted love and *tempus fugit.*

Tempus fuck it. The mortise key was in my pocket. Ultra-Violet was waiting for me on the other side. Everything I felt there. Everything I had been, everything I could be again. I opened my coat to the blunt force of November. The clouds bearing down with their dark bulk. The cold war of the sky. The city below was full of swollen bruises and eyeshadow, buses hissing under bleary streetlights. On Princes Street the shops displayed mannequins in their glass cases like science-fiction astronauts in suspended animation. Yes. I had fortified myself against the season with coffee and chocolate. I had gone to the gym and worked machines whose only purpose was to be worked, and I had burned myself in the sauna for all the heat I missed. My days were full but incomplete. I had shrunk into my work, convincing myself that the part was the whole. But now I stood with the world churning around me, the daily respiration of traffic and toil. I glanced at passersby with their scrubbings and pastings, their armourings of face and hair. This is it, I thought. Here. Now. The North Sea was screaming in the distance. The Castle's flags ripped above me. I could feel every moment giving way to another. The biochemical charge of time. It had been taking the life out of me. Now I was taking it back.

CHAPTER NINE

2006

And this was accomplished, the tour guide said, by blowing paint through hollow bones. Was that how she phrased it? Yes, her voice a confident alto. I remember it clearly now. At the time, though, I simply repeated her words in English, for Aaron's sake. Then I halted at the sight of it. A pair of hands airbrushed onto the wall of the cave. Or rather, the space around the hands. Negative images of left and right, each rendered in a different colour, with thumbs touching. Carbon black. Red ochre. The cracks and fissures in the stone transformed to membrane so vividly it stopped my breath. I wanted to fit my hands to those outlines, but the guide would have called the gendarmes on me, so I folded them over my belly instead. My aching third-trimester mass. And in any case I didn't need to touch the prints to know they matched. No, I thought. Those hands are mine.

"You all right?" Aaron asked, touching my elbow, hair-triggered to any sign of prenatal distress.

Torch beams pulsed and trembled as the people ahead of us moved on, a caterpillar of light. I eased my grip on my own torch, but it didn't make any difference, my hands sluggish by day, throbbing by night. The articulations of Rachmaninoff and Chopin and Bach numbed down to chopsticks. I had been told my dexterity would return after the birth, and until that moment I had believed it. Until then I had been expecting to recover. Until then I had thought I would return to normal, because it was how I had been before and therefore would be always, it seemed. Until then. Until now.

I open my eyes to the dark sitting room, flexing my fingers at the memory. The cave. France. Five years ago. That turning point between my mother-in-law's death and Tessa's birth when I caught the real sense of what was happening, when I understood it was leading to this. You only. Only you. This depleted body, these lost hands. A piano teacher. A part-time academic. A middle-aged mother at home with the shutters closed and lights off, waiting for her cheating husband. And I can't tell anyone. Not even Isobel, who would need a lot more than her philosophy degree to get her head round this one. How does she do it, with Iain down to London every week, getting up to who knows what? Living placidly with three children just beyond the city bypass where the suburbs decompose into the hills, walking distance from nothing, her garden a paradise. A regular mum. Attentive and engaged with her children's daily rhythms down to the timing of their morning snacks. She has no time for Clare's edgy exploits in Berlin, clubbing fervently into middle age because no one cares how old you are, she says, at six a.m. under the pulsing lights. I've tried to follow the meanings of her emails, but I fell out of German music with kabarett, and these days I don't know my weltanschauung from my zeitgeist. And even if I did, it wouldn't help me now. I couldn't seek advice or sympathy from either of them, or anyone else who might understand.

But leave off, Vi. Stop wallowing. You knew it would come to this, but you just didn't know how. And it has already happened, right? Set in stone. You should be doing something, anything, with this clear time. After the sickening business of Natalie Sharples's phone call, which you carried off quite well, actually, you should be playing another piece from *The Well-Tempered Clavier* to settle yourself. You should be finding another temperament instead of dwelling on that earlier one. Yet it keeps coming back, doesn't it?

The hallway touched with a faint glow of streetlight leading to this pocket of darkness. A cave of one's own. How I felt then. How I feel now.

"Ça va, madame?"

The guide's voice snaps me back. I blink at her and realise she has brought the proceedings to a halt. She stands at the head of the group with her torch tactfully averted but eyes fixed on me with a predatory caution. In the chiaroscuro I can see her hair pulled back and braided tightly. Jacket zipped to the throat. Nothing bad will happen on her watch. She hasn't had children and never will—a containment I recognise in other women now—and so she speaks to me with a small measure of condescension. Do I feel faint? Would I like some fresh air? Perhaps I would like someone to escort me out?

I hesitate at the black ice of another language. Please excuse me, I manage to say, but I was overcome by the art.

Her face breaks into instant relief. And to my surprise she bows her head, as if such a profound aesthetic experience must be given its due, before guiding us onward. Or inward. A stale chill. A cold breath running through the cavern's bronchial tubes, all carved out by the flows of an extinct river. We pass whorls and drippings, blisters in the stone's complexion. Alcoves and hollows. Tributaries branching away into unlimited darkness. I stoop through a low passage, against the hard resistance of my stomach, the tight pressure of another life inside me, and then straighten to find the ceiling soaring upward. The people ahead murmuring, their torchlights playing over spikes and spires dangling like icicles, anemones bristling through the rock. My own beam picks out an arch. A flying buttress. A pillar stretched from floor to ceiling like ligament. Aaron points out the shapes of architecture suggested here, the raw fittings of the earth where everything becomes something else and that's why it just happened, why I lost myself at the sight of those hands. This is a primeval funhouse. It's all meant to trigger these reactions, outlandish and irrational. So take a breath.

Think. Be sensible. My hands will come back. I'll recover. Yes. Of course. She would have told me if it was permanent. She would have found a way to warn me. Right?

The guide issues a warning to pay attention to our feet, if we please. The walkway raised half a metre above the scrabbled debris and crumblings that must be protected, taking us on an orderly circuit through galleries and chambers and salons named after the types of figures found within them. Our movement is choreographed, just as Aaron predicted, the space thoroughly civilized with atmospheric sensors and first aid stations and emergency track lighting, heatless lamps trained on images that curators have decided should not be overlooked. Group numbers are limited because otherwise we would destroy the delicate artwork with our humidity, our heat, our breath. Indeed, the guide informs us, Lascaux has been closed because mould was growing on the walls. I translate for Aaron. He nods, doing his best to hide a knowing smile.

She herds us through the next opening and then gathers us along the wall. Now switch off your torches, she instructs us.

There is a difference in the sound here. Amplified but not distorted.

We must understand how these paintings were originally seen, she says, and how they came to life in ancient times. With a deliberate flourish she swings her beam over to a woolly mammoth sketched in thin black strokes, no shading or interior detail but so suggestive of its hair and contoured bulk that for a moment I forget I've never seen one alive. That technique taken from Picasso's line drawings. Or the other way round. And instead of blank canvas it's the natural qualities of the rock providing ridges and bulges, the muscles of the creature itself. Over there a horse's head not drawn at all but instead defined by the ridge of the rock the way Michelangelo said he merely freed the figures contained in the blocks of marble. These things were painted when? Twenty-five thousand years ago. When this was tundra. When pack ice clogged the coast of Spain. She shifts her beam to horses flowing from the surface, the fine outline of muscle and mane bringing out what was already there. What is always there. Farther on there are animals gathered and layered upon each other, a herd of some other existence, their flanks displaying red ochre spots. More negative images of hands printed within them, among them. Those animals that appear to be cattle. I don't understand the word. Aurochs, a man next to me says, in broken but clear English. It is a wild ox. Or was. Extinct now.

These animals display the seasons, the guide says. By the heaviness and colouring of their coats we see the horses as they appeared at the end of winter and early spring, aurochs in summer, stags in autumn. Each one during its mating period. There is a concern with seasonal cycles, with fertility and renewal.

I repeat it to Aaron, and while everyone stands in silent appreciation, I turn back to the guide.

And the hands? I ask. Why are they mixed in? Why are they here?

She smiles indulgently. I will share a theory with you. One of the men studying the caves has pointed out that in order for these designs to be made, one must press a hand against the wall and spray the paint. Like a stencil, isn't it? Such a technique causes the hand to become the same colour, blending into the wall. Disappearing into it. Into the world of the spirits, let us say. If these were spiritual practices, there would be shamans, perhaps, who journeyed to another world. The world in the rock.

"Anything I should know?" Aaron asks.

"Shamans," I say. "Mystical journeys."

I'm not quite sure where we go next. As we pass through another section I notice a rash of spots overhead, also airbrushed. The guide carries on without comment, but the tone brings me to a halt. I snap my fingers for the resonance, the clear shot of sound.

Excuse me? I say.

The whole group comes jostling to a halt, folding together like an accordion.

My voice is loud and clear, is it not?

They nod and murmur in agreement, looking at the stone around them for signs of how this trick has occurred. The guide watches me with the pose of someone who feels upstaged but refuses to acknowledge it.

Have you seen these spots? I ask her, pointing upward. It's like standing in the choir of a chapel or cathedral. Or perhaps a whispering gallery. Has this been studied?

But of course, the guide says with a tight shrug. All aspects of these caves are being studied. Now we must proceed to the next room.

"Troublesome girl," Aaron murmurs in my ear as we move along, even though he hasn't understood a word of the exchange. "You've gone off script."

I raise my head to the vaulted cavern, the upper reaches of the ceiling barely visible in torchlight. The acoustics deep and true. I sing a middle C and work my way up the octave. Do re mi fa so la ti do.

The guide bestows a reluctant smile upon me. Our group shares a laugh.

Did they find any instruments in here? I ask. Any evidence of music?

Well, yes. That is to say, perhaps. A bone flute. We have some scholars who argue the holes are merely toothmarks made by an animal eating its prey. No human design can be proved. Nevertheless an expert at the conservatoire used it to make some lovely melodies. A recording is available in the gift shop.

"What did she say?" Aaron asks.

Or they picked up a chewed bone and blew into it, discovering music in the space where the animal's spirit resided. The sound of its soul. I say it to myself. Or do I think it instead?

And now, the guide announces, in the next chamber we will see an ancient child's footprints preserved in clay.

In the dimness ahead I make out columns bunched together like organ pipes. And a child's tracks. Of course. The full sense of it coming over me in a loss of blood, it seems. A draining of air. Everything dissolving. The world fading out. I hear a torch clattering to the walkway and look down to find nothing, or rather the fringed carpet of our sitting room, the coffee table with its spread of magazines, linens on the sofa for Aaron—all revealed by extra light in the hallway as he arrives. I blink into the sudden brightness. His keys jingling, the rustle of his jacket. The pulse of my ordinary life coming back. Yes, that clattering sound wasn't my torch on the walkway but the door latch. I square my shoulders, bracing myself. My stomach suddenly all nervous and hot. I have another minute or two to settle, I reckon, but he surprises me by coming through the doorway almost immediately.

"Did you miss me?" I can't help saying.

He halts like an escaping prisoner caught in a searchlight. Shocked and disappointed to find me here. Yes, he wanted to be alone. He wanted to wash off his guilt and rehearse his deceptions. His lies. His evasions. All that lament over how I've changed, but what about him? He didn't used to be like this.

"It's as dark as a cave in here," he says.

I manage not to show a sardonic smile. "That seems to be the idea."

"What?"

I don't reply, allowing the silence to take hold. Let him fumble. Let him grope. He makes his way over to the lamp and switches it on as if that will help, as if what he needs is light.

"What are you doing in here?" he asks. "Meditating?"

Squinting in the brightness, I give him a vague reply. But when he asks about the children's whereabouts I have to cover all my live wires sizzling in response—his ignorance of anything he doesn't have to do himself. That must be nice, dipping in and out of their activities. À la carte parenting. Fathers are able to do that, aren't they? They can have full-fledged careers. Other lives out there in the world. Other women. I keep that in mind as I mention the phone call from Natalie Sharples, as I take him to task.

"There's nobody," he says. "Only you. I was considering the flat as a . . . well, I guess for a trial separation. But then I decided against it."

All the nuts and bolts tighten inside me at those words. "Oh. Is that what you decided."

"It's a misunderstanding, Violet. Let's try to make it right." His voice lowered, his face drawn down to the bare edge of emotion. His obvious fatigue, his fading colour. What he's doing to himself. And I almost give in. I can't help it. I can't help myself. But he can't stay here, either. No, not even on the sofa after tonight. I remember that detail most of all. A separate flat.

"After all we've been through," he adds. "I don't want to give up."

I inhale slowly, armouring myself. "We're not giving up. We're taking a break. Maybe you need to have this fling, this affair, whatever. Get it out of your system. Or stay with her permanently. I guess that's what men do at your age."

He gives me a level look, holding down the pain, actually trying to hide it. That way he has of bearing injuries without self-pity. Which only makes it worse. I was expecting an argument. In fact, I was counting on it to make this whole thing easier because this is no time for empathy, no time for backsliding or warm feeling taking me the wrong way, and so I think of them shagging. I think of him fucking her. I think of his ugly and terrible behaviour after visiting the cave. He was still troubled by his mother's death, but it was no excuse for swinging that attitude around in public. At an outdoor café, no less. Yes, remember that. The lunchtime crowd, the plaza ignited in sunlight. The umbrella shading our table with its durable legs and heavy red cloth clipped needlessly into place. The air profoundly still. The hard blue sky of September. The medieval stonework and half-timbered facades, shops set into archways like glass paperweights, a guitarist strumming mournfully for coins I would have given for the sake of stopping those same three chords, and in the background a trickling fountain goading me to seek yet another visit to the toilet. And an older couple at a nearby table, directing smiles our way. Or my way. Aaron facing in the other direction. My parents' age, more or less. American, no doubt. The trainers, the jeans, the forward momentum in their faces. Here comes trouble.

"How about those caves," the man says.

Aaron lifts his head slowly, his face taking on a look I'm glad they can't see.

"We were behind you at the ticket booth," the woman adds.

"The caves," I say, giving them a social smile, "were lovely."

"Are you English?" she asks.

I take the punch as always. "Scottish."

"Scotland!" the man says. "Great place. We were there five, six years ago. Started in Edin Burrow and shot some golf at St Andrew's. What else?" he asks, directing the question not at me but his wife.

"The whisky distilleries," she says.

He nods once. "Then we spent a couple of days in Glass Cow."

Glasgow, I think. It takes more effort than French.

"Beautiful country." He pauses deliberately and cranks up a comical frown to let me know how to receive the next comment. "Too bad about the weather!"

I nod my way through a boat trip on Loch Ness, sadly without a monster sighting, and a catalogue of ruined castles all garnished with his-and-hers matching observations about climate and cuisine and culture—all the while struggling with my croque monsieur and the madness of my dull fingers and the mixed messages from my stomach needing and rejecting food at the same time with these oblivious Yanks nattering on. They share wire-framed glasses and a similarity of color tone across their wardrobe that suggests she shops for him and knows his sizes better than he does himself. They are genial and well-fed, casually prosperous, full of good intentions and unexamined assumptions. You can't marry an American without tolerance for this sort of thing. But Aaron has always been more sensitive, more critical, more unforgiving of

162

what he calls his country's adolescent bluster. And then, not long after watching the World Trade Centre collapse a few dozen times in horrified silence, he pointed to the rising dust and said here it comes. Patriotic fallout. The whole world will be breathing it soon. I don't dare suggest his response might have something to do with his father's reactionary politics, along with the void left by his mother's death. She was a buffer between them—the cartilage preventing bone-on-bone contact, as Aaron once phrased it. But really, I wish he could set all of that aside for just a few minutes. I'm the one who fainted in the cave, after all. I could use some help here.

As if sensing it, the man shifts his attention to the back of Aaron's head. "And you're American, right?"

Still chewing, Aaron turns slightly and nods to him with subsistence-level courtesy before turning back.

"But you took the French tour."

Their gazes wander back and forth between us, searching for a handhold.

"I studied it in school," I say. "And my sister-in-law is from Normandy, so I try to speak—"

"Normandy!" The man's face explodes with delight. "We were there last week. What a place."

Aaron carries on eating. His infuriating habit of ignoring people who annoy him, regardless of the discomfort it might cause.

"You mean," I ask helplessly, "the memorials for the D-Day landing?"

"You bet I do. All those graves." He observes a solemn pause. "It really brings the whole thing home to you."

Of course, getting bombed by the Luftwaffe on a daily basis also brings it home to you, but I keep that to myself. After a polite pause the woman nods toward my stomach. "I think it's brave of you to travel in your condition."

I blink at her. "Well, the ferry is quite pleasant. And the advantage of driving is that you can stop whenever you like."

"Oh, you didn't fly? Smart. Very smart."

The man leans forward. "We booked this vacation six months ago and decided like hell we were going to cancel it. We're not going to let those maniacs stop us. And I have a hunch we'll be seeing some payback soon enough."

"That'll solve everything," Aaron says just before popping the last of his sandwich into his mouth.

They don't seem to hear his comment, fortunately, so I make a show of taking up my fork again. "Enjoy the rest of your trip."

"Say, whereabouts in the States are you from?" the man asks.

Aaron's chest expands. He pivots slightly in his chair. "North Carolina."

"We went to Hilton Head one year."

"That's South Carolina, George," the woman says.

"I just mean the general area. That coastline is beautiful. And we have a place on Cape Cod, so I'm holding it to a pretty high standard."

"I'm inland," Aaron says. "Blue Ridge Mountains."

"Oh. Right."

Aaron doesn't see the microscopic shift in George's expression, the adjustment in his eyes. But he can hear it. A dog whistle of hillbillies and moonshine, incest and outhouses, the regional stereotypes that have always irked him and always will. The Mason-Dixon line, he says, runs deeper than the Highland Boundary Fault. And I can see it happening in his face: his mother's sharp attitude and his father's blunt manner coming together. Lovely combination, that.

Aaron cranes his neck back and gives George a grin. "Y'all should check it out sometime. We got runnin' water and everthing."

I nudge him under the table.

The woman perks forward, hoping to wash away her husband's mistake with goodwill. "So what do you do for work in Scotland?"

"Archaeologist," he says without turning.

"Now there's a coincidence," the man says. "Marge and I visited Stonehenge just last summer."

"And he actually touched one of the stones."

"Don't say that to an archaeologist!" He laughs. "It was illegal. I just scampered over when the park rangers weren't looking and shazam. That's about as close to Indiana Jones as I'll ever get."

Marge takes on a thoughtful look. "They were ahead of their time, weren't they? Those ancient people. So mystical and divine. A religious feeling to the place. Something sacred underneath it all."

And there it is. That moment in the Wild West film when the saloon doors swing open and the jangling piano comes to a halt. In this case, though, the guitarist keeps on playing and Aaron pivots his chair toward them. Oh, god. Don't hurt them, Aaron. Play nice.

"You're right about that," he says. "There was something sacred underneath it all. And you know what that sacred thing was?" He leaves the question hanging for an extra beat. "A drainage ditch."

They both laugh. Marge dots a finger at him. "You had me in suspense there."

I catch the waiter's eye and make a sign for the bill.

"But really, I ain't joshin' you folks. Remember that routeway leading into the monument? That processional avenue? There are long ridges running underneath it. Periglacial stripes is the technical term, because they were formed at the end of the last ice age, when the chalky ground kept freezing and thawing repeatedly. At first they were probably easy to see, like gouges in the earth. By the Neolithic, though, they were covered with enough soil and turf to make them visible only during a drought, when the surrounding grass turned yellow but the strips stayed green where the damp sediment had collected underneath. This occurred mainly during the summer. June, especially. And the funny thing is, those stripes happened to line up with the midsummer sunrise."

He pauses deliberately as the guitarist breaks into an upbeat melody, hitting too many wrong notes to count.

"Markings on the ground," he says, "aimed at the rising sun on the longest day of the year—and in the opposite direction, the sunset on the shortest day because the two events are directly opposite each other on the horizon. A divine inscription. The movement of the sun marked in the land. The axis mundi. The omphalos. Those are Latin and Greek terms for the connection between Heaven and Earth, the navel of the world. At least that's what those noble savages must have thought, because they built up the outer ridges with packed earth and turned it into a processional avenue, and at the end of it they dug a circular ditch and bank. They planted timber posts inside it, but later yanked them out and replaced them with bluestones hauled all the way from the Preseli Hills in Wales, and then, after that, rearranged them to include those spectacular sarsens still standing today. What was it all about? Some say the bluestones had healing properties and the builders wanted to add their magic to that special place, shifting the stones around over the centuries to get different effects with the sun and stars. But really, who knows? This all happened across five or six centuries, so it doesn't necessarily have a single meaning. Beliefs changed, gods retired, dogma and karma traded places. Prehistory is a blessing and a curse because it allows endless interpretation but no hope of finding answers. What were they thinking? What were they feeling? Nobody knows because they're dead. The fullness of their lives has disappeared forever."

To my relief the bill arrives. "Well," I say, taking it up with a grand sigh, "it's been nice chatting with you."

"Meanwhile," Aaron says, ploughing on, "they extended the processional avenue all the way down to the River Avon and, about a mile upstream, built a second avenue where a large scatter of broken flint had collected along a drainage at the bottom of the valley. A broad pathway glinting in the sunlight. And it happened to be perpendicular to the first avenue—or in other words, pointing toward the midsummer sunset. More than a coincidence. It was significant. Meaningful. So they built another circle at the end of it, but this one was made out of timber."

"Did we see that?" George asks, not really wanting to stay in the conversation, it seems, but not sure how to get out.

Marge shakes her head. "We didn't see any other henges."

I drop my purse onto the table. "Aaron, do you have any coins?"

"Stonehenge isn't actually a henge, anyway," he says, with an edge to make it clear that he's ignoring me. "Strictly speaking, a henge has a ditch on the inside, not the outside. So it's the opposite design of a castle with a moat around it. A henge isn't meant to keep anything out. It's meant to keep something in."

Which is the problem. Or was. Or will be. I could go inside to pay the bill, I reckon. Or I could pretend to be ill. But I'm afraid. Yes, I'm afraid he'll go along with it but he won't believe it, which in the long run will only make it worse. Make him worse. And I hate him for that.

"The timber circle was surrounded by dwellings, all made out of wood. A place of habitation and feasting, but only during the winter, when you could stand on that flint pathway and face the sunrise on the shortest day of the year. Stonehenge, on the other hand, shows no signs of habitation. Nothing except hundreds of cremation burials. Timber for life, stone for death. That's what some people say. After all, the two sites are physically connected to each other by the River Avon. Think about all those ancient myths in which a river serves as the threshold between life and death. Those rock carvings in places like Egypt and Scandinavia that show solar boats carrying the souls of the dead to the underworld. In this way Stonehenge and the timber circle complement each other. They function as a single complex."

And it comes back to me now—that morning on the hill. The rising sun, the setting moon. The two places and times working together, linked by a river. His future, my past. It brings a sweet and awful trembling into me, a prickling heat to my eyes. I plunk down money for the bill and look out at a vast blade of shadow sliding across the plaza as I put on my sunglasses, my wide-brimmed hat.

"So here we are," he says, spreading his hands. "It's morning in late December. From the timber circle you carry the body of your loved one down the avenue toward the sunrise. You get into a boat and float down the most winding and tortuous stretch of the Avon, disoriented by all those bends and meanders. One minute you're heading northwest and the next you're heading southeast, spinning every which way—to confuse the dead on their journey to the next world. To ensure they don't come back. Then you disembark and carry the body up the avenue, arriving at Stonehenge to face the sunset at the very moment when it becomes winter. A journey from life to death. Yet this is also when the days begin to lengthen again. The pivot point. The fulcrum. The shift. Over the next six months daylight increases until the summer solstice, when shazam!"

He gestures outward toward the sky.

"The sun rises in the opposite direction, shining down the avenue and all the other stones, forming a corridor to the sarsen circle. And the bluestones. With healing properties. Renewal. Rebirth. That's when you follow the route back to the timber circle to watch the sun set on the longest day of the year. Life has been restored."

He drinks the rest of his lemonade and wipes his mouth with the back of his hand. A blowhard. A verbal bully. Becoming the very thing he hates in them. What would his mother say? I flex my fingers, feeling as if I'm still inside the cave, these fingers no longer mine. Know thyself.

"That's beautiful," Marge says. "It's really poetic. What an incredible ceremony that must have been. To set up all those stones and pathways. They were in touch with the land."

Aaron leans forward. "Except the land lied to them, Marge. It wasn't a divine inscription underneath it all. It was a bunch of frost heaves. They based an entire cosmology on a geological fluke because they needed to believe things happened for a reason. It was just another myth, like Islam or Christianity. And in the end what difference does it make? Why bother spinning the dead around like it's a game of Pin the Tail on the Donkey? It's *death*. It stops them from coming back just fine without our help."

"Right," I say, pushing myself up from my seat. "We're off."

He doesn't move. "Was any of that at the visitor's centre, Marge?"

"Aaron, we're leaving now."

He squints up at me. I stare at him hard-eyed through my sunglasses until he rises from his chair and makes his way out to the plaza with the guitarist still strumming away in common time.

I turn to George and Marge, whose faces have stalled. They don't deserve what he just gave them. Nobody does.

"Sorry," I say, hating my own impulse, my ingrained need to apologise for what I haven't done as I swing round toward the café's toilet because my bladder can't wait and it would do him some good to stand over there in the sun wondering what happened to me—and this is it, yes, this is what I feel years later in the sitting room with him staring straight into my eyes. A need to be lost to him. To conceal my motives. Hidden in plain sight.

"So that's it?" he says, arms stiff at his sides. "You're pulling the plug?"

"I said a break. To sort ourselves out."

"I thought we could do that together. Isn't that the whole point?"

"The whole point is that 'together' isn't working just now."

"Which you want to remedy by living apart."

"Spot on."

He raises his face to the ceiling in exasperation. "So you're fixing a hangnail by cutting off your hand. Congratulations, Dr Wringham."

"Cut the attitude, please."

"Oh, sorry! I should be more cordial when you're trying to kick me out."

"What do you suggest? I move into that other flat while you stay here with the children?" I perk with false brightness at the notion. "Actually, I like the sound of that. You do all the heavy lifting and see what it's like."

"Sure. And you can get a full-time job to see what *that's* like."

"This," I say, whirling a finger around, "is a full-time job. Plus the piano lessons, plus lecturing—two part-time jobs on top of that, you shite. I don't have time for an affair even if I wanted one."

"I'm not having—"

"Spare me. I'm doing you a favour, yeah? A free pass. Open-ended. And for your information it's not *your* hand that's getting cut off. It's mine. It would be easier for me if you stayed and did your share with the children. I'm the one losing out. I'm not sure how I'm going to do everything by myself, to be honest."

"Your mother can help."

"That's a double-edged sword, and you know it."

"Then let's find another way."

"This is the way."

"I don't get it."

"Yes, you do."

"Oh, really?" He passes a hand across his forehead. "Then how about if you let me in on it."

"Verdun," I say.

His face goes dead, as if I've dropped all sense.

"The state of you, all bitter and nasty after your mum died. Stunted. Shut off. Or else emotions coming out in the wrong places. Ranting at those Americans in a café. And meanwhile I was pregnant. You were pulled in opposite directions, and you needed to reconcile them, but you didn't know how."

He remains utterly still and quiet, like an alpine climber sensing an avalanche. "What are you driving at?"

I'm driving at the real purpose of that holiday, which was to lift his spirits after his mother's death. Yet he never seemed to realise it, did he? Instead he believed the pretense—the mission, courtesy of my father, to seek out Cabernets in the south and Champagnes in the north because he couldn't get away from work to do it himself and his daughter had exquisite taste, he said. Especially now. The hormones do wonders for the taste buds, don't they, dear? Yes, it's true. Taste and smell. What I've lost in my hands I've gained

170

in the mouth, sipping and selecting bottles of Cahors we pick up as we make our way along the dry edges of the Massif Central with limestone glaring white through the greenery, soft hollows of farmland and pasture, depopulated villages dug into the cliffs like pueblos. The cave tour is a pleasant diversion, it seems, until I faint in the middle of it and he takes it upon himself to reveal the cosmic truth of Stonehenge to Mr and Mrs Yankee Doodle Dandy.

Driving north afterward through the countrysides and villages and urban knots, I try talking about his outburst while he talks around it, and when we reach Champagne country we take another underground tour—a cellar instead of a cave this time. The cool depths. The manmade hollows glowing in sodium lights underneath a monastery and abbey that no longer exist thanks to the Revolution. We pass old stairways designed by Benedictine monks, with each step carved to match a duplicate overhead so you can find your way in the dark by reaching up and touching it. As above, so below. Stairway to heaven. A chamber shaped like an inverted or upside-down funnel that he likens to the corbelling inside a Neolithic cairn. But he still isn't right. He's pretending to be himself as he points to the rough marks where Roman chisels dug out chalk for building materials, leaving behind passages that seem blank and crudely functional. Yes, man-made. I drag my fingertips lightly along the walls until they become green with penicillin moss, resisting an urge to lick them for the antibiotic, the natural cure that like most things is forbidden for pregnant women to ingest. And that's what does it. That promising green tinge of death. The battlefield as he described it to me, lumped and pocked and overgrown, with its scars and healing visible at once.

As we settle in the car I know what will happen next, all in retrospect.

"Verdun," I say, spreading the roadmap across the dash.

He leans across the gearshift to have a look. "No more Champagne?"

171

"A short diversion." I look at the blank windscreen, feeling it ahead of us. "It's not far."

The motorway runs along shallow bell curves, the land stretching out long and smooth and clear, past farmsteads and fields dotted with sallowing hay bales. Exposures of chalky soil. Trees staked by the roadside in isolation, beginning to take on the stains of the season. A barren fertility everywhere. The baby kicks inside me, andante by my count. Yes. This is what he needs. What we need. At the town itself we follow streets winding down to the river Meuse with its promenade and arched bridges and stone citadel, the embankment holding a piece of monumental artillery in honour of the war to end all wars. After stopping to buy a local guidebook, we carry on across the river, working our way up into the hills and an eerie release of land with slender pines bunched together like the Forestry tracts back home, except these weren't planted in straight rows. In fact, the guidebook informs us, they weren't planted at all. They grew like poppies in the aftermath.

A sign marks a destroyed village that we wouldn't notice otherwise. An empty car park. A sterile silence as we walk along a gravel track. A stone holding a plaque. Simple. Too simple. And nobody in sight. Is it because nobody knows about this place? Or is it because a destroyed village is at once too bland and unsettling? The morbid unease of something neither here nor there. And I see it now—the track widening into what must have been the High Street, the blobs of turf he mentioned to me those years ago. Yes, eerie. Spongy banks all thick and verdant and bristling with weeds. A burn trickling by. Not a single note of birdsong. And for once I'm the one who predicts the future. I know he's going to hop across the burn and climb on one of the mounds and stoop down to dig up a piece of orange roof tile, inspecting it like a scientist and a boy at once—all of which he does. Obeying his own script. Then he scampers along a bit farther and crouches down and starts scraping the moss off a block of stone.

How does it go? Don't you have misgivings.

172

"Don't you have misgivings," I ask, "about trespassing on an historic site?"

Still crouching, he smiles and holds up his hands. "Guess what I do for a living?"

"Really, Aaron, it's probably against the law, not to mention . . ." Do I say the word, or does he?

"Sacrilegious," he says.

I put a hand to my stomach as the baby starts kicking again. He didn't mention this detail. But of course there's no way he could have known unless I tell him. Which I won't do. Instead it's the arrowhead, the potsherd.

"Nobody thinks twice about digging up an arrowhead or potsherd," he says. "In fact, they don't even think once."

I consider the pockmarked ground with all those overlapping shell craters padded and smoothed by a century of growth. Yes, it will be erased. But the blood and bone that was here. The burnt flesh. The ripped bodies and the gales of smoke and broken mortar and lashings of fire. The baby kicking because she senses it, not the words but the music coming through to her, the terrible feeling of truth.

I take a breath. "The grandchildren of the people who made the arrowheads and potsherds don't live in that town by the river."

It seems to catch him harder than I intended. Grandchildren. His eyes flick away as he rises up, brushing his hands on his trousers.

"There's a strange echo up here," he says, as if making a comment about the weather. But I recognise the undertone, the resistance in his voice. "It's actually distracting, all these sounds bouncing back at you."

"That happens in other places as well, doesn't it? A cave, for example. Or a café."

He cuts me a look. I hold steady, fingers trembling like seismograph needles against the baby's thudding. Have I said the wrong thing? I can't remember what's next.

"I should have told our American friends," he says, "that the bluestones make a ringing sound when struck. A research team did acoustical tests on them and produced a whole range of bell tones. Maybe that's why they were considered to be special. Part of whatever ritual took place within the circle. And the sarsens are slightly concave facing inward. They would have amplified the noise."

"Noise?"

He blinks slowly. "The music."

The baby stops kicking. I lower my hand. "Well, it makes sense, doesn't it. Music to accompany the sunrises and sunsets down that . . . what did you call it? A passage?"

"Avenue. Processional avenue."

"Yes, it must have been part of the experience. The healing. And wasn't Apollo a god of both music and the sun? A coincidence, I reckon. Though it all happened before Apollo was invented. And on a different continent, no less."

He glances away—from the thought, perhaps, or the associations with his mother. A wind riffles through the twigged growth surrounding us, a lonely hiss even now, in the brightest sunlight.

"They found a body just a few miles from Stonehenge," he says. "An adult male. Late Neolithic. He was in a crouched position, accompanied by certain grave goods—a member of what we call the Beaker culture. But this guy was special because there were over a hundred items. Bell beakers, arrowheads, daggers, tusks, earrings, wrist guards. The largest collection ever found in a Beaker burial anywhere in Europe. And the lab results for his teeth indicated he came from just over there." He points to the woods.

"Sorry, but I don't have a compass with me."

"Eastern France or western Germany. I talked to someone who saw the paperwork, and he said the middle Rhine is a good possibility."

"Stonehenge built by the Germans?"

He smiles. "It was up and running before he arrived. This guy was a traveller of some kind. An immigrant. A pilgrim. Maybe he thought those bluestones would heal him. Maybe he wanted to bury the ashes of someone he loved."

"But he died there instead."

He closes his eyes for a moment.

"There's a site not far from Stonehenge called Cranborne Chase. It's a round barrow. A huge mound with a single urn inside. They built it by digging up the chalky white soil and then, after depositing the urn, refilling it with dirt carted in from somewhere else. Then they cut turf from the surrounding grassland and piled it up high and wide over the grave. Thirty metres across. And they did it with antler picks. Backbreaking. Brutal. And the pain wasn't just physical. All that productive land for grazing and farming taken out of use. A true sacrifice. When the mound was finished they covered it with a layer of that bright white chalk they had dug up earlier, and then they cut a circular ditch around it. Wide and deep enough to stop anyone from doing what I'm doing now." He gestures at his feet on the mound.

I have to say it. Because I've already said it. "Why?"

"How should I know?"

"But you do."

"You think I'm psychic?"

I watch him evenly without replying.

"They did it that way," he says at last, "because they needed to act it out. What they felt. They needed to make it physical."

"And what about you?"

"I went to the funeral," he says without missing a beat.

"And?"

"And nothing. That's it, Vi. She's dead. She was supposed to have another twenty years. Enjoy life, visit her grandchildren. Our children." He flings his arms out. "But hey, tough luck. Game over."

"She was cheated."

"Damn right. We've all been cheated."

"You especially."

He stalls, feeling it before he understands.

"Because you wanted to make it up to her," I say. "The separation. The distance. Over the years you've been feeling it more and more. Your family getting together so often while you see them once or twice a year at most. Your brothers with their wives and children, getting to know them as grandparents. And on this side, the two of us with my family nearby. You didn't mean to choose one at the expense of another, but that's what's happened. And now, with the baby coming . . ."

He closes his eyes softly as the notion takes hold. "Our daughter was going to close the gap between us. Mom would get to know my life over here in a new way, and she'd realise it was worth the trouble. Because she never quite got it. It never made sense to her."

"And you're angry at her for dying before it could happen."

He goes rigid. "What?"

"You blame her. You think it's her fault she died."

He stands with his chest swelled, nostrils flared. "What is this, Psychology 101? Don't tell me what I think."

"Then stop ranting at clueless Americans just because they don't understand your life. Don't take it out on them. Or anyone else, for that matter."

He turns to walk away, but halts at the downward slope of the mound and then swings back toward me as if I'm the one who has blocked him. "Yeah. Ok. I'm pissed off. All right? I wanted to prove something to her and she . . ." He points a finger as if I might argue with him. "She let me down."

I remember it now. What I need to say to him, because I know how much it will help. "Don't blame her for dying. And don't blame yourself for being angry about it. It's a downward spiral, Aaron. Let yourself out."

His expression curdles, and he starts sobbing, quietly at first, then heavy and loud in the empty woods, the baby kicking again because it hurts me as well. Pain into knowledge. Know thyself. And won't it be easier, at least, to get through the days without his expectations? To live apart? This is what I think in the sitting room. Yes, in his absence I can be just a mummy and not a wife. Plain and simple. A small consolation. It feels easy all the way down to the dry roots of my heart.

"I need you out of here," I say, "because it's what you need. What we need."

He watches me with his arms folded, a grain of animosity coming into his eyes. "You know what? I think you're right. I could use a break from you. From this." He gestures at the air around him.

"You can visit the children a couple of afternoons during the week."

"Well, that's right nice of you."

"And you can have them for a sleepover at the weekend. But I don't want them meeting this other woman."

He leans forward, laughing as if it's the most hilarious thing I could possibly say. I wait for him to stop. I'm good at waiting. "Sure," he says at last. "No danger of that."

I glance at the clock. "They'll be home soon."

His shoulders rise as he takes a breath. "I'll break the news to them."

"By saying what, exactly?"

"You want me to clear it with you?"

"I think we should agree on the best way to describe this situation."

"I believe earthlings refer to it as *separation*."

"If that's your attitude," I say, "then I don't even want you on the sofa tonight."

"News flash. This isn't about what you want anymore. I'm leaving because you've convinced me that I'll be less miserable alone in a rented flat instead of staying here. And that's quite an achievement, Vi. You've outdone yourself."

Yes, I think, my face tightening. The unexpected sense of words he doesn't even recognise. The hot stinging slap of it. That's it exactly. Despite everything, I've outdone myself.

*   *   *

177

Our last stop is an ossuary. A closed cadence. The white crosses stretching away from the building itself, which is a smooth and pale hump, mimicking the landscape but unaccountably ugly, its central tower like a Communist-Bloc penis. Yes, I allow myself this thought: an erect phallus of male misdirection and delusion, all tapering to a sharp point. The white stone porous and chalky—probably quarried from somewhere nearby, Aaron says, or perhaps simply milled up from all the shelling. The Mill on the Meuse. That was the nickname for the battle, according to the guidebook. Over a million shells fired on the first day alone, churning up the bodies over and over until no distinction could be found between one person and another. Hence the ossuary. The bone pile. The remains of at least 130,000 individuals. I enter the hall with a hand covering my nose to stop the smell like over-rich incense, the pall, the chill heavy enough to see our breaths, the blocks in the walls chiseled with the names of the departed with so little time held in the dashes between dates. An eternal flame like a Bunsen burner in a copper urn. The waffled windows of stained glass, all orange, giving a Martian tint to the light. Mars, the god of war. And the smell. I look at Aaron and shake my head.

Outside I inhale a fresh breeze, the white bristles of the killing fields. Aaron takes me round the side of the building to the ground-level windows, where he crouches down, peering through the dirty glass. I know what he can see. And I know what he's thinking because he already told me, in the past ahead of us. Excarnation. Neolithic burial rites. The bones shifted along the chambers of the passage as a conduit into death, into another world.

He motions me over. I kneel on the grass because I already have done it, a fait accompli, and confront a slew of femurs and scapulae and vertebrae and skulls with gaping jaws like the debris of a million Halloweens. He stays there with his hands cupped to the glass. I rise and walk away with my face trembling, the truth sounding in every nerve. The truth of the cave.

She's coming. The older Violet—my opponent, my partner, the one I secretly thanked for making it happen even as I vowed to avoid her fate. As if I could have it both ways. As if I wouldn't meet myself after all.

I wipe my eyes and make my way down the hillside, into the awful symmetry of crosses. The blank lanes open to the sky. No kick inside me. Nothing in my hands. Oh god, please let it be temporary, otherwise it changes everything, everything—the woman I am at the end. What will Aaron make of her? Can we find a way through? Bach's wife inexplicably dropped dead one day, and he married a woman who was eighteen years younger. And everyone who knew him claimed his love for the second never cast any doubt on his love for the first. Together the two women bore him twenty children, half of whom died in their parents' lifetimes. And Bach's last work, composed on his deathbed, was a choral prelude for organ in which the notes on the three staves of the final cadence map onto the Roman alphabet to make the letters JSB. His ego, perhaps. Or an urge to find himself in the nature of things, to unite his fifths and octaves, to make sense from his sound, beauty from his flaws. As if that could save us. Me, her. Together and apart. As if music could prevent here and now from becoming there and then.

CHAPTER TEN

2006/1988

I took the children to the zoo as if nothing had changed. I was living only a few blocks away, I told them, to work on a project similar to an excavation, but instead of digging a hole I was living in one to learn what it was like. This amused Tessa and confused Jamie. Otherwise, though, they really didn't seem to care, which was both comforting and distressing. I reminded myself that there was no scale to children's emotions, that in their short-term minds the loss of a biscuit was worse than the loss of a parent. But I also knew they would have reacted differently if Violet had been the one to leave. Which meant what? I was involved but detached in some crucial way. I didn't do the emotional heavy lifting. I wasn't vital to the fabric of their lives. I was an adequate father—nothing more, nothing less.

After paying the gatekeeper we made our way into a complex resembling a shopping mall, full of primates from various links of the evolutionary chain, all encased in vast terrariums with platforms and riggings and heaps of grass for a wild effect. There was a faint reek of jungle biology despite the ventilation system. Or was it just me? Doorways with protective flaps led to outdoor habitats that seemed spacious and well-managed, but understandably empty in mid-November. It ain't exactly the Serengeti plain, I thought, as they hooted and screamed in dead silence through the transparent wall.

I felt a pair of small hands on my thigh.

"I want some sweeties," Tessa said, craning herself toward the dispenser that stood by the water fountain.

I touched her plump cheek. "Don't we all."

"Daddy!"

Her reprimand. Her plea. Her mini-longing with epic proportions. Five minutes after leaving the building she would forget all about it. But it would be a long five minutes. And in the meantime Jamie was assaulting the dispenser like a junkie desperate for a fix, slapping the glass tank and twisting the crank as far as it would go without a coin in the slot.

I pried him away from it and, with Tessa still hanging on my leg, took them both aside. Would they cooperate with me, I asked, if I gave them some coins? Yes, they said they would. Could they say please and thank you? Yes, they said they could. And as I reached into my pocket they recited the words and appeared to be genuinely grateful in the millisecond before they rushed back to the machine and released its gobstopping chocolates. Even as it was happening I recognized the indulgence of a divorced father, although we weren't even close to being divorced. Of course we weren't far from it, either.

My basement flat was clean and functional, with a look of renovation but little use, as if I had been the first one to tread the floor after the drop cloths had been lifted, the first to place my clothing in the imitation mahogany drawers, the first to twist the updated spigots. It felt more like a monk's cell than a bachelor pad. Solitary confinement. Exile. As expected, there was hardly any natural light. And there wasn't much space. But it was full of time. My own time. Yes, mine. Mine, mine, mine. Without the children I no longer seemed to be running a catering and valet service for vandals. After an unceremonious move, followed by a numb session of staring at the wall, I had taken some pleasure in feeding myself without conflict or controversy, without repeating commands that were ignored, without bruising my heel on scattered toys or clearing out the sink only to turn around five minutes later to find it heaped full of dishes again. The Sisyphean tasks had disappeared. The rock stayed at the top of the hill. In fact, every object stayed exactly where I placed it. I didn't have to hide delicacies from the little bloodhounds I had spawned—the little bloodhounds I missed terribly during those first twenty-four hours even as I relished the absence of their demands. It was a miserable delight.

I was watching them extract riches from the candy dispenser when a great commotion rose up behind the glass wall. The apes contending fiercely. One made a running feint at another while the rest screamed and hopped. A man wearing the zoo insignia explained it was a battle for supremacy. The young challenging the old. Apparently the winner got to choose his mates. Plural. Wry glances passed among the adults—all happy couples with fulfilling lives together—as someone said the law of the jungle seemed better than the one at Scottish Parliament. I forced a smile and went over to the water fountain for a drink, wondering what my younger self would make of me. If he would even want to take over. If he would think this life was worth fighting for in the first place. Not that I would resist. In fact, I'd roll out the red carpet for him. Be my guest. Maybe we could trade partners like it was a square dance. A wife swap. A husband exchange. Why not? At that age I would have appreciated the different pace. An older woman. In fact, it was just the sort of thing I needed back then. And just the thing that Violet needed now. A younger man. Yes, they'd solve each other nicely. Do-si-do, away they go. Swing that lad over to the coal cellar and *voilà*.

My head came up slowly into the thought. He wouldn't have to agree to it. He wouldn't even have to know. Lure him down there on some pretext and shove him through. Then block the passage somehow. All I needed was—

I felt a tug on my arm, Tessa trying to haul me toward the exit, and experienced the full shock of her existence. I remembered holding her slick and slimy body in the delivery room, the deep

demand of her breath, her pulse, her life. The break with Violet
had started then. Tessa's birth. A hairline crack in the porcelain
that grew until the whole thing came apart in our hands. Five
years ago. Yes, her birthday party next weekend would be an anniversary of sorts, not to mention a masquerade with Violet and me
dressed as harmonious parents. But I didn't want either Tessa or
Jamie gone. I just wanted the damage of their existence undone.
As if I could have one without the other.

Outside we made our way along the grey slopes where creatures of all makes and models were penned. There was a playpark
with a climbing frame deliberately mimicking the one we had just
seen in the primate world, and they scaled it together, Tessa and
Jamie, their companionship obvious as they moved among the
other children on the lattices and ramps. Tessa reaching down
with both hands like a trapeze artist to haul Jamie up one of the
steeper inclines. I loved them for reasons beyond biology. I loved
them for themselves. For who they were. They couldn't be traded.
They belonged here.

I touched my fingers to my forehead as if it were simply a matter of thinking, of solving a puzzle. This had been my habit over
the past few days at the office, blaming my distraction on the lingering effects of the illness I had used as an excuse for my time
with ultra-Violet. I had worked raggedly, staring out my window
at the enduring crags to reset myself and occasionally trawling
the internet for data about Metonic cycles and lunar maximums,
or standstills as they were sometimes called, only to discover they
had absolutely nothing to do with each other. Meton of Athens
observed that a period of nineteen tropical years is equal to two
hundred thirty-five synodic months—or almost equal because they
were off by about two hours per cycle, which amounted to a full
day every two hundred nineteen years. And? It was the basis for
the Hebrew calendar. It helped Christians calculate the date of
Easter. It had been useful in flight planning for the Apollo missions. Congratulations, Meton. Lunar maximums, on the other

hand, were simply cycles of the moon itself with no known connection to any other phenomenon.

Except my phenomenon. The coal cellar. Which was a ridiculous location. Why not Inbhir or somewhere else at Kilmartin? Why not Princes Street or the Houses of Parliament? Apparently those sites weren't good enough for the laws of physics. But which laws of physics? And why? The whole thing was beyond me. I didn't have the science. It was like someone five thousand years ago trying to understand an eclipse, wondering why the moon was blotting out the sun. The only thing I felt with any certainty was that the passage led to not only another time but also another world. The older Violet's behaviour seemed genuine, along with other evidence suggesting that nothing had changed here—nothing at home, nothing at work. An online search had confirmed that not even the petrol station at Kilmartin had been altered by my actions, which meant that anything I did in 1988 would stay in that particular timeline. Meanwhile the photography shop had called to say the film from 1988 was spoiled—a victim of the coal cellar, no doubt—so if I wanted to do anything with that carving Violet and I had uncovered I'd have to go back for it. I'd have to go back for her. And him. My younger self. Push him through the passage and seal it off. Swap places. *Voilà.* I shook my head and laughed. Yeah, sure. Of all my half-baked notions, that was the tops. The best of both worlds? No. I was caught between them—between a rock and a hard place. I couldn't leave and I couldn't stay. And so here I was at a frigid zoo with some kind of endangered species braying behind me and my children screaming with joy. I zipped my jacket and folded my arms. There was a milky screen of cloud and the Pentlands vague in the distance even though it was Sunday. Sun's Day. And tomorrow was Moon's Day, when the schedule would be set for the new excavation. To Graeme's nationalist delight the McCain Quarry had awarded us the contract, and I would be returning to those hills, those carvings, that place in time.

When the children finally came down we went to the Wild

Jungle Café, where I bought them extra treats for their good behaviour, promoting their blood sugar to levels that would fall by the time they were home and Violet had to deal with the consequences.

We sat in Graeme's office sorting through the latest round of projects, with mine at the top of the agenda. The site, which we had taken to calling Dualaich in honour of an outcropping located nearby, would be a simple dig. No machinery to hire, no road works or construction to contend with. Just Fergus the Destroyer prowling in the shadows with his backhoe. I would bring the two Alans and Victoria with me for an excavation by hand, documenting our results with our usual rigor and precision. Starting when? Next Monday. A whole week away. As the discussion shifted to other issues I closed my folder and glanced out the window at a footpath leading down through the caked growth to the ravine of Holyrood. It was all bare bones and dead leaves and brown needles and sheddings and bits of rubbish. The sky knotted with dark cloud.

Eighteen years earlier, in the flush of the Inbhir excavation, I had made a carving of my own to learn what it was like, pecking with a quartz hammerstone against a dull grey panel of epidiorite. I had settled into a steady rhythm with the sound ringing hypnotically or perhaps meditatively, losing memory of when I stopped to grind the shape into a better outline or blow away the creamy dust, running my fingers in the hollow to feel my progress, losing time without my watch. The bright white chips sparkling in the sun. The quartz a living substance whose energy I transferred to the carving, giving it a vital presence, an afterlife in rock. It wasn't until I washed it off with water that I saw the results. The carving a reddish-brown hue that would fade gradually, as if the stone were healing. And next week, at Dualaich, I would run my fingers in grooves chiseled five thousand years ago, their shapes becoming mine. The early sunset would leave me working overtime with klieg lights until I switched them off for the slow resolution of the terraced slopes, the folded hills, the flat-bottomed glen that once held the backwash of the sea. I would try to find sense in all that was missing, and I would fail as always, because the true sense came from the work—not the finished carving but the act of making it. It must have brought people together. All that perished love. I would feel it in the cold and darkness, all that has been lost, but after a meal and a few pints at the pub I would drop into anonymous sleep, and it would be a consolation prize for my own life. It would save me a little bit. It would give me a small measure of relief.

"But only if you can squeeze that in by the end of the week, Aaron."

I looked at Graeme with all the wrong lights flashing. "You want me to squeeze something?"

He peered humourlessly at me over his reading glasses while the others laughed, his face taking on the subtle contours of a decision—a reckoning coming my way. I held up my hands in apology. He moved on to another item of business without comment. When the meeting adjourned I didn't even bother to stand up from the table as Victoria, the last one to leave, wisely shut the door behind her. He removed his glasses and sat back with his hands folded over the top of his head.

"Out with it."

"I don't know where to start."

"At the end. I'm in no mood for cliffhangers."

I looked out the window. "Violet and I are . . ."

His hands came unfolded and settled onto the armrests of his chair.

"We're living apart." My throat began to tighten. "For the time being. Sorry, I should have told you sooner."

"Bloody hell, man."

"I called in sick last week because I just couldn't . . ."

As he exhaled through his nostrils I realised his eyes were glistening, reddening at the rims. I found myself touched with both affection and shock.

"It's all right," I said. "Really. We just need some time."

He nodded out of compassion rather than belief, as if I had just assured him an amputated limb would grow back.

"I'm still on for Dualaich. For everything."

There was a silence. Voices passed in the hallway. His computer pinged with email. He glanced at the clock, but I already knew it was late enough for what would happen next.

"Fetch your coat," he said.

The Sheilings had decaying booths and low-wattage lamps and stools with deflated padding. There was a deep suggestion of age in the rails and scuffed wood, in the tarnished fixtures, in the single malts ranged along the shelf. And there were a few framed prints of Highland shepherds and bothies on the walls, but otherwise nothing to earn its name, let alone the reverence Graeme seemed to give it. The cask ales were reliable. The music was traditional folk. When I had noticed Graeme's papers stained with beer one day he let slip that he occasionally did work here. With what, I had asked, a flashlight and earplugs? But now as we settled in a deep corner with a couple of pints it seemed appropriate for the sort of clearance he had in mind.

"I'm not prying," he said, his hand wrapped around his glass as if he were holding it down. "But if you keep it bunged up you'll bust a gut. And I've been through it. Twice. The first time was my fault, the second time hers. Either way it's agony. You think it's only a rough patch at first. You think, aye, we'll sort it out. Keep calm and carry on. Then suddenly you're in a rented room with your heart roasting on a spit."

His eyes went hard and distant for a moment, as if he had pressed too firmly on the scar tissue of his own memory. Then he blinked and lifted his glass.

"How do you know whose fault it was?" I asked.

He wiped the foam from his lip. "When the dust clears you see the timbers leaning a certain way."

"And you blame one partner for that instead of both."

"The beams and supports, the load-bearing walls."

I drank a stout with a burnt and oaty taste that matched my mood. "They're all load-bearing."

He shook his head. "Sadly, no. When all is said and done."

"That's not much help to me now."

"Flummoxed, are you?"

I gazed at the empty rampart of the bar, the television flickering silently overhead, the barman texting on his mobile. There had been fiddle music playing on the speakers when we arrived, but it had trailed off into silence. I lowered my voice as I turned back to Graeme.

"What can I say? Have I been chasing other women? Do I have a gambling addiction? Am I beating the children? No, no, no. Everything is the same. Maybe that's the problem. Continental drift." I felt myself pitching forward, a resolution tumbling out. "We're going back to square one or nowhere at all."

"Don't be hasty. And don't lose the big picture. You made a stretch across the Atlantic and then another stretch across the New Town, the second gap being wider than the first. Give yourself credit for that."

I didn't reply because there was too much to say. Despite my protests over the years he still confused his own class voltage with mine—as if marrying a woman with inherited wealth and expectations had been a stretch for me, when in fact it had been much more of a stretch for her. There were correspondences, of course. I had always been aware that the inflections of Dixie didn't match the clean northern intonations of my country's wealth and power, and in that way I understood Graeme's gut-level resentment of England. But the lineages and ancestries and heraldry and landed this-and-thats made about as much sense to me as a Dungeons and Dragons—a game that raised hackles precisely because it operated on the most adolescent levels of the mind. I had come from a region satirized as narrow, isolated, and inbred, yet I now lived in a place where the elite were defined by those very same qualities. And while my accent had once caused a profound inferiority complex, now it was a free pass, exempting me from the cultural pigeonholes I would have faced otherwise. It happened not only at those occasional gatherings Violet and I attended at her parents' house but also in conversations with repairmen and plumbers who heard my American voice and relaxed into an easy banter. I was both classless and working class. It was my country's only foreign policy success.

As we drank Graeme's eyes took on a clinical distance. "Has anything been off with her lately?"

I blinked at him. "What do you mean, *off*?"

"Medically speaking."

"Are you a doctor?"

"I'm a man," he said, with noticeable reluctance, "married to his third wife. And I'm aware of certain biochemical hazards, shall we say."

"You mean *female* issues?"

"I mean age issues."

It took a moment for me to follow his suggestion, and then I waved it off. "She's miles away from menopause, if that's what you're driving at. And even if that was the problem, plenty of women go through it without sending their husbands into exile."

"Sometimes the prelude is worse than the thing itself."

"A prelude to menopause." I looked around, wanting some kind of audience to consult. "You're making this up."

"Things can happen to a woman at her age. She can change from Jekyll to Hyde." He raised his glass in emphasis. "Except she doesn't change back."

"How come I've never heard of this?"

"Most women haven't heard of it. Or don't want to hear of it. And who can blame them? After all they go through. A woman has a right to expect smooth sailing when she hits her forties, and look what happens. Raw deal, that." He gave his head a shake. "At any rate it hardly bothers some. For others it's a trauma. Edith said it was like getting cancer over and over again. And she changed."

"How so?"

He gave me a look full of grizzle and gristle, like a soldier returned from a battle whose scope I couldn't comprehend. "Jekyll and Hyde. Let's leave it at that."

I clicked back through what I remembered of her. Edith. Wife number two. A brittle and anxious woman whose social reflexes had directly contradicted his. She had been especially sensitive to Violet's pedigree, taking on a self-conscious and restrained demeanor in her presence, whereas Graeme regarded Violet's background as a kind of birth defect to be overlooked. I had always wondered how they reconciled a difference on par with religion. But it made sense if it wasn't the original Edith, if it was a result of some biochemical swerve, if in fact he had married an Edith that the rest of us had never met.

"Ok," I said. "Let's assume this is the problem. Or part of the problem. We solve it with what, medication? Herbs? Folklore rituals?"

"Aye, why not?" His eyes gleamed with humour, but his expression stayed firm. "Introduce her to the *dei teranni*. The earth gods living in the cairns. Take her to Mid Argyll and make her dig."

I felt a smile taking shape, not because it was funny but because it was what I had done with ultra-Violet the previous week. "A heavy dose of Gaelic folklore."

"Gaelic folklore, Celtic myth. It's all about fertility. I'm sure there's something in there for a lass on the downswing. No offense."

I waved a hand to show none taken. We shared an understanding of ancient life expectancies that, at our respective ages, would have made Violet an old woman beyond childbearing, me a doddering wreck, and Graeme dead. But then a thought snagged me, and I halted with my glass raised halfway to my lips.

"Fertility rituals," I said.

He smiled grandly. "The agricultural obsession. Rites to ensure a bountiful harvest. You have Dagda, the chief god, ploughing a furrow in the earth with his penis and inseminating the land. You have the sun god Lugh impregnating Dichtrine inside the passage grave at Newgrange. On and on and on. Mind you, these things never really go away. Nothing disappears. As a schoolboy I had a laugh over Dagda, but then my granddad told me about an old Highland tradition where a man would go outside during a full moon and press his penis into the earth while he pissed. If he could do it without pain, then it meant there was no frost and the ground was warm enough for the spring planting. You can imagine the jokes about that one."

I was sliding along the edge of what he was saying. "Why during a full moon?"

He shrugged. "Why not? The light's better. And a half moon just doesn't seem very special, does it?"

"But why is the moon in there at all?"

"It's always there. The Celts believed the waxing phase was positive, the waning phase negative. And like every other culture they tied themselves in knots trying to reconcile solar and lunar calendrics."

I set down my glass. Dagda plowing the fields with his cock during a full moon. And Lugh impregnating Dichtrine inside Newgrange, which was Ireland's famous counterpart to Maeshowe—another large passage grave in which the sun shone directly into the chamber at the winter solstice, except at Newgrange it came through a slot like a transom window above the entrance to admit the light, and it occurred at sunrise instead of sunset. The effect, though, was virtually the same. The sun inseminating the structure itself. During the solstice. And the bodies inside, disarticulated and shuttled deeper into the passage as they decayed. The reverse of the birth process. In the Bronze age, though, the bodies were kept intact, curled up and lying on their sides as if they were—

"In a foetal position," I said.

Graeme brought his gaze back from the television flickering over the bar and shot me a look. "Say again?"

"The crouched burials. Foetal position. Because the passage is shaped like . . ." I hesitated before finishing the sentence. "Like a birth canal. And the central chamber like a womb."

I braced myself for a tart comment or a dismissal of some kind, but as soon as the words were out I knew they were true. Graeme watched me in silence. He opened his mouth and closed it without speaking. Then he scrubbed a hand over his head as if he were trying to dissolve such a silly notion before it got into his mind.

I sat forward. "You've said it a million times. All those myths didn't come out of nowhere. There was a cultural continuity. An evolution of beliefs. I know, I know," I said, raising a preemptive hand when I saw the look on his face. "It's a complicated gene-alogy. Impossible to trace. We can't reverse-engineer Neolithic myths from a bunch of stories that Christian monks transcribed from Druids who had recast them from Celtic tales three thousand years after the fact. But still."

"But still," Graeme said, coming around to it. "One could say it's like the layout of a Medieval cathedral representing the cross, the symbolic body of Christ." He smiled mildly, taking some pleasure in the speculation, in the conjecture growing outlandishly from the facts. It was why he had hired me all those years ago. Yes. I understood it now.

"But in this case the cairn represented . . ." I wagged a finger. "No, it didn't *represent*. It was a womb drawn from the earth. It was the real thing. A physical transformation. Birth and death. The sky, the seasons. All that cyclical stuff."

He tilted his glass at me. "I'll go with that."

"Like the moon. And the menstrual cycle. Oh, that's it." I slapped the table and sat back in my seat.

Graeme raised his scrubby eyebrows. "That's what?"

"What do you know about lunar maximums?"

He inhaled slowly, his eyes going back to a mental rolodex. "The moon's widest range of declination, which is a fancy way of saying that it swings from far south to far north and then back again for a few cycles before it starts decreasing again. Every 18.6 years, if memory serves. A few sites have arguable alignments, usually to the full moonrise at one extreme or another. And I believe it's happening now. This year. What of it?"

"I was going to ask you the same question."

He spread his hands.

I leaned forward with both elbows on the table. "The moon corresponds to the menstrual cycle, which marks human fertility. And like you said, it corresponds with the agricultural cycle in a certain way. There must be others."

"Aye, probably loads of ways people tried to make it correspond."

"Because," I said, working toward a thought, "because something happens during a lunar maximum. Something that affects women and landscape alike."

He drew up his shoulders and let out a skeptical breath.

"In all these myths Earth and the moon are both female. And the sun is always male. Which makes sense if they were trying to reconcile lunar and solar cycles."

"Not necessarily," he said. "The moon wanders all over the sky. It's a light show. Follow the bouncing ball. Probably a whole slew of myths about that."

"Exactly. That's my point. Myths linked to, I don't know, let's call it *transcendent fertility*. Of course, the rock carvings must have been involved."

"Might have been."

"Oh, come on."

"Take care in how you connect the dots, otherwise you make a whole new myth. Yours instead of theirs. If you don't mind me saying so, this new fertility god is beginning to look a lot like Aaron Keeler."

"But I'm on the edge of something."

"Aye," he said, with a wry wink. "No argument there."

"Come on, Graeme. Think. Help me out here. What am I missing?"

He watched me for a long moment, the furrows of his forehead releasing into a different frame of thought. "What you're missing is a marriage counselor. Now I don't want to make too much of this, but you're in transition."

"Transition?"

His gaze flicked away in regret at the word choice, but then he brought it back. "Uncertain circumstances."

Although he was trying to be fair, I had caught the finality in his voice. He was a man with two dead marriages behind him— but of course he had married a different woman with a different set of obstacles each time. With ultra-Violet, though, I knew the topography. I had a map of our ups and downs, our crevasses and summits, our Tessas and Jamies.

Graeme started to say something else when a burst of fiddle music came from the speakers. The barman called out an apology. Graeme vowed bloody revenge with a smile. And as he turned back to me I found myself awash in a ridiculous but compelling possibility. Could we have Tessa and Jamie again? I didn't know why it came to me with such promise, why it seemed that we could conceive exactly the same children. But I felt it—yes, I felt in my bones. Our children could return to us in that better time, that better place. And could I swap places with my younger self after all? I had dismissed the notion as half-baked, yet that was how the most radical and appropriate solutions seemed, at first, until they suddenly became true.

"Don't worry," I said, to prevent whatever counsel he had been about to offer. "I'm ready for the excavation. Full speed ahead."

Graeme inhaled. "What you find there could stop Fergus's great expansion in its tracks. He'll be rattling every cage he can find. The planning commission will be crawling up your arse about procedure and protocol. You need to be square on your feet." He peered carefully into my eyes. "You ken?"

"Yes," I said, holding my composure. "I ken. I ken it through and through."

He drained his pint. I managed to do the same without spilling it all over me. I was trembling faintly, every nerve lit.

"I'd stay for another," he said, setting down his empty glass, "but my third and final wife is expecting me home. And if you don't mind me saying so, drink is not the thing you need just now. You can tell me to fuck off, but there it is. You need clarity. You need space up here." He tapped a thick finger at his temple. "Besides, my guess is you'll be taking out the weans soon enough, and if you show up foggy with last night's booze, it's about as bad as another woman's lipstick on your collar. Trust me."

I made a vague gesture, like what else was I going to do.

"And try to get some sleep."

"What?"

"I'm going to tell you point blank you look like shite. Understandably. So here's my prescription. Take a couple of days off and eat some bloody vegetables and go to the gym and whatever else it is you do these days with that healthy attitude. I want you back Thursday."

I was about to protest, to express my automatic urge for activity and focus, the distraction of work, before catching myself at the thought of two days of freedom. Two days of ultra-Violet. Two days to find the socket for that stone we had uncovered and learn exactly where it had been positioned. But instead of smiling at the prospect of it all I nodded with false reluctance and thanked Graeme for his kind gesture, his hard advice.

As we were putting on our coats he gave me a deliberate look. "You're on the right track about the cairns. The shape of the chamber. The crouched burials. No accident, that."

True, I thought. No accident. And I had discovered the coal cellar at exactly the right time. No accident at all.

I went shearing through the passage and arrived with nerves ripped and dangling like cut strings. I spent some time on my hands and knees, head lowered, vision blurred. Then I got to my feet and stumbled back and leaned against the wall until everything focused and settled. I was there. I was then. The pulse and breeze of April, the high sun, the garden in its full spread with buds becoming leaves. And the film, I thought. The film.

I pulled out the mortise key and opened the door and felt along the upper threshold until I found the canister exactly as I had left it. I held it in both hands and touched it to my forehead like a holy relic. Then I locked the door and climbed the steps and strolled the streets as if I belonged there, accustomed to the retrograde look and feel of everything, breathing that air, making it mine. I took a closer look at the lost styles around me—the slightly poufy hair, the larger frames to the eyeglasses and jewellery, the clothing cut just a little too tight in all the wrong places—and I tried to remember how it all would drift incrementally, almost imperceptibly, toward the fashions I knew as normal. And when I dropped off the film at the same photo shop I had used earlier, still in business before all those years, I realised the older man across the counter was probably dead in 2006. I forced a smile as he handed me the receipt. Get used to it, I thought. Get used to seeing the dead alive.

I made my way back to my building and lifted the loose stone to find the duplicate key exactly where Violet had said she would leave it. The stairwell echoed with a menagerie of sounds from Mrs McNaught's television. I touched her door ruefully as I passed, smiling at the murky drone of Margaret Thatcher's voice. How quickly it all came back. The political metabolism of the day. The tumult of an unknown future. And Mrs McNaught's heart attack the day after the Berlin Wall came down. A coincidence? As I rounded the next landing I asked myself the hard question.

Could I prevent her death? Was it simply a matter of calling for an ambulance much sooner this time?

At my own door I took a breath. I turned the key. The flat greeted me with its long hallway, its clarity of line and light. I could hear the shower running, but then it immediately stopped, as if cued to my arrival. I didn't want to frighten her so I cleared my throat loudly by the bathroom door and in response she made a low noise of delight. I opened the door and stepped into her steam.

"No, no," she said, shooing me back. She had a towel wrapped under her armpits, her hair in damp cables. "In the bedroom. Let's do it right."

I wasn't exactly sure what she meant, but I backed out obediently and allowed her to pass, following her down the hall like a servant. Her bare legs, her callused heels. She let her towel fall to the floor. I removed my clothes as if they were on fire. I put my hands in her wet hair, and I sucked on her flushed shoulders, her breasts, on every delicious little nook and plain. Afterward she rolled me onto my back and straddled me, keeping her hands on my chest as she watched me come. Then she slumped down and stretched out at my side. Our breaths had barely settled when she said she was late.

My eyes shot wide. I had assumed the same pregnancy would happen, but I hadn't counted on a difference in timing. Which meant it couldn't be the same pregnancy. Or the same child. But what about Tessa? And Jamie? My chest went hollow with panic. I needed to say something.

"Already? I didn't realise . . ." I hesitated, trying to sort out the incubation period, or whatever it was called.

"Realise what? The rector gave me the morning slot, and I can't afford to miss it." She sat up and looked at the clock. "Actually if I catch the bus I should be fine."

I closed my eyes and felt all my pulses and pressures returning to normal. "The rector," I said, "at Tolbooth Church. Where you play the organ."

"Spot on, futureman. Nothing gets by you." She got to her feet and tugged open her wardrobe and started flicking hangars. "How long can you stay this time?"

"'Till tomorrow night."

"Oh, fab." Then she turned and gave me a wince. "Except tomorrow he's coming back midafternoon, so I'm afraid you'll have to leave by then."

I lifted my head. "Wait, what day is it?"

"Thursday."

"It's Tuesday for me."

"When in Rome," she said.

I blinked at the ceiling, wondering if the interval had changed or if the calendar was simply throwing me off. A decimal system would have been a lot easier to track. But there was something else. If the coal cellar was linked to the lunar maximum, then it might weaken as the maximum itself faded over the course of several months, until it stopped working altogether. If, maybe.

"I'll be back in a few hours," she said, "and then we can . . ."

As her voice trailed off I realised she was looking at me with her naked ass cocked to one side, flesh folded at the waist. "How did you get so much time off?"

"Work is a bit slow this week."

"I meant time off from *her*."

I folded my hands behind my head. "Don't worry about that end of it."

"I'm just wondering if she believes you." She turned back to the wardrobe and pulled out a blouse, throwing it onto the bed. "Or if she smells a rat."

"The rat being you, of course. Which reminds me. Last time I forgot to ask if you told him about us. Told me about us. Like you promised."

"Of course I told him," she said, stepping into her underwear. "I delivered it dead serious at first, saying I shagged an older Aaron. But then I started giggling and he kissed me on the forehead because he thought it was such a cute joke, none of which you remember because it actually didn't happen in your time or world or whatever. And to be honest I don't mind if you hang about and have a chat with him tomorrow, but would either of you really enjoy that?"

I settled back. No, neither of us would enjoy that. And still juddering at the thought of losing Tessa and Jamie, I knew it wasn't going to happen. There was too much at risk, too much I didn't understand. My great notion of a switch or trade amounted to an uncontrolled, irreversible experiment on the lives of everyone around me. I couldn't leave my children. Or the older Violet. I blinked at the sudden pressure of the feeling. How much I still loved her despite her foul variations—the results of not only age but also a hormonal meltdown, if Graeme was to be believed. Despite everything, she knew me the way this younger one didn't. She had mentioned Verdun as some kind of rationale for our separation, like it was another emotional push or provocation I needed, and even though I didn't believe her this time, even though it seemed self-serving on her part, I couldn't help remembering how much she had helped me after my mother's death. If we hadn't been together at our particular ages through those years she wouldn't have been capable of such a thing. Was I preventing ultra-Violet from developing in the same way? Was I being selfish? But I wanted her—yes, I wanted this woman, too. It wasn't just the sex. It was the ease of these moments with her, the straight affection, the flair of intimacy in what she said and how she said it, the way she touched me in passing. I wanted her young and old. I wanted her both ways. And I was having her, wasn't I? Maybe this was how I could do it. After all, I had a good thing going with this portal. So why not enjoy it?

I raised myself on an elbow. "Can I watch you?"

She smirked. "You're already watching me."

"I meant listen. At Tolbooth Church."

She paused as if I had just announced a serious illness. "Why?"

199

"Because I didn't do it often enough when I had the chance. All those things I was doing—those things he's doing—seemed so important at the time. But now I don't even remember most of them. They don't matter. Let me go with you."

She blinked. "Except my supervisor is going to be there. Hugh Pearson. Remember him?"

Yes, I remembered him. Gruff, likeable. A taskmaster when it came to her coursework, yet supportive and encouraging as well. "But I thought he handled the academic side of things," I said. "Not performance."

"Well, yes. In this instance, though, performance is part of it. And Hugh knows you. Or him. The young Aaron. Your appearance would pose problems, yeah?"

Yeah. I sank back and closed my eyes for a moment, marking my surrender. Then I realised my eyes had been closed for more than just a moment and I forced them open again.

"Can you do me a favour?" I asked. "I dropped off some film, but it won't be ready until Saturday. I'll give you the receipt."

She looped a bra over her shoulders and bent her arms back to fasten it. "Our double spiral?"

"None other."

"But I thought you took it back to 2006."

"Technical difficulties."

She seemed to evaluate that phrase before she replied. "All right. But in return maybe you can do me a favour while I'm gone and quit ripping the fabric of space-time?"

I let out a drowsy laugh.

"Really, Aaron. Have a kip or something. You look knackered."

My smile drained away because it was exactly how I felt. Knackered. The previous night I had slept with unusual soundness, which in part had to do with the silence and darkness of my subterranean bedroom, but there was something else going on. I murmured in agreement. I tried to keep my eyes open as I watched her dress. Her sharp movements, her fingers working the delicate buttons of her blouse.

"Wear that green one instead," I managed to say.

She glanced at me and then down at herself. "Doesn't match the trousers."

"Then wear it tonight."

"Why?"

"Because it brings out the best in you. And you lost it in Naples about ten years ago."

She put her hands on her hips.

"Ok, ok," I said. "I'll stop."

She came over and lifted the duvet over me and then gave me a sweet kiss on the lips. "I'll be back soon enough."

Yes, I thought, drifting. Soon enough. I turned my head to the damp crater of her pillow, her fragrance of shampoo and body scrub—and emanating from my own covers the faint scent of something familiar that I realised, after a few moments, was actually myself. A different vintage of biochemistry. I had smelled slightly different back then. Or back now. How could that be? I wanted to ask Violet if that was true, if it was real, but my eyes snapped open to an empty room and I sat up with a jolt, heart thudding. The day had shifted farther along, a brighter angle of sunlight in the bedroom. The window open to birdsong and traffic rumbling faintly on cobblestones. I looked at the clock, wiped the drool from my mouth, and reclined again with a hand to my chest. Two hours. I couldn't remember the last time I had napped that long. After my pulse settled I hauled myself up and made some coffee, smiling fondly at the dented kettle, the beans of unfair trade. And then, unable to resist the urge, I made my way into my study, which surprised me with objects shifted and shuffled since my previous visit. Of course. My younger self had been there over the weekend. My ongoing life. At Inbhir this week I was discovering shell deposits that were actually the upper edges of an entire shell midden dating from the Mesolithic. And what else was happening?

Well, right about now I was trying not to watch the curves of Siobhan's ass, the hints of rich exposure in that tight shirt she unzipped at the neck. I was trying not to follow her slim legs and knotty hair she shook out and tied back from time to time, her mouth bent with a smile whenever she glanced up to meet my gaze. I was trying not to imagine her in bed right about now. And eighteen years later I had finally searched for her online, sifting through all her doppelgängers under Smith until I typed in her maiden name and discovered her in Phoenix, Arizona. She was an artist. A ceramic artist. Really? I clicked on an image and peered at it. Yes, really. That was her. And in fine shape, too. Divorced from the petroleum engineer and remarried to an American airline mogul, according to a profile that accompanied her latest exhibition. I believed it all instantly. Despite her postgraduate degrees and specialist training, she had ached for things that were foreign and uncertain. She would periodically fray out and unravel and rework herself into different shapes. I had been a passing interest to her. A diversion. A fringe benefit of the dig. I doubted she had ever thought of me at all.

I closed my eyes. I opened them. I touched the surface of my perished desk, confirming the scratches, the gouge I had covered with a National Trust for Scotland sticker. I touched artefacts that were now in my office at work: a shard of Orkney flagstone, a dish full of flint arrowheads, a mug holding soil from my first dig. Yes, still the same. I stood before the ancient machinery of my typewriter with its indented keys, the letters faded from the friction and impact—as if it were a contact sport, Violet had said once, watching me hammer away. And there was my red notebook with a smoother and brighter complexion. I opened it and wrinkled my nose at the pages. The fresh etchings of my handwriting. And then, inevitably, I raised my eyes to the wall—the grandiose collage that had started on a bulletin board before spilling over the edges. The clippings, the copies, the photos, the drawings. A cup-and-ring with a gutter running out from the centre. A dartboard. An aerial shot of a racetrack. A raindrop hitting the water's surface with ripples fanning outward. An atom with orbiting electrons. Earth with its tilted axis. Saturn with its collars of ignited dust. The solar system. An atom smasher in black and white. A super collider in colour. The pupil and iris of a human eye—Violet's lovely blue. I had believed it was the fundamental shape of the universe until Tessa had enlightened me with that first scribble of hers. We think everything is circular because we make circles everywhere. We think the cause is the effect.

I went to the window with my coffee mug. Timeline or time-circle? I might never have a definitive answer. Bearing in mind that every layer of an excavation must be dated by the youngest artefact found in it, I also reminded myself that by taking the film from its hiding place I had prevented myself from recovering it in 2006, thereby removing the layer itself. And so what? The more I thought about that part of it, the less it seemed to matter. I would keep travelling back and forth. I would have the best of both worlds. And I would bring that stone to official notice in this world before Fergus could destroy it, giving Inbhir a greater significance—the recognition it deserved—while my detailed photos would serve as evidence in case it didn't manifest itself in the other world. Better yet, money wouldn't be a problem. How many elections and sporting matches and technological developments could I predict? The betting parlours would come to fear me if I didn't spread out my transactions. Investors far and wide would begin to notice my moves. I needed to stay hidden. A high profile would ruin it all.

But I had already altered this world with my actions, hadn't I? Like the fabled butterfly fluttering its wings in the rainforest, I had unsettled this existence simply by taking a breath. My predictions, my knowledge, would become less accurate as this world drifted out of phase with the one I knew. Yet the larger pieces, the continental plates, would remain in place. The major triumphs and disasters would still happen. I would still face the sort of ethical dilemmas Violet's father liked to air by the fireplace after his third or fourth glass of wine, wondering what would have happened if someone had assassinated a young Adolf Hitler or prevented Archduke Ferdinand's driver from taking a wrong turn in Sarajevo. Would it make the world better or worse? I rubbed my forehead, thinking of earthquakes and accidents, not to mention a pair of towers in lower Manhattan. I took a slow breath. It would all come later. I had years to sort it out, to perform smaller tests— pilot studies of fate—and then decide. In the meantime I would enjoy these visits to the roaring nineties. The developing internet, the soaring stock market, the carefree gap between the Cold War and the Reign of Terror. How innocent it all seemed now. And how strange to find myself enjoying the certainty, the knowledge of what lay ahead. The large equations that were already solved. It brought a tingle to the air. Yes, the safety of these minutes when the hour was known. Fab, as my young love would say. Absolutely fab.

I was pouring more coffee when the phone rang and I heard my own voice come over the machine, leaving a message for Violet and a sudden memory for me—a reminder of what would happen that weekend. I saluted him as he signed off. Then I went to the window and looked out at a world set in stone.

CHAPTER ELEVEN

1988

This is how it goes, the organ pipes humming with tidal force as I find the pulse and pleasure of it now. The Passacaglia and Fugue in C minor. It's here. At last. The ground bass rising up from the pedals and thinning out in the higher registers of my hands, ethereal and bare, the fine bones of it exposed by the stabbing of each note like a harpsichord before shifting down and massing into a double fugue full of breves and crochets with a counter-subject quavering in and out until it all comes together for the C major transformation that I hit with all my weight at the end, leaning into the vibrations, the fullness and weight and power.

I lift my head to the ribbed vaults as it fades, leaving not a sound but a sense behind it. Something outside itself. An energy beyond its own frame. The pipes holding a silence in the aftermath. The church aching like an empty seashell. I hear the sluggish wing-beats of pigeons somewhere. The low rumble of traffic through the walls. Then my face breaks open, and I start to cry with the seizure of it, whatever it is, in the very nature of things that Bach found. All these patterns and entanglements. An ecstatic presence. In the flush of stained glass I could almost call it God. Touching my sleeve to my eyes I catch a trace of sweat and sex and mineral musk, not quite myself. Her. The older Violet. What is she playing in the future? Something in a minor key. The right hand leading the left. Oh Vi, do you know what I'm thinking? Is this just a memory to you? If so, you'd better watch out, because I want him, I really do, and I'm not waiting eighteen years for it to happen. No way. The higher variations may be yours, but the ground bass is mine.

Eventually I fold myself up and collect my sheet music like an executive, checking the organ to ensure the swell shutters are open, the stops off, the couplers disengaged. And then I descend the stairs to plain air and the breathing world with its purpose and function. The Royal Mile. Pubs sweating out grease, shops clogged up with tartan and tams. People going places, doing things. Untouched, unbothered. I follow a wynd through tenements of medieval stone all ingrown and gnarled, an open court showing its drainage pipes, the gables above me corbie-stepped to heaven. Coming out by the Assembly Hall and the gardens gaping below, I make my way down the Mound with a divine heat in my face. Postcoital in every sense. But it doesn't show. No, it never shows. I pass a few punks with ornamental hair and metal in their faces, a bagpiper in full bronchial blow. I'm plain and proper, it seems. I'm unremarkable. I'm nobody. But maybe I can make the world a slightly better place with my playing, bringing out the transformations I feel in the music. Maybe I can make it real. Is that asking too much? Recognition? Success? It can happen with hard work, with passion, with time, and with a radiant break in the clouds and a wild breeze and gulls in joyful cry I decide to shag him again for good measure and what do you think of that, Violet? I can do what I want. It's my life.

When I come through the door, though, I barely have time to set down my folder before he ushers me into the kitchen.

"You have a message," he says, gesturing at the machine.

For a strange instant I think he's caught me out, as if the message might be from Dr Pearson, inadvertently revealing that I was alone in the church after all. But the odds of Pearson phoning me are practically nil. And when I notice the bright release in Aaron's face, all refreshed by his kip and, judging by the mess on the counter, about a litre of coffee, I know I did the right thing. It was the only way to get him to rest. Otherwise what? He would have dragged along with me until he collapsed, and try explaining that at A&E.

"A message," I repeat, trying to suss out what he's after, "from you?"

"From him," he says in a tone of gentle correction.

I put a hand on my hip. "And you listened."

"Of course. I was standing right here when he left it."

"Why didn't you pick up?"

He shoots a finger at me. "Good one. Now come on, aren't you curious?"

Yes and no. Because it's going to happen whether I want it or not. I raise a shoulder. "Bring on the big surprise."

With a grand gesture he presses the button, activating his own voice. Or the younger variation of it, all American and boyish brash.

"Hey Vi, don't kill me but I can't make it home this weekend. You won't believe what we found. Or what I think we found. Colossal. I need to ask the local curator about it, and he's only around this weekend before he leaves for a conference and then goes on vacation or something. But how about if you come out and visit? Borrow your dad's car. Blame it all on me. He'll understand. And I hope you do, too. Love you, miss you. Come west, young woman."

As the dial tone kicks in I try to force a smile. After all, this is exactly what I want: the younger Aaron out of the picture for a few days so I can enjoy his older vintage. But an uneasy shear runs through me instead. A loss of pressure. A pressure I didn't even know existed. Why?

"I guess I really used to talk like that," he says, leaning against the counter with his arms folded, amused with himself.

Because my parents are going down to the Borders this weekend for Aunt Sally's fiftieth, and Aaron knows about it because he actually recommended some prehistoric sites in the vicinity—all of which he was pretending to forget when he left that message. I could hear it in his voice. And now he stands there expecting me to believe it again. Lying to me twice. He's his own accomplice. The two of them playing me back and forth like a tennis ball. They're hiding something.

"And I guess you really used to act like that as well."

He gives me a puzzled look. "Like what?"

"Callous. Thoughtless. Self-absorbed. Take your pick. You can't wait a couple of weeks to ask this curator a few questions? Or give him a ring, wherever he happens to be?"

"It can't be done over the phone."

"I'll bet it can't."

He goes stiff with caution. "What are you driving at?"

"This wouldn't have anything to do with Miss Jugs and her archaeological assets, would it?"

"I told you, Siobhan is strictly business."

"Siobhan. Mmm, that's right. I had forgotten her name. But you haven't. After eighteen years. Why is that?"

He pauses in the gulf of what I've said. "There's a particular feature I uncovered at the site that the curator needs to see."

"And which has been sitting there for four thousand years, but can't wait a few more weeks. And which takes priority over seeing me this weekend."

"Five thousand. And I want to see you. I mean, *he* wants to see you. We both do." He squeezes his eyes shut and gives his head a shake. "Look, can we stick to the topic? I mean, us? Me and you? I thought you'd be thrilled about the extra time."

"Of course," I say. "It's fab." But it comes out a bit too sharp as I go to the sink and make a show of rinsing out the coffee pot, the bottom thick with sludge. A petulant girl. That's how I must seem to him. The older Violet has got poise, I reckon. She's got composure even in the worst of times.

"I thought I was the one you wanted," he says.

"You are."

"But . . . ?"

I turn toward him. "There's a certain amount of overlap between you."

He breaks into a grin like a car salesman. "And ultra-Violet wants it both ways. Two men devoted to her."

I take a moment to absorb this notion. Yes. Maybe. No. Because they're not really two men, are they? The younger Aaron plans to do this weekend what the older one has already done. They are the same person, claiming to be apart because it suits him now. He's the one who wants it both ways. I feel myself going tight and hard. But then I know what I need to do. I work up a smile as if my intentions have been discovered, my desires revealed, and I make my way over to him and place my wrists on his shoulders. His eyes are pale brown, the same as always, despite the age they carry. With my fingers I trace out the shape of his cheekbone, the wee dent on the bridge of his nose from where his brother whacked him with a stick as a child. And the tiny etchings and weatherings, the mature grain of him. Yes, it's him. All him.

"Ok," I say. "You caught me red-handed. To hell with that young scoundrel. Let's enjoy this time together." I give him a kiss. "And I reckon you have something in mind, don't you?"

His smile deepens, his eyes dropping ever so slightly—almost embarrassed to admit the very thing I'm hoping for.

"I think we should follow his advice," he says. "Or half of it, anyway, and go to Mid Argyll."

Déjà vu with the same car hire, the same packed bags, the same tools nicked from my parents' garden shed. This time, though, I'm behind the wheel, because his hands started shaking as we were loading the boot. Tremors with an electric look to them. Too much coffee, he said, laughing it off. I managed to quell the unease that came over me before starting the engine, surprised by his lack of protest as I took the motorway across to Glasgow and then north along the edge of Loch Lomond with empty campgrounds and stretches of open water, sunlight shattering out of broken clouds. We twist and turn through a village and then rise along the steep flanks of a mountain with safety nets strung out to catch falling rocks, nooks and crevices spilling with recent rains. The glen folded bright green below. At the pass a sign tells us to rest and be thankful, but we do neither. Aaron wants to find the socket for the stone we unearthed last week, and he'll dig like a gopher until he finds it. As the road runs down toward Loch Fyne he tells me why. Fertility. The cairns shaped like wombs. Alignments reconciling solar and lunar calendrics. A fusion of astronomy and landscape.

"Like Maeshowe," I say.

"That's just the midwinter sunset."

"No kidding. You used it to seduce me, remember?"

"Seduce?"

"A golden shaft of sunlight," I say, mimicking his low American register, "penetrates the mound, bringing ecstasy and renewal."

He breaks into laughter. "I think I was smoother than that."

"Apparently," I say, "because here I am."

He rests a hand snugly on my leg. "What I meant was that Maeshowe corresponds only with the sun. Of course the Stones of Stenness and Ring of Brodgar are nearby, which might have had all sorts of alignments with the moon. Or none at all."

"What do you mean, *might have had*? Can't you tell?"

"Some of the stones toppled over, others were shifted and rearranged. One was actually struck by lightning, I think. Anyway, you can't assume the positions are accurate. At Maeshowe, though, the alignment is obviously solar. And I thought Inbhir would be the same until I realised—spoiler alert—that the passage is aligned with a notch in the mountains too far south of the summer solstice to be meaningful."

"Is that a technical term?"

"What?"

"Spoiler alert."

There are a couple of beats as he takes it in. Then he does a slow smile. "It just means I'm about to give something away."

"A forewarning, in other words."

"Exactly."

Yes, I think, as the road begins curling around the inlets of Loch Fyne, the gravel beaches heaped with the muck of low tide, debris and litter caught in thick brown mats of kelp. A forewarning. How appropriate.

"But of course that won't stop the Druids from crawling out of the woodwork. Go ahead, ask me about the Druids."

"Let's skip that one."

He shrugs. "You'll find out soon enough. And go easy on him when he tells you about it, ok? He might seem cocky, but he's looking for reassurance. He's directing his first dig, and it's a heavy responsibility, especially for someone so young, and suddenly he's dealing with a bunch of Hells Angels in bathrobes."

I look away from the road long enough to give him a flat expression.

"Anyway," he says, "I'm thinking Inbhir might have something to do with the moon rising on the summer solstice. A lunar event on a solar occasion. It's possible that the site reconciles the two in some way."

"What about the winter?"

"What about it?"

"You keep mentioning summer, but winter is the best time to see the moon. All that darkness? The long nights?"

He falls silent as we carry on along the slopes and bends in the road.

"Lorna," he says suddenly.

I shoot him a look. "What?"

"On Guy Fawkes Night they drank beers and watched . . ."

I glance over to find him with his hands on the dashboard, his eyes unnaturally wide—a seizure, I think, as I pull over and come to a halt on a muddy track, my stomach hot with panic.

"Are you having a—"

He takes my face in his hands and kisses me like we've been apart for centuries.

"You're a genius," he says.

I ease back into my seat, flushed with utter relief. "Not a genius," I say, recovering myself. "Just smart."

"The full moon. That's what she said. On Guy Fawkes Night. And they could see it from the forecourt at Inbhir."

"Who's *they*?"

"That notch in the mountains, the one the Druids got so excited about, is actually where the moon rises on Samhain. And I'll bet that stone we uncovered originally faced Inbhir and beyond it to that peak in the northwest. Where the moon sets."

"The moon setting where? And who told you this?"

"Lorna. At the pub. They went back to pick up the litter but couldn't find it because they didn't have a torch and the full moon was disappearing behind that peak. That's what she said. Which means the two sites mark the rising and setting of the full moon on Samhain during a lunar maximum year."

"Samhain," I say, groping to remember it—a Scottish holiday of yore which my Yank boyfriend knows better than I do. Boyfriend and husband. "Isn't that a festival of the dead?"

"The first of November. Halfway between the equinox and the solstice. The beginning of winter, according to the old agricultural calendar. The Celtic calendar. Marked by the sun. And during a lunar maximum year it must correspond with a full moon. A coincidence of lunar and solar events, reconciled at Inbhir."

And? I want to ask. What does it all mean? But he seems euphoric with the revelation. Don't spoil it. We need him in good spirits, don't we, Vi? Yes. I can sense her approval.

We gaze through the windscreen at a pasture where sheep are

grazing, lambs trying to hide beneath their mothers' flanks with newborn tails flipping madly. A lorry passes on the road behind us. Then I put the car in gear and back out onto the tarmac.

We pass through a couple of mini-roundabouts to the High Street of Lochgilphead, the grey ranks low and quiet, shopfronts catching a sudden release of daylight on the horizon. With a jolt I notice the hotel where he's staying—the familiar name and number tacked up by the phone. I glance over at him for a reaction, a sense of alarm or caution, but he seems at ease, or perhaps too occupied with the sun and moon to worry about unsettling the past. His past. My future. As we leave town the road runs along the bottom of the glen, the slopes rising up around us. At the sign for the Inbhir B&B he nods and points toward the site, in bold contrast to our previous trip when he seemed to be petrified by the prospect of running into himself. Work is obviously finished for the day. But it's not just the timing, is it? He remembers exactly what he's doing now.

I pull over where we unearthed the stone last week. He hauls himself out and makes his way over to it, still covered with brush and fallen branches. As I help him clear it away I notice a lull in his movements, a leaden delay when lifting the branches. A pinched look to his eyes. I try to share his enthusiasm as he steps back and looks at it between his spread hands like an artist framing a scene—the double spiral clarified by the cleaning he did last week and no doubt all the rain afterward—but I can't help feeling uneasy about the state of him. I bring a knuckle to my lips. Do you know this part, Vi? Do you know what happens next?

I lean against him and give him a nudge. "You all right?"

"Never better."

I hold him against me, tears boiling up in my eyes, but I manage to hide it, reminding myself his condition may have nothing to do with time travel. It may be stress. Or an illness that can be treated. We'll see a doctor. We'll take care of it.

After fetching the spade and shovel, he paces out a patch of ground for us to search. I pull on gloves, wriggling my fingers inside the heavy fabric. And I hesitate in the windy silence. There's a scent of moisture in the air. Muddy fields. The mottled shadows of rain passing in the distance. I glance over at Aaron, already digging intently. What is it? Nothing. Or nothing yet. So I blink it away and lean down and start stripping turf, attentive and diligent, earning some credit that I intend to spend soon enough.

"What were you playing?" he asks.

I lift my head. "Sorry?"

"At Tolbooth."

There's something odd about his interest, something needful, but I smile despite myself. "The Passacaglia and Fugue in C minor."

"And you nailed it."

"Yep, I nailed it. The whole thing fell into place. Now if I could only find a way to make it work on the piano."

He gives me a nonplussed look.

"The transcription. Bach wrote it for organ, so you have to make changes to play it on the piano. Sacrifices. This version isn't working, though. At least for me. I mean it's correct, technically speaking. I can't argue with any of the individual notes."

"But?"

I shrug. "It might be something beyond that one piece of music. Maybe we need another revolution. Something equivalent to the whole Baroque movement."

He goes back to digging. "I thought that happened already. In the twentieth century. All that atonal stuff."

"That was reaction, not invention. The Baroque is when instrumental music came into being. It's when tonality as we know it really developed. Major and minor scales. Functional harmony. Equal-tempered tuning—which was a mixed blessing, in my opinion, but there you have it. A great leap. A fundamental innovation. A revolution. I'm surprised she never told you that."

Or maybe I'm not surprised. She might have had a reason for holding it back. Which would be what, exactly? Let me in on it, Vi.

"Yet another revolution," he says, "started by men in wigs and tights."

"This is more than politics, dear. This is pitch and rhythm. Melody and harmony and texture. This is the stuff of life." I pause, thinking perhaps I should leave it at that, but all this bloody digging for stone symbols is giving me a hard-nosed attitude with something to say for a change. "In the Baroque all these things became developed enough to make music that was satisfying in and of itself, without the need for lyrics. That's why you have all those instrumental forms and procedures. Those apparently fussy structures. Without words you've got to organise the music in a way that makes sense. You've got to have motifs that people can recognise. Sectional relationships. A basic shape. An architecture."

"You're lecturing," he says, with a wry and slightly patronizing tone, it seems to me, as if I could do with a pat on the head. Oh so wise and mature, this one is.

"Well then, I hope you're taking notes." I draw my wrist across my cheek, trying to avoid the rough fabric of the glove. "It wasn't just a single voice and melody fused together. Those early motets and madrigals, the Gregorian Chant—all that monophonic stuff fell by the wayside. Instead they developed a homophonic texture with one voice predominating and others accompanying. And that's where a lot of those instrumental forms came from, actually. The melodies were originally voices, interacting with each other and changing because of that interaction. Baroque composers developed all those things through opera and then fed them back in, using those same instrumental forms in the operas themselves, so you might get something like a passacaglia running underneath a character's voice as she sings."

He raises his head, staring into a thought.

"What?" I ask.

His expression seems to hang in freefall until he forces it into an ordinary composure, a plain face. "Nothing," he says, stooping over to work again.

"Aaron."

He pauses before rearing up in gentle surrender. "Like 'Dido's Lament,'" he says.

"Yes. That's a good example. A really good example." I watch him as he carries on digging. "I'm glad she's taught you something over the last eighteen years."

And that's it—yes, that's how it comes to me. Quite a thing to learn what I'm going say to him this far in advance. But why? What's it all about? A live telecast for me, a rerun for you, Vi. For future reference I could use a hint or two, yeah? Maybe you could tie a note to his leg?

I mull it over, shadowboxing in my head until he shouts and I make my way over to him. Scraping at the dirt, he reveals what he pronounces to be the missing socket. I peer down at it—nothing but a subtle difference in soil colour, it seems to me, but then as my gaze adjusts I realise he's probably right. We lean together in sweaty gratitude, him for his reasons and me for mine, with the wind blowing steadily, the day shedding its final light. Now. The timing is right.

"I have a suggestion for dinner," I say.

"Name it."

"Wherever you're eating tonight."

"Wherever I'm . . ." His arm falls from my shoulders. "Please tell me that's a joke."

I turn toward him. "It's a pub, right? A cheap restaurant. With her."

It sinks in slowly. Too slowly. Because he's faking it. Because he knows exactly what I mean as soon as I've said it.

"I told you it's just professional interest. A harmless flirtation."

"If it's harmless," I say, "then you won't mind me seeing it."

A long moment passes with breezes swishing through distant

trees, the air around us oddly still. I fold my arms. I should feel guilty about this premeditated plan, about springing it on him this way, but everything has become coaxial and recursive, impossible to blame one person for this without blaming the other for that.

"It's too risky. Way too risky."

"Then just tell me where you are, and I'll go there by myself. No harm in that, right? After all, you invited me."

He pinches the bridge of his nose and shuts his eyes. "No, Violet."

"Then I'll find you somehow. I'll ambush you at your hotel. I saw it as we were driving through town. Or maybe you're staying at hers tonight?"

He walks several paces away and then swivels toward me with a finger raised for a reprimand that doesn't come. He recognises the look on my face—a look he has seen quite often, I would guess, over the past eighteen years. A resignation comes into his shoulders, a slight lowering of his head. He lets out a slow breath through his nostrils. I can see him thinking about it, imagining it, letting it happen. Come on, Vi. Help me here. Make him think it's his destiny. Convince him it's his fate.

"If I take you there . . ." he says at last.

I raise my hand. "I promise not to interfere."

He rubs his forehead like a besieged captain. And that's when it begins to make sense. I was asking for a hint when you already sent one, didn't you, Vi? A message from you, the woman left behind. "Dido's Lament."

The pub has lozenged windows and dark timbers and fishing nets, a ship's compass with its needle missing, a throttle set to full by the empty fireplace. The kind of place Aaron has always liked. There's a pleasant murmur with roughly half the tables occupied. He lurks in the back room while I order drinks from a barman with a mustache and the pleasantly rounded features of a seal. Carrying back the pints, though, I discover not just a single room but several stretching back through as many buildings, each chamber dimmer than the previous one, until I find him against the far wall with nary a soul in sight.

I plop down next to him. "Great hiding spot, but doesn't this defeat the purpose?"

In response he lifts an arm and aims straight ahead of him.

I lean over to see an empty table in the front room, framed by the multiple doorways. The contrast in lighting makes it perfect. We're invisible to anyone at the other end.

I pull back and look at him. "You remember where you sat?"

"Where I always sat," he says, lifting his glass, "with excavation notes or just a good old-fashioned newspaper. I didn't really notice these back rooms until about halfway through the summer."

I raise my pint. "Well then, I guess we're safe till July."

We touch glasses and drink. A silence falls between us. I look around at the navigational maps on the walls, the candleholders encrusted with ancient drippings. And an upright piano in the corner. Sheet music on the rack, keys exposed. Drastically out of tune, I reckon, but the alternative is a quiet play of nerves.

"How long have we got?" I ask.

He blinks at me.

"You seem to know the exact timing of everything," I say. "When do they get here?"

"Dusk."

"What?"

He shrugs tightly. "That's what I remember. The colour of the sky as I arrived. And the feeling that came with it. It was a great day of discovery."

I peer out the window at fading daylight, then look back at him sitting with his arms folded like he's waiting at A&E for surgery results. I get up and make my way over to the piano and recognize the score before I even sit down. "Scotland the Brave." I hit middle C and listen to the timbre, then make my way up the scale. Not bad. Not bad at all. It just might help.

"What are you doing?" he asks

"Passing the time."

"Maybe you could pass it more quietly."

With one hand still on the keys I twist around and play the descending line from "Dido's Lament." "Is that quiet enough?"

His face registers just a trace of unrest before he looks away. Gotcha. I turn back and start poking around a bit, going back to Bach and a few motifs from the passacaglia, the countersubject of the fugue I played this morning, a few other stretches with my eyes closed, recalling the sheet music and pondering what it is about the piano transcription, not the notes but something off in the sound. The temperament. Then I feel him standing behind me.

"Have a seat," I say, sliding over.

He sets his pint on the windowsill and sits, weary and washed out, a gnarl of emotion in there, and I'm sorry for what I've done, whatever it is.

"Has she taught you at all?"

He hesitates. "Moonlight Sonata."

"Oh, leave off."

"I requested something famous. And just the left hand. But I had to use both hands, of course, while she did all that stuff over there," he says, motioning toward the treble keys on my end. "I had trouble keeping time—I mean, lining up my notes with hers, so she ended up matching mine instead."

I give him a coy look. "No Bach?"

He gives me a bug-eyed look of disbelief. Which confirms what I thought earlier. Why such a prude, Vi? Why not share the love?

I reach over and play the first eight notes of the ostinato. "Repeat that," I tell him. He eyes me as if suspecting a trick of some kind. I urge him on with a nod. His rough hand hovers between the F and G, but otherwise keeps time. "Good," I tell him. "Now add this." And with a couple more passes he manages to put it together, the entire ground bass more or less intact. This seems like the only way to hold us together just now, to settle into ourselves. "Keep it going," I say. "Keep it natural. This is something you already know." And when I start playing some of the higher notes he falls out of step only slightly, recovering with the next cycle. I skip across the variations, shifting and reversing and improvising all over the place, and of course some of the keys are stiff and there's an E flat/D sharp buzzing like a bumblebee, but I love matching my treble to his bass, my sound to his sense.

"Is this really the way it goes?" he asks, glancing up from the keys.

"Oh no. I'm making it up as we go along."

It becomes jazzy for a bit, a touch burlesque. And then, what the hell, I hit the sustain pedal and give it a romantic nuance. What do you think, Vi? Is this too freewheeling for you?

The bass disappears as he stands suddenly and makes his way over to the window. I come over next to him, cheek to cheek, and watch the younger Aaron striding across the car park all scrubbed and fresh and a bit too smart-casual for the occasion. I pull back and get a jolt of double vision as the Aaron next to me does the same, as if reacting to his own heat. Then we make our way back over to our seats against the wall.

It's nothing remarkable at first—the young Aaron alone with his ale and his crumpled log book, as he calls it, thumbing the pages, occasionally adding a few notes. His expression taking on a certain transparency as he works, his musings and puzzlings on display. I glance at his counterpart by my side. He seems vexed by the sight of his younger self. As if he shouldn't exist. I ask him how he feels. No reply. I nudge him.

He blinks at me. "What?"

"Are you all right?"

"I thought it would be different. Like seeing myself on TV." He turns back to the younger Aaron again and shakes his head. "But I can feel him now."

I watch him carefully. "What do you mean?"

"His breath. His pulse. His heartbeat. Interfering with mine."

I reach over and press my finger to the inside of his wrist. "Your pulse seems elevated. But I think—I think it's just stress, Ok? This isn't something that happens every day. I mean, psychologically . . ."

"I was ready for this. In my head, at least. But it's physical. Something inside me. Like feedback."

I look over at his younger self, flipping obliviously through his notebook, sipping from his pint. "He seems fine," I say.

But then I see her—yes, that must be her standing at his table, because he nearly leaps to his feet. What is he saying? I pick out hints of his voice only faintly in the murmur, the slur of sound. And then they leave the frame. His notebook and pint glass still on the table. Because he's buying her a drink. How nice. No etiquette or refinements, but a primitive grace that's hard to resist, isn't it, Vi, even after all these years? And when they return I really wish I could hear the conversation, and at the same time I don't because they're leaning over his pages now, their foreheads nearly touching, her hair a rich, complicated brown released to its full length, though I bet she wears it up on the site, a withheld temptation. Her snug blouse with the flattering neckline. A bit thick through the midriff, but otherwise nothing out of place. She's his type.

He touches her forearm a couple of times. She laughs and nods.

"I wonder if he's telling her about Maeshowe," I say with a nasty oily sheen in my voice that I relish and regret at the same time.

He swivels toward me. "Shell middens. Votary deposits. Potsherds. You think that's romantic stuff?"

"She bloody well does. And by the looks of it, so do you."

Fickle. Yes, that's it. And that has always been it, hasn't it, Vi? When it comes to women he's like a dog that loves whatever is in front of him. How easily swayed and flattered. How careless of another's love. I let out a hard breath.

"You wanted this," he says. "You demanded it. Now watch it happen. They'll flirt shamelessly, but they won't have sex tonight. Happy now?"

He folds his arms and sits back.

I turn away. Flirt? Such a thin word for what they're doing. And then it catches me—a serrated edge in what he said. I turn back. "Tonight. You said you weren't going to have sex *tonight*."

He remains rigid and silent.

"Answer me."

"You're asking the wrong guy. Take it up with that hotshot over there."

But when I look again I can't see him through my tears.

CHAPTER TWELVE

1988/2006

Violet's lament. The next day she wandered around the site and pretended not to nurse her injury while I took measurements and pretended not to be responsible for it. I had explained and apologised from every angle I knew while at the same time trying not to incriminate myself, or incriminate him—a strategy I regretted almost immediately, but I couldn't backtrack. My words in the back room of the pub couldn't be unsaid any more than his behaviour in the front room could be undone. Eventually I had tried to make amends by telling her about Verdun, the blow-by-blow conversation as I remembered it, emphasising her wisdom and emotional insight and how much she meant to me, our enduring love. A high-risk manoeuvre on my part. But it didn't seem to matter. She had simply listened in glum silence before dropping off to sleep. And now? She was tepid and withdrawn, not avoiding my touch but not seeking it either. His fault. My fault. Then and there, here and now, assuming there was a difference.

From the excavated socket I looked through the tree cover toward Inbhir, using the chapel's steeple as a marker. I was trying not to imagine him there with Siobhan. I was trying to keep my head clear. I was aiming toward that spot on the horizon where Lorna had seen the full moon set on Guy Fawkes Night—or, technically speaking, would see it in 18.6 years—but it was roughly ten degrees too far south. It didn't line up. The configurations weren't right. No matter how I leaned or craned or tilted my head to accommodate irregularities in the stone's setting, or maybe, I thought, incorrect estimates of Inbhir's location through the trees, the two sites seemed to point nowhere. Turning in the opposite direction to imagine what an observer might see from Inbhir itself, I found an unhelpful jumble of hills. The sightline ignored a prominent ridge roughly fifteen degrees to the east and even the run of the glen itself where it twisted toward Lochgilphead. No doubt the sun and moon and perhaps certain stars appeared there at various times of year, but that would be the case no matter where it pointed. Maybe it wasn't connected to Inbhir. Maybe it was an outlier of a stone row or some other monument complex that no longer existed. Or maybe it had been the most important marker in the glen. There was no way to tell anymore. How did it work? What did it mean? Its surroundings had been scrubbed away over the last five thousand years to leave it alone, without purpose or direction, indicating nothing. The bare bones of those structures revealed less about ancient beliefs than they did about mine—my own sense of purpose in the workings of earth and sea and sky. Which was what? What did I want from all this?

I crouched down and placed my hand on the fallen stone. The packed sediments, the layered muds and minerals. The cold results. Set upright in its original position, the larger spiral would have faced southeast while the other would have pointed at a right angle to the northeast—again, toward nothing. I studied the design. The calligraphy of the cosmos. I traced the worn etching outward from the central cup and over to the side where it curled inward again. Something about the corner, the change in direction. The feeling of crossing a threshold. A transition between different planes. Or was that my own agenda—the coal cellar, the time portal messing with my head? I ran my finger back the other way. No. It went beyond my agenda. There was a process in the carving. An action of some kind. It was not only expressing something but also participating in it. Then and there, here and now. Assuming there was a difference.

I stood upright and inhaled a scent of peaty moisture, a suggestion of brine in the air. Tilled fields. Churned mud. Sheep shit. That fresh and complicated sensation of life again, of messy growth. The days were getting longer. I pulled out the camera and went back to the exposed socket and shot a roll of film, using a glove instead of a ranging rod to indicate the scale, until I had captured not only the space itself but also enough context to situate it within the premises of the petrol station in 2006. Of course, the petrol station would be delayed or possibly not built at all once this new stone was officially discovered. As the sun broke through the clouds I realised Fergus McCain would hate me even more in this timeline than he did in the other. I found myself smiling with a petty and grandiose notion that his hatred was a good sign. It meant I was doing something right.

I removed the film and held it between my thumb and forefinger like a vial of some precious elixir before putting it in my pocket. Then I covered up all the excavation work with thick brush and made my way over to Violet, who was leaning against the car with her arms crossed and her glossy raven hair going awry in the breeze, eyes lowered gravely. Her expression turned inward, weighed down. His behaviour in the pub had unsettled her, of course. I had been prepared for that. But I hadn't been prepared for how it would unsettle me.

You're supposed to laugh at yourself in a funhouse mirror—at your grotesque distortions, your slidings and swellings into unreal shape—but I couldn't blame his appearance on warped glass. In fact, clarity was the problem. The corrective lenses of space and time. Their behaviour in the front room had been a mockery of everything I remembered—Siobhan trying to come off as all flippant and casual despite that full charge of emotion in her eyes, the obvious gleamings of her heart. Why didn't he see that? He was taking her at face value, at body value. Idiot. It would all come to light in Edinburgh two weeks later—or two weeks from now—at the Beltane celebration on Calton Hill. The drums and dancing. The May Queen with her White Women. The fire-twirling sprites clad in little more than body paint. It was supposed to be a friendly rendezvous with Siobhan and a cousin of hers, plus Violet and me, but neither the cousin nor Violet had showed up as planned, and the two of us ended up swigging from a whisky flask among the flames. Later we found ourselves at the door of the missing cousin's flat, where the key was stashed under the mat, and Siobhan realised she was out of town, actually; they must have got their dates crossed. The delicious, sexy heat of Siobhan, leaning in close until I seemed to be out of my own skin and into hers, and with my unreasonable resentment at Violet for not being there—her unexplained absence as if it just didn't matter to her, yet I was supposed to obey the rules anyway—I enjoyed the transgression as much as the sex itself until waking the next morning to painful sunlight. Just a bit of fun, wasn't it, Siobhan said, running a finger down my bare chest. A fling. Recreation. A break from my boyfriend and your wife, right? Because you're not going anywhere from that, are you. You're not leaving the love of your life. A slogan she had repeated throughout the summer at Inbhir—those moments she turned to me as if giving in to a craving or a bad habit. I'm leaving my door unlocked tonight. Let's have a bit of fun. It doesn't mean anything. Like cheating on a diet. Like a midnight snack.

She had meant the opposite, of course. I knew that now. And I wanted to tell him the plain truth in retrospect, to stop everything before it happened, to haul him out of the pub and pound some sense into him, come what may, if not for the deep cellular trauma that had taken hold of me, every pulse coming with a backbeat, every breath an added pressure, my impressions split and double-barrelled at once.

"We can't be together at the same time," I said.

Violet halted with the door open. She pulled a strand of hair away from her face, but it blew back instantly, resuming its wrongful place.

"It makes a certain kind of sense," I added. "Like magnets with the same polarity, pushing each other apart."

"Except it didn't bother him," she said.

"You mean it didn't *seem* to bother him. I'm just more sensitive to it."

She touched the back of her wrist to her forehead. "Or you might not belong in this world. A fish out of water. Have you thought of that?"

"I'm adapting."

"Oh really?" She squared up to me. "Is that why you're so knackered and wobbly? Why your hands keep shaking? Why you practically had a seizure when we were loading the car yesterday? It's not getting better. It's getting worse. This world is rejecting you like a transplanted organ."

"I thought I was a fish out of water."

She flared a look of irritation at me, a silent warning to back off, but I could feel a resolution taking shape within her, and I didn't want it to harden.

"Maybe I look worse," I said, "but I feel better. Every day. Every hour. I'm improving. I'm adjusting. It's just taking a lot out of me. Ok?"

She nodded at the pocket where I had stuck the film canister. "And what about your precious photos? Your archaeology porn?"

"Now hang on."

"All your grand digging and discovery. Your stupid obsessions. And once again, some young woman to fuck on the side. How convenient."

"I made an awful mistake with Siobhan. But you—"

"Oh, leave off. You want that stone over there? Well, you've got it. Congratulations. Now let's go."

I blocked her from getting into the car. "He's a selfish fool."

"Him? It's you, Aaron."

"It *was* me. I'm different now."

She drew back and gave me a surgical look. "Are you?"

Before I could reply she brushed past me and got into the car, leaving me with the sound of lambs bleating tenderly beyond the trees, warblers chittering merrily in the sun. The days were getting longer, but all the certainty I had cherished about this world was fading. I was making it different. I was making it a mess.

While she drove I looked out at the farms and Forestry plantations and, on the slope below, a village spread along the shoreline. There was weather clotted high in the bare hills, a crinkled glare of sunlight on Loch Fyne. Fusions of sea and sky. I glanced over at the taut expression on her face and could see hints of the older Violet—or maybe her style rather than her substance. What would she say now? No doubt she'd sound out my deeper motivations, taking me to task for some aspect of this whole scenario I'd overlooked. But ultra-Violet didn't work that way. No. She liked to bunker down and take shots at me until she decided I'd had enough. She liked to dig in. And I always had to wait her out. Maybe it was unfair to expect anything else from her at her age. Did she understand any of this? Did she know why I was here?

"Once upon a time," I said, "there were some young apes who stood upright. They grew taller and smarter. They spread through the rain forests and mountain ranges until they reached the tundras of Europe, evolving into various species along the way. One group in particular, *Homo sapiens*, developed a flair for language and imaginative thinking. They made tools. They played with fire. They painted caves and expressed things beyond themselves. And they displaced all the others. They came to dominate. As the tundras melted they made their way across a land bridge exposed by the retreating ice, following wild herds and fresh vegetation. Rising sea levels isolated them after that, but they weren't too concerned. The fish and game were plentiful here, the edible plants within reach. It required only what it had required over the last three million years. Mobility. Not an aimless wandering but instead a careful tracking of their lifeblood in the land. Of course it involved returning to certain locations periodically, so there was a pattern to it. But there were always shifts and variations. New places. New methods. Their existence was flexible and dynamic. They found a home in every glen, a temple in every cliff—although such distinctions didn't exist. Spiritual practices were inseparable from economic ones. Subsistence and worship were the same. Consciousness was in the tides, in the clouds, in the bloomings and migrations, in the shapes and textures of everything around them. It was both idyllic and hellish. It was raw and brutal and sharp and alive."

I glanced over at her in plain daylight as she drove with both hands on the wheel, her features lifted smooth and her eyes bright with some kind of emotion she didn't want to release. Or couldn't.

"Until we started to dig. A simple thing. After all, it was a skill we already used in our daily lives for minor tasks like securing posts and putting out fires. But now it took place in a more organised and deliberate way. On a larger scale. We used it to control where food would grow and where animals would graze. And little by little we began planting instead of gathering, herding instead of hunting. We became sedentary. We became settled. We learned how to transform the land to suit our needs, or what we thought were our needs. We marked our territory with pits and ditches, channels and furrows, timbers and large stones arranged into permanent structures. We manufactured beliefs with monuments instead of discovering them in caves and cliffs. We transformed raw materials into artificial objects. We turned clay into pottery for storing food, rough stone into polished axes to clear the forests, metal into sophisticated tools and weapons. We buried the dead separately instead of mingled together in communal sites, their bones no longer circulating freely among the living. And over time we developed elaborate methods of cultivation with even firmer boundaries—field systems, enclosed settlements—until the landscape became domesticated. Restricted. Divided. Fixed. Three million years of mobility and open-ended existence brought to a halt. Think of what that first hole cost us. Think of all that has been lost."

I turned to her again. "And sometimes you want it back. Do you understand?"

Her lips were folded tight. Her eyes were wet. Sunlight was blistering through the trees behind her. The world was rushing hard and fast. She gave me a glance that staked my heart and then looked back at the road and we didn't speak after that.

We hit a long reel of traffic at the southern end of Loch Lomond, passing through several roundabouts until we reached some suburban precincts with neighbourhoods branching off here and there, a muddled frontage of shops. Space and light came to us on the bridge over the River Clyde. The wide artery through the heart of Glasgow. Then the bland central belt to Edinburgh. I thought she would return the car immediately, but she parked in front of our building, pulling her bag from the backseat, and glanced back at me before we climbed the stairs to our empty flat. We peeled off our clothes in the bedroom. Then she reached out and clutched my face and kissed me with breathless force as I swung her onto the bed for the straight taste and smell of her, without lotions or creams or fixatives or the brass tacks of age. The sex was blunt and fast, a hot running charge, her voice in my ear crying out. When it was over I lifted myself off her and rolled away to my side of the bed, with my pillow, my table, my clock.

She was sobbing, curled on her side. I enclosed her from behind and murmured in her ear. Eventually she turned and buried her wet face in my chest, all hot and gamey. She breathed and wept. Over her shoulder I watched the sky play itself out. I could feel her pulse, her blood and fire. All the madness of another human body against mine. Eventually she drew away and wiped her eyes and sat up, reaching for her robe—the robe, I realised, that would be torn up for dusting rags in a few years' time.

It was Friday here but it was Wednesday there. I had work tomorrow. And it was my night with the children. A sleepover at Daddy's new digs. But there was no way I could tell her that.

"You're going to be late," she said.

I watched her for a moment. She stood with her back to me and her arms folded, gazing out the window with what seemed like terrible knowledge.

"For what?" I asked.

She didn't reply. The world ticked. The clouds parted, but there was a sadness to the sun.

I swung my feet to the floor and stood up. "I'm starting a new project this week. An excavation. Out of town. I don't know when I can come back."

There was a silence as I dressed. I glanced over, hoping to see her involved in a simple task of some kind, straightening the duvet or picking up her clothes, but she still seemed to be dwelling inside herself. I went over and put my arms around her. In the window's reflection I saw that her eyes were closed. I turned her toward me. She rested her forehead against my collarbone. No, I thought. This isn't the end. This is just another day for us. One of many.

"I left the receipt on the kitchen counter," I said, "for the film I dropped off at the shop. Those photos of the spiral. They'll be ready tomorrow."

It seemed important to enlist her in this errand. To involve her in some kind of plan for our future. Touching a finger to her chin, I lifted her face, all puckered and reddened from crying.

"You'll pick it up for me, like I asked?"

"I won't forget," she said.

Her kiss was full of internal resistance, trapped heat and pressure. I stepped back reluctantly, wanting to set her right before I left, but knowing I could only make it worse. She needed time to absorb everything that had happened. And I certainly could give her that.

At the doorway I turned. "I'm coming back."

She gave me a faint and rueful smile.

Don't argue, I thought. Don't try to prove it ahead of time. Just make it happen. Make it real. Make it right.

I descended the stair, past the sound of televised gunshots coming through Mrs McNaught's door, and emerged onto the stoop. Sun again, clouds again. Wind and trees and aerials and autos, parking meters and cobblestones. The awkward hair, the outmoded clothes. Eighteen years. I took hold of the railing as the tremors returned, the world fracturing and flashing out. I breathed. Was I really a fish out of water, a rejected heart or lung? No. It was the other way around. I was the one on the receiving end. And I was accepting this world. I was taking it in. I was making it mine.

At the coal cellar I remembered the film in my pocket—the fresh roll I had just shot that morning—and stood with the door open and the darkness awaiting me, the dank smell of my underground future. I held the canister in my hand. What did I want from all this? I wanted to give Inbhir meaning beyond the worn placards of a mediocre site. I wanted to vindicate the deep work of my life. And I wanted to prevent that fling with Siobhan from happening. I knew that now. That's why I was here. To save myself. To save both of us. To make everything right.

The film wouldn't survive the passage, so I reached inside the threshold to wedge it in place—for safekeeping, I thought, until I came back and dropped it off at the photo shop. I brushed off my hands. I took a breath. Then I closed the door behind me and stepped into the shearing convulsion of there and then, here and now, assuming there was a difference.

Five days later I was working with Victoria and the two Alans on the slope above the quarry. It was the last week of November. The sun was blotted behind a scrim of cloud. The days were getting shorter—bland and still and frigid—and despite my thermal layers I felt a chill whenever I stopped, but that happened only when I checked to see how the others were doing. We were stripping off the remaining turf and topsoil, working our way down to the base until the entire outcrop was exposed, at which point we would start cleaning. But something had already caught my eye. I was kneeling on a pad with my face nearly touching the gummy residue on the rock's surface, scrubbing at some impacted grime with a paintbrush when I heard Graeme's voice behind me. I sat back on my heels. There he was, hatless, gloveless, his grey hair whipped into spindrift, his skin bright with cold—all giving the impression of an unplanned jaunt up the slope, which I had known was coming ever since he mentioned visiting his aunt in Oban over the weekend. He spent a few minutes hunkered over a patch cleared by the first Alan—or Alan A, as we called him—broad and beefy and bald as an egg, always ready for a light moment, an easy laugh. I couldn't hear the words between them but I caught their music. Graeme's growl of laughter.

I rose to my feet as he approached. "I'm shocked—*shocked*—to see you here."

He grinned. "There's a man who sees right through me."

"Only because you're transparent."

He leaned over the nearest carving and then leaned back, angling his head to catch it in the dull light. "Aye, lovely. Warts and all." He nodded at the exposure by my feet. "I don't reckon you've found something else there?"

"Too early to tell. I'm already beginning to think I underestimated this job. Give me a few more people."

"I'll give you a few more days."

I nodded up at the sky. "You call these days?"

"None of your whingeing now."

"Winter," I said, blotting my forehead with my sleeve even though the real sweat was between my shoulder blades, where it would chill me the most. "It's nice if you're a vampire. Or a mole."

He folded down to his knees and braced himself with his free hand as he ran his fingers over the carving. "Except it's not winter yet," he said.

"I'm on the Celtic calendar."

He flicked his rough eyebrows at me. "Gone native, have you?

"Seriously, Graeme, I need a larger crew."

"Seriously, Aaron, there's none to be had."

As he ratcheted himself up like a drawbridge I understood with a terrible tinge why he was doing less fieldwork these days. It wasn't just his administrative load that had become heavier. It was his body, his bones. I looked down the slope toward the dormant farm, the river shrouded in bare trees along the floor of the glen. Then I knelt and went back to work, letting him think it was the manpower issue on my mind. After a minute or two I glanced up. His hands were shoved in the pockets of his anorak, his lips pursed in a way that meant he had a tale to tell. I wondered if he would get frostbite waiting for me to take the bait.

"*Tempus fugit.* You'll catch your death, as my mother would say."

"Guess what my dear old auntie had on her bookshelf?"

"Books?"

"Aye, Mr Celt, but the devil is in the details."

To my surprise he strolled off, wandering around the perimeter and chatting with the others as he surveyed the work in progress. I assumed he would come back to reveal the great mystery, but sometime later I lifted my head to see him making his way down the slope. I leaned back. Then I stood with my hands on my hips, breath pluming as his car disappeared down the road to Kilmichael. You bastard, I thought. What am I supposed to make of that?

I asked the second Alan, or Alan B, if Graeme had said anything about coming back. He set down a wheelbarrow near me and shook his head. Pale brown in complexion and mood, he had tentative eyes and spoke with great reluctance, habitually clearing his throat. Now, though, he simply glanced at his watch and raised his eyebrows. A request for lunch.

Our small crew meant there was none of the usual infrastructure—the trailer with electric kettle and microwave and space heater—but Lorna had persuaded granddaddy Fergus to provide shelter during our breaks, which satisfied Health and Safety regulations. I called lunch but didn't go with them. A warm lull wasn't what I wanted. The day was too short, my curiosity too sharp, my drive too deep—all of which I recognized now because Violet had brought it up repeatedly over the years—so I pulled an energy bar from my rucksack and tore open the wrapping with my teeth. I understood the implications of drinking coffee straight from the thermos. It earned me a working man's wink from Alan A, a pale glance from Alan B, and a blatant frown of concern from Victoria before she followed them down the slope to Fergus's den. Poor bloke, her expression said. Look what happens when your marriage falls apart.

It didn't seem to be falling apart so much as running down. After coming back through the coal cellar and suffering my usual spasms on the paving stones last week, I had gone to my flat for a quick shower and shave before picking up the children. There had been a brief exchange with the older Violet, frictionless and neutral, like coworkers handing off documents. I had accepted delivery of two overnight bags along with updates of food preferences and various other flight checks. And that was it. You know the routine, she had said to me, without the slightest trace of irony. Yes, I had thought, looking straight into her eyes. And maybe that's the problem.

I had child-proofed the flat before their arrival, raising all precious objects to higher elevations, but Jamie still managed to blow a lightbulb by rapid-firing the switch on a floor lamp while Tessa took great delight in the large spigot that filled the tub much faster than the drain could empty it. At one point she gave me a look, it seemed, of innocent knowing, sensing something that she didn't understand. Were my excursions through the coal cellar affecting them somehow? Was I putting them at risk? Ok, I admitted it. I was gambling with my health, which was an irresponsible thing for a father to do. And the implications of it needled away at me as I fed them and bathed them, as I read them stories with happy endings in the double bed where they dropped off snoring like badgers and I watched them with a knot in my throat. I was insane and selfish—no different from that young swaggering hotshot I had seen in the pub the previous night. I wasn't learning from past mistakes but simply repeating them on a different scale. On a worse scale. Look at them, I thought, as they wheezed and snorted, recharging for another day of life. Your children. From you and Violet together. Make it right again. Repair the damage between you by preventing it from happening in the first place.

And so the next morning, during a catastrophic breakfast and a trail of tears to nursery, I began planning my next trip through the coal cellar until it lifted my spirits enough to carry me into the office, seemingly restored by my time off. No doubt I looked truer than I felt, but it got me through the next two days at my desk and a weekend full of preparations that included online searches for astronomical phenomena that might possibly account for Inbhir's alignment with the new stone. Instead of solid answers, though, the internet offered the usual assortment of space aliens who had designed the Great Pyramids, carved the statues on Easter Island, and built the entire city of Atlantis before mysteriously turning into absentee landlords. Tough luck. We could have used their help with the new Scottish Parliament. And then staring at my blank ceiling in the middle of the night, exhausted yet awake, I remembered ultra-Violet's point about the lunar and menstrual cycles: in a world without artificial light, a full moon coincided with ovulation. Fertility. And what else? Ebb tide. Low seas. Furthermore the moon must have dominated those long winter nights—especially when it appeared and disappeared at those extreme ends of the horizon during a lunar maximum, beyond the sun's reach. Yes, it must have been momentous. Full moon. Full circle. Time and tide. Sex and death in the sky.

I got up and opened my laptop and found my way into some academic archives. One source explained how the interplay between the monthly north-south movements of the moon, the time of year, and the lunar phase cycle all resulted in the rising and setting positions of successive full moons progressing up and down the eastern and western horizons over the course of the year, with the one closest to the winter solstice the farthest north. Ok. Closest to the winter solstice. But not on the solstice itself. Samhain was more likely. It made the most sense. From a farmer's perspective it was a much more realistic marker of winter. Although I could check almanacs and other records, I knew the only way to find out if it really corresponded with Inbhir was to be there when it happened. And the opportunity to do that had already passed. I'd have to hang around for another 18.6 years. I rubbed my face. I touched my fingers to my burning eyes. When I opened them again advertisements were blinking at me from the sidebars on my screen. I switched my laptop off.

It all required a geological lifespan, a glacial patience. I had neither. Instead I had only the calculation and deduction, the hard grind of science, to understand that Earth's orbit wavered above and below the plane it shared with the sun every 100,000 years, the shape of the orbit went from circular to elliptical and back again every 96,000 years, the tilt of our axis increased and decreased within a range of nearly three degrees every 41,000 years, and the direction of the axis itself wobbled like a gyroscope every 27,000 years while the orbit as a whole shifted like a hula hoop spinning around a child's foot every 105,000 years. The cycles clashed and overlapped. They reinforced and cancelled each other out. They changed the length and strength of the seasons. They brought ages of fire and ice. And when the latest rash of glaciers melted 10,000 years ago, causing sea levels to rise, the northern landscape sprung up as it was released from all that frozen weight. The two processes worked in tandem, washing shorelines over and then lifting them away again, beyond the ocean's reach. Raised beaches were still scattered along the headlands of Scotland. Shells could be found beneath the soil of coastal farms. Was it noticeable within a single person's lifespan? Could people have recognised the land emerging from the sea? The knowledge could have been

passed down through the generations, the waterlines acknowl-
edged like stretchmarks in the slow creation of the land. As if the
ocean was slowly giving birth to the world.

I straightened up with a crimp in my back and a pall of sweat
in my thermals, not to mention a touch of indigestion from eating
and working at the same time. As the crew returned from lunch
I stood breathing in the dull cold. The light was colourless, the
heather a bloodless brown. I could hear the River Add running
at the bottom of the slope. The quarry had been silent, I realised,
since we arrived.

"A broken part," Victoria said, "on the something-or-other."

"Fergus must be delighted," I said.

Alan A winked at me. "Bonkers, mate. Good thing you weren't
there."

I smiled despite myself. With any luck this missing part would
give us relative peace and quiet until Friday, which was when the
excavation was originally supposed to end. And those extra days
Graeme had promised would put us to the middle of next week. I
thought about working alone through the weekend, but I needed
to go back to her. Ultra-Violet.

I sat back on my heels. This weekend was Tessa's birthday. It hit
me with a rude jolt. Between the party on Saturday and the drive
back here on Sunday afternoon I wouldn't be able to get away. If
only I could split myself in two for both duty and desire. But the
coal cellar didn't work that way. I was still caught in my life, present and past. I cursed, feeling a backwash of guilt.

We filled buckets. We hauled dirt. We exposed more of the outcrop to find a few additional motifs that kept me running hot. But
a few hours later, with the sun dropping behind the hills and the
light depressed, we staked pins and strung orange mesh around
the site and packed up our tools and overturned the wheelbarrows
and headed down the slope. And when I opened the door of the
van I saw something on the driver's seat. An old hardcover book,
bare and plain, without a dust jacket.

"Yours?" I asked Victoria.

She peered at it and shook her head. I held it up for the two Alans to see in the back seat. They shrugged.

I switched on the interior light to read the title, but the lettering on the spine was faded. I opened it to the title page. "*The Solar Inheritance of Ancient Monuments*, by Mr John Smith." I felt a smile come over my face. "Graeme, you sneaky bastard."

"Something we should know?" Alan A said.

"Something I should, apparently." I flipped a few pages, savouring the loose binding, the musty odour, the library flavour, and saw that it had been published at the end of the nineteenth century. I handed it over to Victoria as I turned the ignition. "Written when your namesake was still on the throne. God save the queen."

There was a brief discussion about the shortage of Alans and Aarons in the royal lineage, the surplus of Henrys and Richards, and then a drowsy silence as I drove to the self-catered cottage we were sharing for the duration of the dig. We had the usual rota for the bathroom, the communal lasagne while the football match played. Afterward Victoria settled down to knit an honest-to-goodness scarf for her daughter while the two Alans and I hashed out precisely why we disliked a certain English team that was on the pitch. We listened to the taunts and cheers of the crowd, the incantations sung out en masse, sectarian, tribal, taking on greater meaning sung together than they would have done alone.

Eventually I kicked back and opened the book, expecting to dispense with it in a few minutes, but instead found myself following the author's disquisition, written in a tone of quiet confidence, about connections between the motifs in the rock carvings and two basic designs that appeared in later Pictish and Celtic stonework. The interlinked cup-and-ring marks bore a telling resemblance, Mr Smith said, to the Pictish "dumbbell," which consisted of two discs connected by concave lines to form an hourglass shape. In addition, the linked triple spirals on the kerbstones of Newgrange, which faced the midwinter sunrise, seemed to be a precursor to the spiralling arms of the triskelion—a motif that became prevalent throughout the Iron Age and early history. A continuity, he said, could be found in each of these resemblances, a belief system inferred along very broad lines. And what was this belief system?

In answer he went to the Roman Empire, when Constantine made Christianity the official religion over various solar cults that included Sol Invictus, the Unconquered Sun. As the Son replaced the Sun, he took on some of his predecessor's symbolism in the form of a halo around his head and rays of light emanating from the centre of the cross that killed him. Truth and light. I knew this part of the story, of course. The mergers and acquisitions of Christianity, assimilating pagan beliefs as it spread. Christmas was grafted onto Saturnalia, Easter onto various rites of Spring. But when it reached the British Isles, Mr Smith pointed out, it found expression not in carvings of Christ but in those Pictish dumbbells and Celtic triskelions, combined at the centre of the cross. And exactly why would this be the case? Why would these symbols have lent themselves so readily to this religion which itself had associations with the sun?

The two Alans yelped and cursed as someone scored a goal. I raised my eyes to the replay, the stadium still roaring as the ball sailed in slow-motion past the outstretched arms of the goalkeeper. But I could barely register what was happening. An assembly of thoughts was taking hold of me. I sat apparently dumbstruck by the goal when it was actually the book I was holding in my hands. The triskelions and double discs must have been brought together because they had similar meanings—or similar enough for a shotgun wedding—that were also compatible with a sunny Christianity. Yes. The spirals were solar symbols. The notion had a circumstantial weight. And it felt right. Furthermore the dumbbell—the two discs joined by a pair of lines—could be the sun. But why two discs instead of one?

I consulted the good book again. Those two discs, Mr Smith said, depicted the sun at opposite ends of the year, six months apart. And with an illustration of the Pictish double disc carved on a standing stone in the northwest Highlands, he directed my attention to two crescent shapes within those circles representing the first and last phases of the moon, effectively bringing the solar and the lunar together. An etching known as a Z-rod, which cut through the centre of the symbol, was in fact similar to the design on star maps showing the sun's path through the sky from one solstice to another. He also pointed out that modern astronomy used a double disc symbol with a connecting rod to represent instances in which the sun and moon are setting directly opposite each other and thus said to be in opposition. Even the notations of our rational science, he said, show the inheritance of the cup-and-ring marks, which might be said with reasonable certainty to be associated with similar phenomena. Similar phenomena, I thought. Yes. And these phenomena were—

"The farther sun and the holy coast," I said.

I raised my head when I realised I had spoken. The two Alans were watching me. Victoria had lifted her eyes from her knitting, her fingers still working automatically. I glanced at the screen and saw that it was halftime.

"The time is nigh, my brethren."

"Amen," Alan A said, eager for a diversion.

"I have seen the error of my ways." I rose from my chair. "And I repent.

"You speak the truth."

I held the book aloft in both hands. "The truth within, my brother."

"Amen," Alan A said again.

I turned to Alan B, who took it up with uncharacteristic volume. "Amen."

Then I looked at Victoria, who peered back at me over her glasses until she understood. "Amen," she said.

Opening the book with theatrical care, I held up one of the illustrations. "Now I say to you, my brethren, behold the Shandwick Stone. Behold its spiiiiiirals and swiiiiiirls." I felt the flush of my native accent, the southern-preacher highlights coming into bloom. "Do you see?"

"I see."

"And do you see the holy circles enclosing them?"

"I do."

"Solar symbolism! The Sun is the Son. Pictish potatoes. Irish eyes. I say po-tay-toe, you say po-tah-toe. Let me see your hands, my brethren."

The Alans obliged immediately and Victoria with a slight delay as she set down her knitting.

"Higher!" I shouted. And as their hands rose higher I was touched with an uncanny hope. "Hallelujah!"

I felt the force of my original voice. The Blue Ridge smoke and fire, the Appalachian thunder. I felt it full in the throat and hot in the chest. I felt the truth inside. The carvings were made on outcrops and standing stones and chambered cairns, reconciling the sun and the moon, the earth and the sky—just as the dead circulated as bones among the living. Yes, I thought. The dead are alive.

"And the Devil," I said, "is in the details. Now is the time to cast him out."

Alan A brought his hands down slightly and started waving me aside. "Och, halftime's over."

I looked over my shoulder. "So it is, my brethren. The endtime has begun."

I had no reason for what I did a few days later—on St Andrew's Day, in fact. I must have dreamt about the carvings. I must have dreamt about the sun. By that point we had stripped the outcrop all the way down to the base and cleaned the surface with soft brushes. The motif I had noticed on the first morning turned out to be a cup with seven concentric rings, while several others were linked with grooves into complex motifs and others fed into natural clefts in the rock. Now and then I would stand back to take them in at various angles and distances and ranges of light. Victoria and the two Alans did the same. Even without the double spiral it would have been a remarkable find—but the double spiral was there, its line running over a cleavage plane in some kind of correspondence with the pattern on the new stone I had uncovered in 1988, which brought both a thrill and a galling heat because I couldn't verify it or even declare it in this time and place. Fergus the Destroyer.

Normally we would use clear plastic overlays to trace the motifs, but since the scale of the outcrop made that impossible even with Graeme's extended deadline we set up a laser scanner to make an electronic map of the whole thing. Perched on a tripod with its viewfinder and plastic gills, the device silently worked its magic while we drank from our thermoses. There would be enough time, I knew, to cut a small trench, maybe two-by-four metres directly in front of the double spiral to search for evidence of activity. Evidence that would merit extending the length of the excavation. Yes, there was more here. But what? And where? I wanted to find it. I needed to find it. Not a solution but a piecing together of something that would bring resolution and understanding, that would keep me intact. An ancient puzzle was more meaningful than a modern one for that very reason, exposing something within ourselves across millennia even if we weren't the same selves then or now and I would solve it, I thought. Goddamn, I will work it out.

As Victoria checked the scanner's progress I found myself staring at a mound about a hundred metres down the slope. It seemed obvious to me then. And it seemed absurd that I hadn't noticed before. I strolled over to it and began pacing its contours, glancing back at the exposed carvings and then down along the vast conduit of the glen toward the sea beyond the folded hills. The sky seemed to be full of squid's ink. There was a threatening scent of moisture in the air. I went down on my knees with a trowel to uncover what I knew was there.

I could see a cup mark almost as soon as I peeled back the turf, the indentation visible in the faecal exposure of mud and slugs and soil roots. And then rings or perhaps the grooves of a spiral as I brushed it all away. I widened the patch, ripping up clumps of growth, grunting and grinning and breathing and sweating and aching until I leaned up and saw the other members of the crew looking at me. I must have been smiling because they were smiling back.

"Come on in," I said. "The water's fine."

They joined me with looks of sly misbehaviour, glancing down at the quarry as if the headmaster lived there. Alan A handed me a pad to kneel on and asked the question that needed to be asked—namely, what authorisation or permission might we need, after the fact, for digging outside the planned area.

"This is the planned area," I said.

"Oh really?" Victoria let out a full laugh.

"Really," I said, quoting a phrase I had included in the initial survey as well as the tender itself, albeit in fine print. "The boundaries of the site may be determined according to the discretion of the excavation director."

"Well done, you."

We worked in silence for a while, exposing a few square metres by the time the rain started. Alan B ran up the slope and packed the scanner into its waterproof case just as the first downpour came hissing through the trees behind us, slapping the stone with cold heavy drops, hailstones coming soon afterward. I felt a harsh chill on my neck. My hands went dead inside my gloves. I looked over at the others, who were working without complaint, and then I straightened up into it, the storm and stress, the gothic mass of cloud. The rock at my feet was crying black tears.

I ordered a retreat to Fergus's shack. In a matter of minutes we overturned the buckets and wheelbarrows and otherwise battened down the hatches and made our way down the slope toward the badlands of the quarry with its frames and skeletal masses all motionless. Puddles were forming in the gravel, streams running past the stolid dump trucks. We came into the office shining wet, our rainproof shells blotted to every inch of our bodies, shaking off like dogs. Lorna cranked the space heater. And to my surprise, Fergus rose from his scrabbled chair and set the kettle to boil. There were schematics and charts spread across his desk as if he were a ship's captain plotting his course. Or the destruction of enemy vessels. So many stones to grind up, so little time. As we sat on the sunken sofa, reasonably dry with hot mugs in our hands, Lorna opened a box of biscuits. We ate. We drank. We tried to be merry, raising our mugs in honour of St Andrew's Day. I felt a raw pleasure in my skin, a hard knowledge in my bones.

"How's it going up there?" Lorna asked, turning her head slightly in the direction of the site. She was wearing an oversized fleece and a thin wool cap with her hair frizzed out to resemble a badminton birdie.

"Wet is how it's going," Alan A said, with his usual wink.

"Yous find more carvings then?"

"Hard to tell," I said, feeling the vague perimeter of Fergus's attention shifting toward me even though he didn't actually look up from his paperwork. "We'll need to clean the surfaces to be sure."

"On that new patch as well?"

I feigned a look of incomprehension even though I knew, with an instinctive dread, exactly what she was talking about.

"The new one," she added, "going just now. I saw yous digging away."

"Oh," I said. "That? It's the same site, really. Though it probably looks different when you're down here." I lifted my mug and blew at it, hoping it was a decent poker face.

Fergus's head came up with a Svengali glare. "What's this?"

"An additional panel," I said. "On an additional rock. That's all."

He drew his arms back and straightened. "Ya bastard, ya." He said it quietly, almost a whisper.

Lorna seemed to crystallize. The others took an extra interest in their tea, sipping with lowered eyes. But I met his glare. I welcomed it. Yes, I thought. Let's do it now.

"You say that," I said, "like I'm the one who carved it. It's an artefact, Fergus. Ancient heritage. Lost property."

"Aye," he said, stabbing the desk with his finger, "and here's the lost property right enough."

"I'm sorry it's eating into your profits."

"Profits! I'm not North Sea Oil, ya fuck."

"And I'm not Greenpeace trying to save a bunch of gannets. Those carvings are irreplaceable. They don't replenish themselves. Once destroyed, they don't grow back. And by the way, they're part of your own culture."

"Oh, aye. Wise counsel from a Yank." He pointed in the direction of the slope. "Look now, aye? That's dead out there, lad. Dead and gone. We'd be standing in Death Valley without the likes of this quarry."

"So you're an economic powerhouse, valiantly keeping everyone alive."

"Doing my part, lad."

"No doubt. And nothing gets in your way, right?" I gave him a theatrical wink. "Hey, I hear the night watchman at Stonehenge is a heavy sleeper. If you grind up a few of those bluestones I bet nobody will notice. They'd look good on the garden paths around here, don't you think?"

His expression seemed to deepen as he watched me. Victoria's teaspoon clicked in her cup. I could hear the space heater buzzing, the rain needling softly on the roof.

He levelled a finger at me. "You can go back to America."

"And you can go back to the Middle Ages," I said, "you vandal."

"*Aaron*," Victoria said, her voice punching out.

Her expression hit me like a splash of cold water. What was I doing? What was I saying? I leaned back and rubbed my face.

Fergus rose from his desk hard enough to make the chair thump back against the shelving behind him. "Outside," he said.

I got to my feet, holding up a hand in truce. "Don't worry, Fergus. You won't see me in here again."

He started to come around the desk.

Lorna braced herself against the armrests of her chair. "Granddad."

"No offence, Fergus, but I'm not fighting someone twice my age. Got it? If you come at me I'll just run away and we'll both look like idiots while you chase me around the parking lot."

He kept coming. His face full of unsettled scores. I tensed against whatever he was about to do, but he brushed past me in a whiff of sweat and gravel and machine oils, and without grabbing his jacket he pushed the door open and stepped out into the rain. I glanced at the others, returning their worried looks. Then I took a breath and followed, wondering what it would take to get him back inside before he caught pneumonia. His death was not something I wanted to add to my crimes.

The rain was instant karma. I hunched my head down and my shoulders up, feeling a razorous chill, a moisture in my skin and bones. Everything was dripping and gurgling and gushing. I stepped over puddles and followed Fergus along the edge of an artery running like a spillway through the middle of the lot. I almost turned back to fetch my waterproof shell but realised that would be a surrender to whatever challenge Fergus had in mind. The sky still held a dull radiance, but the mercury lights along the quarry's funnels and conveyors had come on.

"Fergus, wait up. This isn't—"

"See that?" he said, raising a blunt finger up the glen.

I looked but didn't see anything besides the blurred hills in the distance, the grey shawls of rain.

"One night when I was a wee boy I thought I was seeing the Devil himself come for me down that road. The tarmac twitching.

Like it was alive, aye? I could hear it all scratchy and clicky. Shiny in the moonlight."

I folded my damp arms, hooding my eyelids against the mizzle.

"Rats," he said. "A whole plague. In those days with all the oats and shaves of corn, they'd be moving from farm to farm all together, taking up the whole road. And the king rat in front. A sight, lad. A sight to see. Big and black. Like a dog. I climbed up the dyke as they passed. Thousands. Would of eaten me alive. Instead they ate my family's crops. A whole year growing rat food, it turned out. All for naught."

I nodded heavily. "Ok, I understand the—"

"Before the dyke," he said, "this whole glen was a drainpipe. The Add breaching and that. September one year when all the oats were bindered and all the shaves and stooks were standing in the fields it happened. Washed out to sea. The whole lot." He threw a hand out. "Gone. When they built the dam at Loch Glashan and the hydro over at Tunns some dinnae like it. Myself, I bought rounds. Now yonder it runs like a burn. Nobody loses. Because of the dam. You reckon there were no carved rocks where they built it? No 'ancient heritage'?"

"I know the deal, Fergus," I said, running a hand over my wet forehead. "I know the score. When some carvings are found they're simply covered up again. Or they're destroyed because they would interfere with the best laid plans of rats and men. One time I crossed a stream and discovered the little bridge over it was actually a standing stone someone had toppled over." I nodded emphatically. "I get it."

Fergus paced a few steps away and gestured again. "That road used to be gravel. And you know where it came from? The cairns. The contractor, when I was a wee boy I watched him drive straight in with his crusher. And then farmers lifting stones from the fields in winter and piling them on afterward, no matter they didn't belong. Cart loads, lad. It's all been mucked. Recycled. Always."

"Not all of it." I gestured up the slope. "Not that. It's probably been covered since the Iron Age."

He stood with his arms at his sides. "You don't catch a thing, do ya?" His voice cracked, hitting a higher register. "It's everywhere, lad. *Everywhere.* We're living in it." His lower lip folded. He took a hard breath. And then I understood why we were out in the muck. It wasn't to test my manhood or to punish me. It was because he didn't want anyone to see him break down.

"You'll find what you need no matter where you dig. So why don't ya dig somewhere else?"

I blinked at him through the rain, trying to gauge it, trying to take it in. We were both soaked and trembling. His cotton work fatigues were matted to his limbs. For the first time I imagined him struggling with his conscience as he destroyed that stone, seeing himself without a choice.

"Fergus," I said. "I'm sorry. Really and truly. But these sites aren't like seashells you can just pick up at the beach. Each one is unique and irreplaceable. You'll have to work around it. And I'll help you in whatever way I can. All right? Now come on, let's go inside before we both get hypothermia."

He didn't move. Then without meeting my eye he turned and trudged toward his car, his boots ploshing. I called to him, but he didn't look back. The engine started and the headlights came to life, tyres spraying mud as he peeled away. And then, as I was heading back toward the office, I halted and looked up the glen, where he had been pointing. The water. The River Add. Without the dam it would have run close to these carvings—and close to Inbhir—before reaching the sea.

"They're connected," I said to the rain. "They're linked. Like the carvings themselves. The two spirals joined together and leading to Moine Mhòr."

The estuary. The threshold between land and sea. Unstable, unsettled. A site of transformation. Tides rising and falling with the phases of the moon, which also marked human fertility. Waterways meshing with land governed by the seasons, by the movements of the sun. The monuments worked together here. They reconciled life and death, time and tide.

I peered up the slope but couldn't see it through the static, through the fullness of the rain. Dig somewhere else? I should have said that to him instead of the other way around. It's a fucking quarry, Fergus. You're the one who can dig anywhere. And the more I thought about Inbhir the more I knew what I would find at the base of those new carvings. If only I had more days, more light, more time. If only I could bring the two worlds together through the coal cellar, I thought, then I could sort out everything, including myself.

I walked toward the office feeling enlightened and darkened, dead and alive. The days were getting longer in the grand scheme of things, in the thin consolation of the mind. When Earth was young it revolved every six hours, but the tidal pull of the moon has been slowing it down ever since. The first terrestrial organisms would have needed a twenty-two-hour clock as they were taking root. And 116 million years from now the days will be almost twenty-five hours long, at which point twelve lunar months will coincide exactly with one solar year. The sun and the moon will be reconciled then. But it won't last. It never does. Earth will keep slowing on its axis until it becomes tidally locked with the sun, making the days identical to years, which is another way of saying they won't begin or end at all. Eternal day on one side of the world, eternal night on the other. Darkness at noon. Midnight sun. By that point, of course, there won't be a need for clocks anymore. And anyway the sun will go supernova soon afterward, reconciling everything once and for all. What gave Earth life will give it death. Our ancestors couldn't have known any of this was coming. And maybe it doesn't mean anything, after all. Maybe it doesn't matter. Or maybe it means everything. Our sense of the future ticking away. A feeling in our bones.

CHAPTER THIRTEEN

2006

Nobody calls it The Clockwork Orange. It's simply the Subway or the Underground, but the clickety-clackety rhythm of the coaches follows me up to the surface with a sense of pendulums and chimes in the nature of things, a cuckoo behind a wee door somewhere, ready to pop out. I need the fresh air on my face. The cold comfort of the street. A recovery of sorts after Jamie clung to my leg for the first time ever when I dropped him off at nursery. Does that mean something or nothing? Sensing Aaron's absence, no doubt, after a rough breakfast with both children literally crying over spilt milk and fighting for the same bloody plate and then finding a damaged heel on one of my shoes as I was herding them out the door. And now? My breath hazing out as I walk nearly a mile through Glasgow's raw blocks to campus turning pale with winter, the slopes drained of colour, the pavements lined with hedges roughed to cartilage and trees stripped to the bone. Students around me bristling with West Coast and Highland voices here in the real Scotland, aye, on St Andrew's Day no less. I'm a troubadour filling in for none other than Hugh Pearson, my former supervisor, a gruff declaimer twice my size who doesn't trust his colleagues to make a decent enough job of it, at least when it comes to Baroque tuning, so I'm an honorary guest lecturer for the purposes of his departmental budget. It's like replacing a tuba with a flute. Now if I can just get through it without cracking up.

I know the building. I know the lecture hall. The tiered seats and media system. It's a single thing I slip into, hand in glove. And as I load my presentation I glance at my watch. The Clockwork Orange because the carriages are painted guess what colour and it follows an orbital route in both directions, clockwise and anti-clockwise, without beginning or end. But nobody actually calls it by its supposed nickname. As if they're afraid of linking Glasgow too closely with the book, the film. A dystopian future. Ultraviolence and all that.

Ultra-Violet.

I halt in the backdraft of it. A coincidence. An accidental rhyme of thought. The room rustling and shifting around me. Everyone shedding layers and unzipping rucksacks and settling into place. The projector coming on with a vague wash of light. Sort it out later, I tell myself. After the fact. Stay here, stay now. I lower my eyes to the image on the console and then glance back at its larger version on the screen. Then I look out at the students scattered across the terraced seating—at the plain fittings of their expressions—and I announce that I am not Dr Pearson, which triggers the mild laugh I need, the release of breath.

"The mystery of Bach's tuning," I say, "will never be solved to everyone's satisfaction. Until recently the received wisdom was that he preferred equal temperament, which had been known for at least a century before his birth. After all, in Book 1 of *The Well-Tempered Clavier* he paired the E-flat minor Prelude with its enharmonic key of D-sharp minor for the Fugue, equating the most tonally remote keys where the flat and sharp tones of the Circle of Fifths overlap directly across from C major at six o'clock. Any performance of this pair would have required these keys to sound identically tuned, implying equal temperament for not only that pair but also others throughout the entire work."

I click to an image of Bach's personal copy of *The Well-Tempered Clavier*. The grand calligraphy of his handwriting, the words diminishing in size, margins narrowing down the page and terminating in a great flourish at the bottom. And above it, what appears to be a scroll or cornice with eleven large loops stretching across the top border.

"Yet the sterility of equal temperament contradicts everything we know about Bach. To cite only one example, he insisted on tuning his own keyboard instruments because, according to his first biographer, he found 'all other tunings unsatisfactory.' Furthermore his own tuning reportedly allowed him to play in all keys and to modulate to the most distant ones almost without listeners noticing, thereby avoiding the very problem that equal temperament was meant to resolve in the first place."

I click on the next slide, showing a close-up of the scroll from the top of the title page.

"I believe this drawing is not simply a decoration or a doodle, but in fact a crucial piece of evidence which has gone unrecognised. To put it plainly, this is a diagram for Bach's specific method of keyboard tuning. These linked spirals serve as a guide for adjusting, or tempering, all twelve pitches to the intervals that Bach preferred. This is the key to all keys. It's the Rosetta Stone. I base this outrageous assertion on historical context gleaned from various documents—translated, incidentally, by Dr Pearson—along with the character of Bach's music itself. I imagine quite a few historians and theorists will suffer fugue states of denial at this little hypothesis of mine, so please don't tell them."

There's a ruffle of quiet amusement through the ranks, some anti-establishment smiles. How much humour comes from honesty? I shuffle pages needlessly. I take a breath. I haven't aired this theory because I'm not ready for reactions outside the classroom. The patronizing dismissals. The scorn. Look at her, improvising not only the cadenza but the entire piece. Look at that clockwork orange.

"Notice the letter C, written by the second loop from the right, which I believe signifies middle C on the keyboard. With that as a starting point, each loop corresponds to a successive pitch along the Circle of Fifths and, furthermore, the spirals within the loops indicate how much each interval should be tempered. The best way to read this is actually by turning it upside down."

I click on the next image, which does exactly that.

"Because that's also the best way to draw it without smudging the ink. And of course, as Bach's students made their own handwritten copies from the source manuscript, they would have turned it upside-down as well. Moving from left to right, then, you have five loops with double spirals outward, followed by three empty loops, and then three loops with single spirals inserted on the downstroke before ending with a casual flourish at the end of the line. Quite simply, it tells you how to tune a harpsichord if you start with the tuning pins set at pure intervals. Again starting on the left-hand side, the loops with double spirals indicate pitches to be tuned slightly flatter than they would sound in the pure position—in other words, by twisting the pin ever so slightly anticlockwise. Now, you're probably wondering how I quantify that slight twist. How many degrees is that? What's the frequency? How many hertz? I have to confess I have no idea, measuring the difference only with those period instruments used by Bach and his contemporaries known as 'ears.'"

Mild laughter.

"Moving onward, the empty loops signify no adjustment, while the single spirals show an averaging of the remaining fifths, which I'll explain in a few minutes. But please understand one thing above all: the proof is in the sound. With this temperament the keyboard becomes alert and alive in the handling of tonal music. It affects your phrasing, your dynamics, your timing, your articulation—everything. As each scale is patterned uniquely it takes on a subtly different expressive character, with a natural beauty in the modulations. Did I say beauty? Please don't tell Dr Pearson. The irregularities are sensed as hardenings or softenings rather than deliberate shifts, offering surprises against expectations. In fact, I would argue that the music actually matches the physical layout of the keyboard not only nowadays but also at the time when Bach was composing, so that, for example, when you stretch your finger to play a sharp or flat, the pitch has a peculiar inflection that distinguishes it from a natural, as if the difference comes from your hand rather than the . . ."

I stare down at my hands, blinking in a sudden heat of understanding. My own momentum rushing past me in the silence. And I turn toward the screen to find it there, writ large. In plain sight. All that strife curling inward on my older self for not warning my younger one about the damage of motherhood even as I realised I couldn't be trusted with it, even as I knew our unborn children would have weighed too little in my hands. And resenting the need for a choice in the first place. Why couldn't the older Violet handle it? Why couldn't I? What was wrong with me that I couldn't reconcile motherhood with livelihood? Why couldn't I find a way to do it all? Every turn of thought spiralling down, not knowing who to blame until I blamed both of us, all of us, together in myself.

I turn back to the class, their expressions full of concern, a sympathetic unease. "Sorry," I manage to say, dropping my gaze to the console. "Technical difficulties."

I make a show of hitting buttons when I'm really looking at my ruined fingers. All that has been lost. But who am I, really, in the end? The young pianist or the middle-aged mother? Neither. Both. Yes, this is the ground bass. This is the key. Here and now, there and then. This is how it goes.

I look up at the lecture hall again. Not an audience but students in the terraced seats. Not a performance but a lesson instead. The most important lesson of all. I take a slow breath, tears burning in my eyes.

"All sorted," I say, lifting my hands like a magician. "Now where was I?"

On the way to London. Or perhaps coming back. Yes, after a weekend of concerts and exhibitions without the children. Nearly a year ago. The juddering motion of the train, the landscape stretching and rolling past. The houses and cubed offices, the pitches and playparks, the dead factories with their broken brick and swathes of countryside in between littered with livestock—the dots and dashes of the world. In fading daylight I catch my own reflection floating among it all until a train bursting in the other direction brings me back to myself. I return to the low-level clamour of the interior, complete with refreshments trolley—Ben Hur, as Aaron calls him, crashing down the aisle in his chariot, looking for stray elbows and knees to crack. I feel strangely low. Am I hungover? A bit too much wine with dinner last night and drunken sex not nearly as fulfilling as our more sober session the night before but happy to have two rounds of it in a single weekend, such is the state of our lives. Compound parenthood. Compound fractures. The wears and tears, the causes and effects. And now we're sitting opposite each other across a table, myself facing forward and Aaron facing back.

"It's just like . . ." he says, but doesn't finish. As if he hadn't meant to speak at all.

An aborted comment about Ben Hur, I think, until I realise he's looking at something behind me. I twist in my seat to find the train swinging in and out of alignment as we pass through a series of junctions, the coaches swivelling and straightening out like segments of a telescope with passengers visible in the aisles, or rather a single aisle, all diminished and interchangeable and meaningless. Or maybe I'm just queasy. Yes, hungover.

I turn back to him. "What?" I ask.

He flicks his eyebrows and gives me a dead wry look. And I understand. And it bothers me that I understand.

"Don't be morbid," I say.

"The bodies could be excarnated at King's Cross—"

"I said don't be morbid."

"And installed in first class. Then shifted gradually through the carriages as they decay, with the bones ending up in Quiet Coach.

It works perfectly. And it's not morbid. It's a process of transformation."

"You mean transportation."

"Same thing. From one world to the next. London to Edinburgh. You start English and end up Scottish."

I give him an indulgent smile and make a show of opening my book.

"What's the difference," he adds, "between a train and a passage grave?"

"Is that a joke?"

"An open question."

"Well, let's see. The difference between them. Aside from the corpses?"

"Including the corpses. They dissolve through the successive chambers and circulate among the living." He gestures at the passing scenery. "And throughout the landscape."

"None for me, thanks."

"Oh really."

"Yes, really. I'd prefer not to dissolve just yet."

"Then what were you doing out there," he says with a trickster grin, "just a few minutes ago?"

I take a moment to absorb that statement—his observation of something felt more than seen—before deciding not to dispute it. "But I'm back now."

"For the time being," he says, nodding out the window at something specific to demonstrate the point.

I follow his gaze to a cemetery bristling with crosses and headstones in ordered ranks. The usual containments of the dead. And then suddenly a neighbourhood with brick houses in identical rows, their back gardens cordoned off in regular plots, cars packed neatly along the street, and the juxtaposition, the stark resemblance of living and dead residences must wash all the colour out of my face because when I turn back he looks at me as if delivering an apology.

"The Neolithic Revolution," he says, "is everywhere."

Of all times and places I recognise it now. His life and death, his sharps and flats. His enharmonics. It's never just a theory with him. It's practice. He needs to play it. He needs to be reborn. Yes, this is what comes to me on The Clockwork Orange among the cat-scratched glass and punished seats, the collateral noise of ring tones and raised voices and squealing brakes that force a closure of all sense into thought and memory. I almost miss my stop. As I make my way through the station, though, I can't help thinking I could stay put and it would come around again like, guess what, clock-work. My fingers twitch and ache while I wait for the train to Edinburgh. A sense of things becoming complete. If we make a circle it doesn't matter where we start. But it matters where we end, doesn't it? Because if the beginning and ending don't meet then it isn't a circle at all.

In the stairwell I come to a halt when I see him on the landing outside our flat. His appearance is sharper and brighter, like an enhanced photo. But he seems uncertain about his own presence.

"Is it the wrong day?" Euan asks. "Or the wrong time?"

"Neither. Both." I shake my head and laugh. "Sorry. I think we got our dates crossed."

I step up to him and smile. He blushes and looks away. His hair is trimmed, his coat buttoned to the top, his trousers pressed. His folder in a waterproof sheath. As if he has come for a recital rather than a lesson. But I'm sure he's not in my diary today as I never schedule a lecture and a lesson back-to-back like this, requiring too much teaching in different frames of mind. I glance at the clock. An hour to spare before I have to fetch the children—a precious gap for some tea and, I realise now, a good cry in the midst of all this loss and gain—but I don't have the heart to turn him away. I put my key in the lock.

"In you come," I say.

He wipes his feet on the mat with extra vigour. I point him toward the sitting room and shed my coat and drop my bag. I switch on the heat, the lights. I put the kettle on. And when I come back he has set out his sheet music and positioned himself at middle C as if taking a compass bearing. He seems at once eager and apologetic. He can't quite meet my eye.

"So how are you getting on with it?" I ask.

His chest rises. "I cheated."

"Sorry?"

He points at his copy of the score, scrawled with his note translations, fingerings, bracketings of repeated passages and even pedal markings, though these are much too sparse. I glance through it all, containing my surprise. I didn't actually recommend this, so he thinks he has broken the rules.

"That's not cheating," I say, leaning back. "That's honest work. Well done, Euan."

A smile breaks across his face. "I really liked this one. Especially with the problem I was having. Memorizing too much. Not looking at the score. That's what you said last time. But this one is too complicated for that, so I've just been learning the easier passages by heart and sometimes I look at the score instead of my hands as I play."

I give him an encouraging nod while secretly acknowledging my mistake. I should have offered more guidance with this piece. "Let's hear it," I say.

Of course it's a simplified and truncated version of that famous first movement, the adagio sostenuto, transcribed from the complicated footing of C sharp minor to E minor, brought down from four sharps to one. He simply couldn't handle all those black keys. It would be like asking him to walk on stilts across a frozen lake—which is Beethoven's agenda, of course, those motifs ruggedly repeating and turning dissonant and threatening to break down before scrabbling toward a resolution across the keys, that tough passionate megalomaniac bastard who laughed at people moved to tears by his playing, who went at his pianos with such force that he needed an assistant to pry the hammers away from the strings during performances, declaring to anyone who questioned him that if you want Herr Mozart you'd better start digging because I am Ludwig van Beethoven.

Euan plays it gently, having some trouble with those first octaves in the left hand but otherwise following the more difficult changes, only a few wobbles here and there, some pauses as he shifts, a wrong note that he misses and then another that he doesn't, backtracking to correct himself. But he gets that tricky bit at the end, with the bars shrunk down to fit the page. I've underestimated him. His only real problem is his pedaling.

"Do you hear that?" I ask.

He halts with his gaze averted, as if listening to something in the street.

"You're keeping the sustain pedal down too long. Try lifting it between bars, or most bars, which correspond to the harmonic changes. Like taking a breath. That way you won't get that resonance—that hum—building up as the piece progresses and turning into dissonance. Because all the notes linger after you play them. Especially the wrong notes. You don't want your mistakes to resonate."

I hesitate at my own words, but then blink it away and give him a smile. His face takes on a grateful flush. And something else. What? I ease back and watch him as he runs through it again, much more haltingly, with more pronounced mistakes, his ears bright red, his expression folded and tensed.

"You're getting it," I say, hoping to ease him down. "Spot on. It's difficult at first, but that's the way with everything. Now let's use it to good advantage, shall we? Those octaves at the beginning—you can lift your hand from each one much sooner and float it over to the next. Like so."

I reach over and show him. He stiffens with attention, as if he might miss some nuance.

"Breathe," he says.

"Sorry?"

"That's the note, right? A breve? I thought you were supposed to hold it the whole time."

"Ah. Yes. Technically speaking. But it only needs to *sound* like you're holding it for the entire bar. That's the advantage of the sustain pedal. Aside from the resonance of course. The lovely blur of the notes."

"It's beautiful," he says, his voice nearly a whisper.

I lift my foot, releasing the piano into silence. For a moment the room takes on the faint rumble of traffic. A siren in the distance, that lonely sound.

"Now give it another go," I say, rising from the bench. "And I'm just going to listen this time." I stand at the window with my mug of tea, looking out at the garden all ribbed bare while he plays. The jerkiness less pronounced now, as I suspected. Less self-conscious if I'm not watching. As a girl I knew I was playing well when Mrs Parker made her way over to the window and corrected my phrasings or articulation without even glancing back, her ears as sharp as flint. I didn't appreciate it at the time. Her balanced engagement, knowing what to assign and how to assign it along with anecdotes to keep that wee canny head of mine interested in the life of the music which in this case is actually entitled Piano Sonata Number 14, quasi una fantasia, in the manner of a fantasy, and not the Moonlight Sonata. A title somebody ascribed to it five years after Ludwig died. After the fact. I halt with the teacup at my lips. Moonlight Sonata. Oh my god.

"Mrs Wringham," he says. "Would you like me to play it again?"

I stand in the hum of the final chord. As he takes his foot off the pedal the world comes back, as full and false as a cinema screen once the film is over. I turn to him, hoping my face doesn't reveal my self-inflicted injury, my subtle shock.

"Euan, I don't remember. . . . Did I choose this piece for you? Or was it something you requested?"

He hesitates as if it might be a trick question. "You picked it out. And asked me if I might like it. If I might be up for a challenge."

I smile at myself. At the trickery of my own mind. "Well done, Euan. You've surpassed yourself."

"Thank you, Mrs Wringham." The words seem to come out by rote, in contrast to what he feels. Like all good etiquette. His mother has taught him well.

"Mrs Wringham," I say, in an easy voice, "is my mother's name. You can call me Violet."

"Violet," he says, his eyes enlarging, his features filling out.

And that's it. After the fact. Always after the fact. How difficult is it to recognise a teenage boy with a crush on his piano teacher? Violet, you bloody stupid girl.

On Saturday Aaron arrives as scheduled, standing uncertainly in the hallway but trying to appear at ease until Tessa comes running and he forgets himself, or maybe remembers himself, in her embrace. As he comes upright and meets my eye his smile takes on a reduced measure, tempered by our complications. Formal or casual, together or apart. What are we? He seems to be watching me for a lead. I put a hand on his forearm and give him a small kiss, resisting an urge for more and less at the same time.

Tessa starts towing him to the kitchen to see the cake, still encased in cardboard, while at the same time Jamie tries to enlist him in some activity with his dinosaurs until a competitive clamour rises up between them and he placates it by bringing in the stegosaurus for a feast, satisfying both at once. They cling to him like groupies as they seem to realise he has been gone only when he comes back—a retroactive trauma. It was worse after that London trip as they were reportedly angels with my parents all weekend and then devils when they saw us again. Or rather, when they saw me again. The Mummy Returns, Aaron said. The Curse of the Mummy. The Mummy's Tomb. How appropriate you married an archaeologist.

"We've got to leave now," I tell him, "if we want to arrive before our guests."

Aaron claps his hands sharply. "Attention!"

Tessa and Jamie snap upright with arms stiff at their sides. A military playtime scenario they've acted out before.

"Who's going to the birthday party at Mongo Bongo?"

Meeeeee, they sing out.

He cups a hand to his ear. "I can't hear yooooooooou."

They scream it again with blunt joy for the troop leader, the sergeant-major of recreation, or so it seems when he isn't the one who feeds them breakfast and gets them dressed every morning. As he ushers them back out to the hallway I linger deliberately with a glass of water so he can be reacquainted with all their friction and fuss as he struggles them into their shoes, their coats. An edge of impatience coming into his voice. But then the door swings open and they're heading down the stairwell with him leading a chant of BYOC, bring your own cake, the only item we need for the venue booked months ago—before it all started, from his perspective. On the pavement I hand over the car key as we strap them in their seats like RAF pilots. And it feels almost normal as we drive together. We look like a family, cohesive and true. No one would know.

As always, the soft play centre is hard to take, with its pits and pendulums of indoor exercise for children on these foul winter days. The vast space is too warm, the light too bleak, the acoustics layered with hellish cryings and screamings and shrillings and canned music pulsing in what would otherwise be blissful gaps. The only situation, aside from airline travel, when I wish I were deaf. Just beyond the entry we find Mum and Dad waiting for us, still wearing their coats, as if needing our help to establish a beachhead on foreign territory. Dad spreads his arms and hoists up the birthday girl, complaining ironically about her weight.

"Good to see you," Mum says, aiming her gaze deliberately at both of us as she pats Aaron on the forearm—not subtle at all,

263

it seems to me, but an instant later I realise that's exactly what she wants. To make a show of endorsing our marriage after all these years of hiding her fear that it wouldn't last. When I told her about the separation my voice didn't crack nearly as much as I had feared, but she quavered like a girl at her first recital. The bleeding emotion in her eyes as she offered support in the form of sewings and darnings, washings and shoppings, the works and days that still seem to equal life in her mind. She gave me a bony hug at the end. And then, in the silence of her kitchen, we both cried.

As we cross the main hangar she chats up Aaron about the latest turns of her gardening committee, the depths of a blood drive. Could he spare a pint for a good cause? I flinch at the thought of it. No doubt she attributes his shadowed and shaky appearance to the troubles between us, a lack of sleep and proper meals with his family. How much can he take? How much can I?

"You bearing up all right?" Dad asks on the other side me, still carrying Tessa in his arms. A casual lilt to his voice, but with a knowing charge.

"Getting on," I say, tending to Jamie wobbling along beside me. And then, wanting to suggest something positive, I glance up again. "We're sorting through things."

He nods firmly, with a firm stretch of the lips. The news seemed to hit him hardest of all, the air leaving his body as he sank into a chair. Not quite admitting to anyone for fear of favouritism how much he enjoys hashing out the workings of ancient humanity with Aaron. Now more than ever I wonder what urges and curiosities of his were diverted into law. And what else? Something about our marriage has always pleased Dad for reasons beyond my happiness, as if it were evidence of something deeper about me or the way he raised me, secretly taking credit for how well it all turned out.

We reach an alcove with a long table and an overseer who greets us with a trolley full of party bags and various tools of fun, twisting balloons into amusing shapes. There's the usual exchange of pleasantries and jokes with other parents as they arrive, some well known to us and others virtual strangers, all touched with delight at legitimately abandoning their children for two hours. And Isobel? As expected, or rather half-expected, I feel a buzz in my pocket—a text apologising for her absence because Maggie is vomiting. Another mishap. Never tragic, but always serious. Our children give us more to talk about while they keep us apart.

Soon enough they all remove their shoes for the great framework of padded rigging—the platforms and catwalks and gantries stretching in every direction, strung with safety netting. Jamie is shunted into the toddler portion with extra bulbous fittings while Tessa and her older friends go scrambling among the more challenging lumps and tumours. They push through a gauntlet of hanging tonsils. They tumble over multi-coloured cysts. And I stand with my arms folded at the entrance to it all.

"Paradise," Aaron says, returning from the counter with a large mug of coffee in one hand and a cup of tea in the other.

I give him a smile as he passes the tea over to me. Despite the rueful slant to his expression he seems relaxed—a sense of outdoor vigour in his stance, a spacing to his limbs that comes from excavations rather than the orderly exertions of the gym. It helps to offset that awful drain on his health, which at any rate will end soon.

"Off you go," Mum says, shooing us with downturned hands. "Your father and I will stand watch."

It isn't necessary, of course. No lifeguards needed under these conditions, but it serves as a good pretext. And it was almost comical, the way she sidetracked Dad when he suggested stopping by the flat so we could all drive over here together. The two of us alone. The reverse of my teenage years when the last thing she wanted was to leave me unsupervised with a member of the opposite sex.

We take seats at an empty table where I set down the large cup of juice Jamie demanded but hasn't touched. There are promotional menus and cartoon adverts accompanied by declarations that no food purchased outside the centre is to be consumed on the premises. The staff, who don't enforce the rule because nobody is brazen enough to break it, are roughly the same age as my students, minimum-waged and armoured in fluorescent t-shirts. Attitudes of bright endurance. No children of their own, of course. That must be how they do it. This is a job for them, underpaid but paid nevertheless.

There's a lull between us as we watch the structure where Tessa and Jamie are playing. Our children. Their painful harrowing dreary exuberance we've made together. This is where love has led us.

"I've been a tough row to hoe over the years," he says, his eyes tracing Tessa's movements. "And so have you. I understand that now. In a new way. But one way or another we need to start over. Or we need to finish." He shifts his gaze to mine. "I'm getting to the point where I need to know which one it is."

I feel a rising heat, a flood into my face but I manage to hold it back. I nod to him in a way he seems to understand. Then I turn back to the wash of commotion. Too much to think and feel at once. A few beats pass.

"The excavation has been extended," he says, giving the words a careful balance as he speaks them. "And I'm driving back tomorrow so I can be on site first thing Monday morning. In case you need to reach me."

And this is how it happens. I play it naturally, without hesitation. "Enjoy the sunrise, then. Assuming you have a chance to stop at Inbhir before work."

He slides me a look as he lifts his coffee cup, not sure whether or not to take it as a joke. Such a basic detail that I've got wrong. "Not this time of year. It's the *summer* sunrise you're thinking of."

"Ah, of course. Right. It's pointing in the wrong direction, isn't it? I guess I had this sentimental notion you might watch the sunrise to mark our anniversary."

His forehead wrinkles up in confusion. Because it hasn't occurred to him. Of course not. Another twist, as it turns out—another note I never realised was mine.

"Our anniversary," I say, "of the night we met. Twenty years ago Monday. Instead of the sunset down the passage at Maeshowe it could be a sunrise at—"

A cry yanks me out of it and I turn to find Jamie at my legs, pointing at his cheek as if his own tears are the cause of his distress. There has been a mishap, it seems, on one of the chutes. Mum and Dad lost on the other side of the apparatus. They probably don't even know he's here. I take him onto my lap for the usual comfort, the usual wee kiss. His face flushed with heat. And without warning he lunges for the juice and spills it in a great slick across the table toward Aaron who lifts his hands like a holdup victim. Then he looks my way without missing a beat.

"Guess what I do for a living?"

The laugh comes ripping through me and I slouch forward with Jamie still on my lap and Aaron's shoulders shaking because he can't contain it either. Everything resounding. Every joy, every mistake. Remember me, but forget my fate.

CHAPTER FOURTEEN

1988/2006

She wasn't there. I stood dripping in the hallway listening to the heavy swish of traffic passing on the street outside until I confused her absence with it—with the rushing sense of loss it left behind. I called her name again. The flat remained silent in grey daylight, the windows weeping with rain. Of course I had always known that if I stopped by without notice she might not be around. But it was Monday, according to my calculations. My younger self should be digging at Inbhir and she should be home by now. I went over to the sitting room, leaving damp footprints on the carpet, and glanced at the clock to find it several hours earlier than expected. Which meant, what? The connection inside the coal cellar was breaking down. As I feared. But the difference was only a few hours, not days. I still had time.

In the bathroom I took off my winter jacket and spread my arms like a bird pulled from an oil slick. After running a towel over my head I gave myself an unpleasant look in the mirror. I had ended up on my hands and knees in a puddle outside the coal cellar with my bones throbbing and every membrane swelled to bursting, wiping the rain from my face as I tried to comprehend how I could have possibly tripped a sprinkler system in there. Out here. Blinking dumbly at the sky, at the April showers that would bring May flowers as my nerves settled down. Eventually I had hauled myself up and climbed the stairs and fitted my key to the main door with the unsteady hand of someone who had spent all day at the pub instead of Mongo Bongo Fun Centre where the true soft play, I now realised, had been in impersonating Tessa and Jamie's harmonious parents.

My fault for believing it—our shared moment at the table, her emotional weathervane swinging in my direction. After driving home together and unloading the gifts and bathing the children and reading them bedtime stories with just a faint notion that I might not be leaving right away or in fact at all that night, she had given me a polite and arid dismissal. Our job was done. She had thanked me for my help. I had told her she was very welcome, the least I could do, before heading out to the sleety dregs of December and straight down to the coal cellar despite the little time I had to spare because even a small dose of Ultra-Violet, I realised, was better than none at all. I had paused only to stash my mobile and wallet in the stonework like a gangster checking his weapons at the door. And now I was here. Now I was now.

On the kitchen table I spotted a newspaper headline about protests to mark the second anniversary of Chernobyl. I flipped it over and checked the date. Wednesday 27 April. Which gave me a hot and queasy jolt. Two days off. Unless I had miscalculated? I counted the dates on my fingers like a child. No. The connection inside the coal cellar was shifting even faster than I had thought. Than I had feared. I rubbed my forehead with a trembling hand. The times were out of joint. And so was I. This jump had hurt more than the others and it suddenly seemed like a good thing that Violet hadn't seen me staggering though the door in this condition.

The rain reared up and gusted, rattling like birdshot against the windowpanes. Was she caught in it? I paced the old tile floor, searching absurdly for some clue to where she might be or when she might be back even though what I really wanted was an emotional checkpoint of some kind, a reassurance or remedy for the way she had been the last time we were together. Ten days ago. Too long. The fateful night of the Beltane was coming up and I needed to warn her about it so she could stop him—or stop me—from having that fling with Siobhan. If Violet had simply shown up as planned then it wouldn't have happened. I was sure of it. And besides, I was overcome with an awful ache for her. I had been denying and evading it. The double impact of travelling back and forth through the coal cellar so quickly seemed a small price to pay for even an hour with her. Except she wasn't here. And I had nearly drowned in a puddle. Ridiculous way to die.

I reached down to remove my shoes and socks. I tugged at the leaden legs of my trousers like stovepipes and shook out my shirt sleeves, still damp at the cuffs. I glanced ruefully at the corner where our tumble dryer would be in 2006. And then I laughed at the plain solution. He wouldn't notice. He would never know. I made my way over to the bedroom and picked out a two-tone shirt that had long since expired, a pair of sweats that had been my favourite before holes had grown large enough to make them flap and flare ridiculously as I walked. But not yet. Not now. I checked myself in Violet's full length mirror. Although the sweats were fine, the shirt was strangely snug in the shoulders and loose in the wrists. It hadn't been that way before. Because I hadn't been that way. I looked like a stage comic doing an impression of myself.

I glanced at the clock again. I looked at the rain again. I wandered over to the bed and took up her pillow and held it gently to my face. Her stale sweet musk. I opened her top drawer and found her silk underwear lodged at the bottom, below the practical cotton, wanting its touch rather than its scent, its associations with her skin, and then I opened her wardrobe and ran my hands over her dresses and blouses and trousers and skirts for the fullness of their suggestions, the absent presence of her. I picked up her shoes with all their rooty residue. I held her empty stockings to my cheek. In that moment it seemed that I had always been alone.

I brought myself out of it with logical considerations, with tactics and strategy. Could I leave her a note? It might do the trick. Or it could backfire, triggering some kind of resentment and

270

thereby causing her to avoid the Beltane out of spite. I rubbed my head. No, I had to talk to her directly. I had to make sure she understood. And in the meantime, what? The photos. In the rainy confusion of my arrival I had forgot to check for the film canister hidden in the stonework—in the same cleft where I had left my mobile and wallet back in 2006—but Violet must have picked up the prints from that first roll. Assuming they turned out. I searched all the drawers again. I rummaged through the debris of her bedside table. I went down the hall and carefully ransacked several centuries' worth of music in the room where I normally tidied up Jamie's toys and then I swept through the kitchen like a health inspector, occasionally pausing at the items that would disappear. They carried not so much memories but sediments of life within them, an everyday wash of feeling I had forgotten or lost. Eventually I ventured over to my study, the least likely place, and gave it a suspicious stare. My desk and bookshelves and paraphernalia. My file cabinets where Tessa's dresser would be.

Nothing. No photos. No Violet. No hope. I sat staring at the wall until the rain slackened and the sky brightened, bringing an enamel to the slate rooftops, the gutters and drainpipes gleaming like exposed ligaments on the stones. I went back to the bedroom and changed back into my soggy clothes with the glum acceptance of what I was—a man having an affair with a woman nearly half his age. The truth was that even if the coal cellar remained stable and I kept zipping back and forth as I had planned, she would find me less viable than the young Aaron as we both aged and he became me. In the end I couldn't compete with myself.

In the stairwell I halted at the sight of Mrs McNaught's open door and reeled back as she appeared on the landing, but her head was canted oddly in my direction. Her milky gaze settled on me. I forced myself forward and gave her a nod as I passed, conveying what I hoped was an impression of civilized urgency—a man hoping to catch a bus, perhaps. Her vision was bad, I told myself. And the stairwell was dim. And furthermore my modeling session at the mirror had emphasized just how different I looked now, especially with this older haircut. She wouldn't recognize me.

"Oh Aaron?" she said.

I stopped halfway down the next flight of stairs with my shoulders scrunched. I turned my head but not my body, showing only my profile.

"Yes?" I said, with a careful neutrality in my voice.

"Would you mind terribly lifting my suitcase for me? I'd prefer to have it waiting on the stoop when the taxi arrives. I would be ever so grateful."

I turned and faced her fully. Her rain scarf was tied over her head, her jacket zipped to her throat. She was gripping the doorframe with a cane hooked over her forearm as if it were an umbrella she might not actually need. Her gaze slightly misaligned with mine—not quite eye-to-eye, I realised. Partly it was her vision but partly it was also that camouflaged pride of hers. Of course. She must have heard me through her ceiling and left her door open in the hope of catching me as I happened by.

No trouble at all, I said, flattening out my accent as I climbed back toward her. American, I told myself. Remember the drawl. But I was already thinking ahead to the sidewalk. The full light of day. She might notice my features more closely out there and realise something was amiss. Or someone else would catch sight of me. Maybe I could pass myself off as my older brother? I followed her warily into her flat. The exposed flagstones, the unpapered walls, the single radiator in each room for those cold winter nights—but now the deep rich seasonings and taperings of the furniture revealed their Georgian pedigree where I had noticed only outdated austerity before. Her wealth unrealised, unspent. I recalled some kind of struggle between her two sons in the aftermath of her death—items not listed in the will and therefore up for grabs.

The suitcase lay flat on her bed, ready to go. I grabbed the handle and nearly fell forward as I lifted it.

Her hands went to her face. "Oh sorry, I meant to warn you."

"No harm done," I said, smiling as I took it more firmly. "I'm used to lifting rocks."

"Coins," she said, with a tone of tart dismissal.

I hesitated, thinking maybe it was an old Scots curse of some kind, but then decided to take it at face value. "Most people pack clothing."

"Not for this journey, I'm afraid. I'm going only as far as the High Street." And then, sensing rather than noticing my confusion as we made our way back down the hallway, she explained. "It is a collection of some value which I am finally liquidating, or rather re-liquidating, as it seems one must trade currency in order to receive more currency these days. I have been told it will pay my living expenses into the twenty-first century, though that gives me cold comfort in light of what it did to Charles."

She tugged the door shut and picked through her keys with trembling hands and engaged the mortise lock with a full twist of her upper body. Her reference to the twenty-first century had been ironic, but it stung the heart. A woman who would reach only the edge of the 1990s.

"I'm sorry," I said. "I mean, about your husband. I never had the pleasure of meeting him."

"Well, it was many years ago. Before your time. And before his time, to be honest. All for some old shillings and guineas. In mint condition, mind. Heaven knows how they survived in such a state down there."

Her words took on a disturbing undertone as we descended the stairs.

"Down there," I repeated.

"In our coal cellar. I always reckoned it was digging in such a foul place that did it. The mould, perhaps. Some kind of fungus."

I halted and turned to her. She came up short and lifted her waterproofed head, her eyes swimming in their lenses.

"Mrs McNaught, I hope you don't mind me asking, but how did your husband die?"

"Oh that's the issue, you see. That's it exactly. He never received a proper diagnosis. His health declined in a matter of weeks and then he suffered a seizure. Or something to that effect. They never quite sorted it out."

The stairwell became airless. For a moment it seemed as if I had lost my lungs. "And this happened," I managed to say, "after he spent a lot of time in the cellar. For these coins. In mint condition. Like new."

She blinked at the oddity of my interest. "That's right."

"Did he ever take anyone with him? Into the cellar, I mean?"

She shook her head with sad gravity. "He always insisted on going it alone. He was quite thorough and meticulous, I must say. He feared someone else would muck it up."

"So he took multiple trips, then?"

"Oh yes. He didn't find them all at once—in a single cache, as it were. He kept discovering wee pockets of them. Just a bit here and there, every few days or so."

I brought my free hand to my brow, knowing the answer before I asked the question. "By any chance are these coins all from the same time period?"

She nodded. "Why, yes. Roughly speaking. Early nineteenth century. When this building was first constructed, as a matter of fact. That was part of the appeal, or so he claimed. Now, Aaron, are you all right?"

"Fine," I said, forcing a pale smile. "Just a bit of fatigue."

We soldiered onward and outward to where the taxi was waiting. I helped her inside and set the precious cargo at her feet. And just before shutting the door I had the sense to ask the crucial question.

"Did Charles pass away in 1969, by any chance?"

She peered at me, dumbstruck. "As a matter of fact he did."

"Late in the year," I said. "November or December."

"Why, yes. How did you know?"

I closed the door and patted the roof. The taxi pulled away. I stood casually in a world where I didn't belong, in the rhythms of its passing traffic, its crisscross of activity and regular life. How did I know? Because it was easy to subtract 18.6 from any given year. As I turned and walked to the wrought iron gate in my soggy clothes I estimated how many cycles poor Charles had traversed all the way back to the early nineteenth century. At least half a dozen. That must have hurt, I thought. Yes, it must have been grueling to stretch that far. And deadly. I tried to take some comfort in that hypothesis—the notion that a shorter time frame wasn't as damaging to my health—as I descended the slick steps. At the bottom I gave the McNaught cellar a morbid glance. It was adjacent to ours. The decrepit doors ranging in either direction taking on a more suggestive and menacing look, like bottomless wells. Did they all connect to the same era with each lunar maximum, or did they branch off separately? I was in no condition to find out.

I pulled the key from my damp pocket and opened the door. Remembering the canister of film, I reached up and found it still wedged in the crack above the lintel. I brushed off the grit and held it in my fist. Did it matter anymore? Was it worth the effort? I backed out with a kind of sluggish determination and followed the streets to a photo shop where the clerk promised best possible results. My hand juddered madly as I took the receipt from him. And as I strolled home the rain returned, windless this time, a soft static in the air. The street globes coming on with an astral glow. Unlocking the coal cellar again, my vision trembled. My nose started to bleed. I pinched my nostrils and tipped my head back and found myself looking at the dark windows of our flat with a sense of quiet terror in every heartbeat and eyeblink, in the ticking of my thought. I brought my head forward. Then I wiped my face and took a deep breath and ran the gauntlet of time.

The next day I slept through my alarm and woke with more blood on the pillow. In the shower I held out my hands and watched them misbehave for a while. I stabilised myself with peppermint tea. I ate fresh fruit and muesli. Nutrition. Health. Then I had a few cups of coffee for good measure. Packing my bag for Mid Argyll, I recalled a dream or half-awake musing in which it seemed to me that Charles hadn't counterbalanced himself, that he hadn't replaced his older self with a younger one or even someone else, another living human, to offset his absence in his original time and place. That might have been the source of the trouble. But still, it seemed obvious now that I couldn't risk even one more trip no matter how much I wanted to prevent Fergus from destroying the stone or my younger self from destroying my marriage. Which meant what? End of story. End of the affair.

I drove with thundering hip-hop and hard rock on the speakers, all guitars and drums and common time, exceeding the speed limit, breaking the law. There was a low shear of sunlight on the motorway toward Glasgow and a westerly gale offering pockets of resistance through the twistings and turnings of the glens as I headed northward but not a single cloud anywhere, it seemed, as if the sky had run out of ammunition. By the time I arrived at the McCain Quarry it was mid-afternoon, which in December meant it was both early and late. The entire valley was in deep shadow with high sheds of blue sky above the darkened hollows and cavities, night-in-day, day-in-night. The parking lot was empty, of course. The machinery dormant. No doubt the crusher was still broken. And it was Sunday. Sun's Day. I climbed up to the site and checked the condition of the carvings even though the protective fencing was undisturbed. Fergus's days of sabotage seemed to be over. I folded my arms and watched the sunset, the sad bleeding of the light.

Exactly twenty years earlier I had been coming back from Orkney in a van with a handful of other archaeology students. At that point I hadn't even known Violet existed. And if someone hadn't spilled a drink across the bar the following night, I still wouldn't know. Maybe. How many times I wondered if I would have noticed her otherwise. Her plain clothing that night. Her lack of makeup. No sexual snag to her. But after the first look I couldn't stop. A sultry variety of expression as she spoke. And that ass, that arse, as she walked away. I laughed out loud and felt a kick in the opposite direction, tit-for-tat, with each intake of breath until my eyes welled up and I couldn't tell one thing from another.

I walked down the slope and drove into town and bought groceries and ate alone in the rented cottage and read through some of the old reports on Inbhir, unsure if I was reviewing or reminiscing, and fell asleep with the lamp in my eyes. The next morning I was awake early. Monday. Moon's Day. Happy Anniversary. All right, I thought. Fine.

The Inbhir Bed and Breakfast was in vacant winter mode. The chapel stood with its bare-knuckled stone. I made my way over to the cairn just becoming visible in the dawn—the broken shapes and nubs, the exposed length of the interior, the vertical ribs of the orthostats—and I stood with my hands on my hips in the forecourt looking toward the petrol station with its square hoodings and surfaces all rimmed in fluorescence. The hills to the south backlit against faint daylight. Then I swivelled and checked the other direction. My estimated alignment in 1988 had been correct. Unfortunately. The orthostats always suggested to me slots or viewing positions, one of which would line up with the new stone, but the two points didn't indicate anything notable. Ordinary horizons. Indistinct features of landscape. They didn't correspond to anything.

I listened to the low rush of water just down the slope. The River Add. The link with Dualaich. I shuffled my feet and watched the glow in the southeast slowly taking on the fullness of day. Too slowly. And it was bright enough to dig now. To hell with sentimental occasions, I thought, walking toward the car. Dualaich was where I needed to be.

Or not. I halted as I saw it happening—the light concentrating at the particular jumble of hills where I had been looking only a minute earlier. I backtracked to the forecourt and positioned myself at the most prominent orthostat and faced the petrol station, watching the sun clear the shoulder of an anonymous hill, coming directly in line with the new stone. And with Inbhir. And with me. I brought both hands to my head and squinted at the sharp exposure of it until I finally had to shut my eyes, clicking through the possibilities, the solar occasions, but there was no solstice, no equinox, no cross-quarter day. And due to precession this wouldn't have been an exact alignment at the time the monument was built. It didn't make any sense. The fourth of December wasn't special to anyone besides Violet and me. It wasn't anything at all.

On my way back to the car I told myself the odds weren't as outrageous as they seemed because there would always be a couple of trees, a couple of houses, a couple of sheep aligned with the sun at any given moment of any given day. So get over it. I put on my seatbelt. I started the engine. Then I switched it off and climbed out, needing something in the other direction. The chapel. And the graves. I paced among the markers all worn and slanted and mismatched, the formal cuts of sandstone and epidiorite with their inscriptions lost to erosion and mossy eczema. A different set of standing stones. They didn't mark the sun or moon. They marked only the bodies beneath them. They referred only to themselves. Straight rows. Christian coordinates. Euclidian geometry. And there was one barely legible: a name and a pair of dates. And a dash between them. A load-bearing hyphen. What's the tensile strength of that line? Something my father would ask. Because that line is your life. That's what it amounts to. That's what you are. Everything you think and feel. Now get over it.

B y the time the crew arrived from Edinburgh I had cleared a trench at the base of the new carvings. Don't ask why, I told Alan B as he knitted his brows. I marked out another rectangle and set them to work. There was the usual banter, the exchange of weekend pleasures or lack thereof, the minor joys and complaints that helped me to feel almost normal. We all expressed gratitude for a clear and still sky. And I kept seeing the sunrise in my thoughts, in the burnt retina of my mind's eye. Which might have been why I didn't notice the first hunk of quartz. Or maybe I was expecting it so naturally that it didn't register. It wasn't until I found a second one that I recognised the first. I sat back on my heels and rubbed it against my trousers until its whiteness shone. I held it up like a trophy.

"We have a winner!" Alan A shouted out.

The troops gathered for admiration. Then they settled around me and began uncovering more. The pieces were knapped or shattered in the upper layers, having the obvious look of deposits, while the deeper ones seemed to be unshaped chunks mixed with rock cobbles, all roughly fist-sized. Structural, I thought. And of course it became less dense as it extended from the outcrop. We set half-meter grids across the trench to record it all. Flakes, scrapers, hammerstones. This wasn't simply functional debris. This was sacred debris. This was a ritual site.

At one point everyone seemed to be gone and then they were back, with Alan B handing me an energy bar and Victoria a thermos full of tea. Drink, she ordered. Eat. Or we all quit.

I obeyed. As the sun declined and my vision blurred—with fatigue, I told myself—we packed up our tools and fenced off the site. We made our way collectively down to the vehicles.

I nodded at Fergus's shack. "How is he?" I asked.

"Sweetness and light," Victoria said, "since the crucial machine part arrived and the crusher will be fixed tomorrow morning. He's gone off to some warehouse to fetch it himself."

"Did you tell him about the quartz?"

Alan A laughed. "We're going to draw straws for that."

"Don't bother," I said. "It's my job. Besides, I need to make amends with him. If possible. But only if you make your pasta bolognese tonight."

Alan A shot me with his finger. "Deal."

They piled into the van bound for the grocery store, joking about the budget for red wine. A minor celebration was in order. I sat in the car for an extra moment with it all lit in my mind. The two sites. The quartz deposits. The carvings. The river. A monument complex I would parse for the pleasure of parsing rather than the result. The lack of fulfilment was the fulfilment itself. Know thyself, Mom would say. Know your life.

On my way back to the rented cottage I saw the access road to Inbhir and thought why not. A moment of reflection. It would help to set everything in context. A coincidental sunrise on the day when I found quartz at Dualaich. One excavation informing the other. It seemed right.

I stood in the forecourt with my hands in my pockets. There was a rural silence. The resolution of the night, stars sharpening above me. And that's when I realised I should have checked the almanac. That's when I realised I should have known, because it appeared so inevitably—the white edge of it, like the tip of a fingernail, emerging behind a hill to the northeast, and then the entire disk rising full and clear, in direct alignment with the entrance to Inbhir's passage. I held out my arms to the moonlight, feeling something restorative in it, something healing, an unreasonable fulfilment in what was happening now, this meaningless significance in earth and sky.

As the others returned to the cottage I met them with news of an emergency in Edinburgh. I couldn't go into any detail but I had to leave immediately. Could Victoria take over while I was away? Yes, of course, of course. There was much nodding and murmuring of concern. There were assurances of careful procedures and updates, for which I thanked them in advance, saying I would be back as soon as possible. Not to worry, they said. It was all in hand.

So this is how it feels to be truly reckless, I thought, driving in the dark. This is what it's like to ride your instincts like a rodeo horse. Inbhir caught the sunrise and the full moonrise, reconciling solar and lunar events on my own private day of reckoning.

The proper response, of course, was to marvel at the odds. It was to have a drink and say to myself, it's not about you. Get over it. Move on. Yeah, yeah, yeah, I chanted to myself as I drove. *Tempus fuck it*. But the carvings at Dualaich had a southwest-northwest orientation that would be significant at a different time of year—say, late April or early May. And, assuming the interval between the two worlds was still the same, then the 4th of December here was the 30th of April there. Which also happened to be the eve of Beltane, a date directly opposed to Samhain on the calendar. Celebrating guess what? Fertility. And my sexual escapade with Siobhan that night. My grip tightened on the steering wheel as I stared into the darkness just beyond the reach of the headlights. One more trip through the coal cellar. I would send Violet to meet my younger self while I went to Dualaich for the moonset and sunrise. Of course I could get online and look up the almanac figures for 1988 to confirm the alignment, but I already knew the answer. I needed to be there. I needed to experience what would happen at the site. It would cure me. It would restore me. It would make everything right.

I stopped for a double shot of espresso and gave myself a pep talk as I followed the motorway into Edinburgh, the roundabouts like sluices and gates and locks. When I reached our neighbourhood I parked in a side lane where I hoped the car wouldn't be noticed and tried to avoid the street lamps as I approached our building. The windows of our sitting room were lit, the children's shutters closed. I thought of them sleeping or, more likely, resisting arrest as Violet read them stories. How many times I had wished for a tranquilizer gun like the manager of a wildlife preserve. Bang bang, good night.

The coal cellar took me with its usual blunt force and spat me out to fading daylight. Dusk. I raised my head to the scent of growth and warmth in the air. Surprisingly warm. And a clear sky. I couldn't see the moon yet, but I didn't need to. As I staggered to my feet and wiped the blood from my nose I realised I hadn't even considered the possibility that it might be raining or overcast, and I climbed the stairs worrying about not my health but how long the good weather would hold. And then I halted on the landing outside our flat. If the dates between the two worlds had wobbled even further, then it wasn't April 30. He might be here. I stared at the door. And then I thought, to hell with it. This is what I need, whatever it is.

She came out of the kitchen wiping her hands on a tea towel and frowning at me—or at him, I realised, until she realised he was me. Her eyes widened. Then she rushed forward and held me. I seemed to fall into her, into everything I had missed.

She drew back and put a hand to my face. "You look like hell."

"And you look like heaven. The makings of a great . . . hey, come on."

Her face was buckling, eyes filling with tears. "You've got to stop doing this."

"It's the last time, I promise. I just need to go to Dualaich."

"Where?"

"Mid Argyll. It's urgent. Please do me a big favour and ask your parents if you can borrow their car tonight."

She lowered her chin and rapped her fist gently against my chest. "You don't understand. I can't just leave. It's Saturday. He's here. I mean, in town. There's an event at Calton Hill—"

"And you're going to meet him there."

She let out a breath. "Well, yeah. That's the plan. But now you're asking me to run off again."

"I'm not asking you to run off. In fact, I want exactly the opposite."

"Sorry?"

"You meet him at the Beltane while I drive to Dualaich."

She pulled back as if I had spit on her. "You're not driving in this condition."

"Don't worry about me. You just show up like you're supposed to."

"While you kill yourself on the motorway? And maybe someone else besides?"

I took both her hands in mine. "I'll be fine."

She shook her head slowly, eyes narrowed hard and firm. "Vi, please."

"If you go, I'm going with you. And I'm driving every inch of those roads."

"What if . . . what if I hitch a ride or pay someone to drive me there? Will that work? That way you can meet him as planned."

She drew a contemplative breath. "I'll go to the Beltane if you return to 2006 immediately. For your sake, yeah?"

I clenched up. "But that's why I need to go there. It's going to help me, repair me somehow. I can feel it. Trust me on this."

"All right, then," she said with a brisk inflection. "Settled. I'm driving you. I'll ring up Mum and beg the car off her."

I stepped away from her and turned to the wall, a pale soothing green that would turn a bright blue later. Could I live with myself if I told her? Could I live with myself if I didn't?

I turned back. "Siobhan is going to be there. And tonight is when . . ."

To my surprise she took it in smoothly, her expression filling with gentle recognition. Her eyelids fell with a slight nod. It was almost beatific.

"Stop him," I said.

"He's already done it."

"No, I've already done it. But there's still a chance for him. For both of you."

"I could prevent him from acting it out. Physically, I mean. But that's all."

"What do you mean, 'that's all'? Doesn't it mean something to you?"

"Not as much as you mean to me."

"Forget me. I'm from La-La Land, remember? A parallel universe. This is the world that counts for you."

"It all counts. It all matters. It's all connected."

I sagged, dropping my head in deep confusion and fatigue. "I can't keep anything straight anymore."

"Oh Aaron, don't you understand?" Her eyes were still red-rimmed, but now they seemed to be touched with a sad wisdom. "It was never straight in the first place."

I told her what had happened at Inbhir. I told her what would happen at Dualaich. There and then, here and now. It was bringing everything together. It was making us right again. She give me a lingering look as she drove—on the road again, in the dark again, with a different hue to the night—and apologised about the photos. They didn't come out, she said. The clerk at the shop had showed her the blank results. I let my head fall back against the seat and closed my eyes. A couple of hours later she woke me as we were entering Lochgilphead so I could direct her to the site, or where the site would be in eighteen years.

The quarry had a youthful appearance—a look of bright industry to its unworn tubes and girders and crushers and scoops, a fresh hue to the paint under the sodium lights, a healthy vigour to the trucks. There weren't any paths or cycling trails yet, so we forded the weeds and tramped through some heather, crackling and snagging our shoelaces as we ascended the slope. The lights of the quarry were doused behind the lower slopes. The moon fierce and bright above us. And full. White light, sharp outlines. Everything visible in the dark. I recognised the shape of the mound. The Sitka saplings that would grow to maturity only to be uprooted by that Halloween gale. There was a lingering warmth in the air. No midges. Too early in the season. We couldn't have asked for a better night, I told her, spreading a blanket on the turf directly over the carvings and motioning for her to sit with me. It was just past midnight. We had some time to kill. On the ground she eased back against me, hooking her arms around my raised knees and feeding me bits of trail mix as we talked. The moon was going where it needed to go. She asked how I was feeling, like a doctor checking my symptoms, and then asked me to describe the sunset and sunrise at Inbhir again. And why, she wondered, did I happen to be there on that particular day? I told her. There was a long silence.

"You can't come here anymore," she said.

"That's what I thought. But if this works—I mean, if my condition improves after tonight—then maybe I can handle a visit to this world once in a while. And maybe you can come to mine."

She sat forward and faced me as if I had touched her with a branding iron.

"A single trip," I said. "It wouldn't be harmful. In fact, I think it would be healthy, in a certain sense."

"Why?" she said in a whisper.

She was staring into me. I thought I was ready for that question, my mind loaded with all kinds of vague and evasive responses to stimulate her curiosity, her sense of adventure, her urge to know the hazards in advance. But I couldn't say anything like that now.

"Because you need to meet her. Or at least see her the way I saw myself at the pub a couple of weeks ago. You should know what you might become."

She rose and stepped back with her hands bridged over her mouth as if considering not simply what I had said but what it implied about everything. Then she turned and went out to the edge of the mound. The moon directly above her. The fierce grit of the stars. All the wild and smooth shapes of the hills in darkness and her own silhouette. All the life she contained. I went up behind her and put my arms around her.

"Come back with me."

"I'm already there."

"She's there. The other Violet. But you're not."

She turned out of my arms and gave me a look as if trying to see all the way to the back of my mind. "Are you sure about that? Or do you think maybe you haven't looked carefully enough?"

I couldn't reply. It was too simple, too complicated. I closed my eyes, feeling something in that moment between us until she took my hand and towed me over to the blanket where we started kissing and stumbling as we worked off our clothes, finding our way down to the ground. There was a bristly mat of heather somewhere under the blanket, the prongs of a fallen branch somewhere else, and it seemed too technical for a while, too mechanical, like the awkward contortions of teenagers in a parked car until she tapped an index finger on my forehead and told me to stop. We lay there breathing for a few moments. I thought it was over, the failure I hated most. But then she eased me onto my back and straddled me, reaching down to touch herself, wriggling her hips, adjusting and experimenting. And with the moon shining behind her she seemed different to me then, but also deeply familiar as I held her thighs in rising ecstatic confusion of younger and older, a silky heat all loose and vibrant as we came at nearly the same time and she seemed to float down over me afterward with her hair settling on my face. I held her naked breathing body, her pulse and heat, her layered life against mine. All of her. All she had been and would be. It wasn't a thought. It wasn't a feeling. It was a knowledge in the blood and bone. Flawed love. And now I accepted it in her, in me, in both of us, all of us, for the first time.

Eventually we put on our clothes and sat huddled together as the sky grew pale. The stars dimmed and the world took shape again. There were chirpings and cheepings around us, a deer detaching itself from the scarp below and making its way toward the river with high leggy steps. The moon fading as it dropped. We were facing the mound where the lower set of carvings was still hidden, covered beneath a woody heather too thick for its own seeds to reach the earth. I remembered the forests had been cleared, taking the insects with them, the leaf moulds no longer digested into fertile nutrients but condensed into rubbery peat instead. The vital predators eliminated, the food chain broken. The glens stripped by grazing. The rivers redirected, the fields reshaped. The ecological cycle altered in a downward spiral of cutting and digging and hunting and herding until it left the land practically sterile with these exposed shoulders and bony flanks, these naked coastlines and dark lochs everywhere. Earth laid bare. The hard beauty of living with the dead. It must have troubled the earliest beatings of the heart, the first gleamings of the mind. And we resolved it in the sky, we resolved it in the land. We set it in stone and we carved it in rock. Did it matter that the solutions changed across time and space? Or was the process of making different solutions the solution itself? Had I been solving the sites, or had they been solving me?

It was happening now. The sun was rising behind us while the moon was setting directly ahead. There was a blue aura coming up from the sea. There was a stillness to the islands in the distance, a scent of brine and kelp and tidal sands. There was a clarity to the hills and glens. There was a composure to the outcroppings and sharp juttings of land. There was growth in the maples and ashes along the river, in the heather and bracken and peat. The sun and the moon facing each other in opposition, in harmony, with the carvings as solid reflections underneath. The land in the sky, the sky in the land. It was mourning and healing at once.

As the moon disappeared below the horizon she turned to me with a bright sad smile, searching my eyes. She said she loved me. I no longer felt the urge to ask which one, the young or the old, because the notion didn't fit anymore. Neither. Both. Here and there, now and then. I said the only thing I could say. I love you too—a constant changing through the ages, it seemed to me, as we walked back to the car holding hands.

CHAPTER FIFTEEN

1988/2006

So that's how it goes. The slow pulse of Sunday morning through the glens and braes and silent towns, the lochs glowing in early daylight. My feet on the pedals. My hands on the wheel. The inevitable surprise at the end—the tonic, the release. It's the coal cellar, he says. The passage between here and there, now and then. I laugh at the ordinary strangeness of it, like the way he appeared to me in the first place, which he also seems to think needs an explanation, running through the possible whys and hows, until he finally trails off. He has his own flat in that world, he says, where we can gather ourselves and sort out a strategy for making it happen. How I might meet her safely. Would I be up for that? Yes, I say, meaning not what he thinks but instead that I've found a way to end it, to mark the ending at last. And what will happen. Our separation. Our estrangement. It needs to be that bad. We park outside our building and follow the steps down into the trench. The row of doors weathered and dull. This is the one, he says, drawing the key from his pocket. Minor, major. This is how it happens. This is how it goes.

The door swings out roughly on its hinges. I look into the dank scrabblings of the interior—the dregs of coal and filth—and give him a doubtful look, but he crosses the threshold and motions me inside, pointing at a scrap of wood by his feet.

"One more step beyond that and . . ." He spreads his fingers. "You're gone."

The cellar turns dim as he tugs the door shut behind us, barred daylight coming through the slats. He fits the key into the lock.

"Hold on," I say. "Do you really have to do that?"

"It's the only way to keep the door closed."

"Then leave the key in it, at least."

His chest fills with resistance.

"I'm feeling a bit claustrophobic. And you said you had another key in 2006, yeah? What if something goes wrong and I get trapped in here?"

"We should take it with us."

"Then let me hold on to it."

Another moment passes as he weighs the hazard, the existential risk.

"Please, Aaron. I'm not Houdini."

He exhales through his nose. Then he passes it over and watches uneasily as I tuck it in my pocket.

"All right." He takes my hand. "Ready?"

I peer into the darkness.

"It'll be fine, I promise."

"Turn this way." I twirl a finger. "Facing me."

"You want me to go backward?"

"I want you in front. Against me. So I can bury my face against your chest as I scream."

He lets out a laugh despite himself and, turning carefully, sets his feet at the invisible threshold. He puts his arms around my waist and gives me an apologetic look. "This is going to hurt."

"I know," I say, raising a hand to his face. "I'm sorry."

I dig hard enough to draw blood. He flinches with a wild shock in his eyes, teetering back.

I put both hands on his chest. "See you later."

"Why did—"

His voice cuts out as I shove him into a soft suction of air, leaving not a sound but a sense behind him. The ache of an empty frame. I sink down with a hand clamped over my mouth as the

289

throbbing mad loss takes hold of me. How long do I stay here? How long sobbing on these grimy stones? The cellar holding my pain like an empty seashell through the years with the key hidden in the storage cupboard, our children present before they are born, the time signatures and movements I follow all the way up to the Halloween storm and then back to that bright young Violet with her nimble hands, undamaged and unhindered in ways she can't understand. I feel something of her now. Yes, I feel her again. Is it possible? Her temperament coming into mine unexpectedly in the dull murk of December, in the Passacaglia and Fugue in C minor transcribed for piano, the intervals true. We're here. We're now. This is how it goes.

The entryphone doesn't buzz this time. It's simply his key in the lock. The click of the latch. The children are busy making a tent with sheets and blankets in Tessa's room down the hall, so they don't hear him. And I don't stop playing. I don't look back. The double fugue of breves and crochets with a countersubject quavering in and out until it all comes together for the C major transformation at the end, leaning into the vibrations, the fullness and weight and power.

I feel him standing behind me as it fades. I wipe my eyes. Then I reach for the cotton balls and hydrogen peroxide before swinging my legs over the bench to face him.

The slash on his cheek. The fresh blood. Haggard and sleepless and unshaven. I forgot how rough he looked at the end.

"You," he says. "Always you."

"My fingernails were clean," I say, motioning for him to sit on the sofa, "but let's not take any chances."

He gestures at the wound in bittersweet recognition, like a chess master recognizing the pattern of his own defeat. "A message to yourself. Through me."

I give him an apologetic smile.

"The whole time," he says. "The *whole time*. Both of you working together, knocking me back and forth like a tennis ball."

"You make it sound like I was in control. It was a foursome, Aaron. A mixed doubles match."

He starts to speak but then falters, grappling with the notion.

"We had affairs on either side," I say. "We told lies. We could compare score cards but let's just call it a draw, shall we? And just in case you think it was all fun and games for me, try to imagine how I've felt lately. Helpless. Resentful. And isolated. My husband is having an affair—with me. It's not exactly something I can share with Isobel over coffee. Meanwhile I had to play my end of it, knowing what you were up to."

He twists slightly, taking aim with his reply. "What *we* were up to. You and me."

"That's what I thought at first. Back then. It seemed like a great idea. Kinda fun, yeah? Sharing you with my older self? But as it drew closer, it began to feel different. Worse. Much worse. I became the other woman despite myself. It wasn't what I thought it would be. I wasn't sharing you. I was losing you. And I couldn't even blame another woman like Siobhan this time."

His face changes as it sinks in. "You've known about that . . ."

"For eighteen years."

"I meant to tell you."

"No, you didn't. I gave you loads of opportunities. But you just wanted to bury it. As if it didn't count for anything. I know you're sorry but you were also a coward."

"I thought you weren't keeping score."

"I'm calling a spade a spade."

His jaw goes rigid. "You could have just come out and said it."

"That I knew about her? It would have been like playing the coda in the middle of the piece. It would have destroyed everything."

He gives me an exasperated look. "This isn't music."

"It's what music comes from."

"That doesn't make any sense."

"To me it does."

"Well that's right nice, Vi." He rubs his forehead. "So this is what, a symphony? A concerto?"

"A passacaglia."

"Of course. How silly of me. But I guess that leaves room for an encore, doesn't it?" He pats his pocket, his eyes going sharp. "I still have that other key, you know. I could go back."

"You won't," I say. "Because you didn't."

The truth of it washes over him heavily. He goes to the window and stands with his face ghosted in the dark reflection of the pane. "I wanted her at first. The way she was. The way you were back then. By the end, though, I knew that wasn't really it. Instead I wanted . . ." He turns back to me. "I wanted to bring her here."

I let my eyes close for just a moment, hoping it will sound true. "And that's what you've done."

His expression takes on the warmth of a recognition. The floating sense of it coming into the pulse and breath of everything. The whole world. Life, time. Is that possible? I had forgotten how it feels to be together. This quiet joy.

Just then Tessa shouts down the hallway. "Who goes there?"

Jamie yells out a phrase in response. Sign and countersign—a castle guard scenario Aaron invented. He lowers his head laughing and then gives a nod in their direction as if it has just proved a point.

I hold up the bottle of hydrogen peroxide.

He comes over to the sofa and sits facing me. "Well," he says. "Ain't we a pair."

I dab at the wound, which turns out to be much deeper than I intended. "Poor you," I say, trying to make light of it, but feeling unsettled at the sight of my own handiwork. "I'm afraid this will leave a scar."

"No kidding, Catwoman. You could have just given me a love bite on the neck, you know."

"Really?" I fix the plaster to his cheek with my hand lingering afterward for the feel of him, the warm contact. "Well, then. Better late than never."

I lean in for a wee nibble, tasting him again, the firm cords and stubble on his skin, all that salty rigorous life. To be known at last. As much as possible. That's what we want, isn't it? His chest arcing forward, his hands in my hair, lifting my face for a long hot kiss. He pulls back slightly, his eyes in mine.

"Ultra-Violet," he says. "It's you."

And I'm about to push him back onto the sofa, I really am, when Jamie enters in a full-throttle burst. His smiling face, lips smeared with jam. Aaron rises and spreads his arms wide. As Jamie comes waddling forward Tessa appears behind him with all that serious love of hers almost like an attitude, a challenge, so obvious where she gets it now.

She halts, staring at his cheek. "What happened, Daddy?"

"He cut himself shaving," I say, before he can fumble out a reply.

He glances at me. "Yes. I wasn't careful. I wasn't paying attention to what I was doing."

"And now," I burst out, "it's question time! Do we want Daddy to come home?"

A scream of assent from the children. There's a celebratory tussle on the floor until Aaron ends up wrapping them together in a bear hug. They break free, scrambling and regrouping and skirmishing again until I finally call a truce by announcing chocolate treats which I've strategically placed on the kitchen table in advance. There's a rushing surge as they clear out, the room settling afterward like water in a swimming pool.

He stands with his clothing all skewed and untucked, watching the space they've left behind. His eyes in gear, working out a thought. And then, straightening his shirt, he discovers something and pulls it out of his pocket. A receipt. Yes, I've been waiting for this part. How many times have I rehearsed it in my mind?

"What are the odds," he says, with an ironic smirk, "that the photo shop is still holding the prints from that film I dropped off in 1988?"

I stand up and raise the lid of the piano bench. The sheet music, the exercise booklets. And the photos. The air comes alive behind me. When I turn back to hand over the envelopes he seems freeze-framed. He stares at them, sealed for eighteen years.

"But you said . . . in 1988, when I asked . . ."

I cup a hand to his face. "I lied, ya dope."

"I left the second one at a different shop, though. And I never told you."

"The manager was an old schoolmate of my mum's. He happened to see her at some charity event a few months later when he recognized your surname from one of the unclaimed packets."

He takes them and goes over to the coffee table and tears them open with frantic delicacy, separating each individual photo, sorting and examining them under the light.

"How do I explain these? To other people, I mean." He looks over at me. "It doesn't make any sense."

I tilt my head slightly. "Maybe this isn't for other people to see. Like the sun and moon together at a special time and place."

"Except that was a coincidence. A hell of a coincidence, I admit. But come on, Vi. You realise we were just lucky, right? Unlike me, you've had eighteen years to mull it over. Those monuments weren't built for us."

"And Bach didn't write his music for me either. Does it matter? Does it lose meaning because of that?"

He slants his eyes and gives his head a little shake, as if I'm the one who doesn't get it. Silly Vi. I go back to the piano and pat the bench next to me in invitation. He gives me a wary look. I beckon him over with a crooked finger until he joins me and then I draw him in closer until our thighs are touching. I reach over and start playing with my left hand—a sequence of fifths sprinkled with oddities here and there. Not too complex. But different. I play it over and over again to make sure it's true before passing it over to him. He takes it up slowly, looking down at his hands as he plays, a bit too choppy at first, until he finally relaxes and opens it up. Yes, that's it. This is how it goes. I find something to complement it on my end of the keyboard, a place that seems like home. Some broken chords, a surprising sharp or two, open cadences everywhere and motifs that return in variations, in new sequences, in refrains. I match it with his ground bass, the motifs blending together in places, concealing the beginning, withholding the end.

"This is beautiful," he says. "What is it?"

It brings a luminous feeling to me, a stretch of blue sky and bare green hills and endless sun. Remember? Remember how it felt? A time in my life when anything could happen. Yes, it's here again. It's back. That tingle of possibility, a sense of promise in everything ahead. It's always happening now.

"I'm not sure," I say, open to the moment, in love with every breath. "I'm making it up as we go along."

Acknowledgments

Thanks to:

Allyson Stack, Nicole Stack, Callum Legendre, Connie McGovern, Kathryn Nicol, Judy Moir, Alison Moore, Angus Farquhar, Simon Brown, Alan Gillis, Patricia Murphy, John Barbour and Graeme Cavers at AOC Archaeology, Debbie Moss, Lyn Heath, Aaron Watson for guidance to rock carvings, Sharon Webb at Kilmartin Museum, Creative Scotland, Glasgow Museums Resource Centre, Society of Authors, the School of English at the University of Nottingham.

Earlier versions of chapters 1 and 3 appeared in *Edinburgh Review* and *Superstition Review*.